The
Taxidermist's
Daughter

ALSO BY KATE MOSSE

The Languedoc Novels

Labyrinth

Sepulchre

Citadel

Gothic Fiction

The Winter Ghosts

The Mistletoe Bride
& Other Haunting Tales

Nonfiction

Becoming a Mother

The House: Behind the Scenes at the
Royal Opera House, Covent Garden

Chichester Festival Theatre at Fifty

Plays

Syrinx

Endpapers

Dodger

The Taxidermist's Daughter

KATE MOSSE

WM

WILLIAM MORROW

An Imprint of HarperCollins*Publishers*

First published in Great Britain in 2014 by Orion Books,
an imprint of The Orion Publishing Group Ltd.

FIRST WILLIAM MORROW EDITION PUBLISHED 2016.

Library of Congress Cataloging-in-Publication Data has been applied for.

Illustration © 2014 by Jack Penny
Map © 2014 by Mike Hall

ISBN 978-0-06-240215-8

16 17 18 19 20 OV/RRD 10 9 8 7 6 5 4 3 2 1

As always, for my beloved Greg, Martha and Felix

Also for my wonderful nieces and nephews,
Emma, Anthony (aka Gizz), Richard, Jessica,
Lottie, Bryony, TH, Toby, EH and Zackary

I do remember an apothecary and hereabouts he dwells . . .
and in his needy shop a tortoise is hung, an alligator stuff'd
and other skins of ill-shaped fishes.

—William Shakespeare, *Romeo and Juliet*, 1597

'Tis now, replied the village belle,
St. Mark's mysterious eve,
And all that old traditions tell
I tremblingly believe;
How, when the midnight signal tolls,
Along the churchyard green,
A mournful train of sentenced souls
In winding-sheets are seen.
The ghosts of all whom death shall doom
Within the coming year,
In pale procession walk the gloom,
Amid the silence drear.

—James Montgomery, "The Vigil of St. Mark," 1813

Let your fiction grow out of the land beneath your feet.

—Willa Cather, circa 1912

CONTENTS

PROLOGUE
April 1912   1

PART I
Wednesday   11

PART II
Thursday   129

PART III
Friday   271

EPILOGUE
April 1913   401

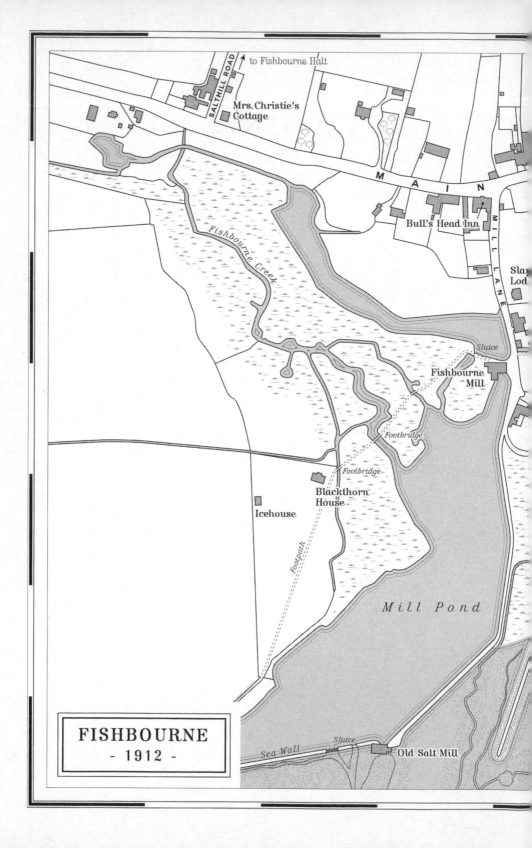

to Fishbourne Halt

SALTHILL ROAD

Mrs. Christie's
Cottage

M A I N

MILL LANE

Bull's Head Inn

Sla
Lod

Fishbourne Creek

Sluice

Fishbourne
Mill

Footbridge

Footbridge

Blackthorn
House

Icehouse

Footpath

Mill Pond

Sea Wall   Sluice   Old Salt Mill

FISHBOURNE
- 1912 -

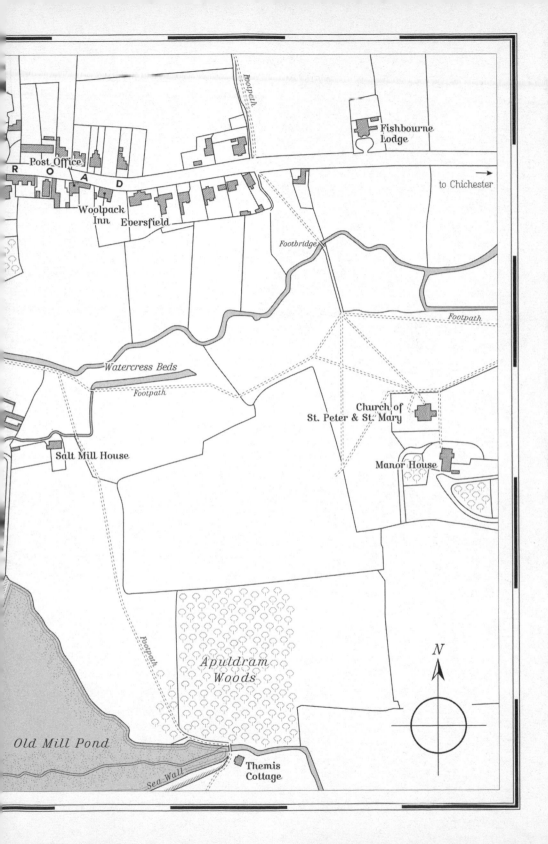

PROLOGUE

April 1912

The Church of St. Peter & St. Mary
Fishbourne Marshes
Sussex
Wednesday, April 24th

Midnight.

In the graveyard of the Church of St. Peter & St. Mary, men gather in silence on the edge of the drowned marshes. Watching, waiting.

For it is believed that on the Eve of St. Mark, the ghosts of those destined to die in the coming year will be seen walking into the church at the turning of the hour. It is a custom that has long since fallen away in most parts of Sussex, but not here. Not here, where the saltwater estuary leads out to the sea. Not here, in the shadow of the Old Salt Mill and the burned-out remains of Farhill's Mill, its rotting timbers revealed at each low tide. Here, the old superstitions still hold sway.

Skin, blood, bone.

Out at sea, the curlews and the gulls are calling, strange and haunting nighttime cries. The tide is coming in fast, higher and higher, drowning the mudflats and saltings until there is nothing left but the deep, shifting water. The rain strikes the black umbrellas and cloth caps of the farm workers and dairymen and blacksmiths. Dripping down between neck and collar, skin and cloth. No one speaks. The flames in the lanterns gutter and leap, casting distorted shadows up and along the flint face of the church.

This is no place for the living.

The taxidermist's daughter stands hidden in the shadow of the cypress trees, having followed her father here across the marshes. Connie can see Gifford in the knot of men at the porch, and is surprised. He shuns friendship. They live a solitary life on the other side of the creek, in a house filled with fur and feathers, bell jars and black beaded eyes, wire and cotton and tow, all that is left of Gifford's once celebrated museum of taxidermy. A broken and dissolute man, ruined by drink.

But tonight is different. Connie senses he knows these men and they know him. That they are bound to one another in some way.

> . . . when the midnight signal tolls,
> Along the churchyard green,
> A mournful train of sentenced souls
> In winding-sheets are seen.

The words of a poem learned in a classroom slip, unbidden, into her mind. A glimpse from the vanished days. Connie struggles to grasp the memory, but, as always, it fades to smoke before she can catch hold of it.

The rain falls harder, ricocheting off the gray headstones and the waterproof wrappers and coats. Damp seeps up through the soles of Connie's boots. The wind tugs at the skirt around her ankles. She tries not to think of the dead who lie in the cold earth beneath her feet.

Then, the sound of a man whispering. An educated voice. Urgent, anxious.

"Is she *here*?"

Connie peers through the leaves into the mist, but she cannot tell from whose mouth the words came and if the question was intended for anyone in particular. In any case, there is no reply.

She is surprised by how many have made their way here, and on such a night. Most she recognizes, in the glint of the lamp that hangs above the porch. The old village families— the Barkers and the Josephs, the Boys and the Lintotts and the Reedmans. There are only one or two women. There are also, so far as she can make out, three or four gentlemen, the cut of their clothes setting them apart. One is particularly tall and broad.

She does not recognize them and they are out of place in this rural setting. Men of business or medicine or property, the kind whose names grace the pages of the local newspaper during Goodwood week.

Connie shivers. Her shoulders are heavy with rain and her feet numb, but she dare not move. She does not want to give herself away. Her eyes dart to her father, but Gifford is no longer standing in the same place and she cannot pick him out in the crowd. Is it possible he has gone inside the church?

The minutes pass.

Then, a movement in the far corner of the graveyard. Connie catches her breath. The woman has her back to her and her features are hidden beneath her Merry Widow, but she thinks she's seen her before. Drops of rain glisten on the iridescent feathers of the wide brim of the hat. She too appears to be hiding, concealing herself in the line of trees. Connie is almost certain it is the same woman she saw on the marshes last week. She certainly recognizes the coat, double-seamed and nipped tight at the waist.

No one comes to Blackthorn House. They have few near neighbors and her father is not on visiting terms with anybody in the village. But Wednesday last, Connie noticed a woman standing on the path, half obscured by the cattails, keeping watch on the house. A beautiful blue double-seamed woolen coat and green dress, though the hem was flecked with mud. Willow plumes and a birdcage veil obscuring her face. A tall, slim silhouette. Not at all the sort of person to be walking on the flooded fields.

She assumed the woman would come to the front door and present herself, that she had some purpose in being there. Someone new to the village, coming to deliver an invitation or an introduction? But Connie waited, and after a few minutes of indecision, the woman turned and vanished into the wet afternoon.

Connie wishes now she had gone out and confronted their reluctant visitor. That she had spoken to her.

"*Is* she here?"

Whispered words in the dark bring Connie back from last week to this cold, wet churchyard. The same words, but a different question.

The bells begin to toll, echoing across the wild headland. Everyone turns, each set of eyes now fixed upon the western door of the tiny church.

Blood, skin, bone.

Connie finds herself staring too. Is she imagining that the crowd stands back to allow those who have come—apparitions, spirits—to enter the church? She refuses to give in to such superstition, yet something is happening, some movement through the mist and air. An imprint of those who have felt Death's touch upon their shoulder? Or a trick of the light from the wind-shaken lamp above the door? She does not consider herself impressionable, yet this promise of prophecy catches at her nerves too.

This is no place for the dead.

From her hiding place, Connie struggles to see past the men's shoulders and backs and the canopy of umbrellas. A memory, deeply buried, sparks suddenly in her mind. Black trousers and shoes. Her heart drums against her ribs, but the flash of recollection has burned out already.

Someone mutters under his breath. An angry complaint. Connie parts the branches with her hands in an attempt to see more. Shoving and jostling, male voices rising. The sound of the door of the church flung open, banging on its hinges, and the men surge inside.

Are they looking for someone? Chasing someone? Connie doesn't know, only that the graveyard seems suddenly emptier.

The bells toll more loudly, catching their own echo and lengthening the notes. Then a shout. Someone curses. Hands flailing against the wet evening air. A hustle of movement, something rushing out of the church, frantic motion. Connie takes a step forward, desperate to see.

Not spirits or phantasms, but birds. A cloud of small birds, flocking, flying wildly out of their prison, striking hats and graves and the stones in their desperation to be free.

Still the bell tolls. Ten of the clock, eleven.

In the confusion, no one observes the black-gloved hand. No one sees the wire slipped around the throat and the vicious twist. Savage, determined. Beads of blood, like a red velvet choker on white skin.

The clock strikes twelve. Beneath the crack and fold of the wind and the remorseless toll of the bell, no one hears the scream.

*

The last discordant note shimmers into the darkness. For a moment, a vast and echoing silence. Nothing but the sound of the relentless rain and the wind, the ragged pulsing of Connie's blood in her head.

The ghosts of all whom death shall doom.

Time hangs suspended. No one moves, no one speaks. Then, a rustling and a shifting of feet. The click of the inner church door, opening or closing, Connie cannot tell which.

"That's the last of them," someone says. "They're all gone."

A restlessness runs through the crowd remaining outside. They feel they have been played for fools. That they have been the victims of a hoax. Connie, too, feels she has awoken from some kind of trance.

In pale procession walk the gloom.

She remembers, now, a woman's voice reciting the poem out loud, a long time ago. Connie writing down the words to help commit them to memory.

Most of the birds are injured or dead. A man lifts one of the finches from a tombstone and throws the corpse into the hedgerow. People are talking in low voices. Connie understands that they are embarrassed. No one wishes to admit to having been duped into thinking that the sudden midnight apparition was anything other than the flight of the trapped birds. They are eager to be gone. Lifting their hats and hurrying away. Taking their leave in twos and threes.

Not ghosts. Not images of the dead.

Connie looks for the woman who'd kept watch over Blackthorn House. She, too, has vanished.

Connie wants to go into the church herself. To see what, if anything, has taken place. To see with her own eyes if the hymnbooks are all in their usual places, if the striped bell rope is tethered to its hook, if the pews and the polished plaques and the lectern look the same. To try to work out how so many birds could have become trapped inside.

Keeping to the shadows, she steps out from her hiding place and moves toward the church. All around the porch, tiny bodies litter the ground. Chaffinch and siskin, silent now. Brambling, greenfinch, linnet. In different circumstances, Connie might have taken them, but her duty to her father is not yet discharged. She still can't see him and is worried he has slipped away. Frequently she is obliged to follow him home from the Bull's Head to ensure he doesn't slip into the dangerous mud on the marshes and come to harm. Tonight, despite this strange ceremony in the churchyard, is no different.

Finally she does catch sight of him. She watches as he puts out his hand to steady himself, staggering from the church wall to a sepulcher tomb. In the single lantern left burning, she sees that his bare hands are red, raw, against the stone and lichen. Dirty, too. His shoulders slump, as if he has survived some elemental ordeal. A pitiful sound comes from his throat, like an animal in pain.

Then Gifford straightens, turns and makes his way down the footpath. His step is steady. Connie realizes that the sharp rain and the cold and the birds have sobered him. For tonight, at least, she need not worry about him.

Blood, skin, bone. A single black tail feather.

A black glass bead is blowing back and forth on the path. Connie picks it up, then hurries after her father. She does not notice the dark, huddled shape lying in the northeast corner of the graveyard. She does not notice the twist of bloody wire.

Connie does not know that a matter of yards from the broken bodies of the songbirds, a woman now also lies dead.

PART I

One Week Later
Wednesday

Chapter 1

Blackthorn House
Fishbourne Marshes
Wednesday, May 1ˢᵗ

Connie looked down at the scalpel in her hand. Quicksilver-thin blade, ivory handle. To the untrained eye, it looked like a stiletto. In other houses, it would be mistaken for a paring knife for vegetables or fruit.

Not flesh.

Connie cradled the dead jackdaw in her hands, feeling the memory of warmth and life in its dead muscle and sinew and vein, in the heavy droop of its neck. *Corvus monedula*. Black glossy birds, with ash-gray necks and crowns.

Pale eyes. Almost white.

Her tools were ready. An earthenware bowl with a mixture of water and arsenical soap. Several strips of cloth, and a pail on the floor at her feet. Newspaper. Pliers and scalpel and file.

Gently Connie laid the bird down on the paper. With her fingers, she parted the sooty feathers and lined up the blade at the top of the breast bone. Then, with the anticipation she always felt at the moment of incision, she maneuvered the tip into place, looking for the best point of entry.

The jackdaw lay still, accepting of its fate. She breathed in and slowly exhaled. A ritual of sorts.

The first time Connie had been taken inside her father's workshop, the smell made her nauseous—of flesh and undigested food and rotting carrion.

Blood, skin, bone.

In those early days, she'd worn a handkerchief tied across her nose and mouth. The perfumes of the trade were pungent—alcohol, the musty odor of flax tow, linseed oil, the paints for the claws and feet, beaks and mounts—too strong for a child's sensibilities. Over the years, Connie had become accustomed to them and now she barely noticed. If anything, she believed that acknowledging the scent of things was an integral part of the process.

She glanced up at the high windows that ran the length of the workshop, tilted open today to let in the fresh air. The sky was a welcome shock of blue after the weeks of rain. She wondered if she might persuade her father to come down for lunch. Perhaps a cup of beef tea?

Since the events in the churchyard a week ago, Gifford had barely left his room. She heard him pacing up and down until the early hours, muttering to himself. It wasn't good for him to be so cooped up. Last night she'd come upon him standing on the half-landing, peering out over the darkening creek, his breath misting the glass.

Connie was accustomed to his dissolute condition in the days following a bout of drinking. Even so, she'd been alarmed by his physical deterioration. Bloodshot eyes, his face gaunt and six days' worth of stubble on his chin. When she asked if there was anything she might do for him, he stared at her without appearing to have the slightest recollection of who she was.

She loved her father and, despite his shortcomings, they rubbed along well enough. Taxidermy was not considered a suitable job for a woman, but Gifford had—in secret—gone against tradition and passed on his skills to her. Not merely the cutting and the stuffing and the dexterity, but also his love and passion for his craft. The belief that in death, beauty could be found. The belief that through the act of preservation, a new kind of life was promised. Immortal, perfect, brilliant, in the face of the shifting and decaying world.

Connie couldn't recall precisely when she had gone from passive observer to Gifford's apprentice, only that it had turned out to be essential. Her father's hands were no longer steady. His eye was no longer true. No one was aware that it was Connie who carried out the few commissions they still received. Business would have declined in any case. Tastes had changed, and the mounted animals and birds that once graced every parlor had fallen out of fashion with the new century.

All the same, even if they never sold another piece, Connie knew she would continue to do the work she loved. She held within her the memory of every bird that had passed through her hands. Each creature had left its imprint upon her as much as she had left her mark on it.

Through the open windows, Connie could hear the jackdaws chattering in their new colony in the poplar trees at the end of the garden. Earlier in the spring, they'd set up residence between the chimney stacks of Blackthorn House. In March, a nest had come down into the drawing room, a collapse of twigs and hair and bark sending the cold remains of the fire billowing out onto the furniture. Particularly distressing were the three speckled, partially hatched blue-green eggs and the one tiny chick, tangled in the debris, its beak still open. The distraught cawing of the mother had haunted the house for days.

Connie looked down at the bird on the workshop counter.

Unlike its living companions, this jackdaw would never age. Thanks to her care and skill, it would be preserved at one dazzling moment in time. Eternal, forever poised for flight, as if it might at any moment come back to life and soar up into the sky.

*

Pushing everything else from her mind, Connie lined up the scalpel, and cut.

At first, a gentle shifting, nothing more. Then the tip of the blade pierced the skin and the point slipped in. The flesh seemed to sigh as it unfolded, as if the bird was relieved the waiting was over. The journey from death back to life had begun. A leaking of liquid and the distinctive coppery smell of meat. The feathers held within them a scent of dust and old clothes, like a parlor left unaired.

The cloudy eyes of the bird stared up at her. When Connie was done, its eyes would be ivory again. Glass, not jelly, shining as brightly as they had in life. It was hard to find a good match for a jackdaw's eyes. Pale blue when young, like jays, then shifting through dark to light.

Connie let her shoulders drop and allowed her muscles to relax, then began to peel the skin from the flesh with her fingers. Cutting, pulling back, cutting again. The deep red of the breast, the color of quince jelly; the silver sheen of the wings. She took care to keep the intestines, lungs, kidneys, and heart intact in the abdominal sac, so she could use the body as a guide for the shaping to come.

She worked slowly and methodically, wiping the tiny pieces of tissue, feathers, blood and cartilage from the point of the blade onto the newspaper as she went. Rushing, the tiniest slip, might make the difference between a clean job and a possibility ruined.

Connie allowed two days for a carrion bird—a jackdaw like this, or a magpie, rook or crow. Once begun, it was important to work fast, before the natural processes of decay took hold. If all the fat was not scraped from the bones, there was a risk of maggots destroying the bird from within. The first day was spent skinning, washing and preparing; the second, stuffing and positioning.

Each task was mirrored left and right; she followed the same sequence each time. Either side of the breastbone, the left wing and then the right, the left leg and the right. It was a dance, with steps learned through trial and error and, in time, perfected.

Connie reached for her pliers from their hook and noticed that she would have to order some more wire for mounting. She started to loosen the leg bones. Twisting back and forth, the scraping of the side of the scalpel as the flesh came loose, then the snap of a knee joint.

They knew each other now, Connie and this bird.

When she had finished, she placed everything she did not need—tissue, stray feathers, damp scraps of newspaper—into the pail at her feet, then turned the bird over and moved on to work on the spine.

The sun climbed higher in the sky.

Eventually, when her muscles were too cramped to continue, Connie folded the bird's wings and head in on itself to prevent the skin from drying out, then stretched her arms. She rolled her neck and shoulders, flexed her fingers, feeling satisfied with her morning's work. Then she went out through the side door into the garden and sat in the wicker chair on the terrace.

From the roof of the icehouse, the colony of jackdaws continued to jabber and call. A requiem for their fallen comrade.

Chapter 2

North Street
Chichester

Harry Woolston stood back and looked at the partially finished painting.

Everything was technically correct—the color, the line of the nose, the hint of dissatisfaction in the lines around the mouth—yet it was not a good likeness. The face, put simply, had no life in it.

He wiped the oil from his brush with a cloth and considered the portrait from another angle. The problem was that his subject was flat on the canvas, as if he had sketched her from a photograph rather than from a living, breathing woman. They had worked late into the gray, wet night, then Harry sent her home and continued on his own, before heading to the Rifleman for a late, quick nightcap.

He had ruined the painting. Or rather, it had never worked at all.

Harry put down his palette. Usually, the smells of linseed oil and paint filled him with expectation. Today, they taunted him. He was tempted to think it was his subject's fault—that he should have found someone with more promise, with a more distinctive face and unique expression—but, though he tried to blame his sitter, he knew that he was at fault. He had failed to find the essence of the woman, failed to capture the shadows and lines and curves to preserve for posterity. Rather, he'd produced a list of painted characteristics: a nose just so, hair of such-and-such a color, eyes of this tint rather than that.

All true. Yet all completely false.

Harry put his brushes into the turpentine jar to soak and wiped his hands. He took off his blue working smock, flung it over the back of the armchair and put his waistcoat back on. Glancing at the carriage clock, he realized he was running late. He drained the last of his cold coffee, stubbed out his cigarette, then noticed with irritation that there was a smudge of paint on his right shoe. He reached for a cloth.

"Damn," he said, as he succeeded only in smearing the vermilion over the laces. He'd have to leave it for now.

"Lewis?" he called, walking out into the hall.

The butler appeared from the back of the house.

"Yes, sir."

"Has my father come in?"

"He has not." Lewis paused. "Were you expecting him, sir?"

"I'd thought he might return for lunch."

When he'd bumped into his father at breakfast, Harry had asked if they might talk. The old man hadn't committed himself either way.

"Did he say what time he'd be home this evening, Lewis?"

"Dr. Woolston gave no reason to assume that it would not be at the usual time, sir."

"That's it?"

"His only instruction was that, should you find yourself detained, dinner should be served at seven thirty."

Harry knew—and Lewis knew—it was intended as a reproach for the fact that Harry had failed to come home for dinner on several occasions recently, each time without sending his apologies. The Castle Inn was so much more appealing than another formal, silent meal alone with his father, struggling to find a topic of conversation that suited them both.

Harry took his hat from the stand. "Thank you, Lewis."

"So will you be in for dinner this evening, sir?"

Harry met his gaze. "I should think so," he said. "Yes."

*

Harry walked slowly past the Georgian facades of the private houses at the top of North Street, heading toward the shops closer to the stone Market Cross that stood at the junction of Chichester's four main streets.

He had taken the morning off, pleading illness, in order to work on the painting—pointlessly, as it turned out. Now he resented having to go to the office at all, especially since it was a pleasant day for once. Ceramic plates and serving dishes and milk jugs, Spode and Wedgwood imitations, lists of container carriers and shipping lines, moving goods from one end of the country to another to grace middle-class dining tables: this was not what Harry wanted to do with his life, working his way up in a business that bored him rigid, and for a man he loathed.

He still didn't understand why his father had insisted he find employment with Frederick Brook. Staffordshire born and bred, Brook was a self-made man and successful at what he did, but there was no common ground between him and Harry's father at all. Dr. Woolston was a great believer in everyone knowing their place. He mixed only with other professionals and looked down upon those who made their money in trade.

Harry couldn't stick it out any longer. He didn't care how

much of a favor Brook was doing his father, nor how many times he told him so. He was going to chuck it in.

Harry drew level with the Assembly Rooms, then moved on toward the Market Cross. The street was busy, women with shopping baskets and baby carriages, men loading bottles onto a delivery cart outside the wine merchant, everyone enjoying the promise of a summer's day free from umbrellas and mackintoshes or the need to scuttle from one shop to the next.

A crowd of people was standing outside Howards. The usual selection of skinned rabbits and poultry was hanging in the butcher's window, raw and bloody, but when Harry drew level, he saw that the glass had been smashed.

"What's going on?"

"Break-in," one man said. "Took some knives, a few other tools."

"Cash from the till," another put in. "Smashed the place up a bit."

Harry glanced at the jeweler's shop next door. "Funny place to go for."

"They reckon it's down to a chap who got sacked," a third man offered. "Got out of prison last week. Sore about losing his position."

Harry turned right at the Market Cross into West Street, heading for his father's consulting rooms. No time like the present. Wherever or whenever the conversation took place, it was going to be difficult. He might as well have it out with him. At least he'd know for certain where he stood.

Harry intended to enroll in the Royal Academy Schools; he'd made his application. He could live without his father's approval, but not without his financial support. He'd be stuck working for Brook for years before he made enough money to fund his studies out of his own pocket.

He straightened his jacket and checked his tie was properly knotted, then mounted the stone step. He noticed how the brass plaque was brightly polished: DR. JOHN WOOLSTON, MD. Today, even that made his spirits sink. His father didn't see patients anymore—he was strictly a paperwork man—but it was all so visibly respectable, so predictable.

He took a deep breath, pushed open the door and walked in.

"Morning, Pearce. The old man in?"

Harry stopped dead. The reception room was empty. His father's clerk was as much a part of the fabric of the building as the tables and chairs. In all his life, he couldn't remember a time when he'd arrived without seeing the avian profile of Pearce peering with disapproval over his half-moon spectacles.

"Pearce?"

From upstairs, he heard the sounds of someone walking about.

"I'm telling you, get out. Damn you!"

His hand on the highly polished banister, Harry froze. He'd never heard the old man swear, or even raise his voice.

"I wanted to give you a chance," a man said. A soft voice, educated. "I'm sorry you chose not to take it."

"Get *out*!"

Harry heard the sound of a chair being upended.

"*Get out!*" his father shouted. "I tell you, I don't have to listen to such filth. It's a disgraceful slur."

The whole situation was so extraordinary that Harry couldn't decide what to do. If his father needed help, he would of course intervene. But at the same time, the old man hated to be embarrassed in any way and would almost certainly resent his interference.

The decision was made for him. The door to his father's consulting room was flung open with such violence that it hit the wall, then rattled on its hinges. Harry bounded back down the stairs two at a time and hurled himself into the recess behind Pearce's desk, only just in time. The visitor came quickly down and disappeared into West Street. Harry caught no more than a glimpse of his clothes—workingmen's trousers and broad-brimmed farm hat, and small, clean black boots.

He was about to set off after him when he heard the floor-boards again shift overhead. Seconds later, his father came down the stairs as fast as his stiff knee would let him. He took his hat and coat from the stand beside the door, put on his gloves and left.

This time, Harry didn't stop to think. He ran after his father, tailing him through the cathedral cloisters, down St. Richard's Walk and into Canon Lane. Despite his bad leg, the old man was walking fast. Right, into South Street, past the post office and the Regnum Club, all the way down to the railway station.

Harry held back as Dr. Woolston climbed into a Dunnaways cab. He heard the crack of the whip and watched as the carriage pulled away, then ran across the concourse.

"Excuse me, can you tell me where that gentleman was going?"

The cabman looked at him with amusement. "I'm not sure that's any of your business, is it, sir?"

Harry fished a coin from his pocket and forced himself to stand still, keen not to give the impression that the information was worth a penny more.

"The Woolpack Inn," the cabman said. "So far as I could hear."

"And the Woolpack is where?" Harry tried not to sound impatient.

"Fishbourne." The man tipped his cap back on his head. "Might you also be wanting to go there, sir?"

Harry hesitated. He didn't want to run to the expense of a cab; besides, he didn't want his father to see him. He had no idea what the old man was up to, but he wanted neither to compromise him nor to fail to help him if he was in some sort of difficulty. Despite his current frustrations, he was fond of the old man.

"No," he said, and rushed instead to the ticket office.

Harry all but threw his money at the clerk behind the counter, then took the stairs two at a time over the bridge to the opposite platform, just a moment too late to make the Portsmouth train.

"Damn it," he said. "Damn."

He stalked up and down the platform, waiting for the next local service to Fishbourne, still wondering where his strait-laced father might be going in the middle of a working day. He realized too that, in his rush to follow, he'd omitted to inform Brook of his whereabouts. Then again, if he was fired, it would force his father's hand.

"Come on," he muttered, looking up the track, though the train was not due for another twenty-five minutes. "Hurry up, come on."

Chapter 3

Blackthorn House
Fishbourne Marshes

Connie drank her coffee on the terrace, making the most of the sunshine before going back to the workshop.

Her journal and a fresh jar of blue ink sat on the table in front of her. So far, she had written nothing.

She took a deep breath, filling her lungs with fresh, sharp sea air. She was pleased with her work this morning and, for the first time in some days, felt at peace with the world and her place in it.

Who killed Cock Robin?
I, said the Sparrow
With my bow and arrow.
I killed Cock Robin.

The maid's voice floated through the house and out of the French windows onto the terrace. Connie smiled. Mary often sang to herself when she thought no one was listening. She was a sweet creature and Connie considered herself fortunate to have secured her. Her father's profession was strange enough to excite distrust these days, and most of the village girls she'd interviewed when they first arrived were scared, or claimed to be, by the bell jars in the workshop, the bottles of preserving solutions, the trays of sharp glittering eyes and varnished claws. The first maid Connie engaged had given notice after only two weeks.

> And . . . all the birds of the air
> Fell a-sighing and a-sobbing
> When they heard of the death
> Of poor Cock Robin.

Connie put down her pen and sat back, feeling the sigh of the wicker garden chair beneath her.

For the first time in weeks, she had woken shortly after five o'clock to the sound of birdsong, then the sound of silence. Loud, astonishing silence. She could no longer hear the wind howling around the house or the rain smattering against her windowpane.

The past winter and early spring had been long and harsh. Black clouds and purple skies, the endless shifting of the mud-flats and a pitiless wind shaking the house to its foundations night after night.

In January, Mill Lane and Apuldram Lane both had flooded. Ghost lakes forming where once were fields. The roots of the wych elms rotting where they stood. In February, Connie had been kept awake by the frantic rumbling and turning of the wheel of the Old Salt Mill in the center of the creek, spinning and booming and thundering in the surge of the spring tides. In March, one of the branches of the oak tree had come down in the gales, missing their workshop by a matter of inches. April and the endless squalls, rain falling vertically and the land sodden underfoot. The water meadows hadn't dried out yet. Connie had set up a line of pails in the attic to catch the water. She made a note to remind Mary to bring them down, if the weather looked like it was holding.

Today, the surface of the mill pond was flat and the marshes were alive with color. Blue-green water, tipped with foam by a gentle breeze, glinting in the sunshine. The oaten cattails like the underside of velvet ribbon. The blackthorn and early hawthorn shimmering with white flowers. Red goosefoot and wild samphire, purple-eyed speedwell and golden dandelions in the hedgerows.

Connie looked back over her shoulder to the house itself. Often it appeared inhospitable, so isolated and exposed on the marshes, some quarter of a mile from its nearest neighbor. Today, it looked splendid in the sunshine.

Fashioned from the same warm red brick as several of the finest houses in Fishbourne, it had a steep red-tiled roof and tall chimney. At the back of the house was a kitchen with a modern black-lead range, a scullery and a walk-in larder. On the first floor were four bedrooms and a night nursery over-looking the water. A narrow flight of stairs led up to the servants' quarters on the top floor, unoccupied since Mary's mother insisted on her living at home.

But what had persuaded her father to take the house was the long and light conservatory, which occupied the entire west side of the house. He had turned it into their workshop. And in the farthest southwest corner of the garden, there was a large rectangular icehouse made of brick, which they used as a storeroom.

The gardens to the south and the east were set to lawn. A wooden village gate, cut into the blackthorn hedge at the north-east corner of the property and bordered by one of the many tidal streams that fed into the head of the creek, opened directly from the kitchen garden to the track leading to the village.

The main entrance was farther down the footpath. A black wrought-iron gate led to the front door of Blackthorn House, which faced east toward the Old Salt Mill. On a clear day, there were views all the way across the creek to the water meadows on the far side of the estuary. There were no beaches where children might play, no dramatic cliffs or outcrops, just miles of mudflats and saltings, revealed at low tide.

There, just half a mile as the crow flies across the water, the tiny Church of St. Peter & St. Mary was hidden in the green folds of willow and beech and elm. Beyond that, another mile to the east, the soaring restored spire and Norman bell tower of Chichester Cathedral dominated the landscape.

Who'll dig his grave?
I, said the Owl,
With my pick and shovel,
I'll dig his grave.

Connie ran her hand over the surface of the table, still thinking about her father. If only she could persuade him to leave his room. It wasn't simply a matter of his health, but also because she wanted to ask him why he had gone to the church a week ago. He hated to be questioned, and usually Connie did not press. She did not like to distress him. But this time was different. She'd been patient, knowing she had to choose her moment wisely, but she couldn't allow another week to slip by.

In the past couple of weeks, Gifford's demeanor had changed. He seemed to be in the grip of some complex emotion. Fear? Guilt? Grief? She had no idea, only that when he did emerge from his room, he walked quickly past each window and repeatedly asked if any letters had been delivered. Twice, she had heard him weeping.

She was worried for him. About him too, she realized.

A sudden glint from the middle of the channel caught Connie's eye. A bright flash, like a ship's warning lamp. Had it come from the Old Salt Mill? She shielded her eyes, but she couldn't see anything. Just the few small houses dotted on the Apuldram side of the water.

Trying to quell her anxious thoughts, Connie opened her journal at the entry for the twenty-fifth of April and flattened the pages. She had recorded her impressions immediately after the visit to the church—as she did with all her private reflections—trying to make sense of what had happened. She'd set down the names of those she recognized, done pen portraits of those she had not. The woman in the blue coat too, though Connie had soon realized that although she could describe her clothes and hat, she had no idea at all what she actually looked like.

She drained the last of her coffee, then began to read.

A Fishbourne village tradition or not, Connie hadn't accepted then—and still did not—that so many people would have made their way to the church on the Eve of St. Mark without some kind of prior arrangement. And she was certain her father would not normally have been among them. She had never known him to attend a service—not at Whitsun, not Christmas, not even on Easter Sunday.

And that strange whispered question, overheard as the bell began to toll again. "Is she *here*?" An educated voice, not a man from the village. "*Is* she here?" The meaning was quite altered with each different intonation.

Who'll be the parson?
I, said the Rook
With my little book,
I'll be the parson.

Mary's song continued to swoop and soar around the corners of the house, the notes floating in the sweet afternoon air.

*

Connie heard them before she saw them.

She looked up as a pair of mute swans flew low overhead. Their long necks stretched, the orange flash of their beaks, the steady beating of their wings against the air. She turned to follow their flight.

A swan. White feathers.

She was pricked by a sudden, vivid memory from the vanished days. Herself at nine or ten, long brown hair twisted through with yellow ribbon. Sitting on a high wooden stool at the ticket counter at the museum.

She frowned. No, not yellow ribbon. Red.

The painted wooden sign above the door—GIFFORD'S WORLD-FAMOUS HOUSE OF AVIAN CURIOSITIES—and her palms hot and sticky from the farthings, halfpennies and the occasional sixpence. Issuing printed entrance tickets—*billets*—on a grainy and coarse blue card.

Another shift of memory. The swan once more. With its grief-clouded eyes.

Of all the taxidermy exhibits in the collection, she had only hated the swan. Standing inside the main entrance, its wings spread wide as if to welcome visitors in, she was terrified of it. Something about its size and its breadth, the breast feathers molting in the sun through the glass. The moths and the beads of fat, like blisters on the surface of its skin. Another memory. When she had been told that swans paired for life—who might have told her that? Connie remembered how she had wept and become quite ill with the idea that the mate of the preserved cob might be searching in vain for her lost love.

She waited, willing more to come back to her, but already the memory was fading. She did not think the swan had made the journey here to Blackthorn House, as a few of the museum exhibits had. The image of her young self slipped away, unseen again, back into the shadows.

The vanished days.

Her life was divided into two parts. Before and after the accident. Connie had dreamlike memories of long and blurred weeks, drifting in and out of sleep, a gentle hand stroking her forehead. Hot air and all the windows open. Her dark hair shorn and rough on her scalp. A scar on the right side of her head.

When she did recover, her past was lost to her. The first twelve years of her life almost completely wiped from her mind. People, too. Connie had never known her mother—she had died giving birth to her—but she had the memory of being loved. A female voice, gentle hands smoothing the hair back from her face. But who was she? An aunt, a grandmother? A nurse? There was no evidence of any other family members at all. Only Gifford.

From time to time, there were glimpses of another girl. A cousin? A friend? Eight or nine years older than Connie, but with a youthful, spirited air. A girl with a love of life, not bowed down by tradition or proprieties or restrictions.

At first, Connie had asked questions, tried to piece things together, hoping that her memory would return in time. So many questions that her father could not—or would not—answer. Gifford claimed the doctors advised that she should not try to force herself, that her memory would come back in due course. And although Connie recovered her physical strength, she suffered episodes of petit mal. Any stress or upset could trigger an attack, sometimes lasting only a minute or two; other times half an hour might pass.

Her father refused, therefore, to talk about anything other than the accident. Even then, he limited himself to the barest facts.

Spring 1902. April. Gifford was working late in the museum. Connie had woken from a nightmare and, seeking reassurance, had left her bedroom and gone to look for him. In the dark, she lost her footing and fell, from the top of the wooden stairs to the stone floor at the bottom, hitting her head. She'd only survived thanks to a doctor's urgent ministrations.

After that, her father's account became vaguer still.

Gifford sold up and they moved away, finally settling in Fishbourne. He did not want to be reminded every day of how nearly she had died, and did not want her to be distressed. Besides, the sea air and the peace and quiet of the marshes would do her good.

The vanished days. Lost, as if they had never been.

And now?

Connie couldn't be certain, but she thought her flashes of recovered memory were becoming more substantial, more frequent. At the same time, it seemed that the moments when time appeared to stop, and she was sucked down into a black unknowing, were becoming less common.

Was it true? Did she want it to be true?

*

Connie watched as the swans came in to land in the orchard of Old Park, where sixty or more nesting pairs had made their home.

All the birds of the air
Fell a-sighing and a-sobbing
When they heard the bell toll
For poor Cock Robin.

As the sun moved around behind the oak tree, dropping the terrace into shadow, the ghost child was still there, waiting on the edges of Connie's memory. A girl.

A girl with a red ribbon in her hair.

Réaumur received birds from all parts, in spirits of wine, according to the instructions he had given; he contented himself by taking them from this liquor, and introducing two ends of an iron wire into the body behind the thighs; he then fastened the wire to the claws, the ends, which passed below, served to fix them to a small board; he put two black glass beads in the place of eyes, and called it a stuffed bird.

TAXIDERMY: OR, THE ART OF COLLECTING, PREPARING, AND MOUNTING OBJECTS OF NATURAL HISTORY

Mrs. R. Lee
Longman & Co., Paternoster Row, London, 1820

I am watching you.

You sense this, I think. Somewhere in the depths of knowledge and emotion, you know. Somewhere, buried deep in the thoughts you think you have lost, you know and you remember. Memory is a shifting, dishonest and false friend in any case. We cherish what does us good and bury the rest. This is how we keep ourselves safe. How we make it possible to carry on in this decaying, corrupting world.

Blood will have blood.

The time of reckoning is coming, getting closer with each sunrise and sunset. But it is their own deeds that will be the cause of their undoing, not mine. I did offer them a chance. They did not take it. Even as I imagine the misery that will follow these revelations, I have the consolation that you will read these words and know the truth. You will understand.

What, then, can be said without dispute?

That the spring of nineteen hundred and twelve has been the wettest on record. That the horse chestnuts are late in leaf. That the waters rose higher and higher, and are rising still.

And the birds. The white birds and the gray and the black. Feathers of ink-blue and purple and iridescent green. The jabbering, cawing and threatening of jackdaw, magpie, rook and crow. For all those years I was away, I heard them in my dreams, calling from the trees.

I am watching you.

So here I set down my testimony. Black words on cream paper. It is not a story of revenge, though it will be seen as that. Dismissed as that.

But no, not revenge.

This is a story of justice.

Chapter 4

The Old Salt Mill
Fishbourne Creek

Dr. John Woolston stood in the tiny attic room in the Old Salt Mill in the center of Fishbourne Creek and looked across the water to Blackthorn House.

"Any sign of Gifford?"

Joseph shook his head. "No."

Woolston gestured impatiently for the field glasses.

"You can't possibly see," he said irritably, wiping them with his pocket handkerchief. "The lens is filthy."

He put the cream envelope Joseph had handed him onto the chair, removed his spectacles and raised the binoculars to his eyes. He adjusted the focus until he had Blackthorn House in his sights. It sat on a substantial plot of land, surrounded by open fields. Woolston shifted his gaze. The only access, so far as he could see, was a narrow footpath on the northeast side of the property.

He returned his scrutiny to the house itself. There was an attic—he observed the steep pitch of the roof—and a peculiar rectangular structure with a dome in the south-facing garden. An icehouse, he assumed, though that was unusual for a property so close to the water.

"Just sitting on the terrace."

"What?" he said, startled to find Joseph standing so close.

"The Gifford girl. Came out after lunch. Barely moved."

Woolston lowered the field glasses and handed them back to Joseph.

"You're absolutely certain there's been so sign of Gifford?"

Joseph shrugged. "As I said, I've not seen him."

"There's no possibility he might have left without your noticing?"

"Not since it got light. Can't answer for before that."

Woolston stared at the litter of spent matches and cigarette ends on the floor. He had no way of knowing if Joseph was telling the truth and had been at his post all the time. He hadn't engaged the man, though after the events in Fishbourne churchyard a week ago, he had agreed they had no choice.

"What about visitors?"

"Maid arrived at seven," Joseph replied. "Brought a table and chair out to the terrace about one, give or take. No one else gone in or out."

"Deliveries?"

"Nutbeem's doesn't come out this far."

"Door-to-doors?"

"I'm telling you, nothing."

Woolston looked back through the window, across the creek and the mill pond, to where Blackthorn House stood, peaceful in the sunshine.

"You are . . . prepared?" he said, then immediately regretted asking.

"Ready and—"

"Not that there is likely to be any need," Woolston cut across him.

"Waiting," Joseph finished, patting his pocket.

Woolston disliked the man's attitude, but Brook had assured

him that Joseph knew the village like the back of his hand and was the best man for the job. Did what he was told, no questions asked. Woolston hoped Brook's confidence was not misplaced. He thought it a mistake to put their trust in such an individual, but it had not been his choice to make.

He put his hand in his pocket and handed over a plain cotton bag.

"Thanking you," Joseph said, then tipped the bag upside down.

"It's all there," Woolston snapped. "The sum we agreed."

"Best to be sure, sir. Saves any unpleasantness later."

Woolston was forced to watch as Joseph counted the coins, one by one, before slipping them into his pocket.

"A couple of smokes to keep me going? Manage that?"

Woolston hesitated, then handed over two cigarettes with barely concealed anger.

"Your instructions are to stay here."

"It's what you and your colleagues are paying me for, isn't it?"

Provoked beyond endurance, Woolston stepped forward. "Don't make a mess of it, Joseph. This isn't a game. If you do, I will break every bone in your body. Is that clear?"

A slow, contemptuous smile appeared on his face.

"Aren't you forgetting something," he said, picking up the envelope and holding it in front of Woolston's face. "Sir."

*

Joseph listened to the doctor's angry footsteps on the narrow wooden stairs. He waited until he heard the latch of the door at the bottom of the mill click shut, then made an obscene gesture with his fist.

As if he'd be intimidated by so feeble a specimen as

Woolston. Or even by the men behind him. Scared of his own shadow. He'd met plenty like him before, men who never got their hands dirty. Pillars of the community, so called. He'd had to bow his head to enough of them, up before the City Bench. Yet the instant there was trouble, they came knocking same as anyone else. Brothers under the skin.

He cleared his throat, spitting the filaments of loose tobacco out of his mouth, then took one of Woolston's cigarettes from behind his ear and lit it. Joseph didn't care why he was being paid to spy on a wreck of a man and his daughter. Not his business. He turned the coins over in his pocket. He couldn't deny the money was good.

He smiled. It paid to listen.

He blew a ring of smoke up into the air, pierced it with his finger, then blew another. Joseph made it his business to notice things. So he knew about the maid, Mary Christie, what time she arrived each day, what time she returned to the modest row of cottages nearby the pumping station where she lived with her widowed mother and kid sisters. That they were stalwart members of the congregation of St. Peter & St. Mary. He knew that Archie Lintott waited for the girl at the end of the lane every Saturday afternoon.

He knew Gifford by sight from the Bull's Head. He could have told Woolston where the man could be found most afternoons, between four and ten, slumped at the table in the corner. No need to set up surveillance on the house. But no one had asked him. And why do himself out of easy earnings?

Joseph heard rumors about Blackthorn House, same as everyone. Stories of the stink of rotting flesh when the wind was in the wrong direction. How the workshop was filled floor to ceiling with stuffed birds and moth-eaten foxes, skeletons. Monstrosities. A two-headed kitten in a glass jar, stolen from some museum over Brighton way. An unborn lamb suspended in liquor. Then, last week, Reedman's lad claimed he'd heard unnatural sounds coming from inside the house. Joseph grimaced. Everyone knew Davey Reedman would make up any kind of wild story to talk his way out of a hiding. Been out poaching likely as not.

"And what of it?" he muttered. God helps those who help themselves, wasn't that what old Reverend Huxtable used to preach from the pulpit? Same sermon every Sunday, rain or shine. The new rector had a bit more variety, or so they said.

Joseph smoked his cigarette down to the end, sending a final ring of smoke into the air, then opened the window and flicked the stub out and down onto the exposed mudflats. He wondered if the tide would take it, then shrugged. Not his problem.

He pulled the chair back into position at the window, propped his muddy boots up on the sill and raised the glasses to his face. No sign of Gifford, but the girl was still sitting out on the terrace.

Motes of dust floated suspended in the lazy air; the warm afternoon sun filtered in through the window. Over the creek, the gulls continued to wheel and cry overhead. The lethargy of the afternoon pressed down upon him. As his eyes closed, Joseph was imagining the first mouthful of ale hitting the back of his throat.

*

Woolston stood outside the door, feeling every one of his fifty-eight years. He couldn't imagine what had possessed him to threaten the man. He'd never laid a finger on another living creature, not even bare-knuckle fighting in his school days. He was rattled, that was it. His visitor this afternoon, the menace. The idea that someone knew what he'd done. Had the others had a similar visit?

He was losing his sense of judgment.

Woolston took a deep breath, then looked down at the envelope in his hand. He also couldn't imagine why Brook had chosen to communicate with him via Gregory Joseph, rather than simply sending his clerk across West Street to deliver the letter in person. Were they not due to meet tomorrow anyway? Perhaps Brook had decided it was better to meet away from West Street, careful for once. Woolston supposed he should be grateful for that.

He read the brief note once, frowned, then read it again to make sure he hadn't misunderstood. All these contradictory instructions and changes of plan seemed needlessly complicated.

Folding the letter and putting it in his pocket, Woolston looked out over the estuary. The short stretch of open footpath leading to the Old Salt Mill was exposed, but he could see no one in the fields or footpaths on either side of the creek who might notice or remark on his presence. Just above the waterline, a flock of gulls swooped and skimmed, then soared up again into the sky. He hated all birds, but gulls were particularly aggressive. Hadn't he read in the newspaper last week that a boy fishing off the pier at Bognor had been attacked?

Woolston pulled his hat low over his brow and walked as quickly as his knee would allow him along the uneven foreshore. Back into Mill Lane and up to the Woolpack Inn, where the carriage and pair was waiting. He climbed in, pushed himself back into the seat and gave a deep sigh of relief.

One mistake. August 1902. His brigade recently returned from the Transvaal. All the flags out along the Broyle Road and girls cheering to welcome home the Royal Sussex Regiment. A funfair on the Militia Field.

How flattered he had been to be invited. Asked to make up a four at cards. He'd been looking forward to a rubber of bridge or two. Fine cigars and brandy. Feathers. Men, as he'd thought, with similar experiences. The promise of some special entertainment, not in the usual round of things; Woolston hadn't paused to consider what that might mean.

He hadn't done anything, but he had been there. He had been drunk. He'd done what he could to put it right. But in the end, he hadn't stopped them, and he had held his tongue.

"Where to, guv'nor?"

Woolston was pulled back to the present. He thought of the letter in his pocket.

"Graylingwell Hospital," he said.

The driver clicked his tongue and the horse pulled off in a rattle of clinker and bridle. It was slow going to start with. The road was claggy with mud and deeply rutted from the endless rain, though they picked up speed as they drew closer to Chichester.

It was a damnable business. More than anything he wished he could put the clock back. He put his hand to his breast pocket, where his old Boer War pistol was wrapped in a handkerchief. When he'd asked Joseph if he was prepared, it wouldn't have taken a psychiatrist to realize he actually had been thinking of himself.

Woolston shut his eyes and thought of his son.

Chapter 5

**Blackthorn House
Fishbourne Marshes**

"Is that you, girl?"

Connie jumped. She turned around to see her father standing in the open French doors. He was unsteady on his feet and, even a yard or so away, she could smell the sour ale on his breath and the tobacco sweating through his skin. Her heart contracted first in despair, then pity.

"Cassie?" he said, peering at her through sore, milky eyes.

"It's me. Connie."

He often woke from a drunken sleep confused or calling her by the wrong name, but he usually came back to his senses soon enough.

"Sit down," she said gently, as if talking to a child. She pulled the chair from under the table. "The sun's come out for a change. It will do you good to be in the fresh air."

She could see beads of sweat on his forehead and temples and realized that he was still very drunk. She saw the effort it was taking to stop himself from pitching forward on the uneven stone paving of the terrace. Six days of stubble on his lined face and smudges on his cheeks, as if he had been crying.

"Come and sit down," she said again, worried that he might

fall and hit his head. He was still wearing his boots, she noticed, thick with mud from a week ago. Had he changed his clothes at all?

She stood still, knowing the pattern things would take. No sense rushing him, it only made it worse. Sometimes he lashed out when he became frightened about not knowing where he was.

He rubbed the flat of his broad red hand across his face, almost, Connie thought, as if he was trying to erase his own features. Then he held both hands out, turning them over and back again, peering at the dirty skin.

"Come," she said, dropping her voice even further. "Sit here."

He was still in the grip of whatever nightmare had woken him and driven him downstairs. Without warning, he jerked his head up and stared directly at her.

"Work . . ."

The word exploded out of him. Connie had no idea what he meant.

"Dress," he said, half pointing at her clothes.

She looked down at her plain black skirt, her white collared blouse and black tie, trying to work out what he was seeing. *Who* he was seeing. Then she realized that her sleeves were still folded up from being in the workshop earlier.

"I found a jackdaw—" she began, but he cut across her.

"Schoolroom . . . go on with your lessons and your . . ."

Connie knew there was no point trying to understand what he was saying or follow his train of thought when he was in this state. Words would fall from his mouth, without order or meaning, like notes played out of sequence. Other times he might come up with snatches of ragged philosophy or theology. His mood could vary too. Sometimes he woke from his drinking sleeps full of self-pity, others times shaking with rage, storming against those who had stolen his livelihood from him. Very occasionally, he woke angry. Then there was little she could do except stay out of his way.

He started to laugh. A racked sound, no mirth or joy in it.

"Please," Connie said sadly, "come and sit with me here."

"Blue . . . thought it was her, but ghost . . ." He stumbled. "Got a letter telling me. How can she be dead? Don't understand. After all the waiting, not right . . ."

His balance was deteriorating. Now he was paddling from foot to foot, an uneven march to try to keep upright, before staggering over the threshold and onto the terrace. Connie leaped forward, ready to catch him if he fell.

"Blood . . ."

Connie's eyes widened, watching in horrified fascination as her father waved his hand, then let a finger come to rest on her sleeve. When she looked down, she saw that the cuff of her shirt was stained.

"Remember, I found a jackdaw," she said patiently. "Beautiful. Not a mark on him. I've been in the workshop. You see?"

She managed to take his hand and half lead him, half pull him to the garden chair. The wicker complained under the sudden weight, but he settled himself back and sat still.

"There," she said with a sigh of relief. "Now, I'll fetch us some tea. Stay here. Don't worry about a thing."

She didn't want the maid to see him like this. Mary wasn't a fool; she knew perfectly well what was wrong with Gifford, but Connie didn't want him to be humiliated. She had to find a way of giving him something settling to drink, and perhaps some toasted bread and butter. She also had to get him out of his unwashed clothes. She couldn't make him bathe, though if she could persuade him to rest for a while in the drawing room later, she could at least get into his room and clean it. She shuddered to imagine the kind of state it would be in after seven days.

"'. . . all that old traditions tell,'" he muttered, a sound something between a growl and a song, "'I tremblingly believe . . .'"

Connie pulled herself up. He was quoting the same verses that had slipped into her mind in the wet, dark churchyard. She crouched down by his chair. "Where did you hear that, Father?" she said, trying to keep her voice calm. The half-remembered classroom, the voice reading out loud. She clutched his arm. "Can you tell me?"

"Schoolroom, all those lessons, good for nothing in the end." He gave a long sigh. "That's it, that's it. Chalk. Back to the classroom. Not in with the birds, not until after lessons . . ."

His eyes were starting to close. Connie shook him. She couldn't let him stop now that he was actually talking. About the vanished days, telling her something while forgetting she did not know.

"'Two little dickie birds, sitting on a wall' . . . no, that's not right. Younger before." He flapped his hands in the air in front of him. "'Fly away, Peter, fly away, Paul.'"

Connie repeated the lines, hoping to return him to his original spiral of thought.

"'Tis now, replied the village belle,'" she quoted. "Isn't that how it starts? Do you remember?"

"Can't remember," he mumbled. "Village belle, yes."

"Remind me," she said softly, keeping the desperation out of her voice for fear of jolting him back to the present. "Remind me how it goes."

If he knew the same poem, then the vanished days might not be completely lost. If there was one shared memory, why not others? But he was sitting silently now, his face slack.

She closed her eyes, trying to drag out of her locked memory, like Ariadne's thread, the words she once must have known well. Steeled herself to remember an older girl's voice, and her own, child's hand shaping the letters on the page to better learn the lines.

"'Tis now, replied the village belle, St Mark's mysterious eve . . .'" She squeezed his arm. "Your turn."

"'How . . . how, when the midnight . . .'" His words were halting and indistinct, running one into the other, but Connie knew they were right. "'Green,'" he murmured.

Connie took up the next couplet, then Gifford the next, each remembering a word, prompting a line, until they had recited the poem between them.

"'Amid the silence drear.' There," she said. "That was good."

Gifford nodded. "Very good." He gave a small, soft laugh. "Top marks."

Connie drew in her breath, knowing this was the moment, but fearing that if she said the wrong thing, or even the right thing but in the wrong way, the spell would be broken and Gifford would come to his senses.

"How wonderful that we can remember after so long," she said, keeping her voice as light and level as she could. "We did well, didn't we?"

She saw that the fight and confusion had left him. His shoulders were relaxed and his dirty hands resting, still, on his lap. His eyes were closed.

"After all these years," she said, desperate not to let him drift into sleep.

He laughed again, this time with warmth.

"She made you say it over and over again," he said. "Verses, poetry, rhymes, very keen on all of that. 'A good mental exercise,' that's what she always said."

Connie could barely speak. Her heart beat harder. "Who said?"

"Could always hear you. From the museum, I could hear you. Doing your lessons. Windows open. 'A good mental exercise, Gifford.' Like a sister to you."

"Who?" she said again.

But he was smiling now, his eyes firmly closed. Connie knew he was lost in the gentle arms of the past, safe from everything that troubled and tortured him. She felt cruel trying to bring him back, but she had to know. Carefully keeping her voice low and quiet, she asked the question in another way.

"Where is she now?"

For a moment, she didn't think he'd heard. Then the color seemed to drain from his face and his expression folded in on itself. Haunted.

"Gone. Got a letter. Dead, so they say. All for nothing."

"Who's dead, Father?"

A terrible wail escaped from his lips. As if he'd been struck, Gifford suddenly lurched up out of the chair, flapping hands by his sides. Connie sprang back in alarm.

"Is she here?" he cried, his eyes wide with terror. "*Is* she?"

"It's all right," she said urgently, as he struck at the air with his raised fists. "There's no one else here. Just us." She managed to catch his wrists in her hands. "It's just us, like always."

For a sudden, clear, lucid moment, Gifford met her gaze. Seeing her as she was, not through a haze of drink or as someone else. Her, Connie. Then his eyes clouded over. Grief, guilt, a pain so deep that it would never leave him.

"Who is she?" Connie asked. "Please, Father. Please tell me."

"Don't remember," he shouted.

Before she could stop him, Gifford was blundering over the step and into the drawing room, lurching from piano to armchair to banister, then the sound of his bedroom door slamming.

Connie sank down onto the low stone wall that divided the terrace from the garden and put her hands on her knees. She hated these scenes. She was desperately sorry for him, but also angry that he let himself get into such a state.

But this time, her dominant emotion was relief. Her instincts were right. Whatever had happened in the churchyard had affected him profoundly.

"Is she here?"

The same, whispered question she'd overheard at midnight in the graveyard. And a new name. Her father had got Connie's name wrong many times before when he was overcome by drink, but she didn't think she'd heard the name Cassie before. And spoken so clearly, without hesitation.

A strong memory of being loved, of being cared for. Not by her poor unknown mother, but by someone who had taught her things and who'd cherished her like a sister.

Connie looked back into the dark drawing room, through the French windows. She wanted to go after him, but she knew there was no point. He would either fall deeply asleep, waking later without the slightest recollection of what he'd done or said. Or else—and she hoped this wasn't the case—he would seek solace in his brandy and try to drown the darkness inside him. If that happened, her chances of learning more were reduced to nothing.

Connie stood up, smoothed down her skirts, picked up her coffee cup and saucer. The afternoon was moving on. If she didn't go back into the workshop soon, the jackdaw would be ruined.

Her father's last words before he'd staggered out of the room, were they an apology or an instruction?

"Don't remember."

Chapter 6

Salthill Road
Fishbourne

Harry Woolston was the only person to alight at Fishbourne Halt. The tiny station was simply two narrow strips of platform. Set in the middle of fields, it was flanked by trees filled with nesting black birds. Rooks, were they? Barely a mile and a half from Chichester, and he was in the heart of the countryside.

The driver blew his whistle. A belch of smoke. The fireman, standing on the plate, raised his hat to Harry as the motor steam engine pulled away. The rails began to hum.

Harry was already regretting the impulse that had made him come chasing out here. It was early afternoon, and here he was, in the middle of nowhere. He looked around for a porter or anyone from whom to get directions, but there wasn't a soul about.

He made his way along the platform. As he reached the road, the door of the keeper's cottage opened and a rickety old man in the uniform of the South Coast Railway limped out and began to open the crossing gates. One by one, by one by one. It was a slow business.

"I'm after the Woolpack Inn," Harry said.

"Straight down," the keeper said, pointing south. "All the way to the bottom of Salthill Road."

"This being Salthill Road?"

The keeper nodded. "When you reach the main road, turn left. Five minutes' walk, young man like you, give or take. Two minutes. First tavern's the Bull's Head, that's not the one you want. Keep following the road round, past the Methodist chapel, and you'll see the post office. Woolpack's next to it on the far side of the road. You can't miss it."

*

Harry set off down the lane. The ground was soft underfoot, after the endless rain, but the hedgerows were full and it was pleasant.

Cow parsley as high as his shoulder. Nature didn't interest him—he was a portrait painter rather than a landscape artist—but he appreciated the colors. Deep moss greens to filigree silver leaves, yellow buttercups and celandine. From time to time, the palette was broken by a tree with magnificent purple leaves, the color of claret. He thought back to the painting on its easel in his studio, to the woman frozen lifeless in time, and realized it was the color of her skin he'd got wrong. Too pink, no hollows and shadows. No life in it.

Harry kept walking, still thinking about his failed portrait. Past a small white cottage and a flint-faced building at the junction with the main road. A laundry by the looks of it. Billows of steam and the smell of hot, starched linen. That was another thing. The woman's bonnet was drawing the attention away from her expression. She seemed like a mannequin, rather than a representation of a real person. Perhaps if he muted down the color, a pale blue or green, that would shift the focus of the painting?

He turned left and walked east along the main road, such as

it was. Here, cottages were tucked in between larger plots with modern, detached redbrick houses. He saw the Bull's Head on the south side of the road, as the porter had said. A large gabled building with a pleasant facade, a few trees and a low, thatched wooden barn behind, it was rather charming.

On the corner, a gaggle of children stood outside a sweet shop. Girls with smock pinafores over their dresses, hair tied back with ribbons; the boys with grubby collars visible above their jackets.

Harry stopped on the opposite side of the road from the Woolpack. If the Dunnaways man was right, this had to be the place. But the idea that his father might have a rendezvous in this spit-and-sawdust tavern, a workingmen's bar, was absurd. His father was fastidious. The kind to put his handkerchief on a park bench rather than risk getting a speck of dirt on his coat. And on occasion, when Harry came into dinner without properly cleaning the paint from his hands, the old man would fidget and struggle not to comment on it. Harry smiled fondly. John Woolston was as predictable as clockwork. He never acted on impulse; he was formal and rather dull, did everything by the book. Absolutely Victorian in his outlook. Obedience, respectability, duty, everything planned to the letter.

Except here Harry was, standing outside a disreputable-looking place in Fishbourne, wondering if his father might or might not be inside.

The smile faded from Harry's face.

There was no sign of a taxi outside, though there was a tub trap with a mule in harness. A group of five or six men were standing in the shade—caps, weather-worn faces, short workingmen's jackets. At their feet, a black-and-tan terrier slumbered, oblivious to the danger of hoof and wheel.

Harry was stumped. If he went in and his father saw him, it would be obvious he must have followed from Chichester. So whatever his father was or was not doing—even if it was a blameless game of dominoes—the situation would be awkward for both of them.

Aware that he was attracting attention, Harry continued on to the outskirts of the village, where the houses stopped. There, he crossed over and ambled back on the south side of the road. There was a pleasant low cottage, set at right angles to the road, and several substantial houses. At the end of the row was a rather attractive white house with its own stable and coach house. Set behind wrought-iron railings, flanked by mature trees and bushes, with a square portico, it gave almost directly onto the street.

Harry stopped and lit a cigarette, wondering what the devil to do next.

*

Connie went back to the jackdaw, hoping she had not been away from the bird for too long.

When she'd left the workshop earlier, she'd protected the skin from drying out by folding the head and wings in on themselves, and had placed a cloth over the carcass. But any number of parasites, invisible to the naked eye, could have burrowed their way into gaps between the skin and the exposed flesh at the tips of the jackdaw's wings, leaving no sign. Only if the bird began to rot would any damage become clear.

Connie turned the jackdaw over in her hands, examining it thoroughly, and decided to continue. The flesh hadn't become sticky and it was a beautiful creature; she didn't want to let it go to waste. This was the moment when it would begin to transform from something dead into an object of beauty that would live forever. The essence of the bird, caught by her craft and her skill, at one distinct moment.

Immortal.

She sprinkled a little water on the skin to make sure it wouldn't shrink or tear, then continued where she had left off before lunch. She worked her way down the spine, the scalpel squeaking as she scraped flesh from bone, fat from cartilage, wiping the tiniest feathers on the edge of the newspaper. The white tail bone, and a sharp point in the right wing, set at an angle, as evidence of how the bird had died. Shot by the game-keeper at Old Park, Connie suspected, leaving the jackdaw just enough strength to fly home to die. She had found it lying beside the hawthorn. It would require a certain amount of skill to disguise the disfiguration when the time came to stuff and present the bird.

Connie was shaken by the scene with her father—the new information he had let slip, as well as the tantalizing glimpses of how much more he might tell her if he chose to. She was aware, too, that she must not allow herself to brood. When she was worried or upset, she was more likely to slip between the cracks in time. Those disabling, alarming petit mal episodes had been the reason her father had given for not sending her to school once she had recovered after the accident.

Connie began to skin the flesh from the neck until, finally, she was ready to turn her attention to the skull. This was the part of the process she liked the least, the texture and smells reminding her that without death, there was no new form of life. No beauty.

She wondered if, when it was done—and provided she was

pleased with her work—she might try to sell the jackdaw. The last commission had been in the autumn—a preserved rook for a barber in Chichester, wanting something unusual in the shop window to attract customers' attention—and although her father refused to talk about their household finances with her, she suspected any contribution would be useful.

She sighed, wondering how she might achieve such a thing without her father's knowledge. But the truth was, regardless of what happened to the piece, the work itself calmed her. Connie felt most herself when she was alone in the workshop. She and a bird, working together to create something new and extraordinary. The process itself was its own reward. The business of skinning and cleaning and stuffing rooted her in something tangible, kept her tethered to the real world.

She put down the scalpel and picked up her forceps. Pressing the jackdaw's skinned head to the table, she inserted the points into the left socket and squeezed. As always, the eyeball was sticky at first. Then, it popped out with a leaking of inky dark liquid. Round on three sides, the surface closest to the socket was flat, the shape of a blueberry. Connie placed it on the table, beside the bird's thin, black strip of tongue.

The right eye came more easily. When she had finished, she wrapped it all in a scrap of newspaper and put it in the pail.

This, now, was the worst of it. She breathed in, trying not to draw the noxious odor too deeply into her lungs. With a blunt knife, she carved a square in the back of the skull. Then, delicately, she began the process of pulling the gray matter of the jackdaw's brain out of the opening with the same delicate forceps. Little by little by little, a time-consuming and messy process. She let her shoulders drop, rolled her neck, knowing that soon it would be over.

She would wash and preserve the bird. Then, tomorrow, the process of bringing it back to life would begin.

Blood, skin, bone.

Mauduyt, however, did not point out any means of preservation.
Sulphurous fumigations appeared to him the ne plus ultra *for*
killing destructive insects. Sulphur does still more, it destroys the
skins themselves . . . their upper parts were burned; the sulphurous
vapour had changed the red into a dirty yellow, faded the yellow,
blackened the blue, soiled the cases, and even the glasses which en-
closed them.

TAXIDERMY: OR, THE ART OF COLLECTING, PREPARING,
AND MOUNTING OBJECTS OF NATURAL HISTORY

Mrs. R. Lee
Longman & Co., Paternoster Row, London, 1820

It has been hard not to reveal myself these past weeks, almost the hardest thing in this long and terrible business. There was a time when a different story might yet have been told. But I lacked the courage and the moment slipped away.

Dead for all these long and many years. The smell of sulphur and the grave. The smell of rotting and unpreserved flesh. The darkening glass. They sullied the beauty of the place. Destroyed all that was wonderful and made it dark.

Old sins have long shadows.

I am embarked now on this road, and now there is no choice but to follow it to the end. It is a tale that begins, as it will end, in a graveyard where the bones and the spiders and the worms inhabit the cold earth. I give each a chance to do what is right. A chance to make reparation.

I do not believe they will listen.

I make no plea for exoneration or sympathy. This is not an attempt to soften your attitude to me in the name of pity or sorrow or remorse. They will choose their fates and I do not expect them to choose well.

I am watching you.

Chapter 7

Blackthorn House
Fishbourne Marshes

The scream shattered the peace of the workshop.

Connie dropped the forceps. Another scream and she was on her feet. Her first thought was fear for her father, then she realized the sound was coming from outside. Mary, not Gifford.

Throwing a sheet of newspaper over the jackdaw, she picked up her skirts and ran. Out through the scullery and into the kitchen garden.

"What on earth is the matter?"

Mary was hunched over by the washing line, her hands clutched across her chest. The pegs were scattered over the ground and a basket of clean linen was half upturned. The best linen tablecloth, two handkerchiefs with CG embroidered in blue, the tea towel with green trim—all lay in the mud.

Connie dashed toward her. The girl was still screaming, but her voice was oddly rhythmic, like single, shrill repeated blasts of a whistle. There was no one else there and Connie couldn't see anything that might have terrified her to such an extent. She put her hands on Mary's shoulders.

"What on earth is the matter? Are you hurt?"

The maid stared at her with wide, unseeing eyes, but her mouth fell thankfully silent.

"What happened to send you into such a state? Tell me."

Mary gulped at the air, half sobbing.

"You won't be in any trouble," Connie said, feeling the girl's whole body shaking. "Tell me."

Connie felt the maid wriggle out of her grasp, heard her take a deep breath. A few moments more, then Mary turned and pointed to the small stream that ran along the northern boundary of the garden. One of the many tributaries leading away into the creek.

Surely it wasn't possible she'd been frightened half to death by a water rat? Or one of the thick black eels that lived along the riverbank? Davey Reedman was always out there, fishing with his home-made rod. They were revolting, and there were a great many more of them this spring than usual, but they were harmless.

"Show me," she said. After the incident with her father, she had no patience left for melodramatics.

"No . . ." The girl backed away, shaking her head. "I can't. It . . . Down there."

Connie took a handkerchief from her cardigan pocket and held it out. "Wipe your eyes. Whatever it is, I'm sure it's not as bad as you think."

*

At first Connie saw nothing out of the ordinary.

Then her eyes fixed on a flash of color in the middle of the reeds. Cloth. A blue doubled-seamed woolen coat, floating in the brackish water. Visible beneath, a plain green skirt swaying lightly in the current.

Connie took a deep breath. "Go quickly to Slay Lodge," she said, thinking of the nearest house. "Find Mr. Crowther. Inform him . . . Explain that we need—" She broke off, feeling a wave of nausea rising in her throat. She swallowed hard. "In fact, no. Go into the village and fetch Dr. Evershed. Tell him what's happened. Ask him to come. Quick as you can."

"Is she not . . . dead, then?"

Connie faltered. She looked with sympathy at the girl. Mary was shaking, her arms wrapped tight around herself. She'd only just turned sixteen. Connie couldn't be sure she'd even heard her instructions, let alone taken them in.

"Mary," she said sharply. "Go to Eversfield and ask if the doctor is at home. The white house, you know it?"

This time, the girl nodded.

"Of course you do. Good girl. Fetch Dr. Evershed. He will know what to do." She gave her a gentle push. "Now."

Mary's eyes held Connie's gaze for a moment or two, then without another word, she ran, out through the gate and onto the footpath.

"Don't fall," Connie called after her, knowing the wooden bridges were slippery from the endless rain. But the girl was already out of earshot.

*

Connie steadied herself, then walked back to the swollen stream. For a moment, she allowed herself to believe it was merely a mistake. That all she had seen—all Mary had seen—was a coat trapped in the reeds, and imagination had done the rest.

She looked into the water. The body was still there, face down, arms being swayed this way and that in the current, its position leaving no possibility that the woman could be alive. Connie forced herself not to look away. A cloud of chestnut hair, come loose from its pins. The blue coat, bright and water-logged against the pale stalks of the cattails.

Bare hands, bare head.

Connie stepped back from the water's edge. She glanced up at her father's bedroom window. It was shut and the curtains drawn, but surely he could not have failed to hear the commotion? Mary had screamed so very loudly. Already regretting having sent the girl straightaway to fetch help, Connie realized she had to talk to Gifford before anyone came. She didn't want him, in his inebriated state, to say anything foolish or humiliate himself, do something that might be misinterpreted by Dr. Evershed or even by Mary. Not that she thought he was involved, of course she didn't, but his earlier words had been wild and distraught. She would blame herself for not warning him.

At the same time, Connie couldn't shake from her mind the image of her father staggering out from the church a week ago, his hands naked and raw. Gifford, the last to leave, tramping down the path through the broken bodies of the songbirds.

Had he seen the woman in the churchyard too? Had he also seen the woman watching the house?

Connie ran back inside and upstairs to the first floor.

"Father?" she said, knocking on his closed door. "I'm sorry to disturb you, but I must talk to you."

There was no sound from inside the room.

"Father?"

She banged harder and rattled at the handle, unwilling to accept that he could have fallen into so deep a sleep in the short time since they had parted company. To her surprise, the door opened.

"May I come in?"

Inside, the atmosphere was even worse than she'd anticipated. A sweat of stale beer and tobacco and spent matches washed over her. And something else.

Despair. The smell of despair.

"Father, before anyone comes, I must talk to you."

As Connie's eyes adjusted to the gloom, she picked out a lumpen shape in the bed. Quickly, she crossed the room and drew the curtains, unlatching the window at the same time to let in some air.

"Wake up," she said, her voice now sharp with anxiety.

She reached out her right hand, hovering it over the bed for an instant, then let it drop onto her father's shoulder. Soft, not hard. She threw back the covers to see an old pillow and her father's mothballed frock coat rolled up in the center of the mattress.

For a moment, Connie stared at the bed, unable to accept the evidence of her own eyes. Then she ran back to the window and looked out, her sharp gaze scanning the landscape for as far as she could see. A shaming image of him staggering into the Bull's Head, drunk and unkempt, came into her mind, quickly crushed. He couldn't have gone onto the footpath without her noticing. She and Mary had been in the back garden the whole time. They would have seen him leave. The only way he could have gone was to the south, or to the open sea, or to the fields to the west toward the large estate of Old Park. And why would he?

Connie took a deep breath. She couldn't lose her head. There was no question of going to look for him, when Mary could arrive with Dr. Evershed at any moment. Besides, where would she start? Another unwanted picture of her father, stumbling into the marsh, his nose and mouth filled with choking black mud. She pushed this image away too. It was broad daylight, the sun was shining. Even in his inebriated state, there was no reason he should fall.

Trying to persuade herself that it was, in fact, fortunate he would not be here when the doctor came, Connie cast her eyes around the squalid room for clues as to why he had left so abruptly. Was it their conversation that had caused him to bolt? Or had the same secret distress that had led him to take refuge in his bedroom now driven him to leave it?

Her sense of dread grew stronger. Had Gifford looked out and, in the rising tide, also noticed that same blue coat floating in the water? Or even worse to contemplate—and she felt disloyal for allowing the thought to come into her mind—had he known all along that the body was there?

With a knot in the pit of her stomach, Connie shook out the bedclothes. She returned the frock coat to the wardrobe, noticing that his daytime coat was not on its usual hanger. The floor was littered with empty beer bottles and broken glass. There was nothing large enough in which to carry all the detritus downstairs, so she pushed it under the bed with the tip of her boot. She would return later to clear it up properly. There was nothing to be done about the smell—the whole room needed a thorough airing—but she emptied the ash and spent matches into a brown paper bag and stacked the dirty saucers ready to take back to the scullery.

Then, she stopped.

She put her hand back into the bag and fished out the fragment from the remains of the cigarettes and matches. Plain cream writing paper, of adequate quality, nothing distinctive about it. Black cursive letters.

Holding the remains between her thumb and forefinger, she blew off the warm ash. She could make out only six letters:

DRA CRO. There was no way of knowing if it was a name or part of the address, or what came before or after. There appeared to be a small space between the third and fourth letters, but she couldn't be sure.

The only word that was clear, at the top right-hand corner of the piece of paper, was ASYLUM. Had the letter come from Graylingwell? If so, from whom? He had no contact with the place, so far as Connie knew. She had never once heard him mention it.

Time seemed to slow. The familiar sense of everything darkening, fading to black. Connie fought it. She would not let herself be pulled under. She would not let her father down; whatever he had done or wherever he was, she had to keep her head.

She sat heavily down on the bed and tried to focus on the scrap of paper.

Chapter 8

Gifford raised his head from the ground, tasting dirt, straw and blood in his mouth. He felt like he'd gone fifteen rounds with Jack Johnson. His knuckles were cracked, his lips too. When he tried to blink, he realized his left eye was swollen shut.

A few moments passed, then, gingerly, he tried to push himself up into a sitting position. He managed it, but the effort left him gasping for breath. He slumped back against the wall, his chest tight and his ribs sore.

After a few moments, he got himself more comfortable on the tiles, legs straight out in front of him, and tried to remember what had happened. For years, he had been waiting, one day knowing he would be called to account. Finally, that day had come.

His sins had caught up with him.

At first, he'd stayed in his room to avoid Connie, not wanting to lie to her. Trying not to drink, failing. Knowing that his loosened tongue was dangerous. Connie always could see through him in any case, sharp as a tack, even when she was little. Used to call him Gifford from time to time, made the customers laugh. And hadn't he noticed in the last few days the different way she looked at him, when she thought he wasn't watching? He knew she was trying to remember. He wished he could tell her why it was safest to forget.

It was the one thing he feared more than anything. Because then, like a crack in the seawall, once her memories came flooding back, who could say where it would end?

What had he given away earlier in the afternoon? In his drunken meanderings? They had talked, that he remembered. But as to what had been said, it was a blank. She had made him talk and say things he should not have said. He felt cold with fear. What secrets had he betrayed?

He felt bad, bruised from top to toe. He should have stayed in his room, only he hadn't been able to bear it any longer, cooped up with only his accusing thoughts for company, and his grieving heart.

Ten years. He'd been living with the consequences ever since. No harm in it, so he'd thought. Four fine gentlemen looking for a special night. A night to remember.

Gifford covered his face with his hands.

All these years and he hadn't talked. All these years, he'd taken their money and used it well. Used it right. They had no cause to come after him, had they? He stopped, the effort of remembering making his head throb.

That glimpse of chestnut hair in the water.

Not possible. In the churchyard, not possible. She was dead. He'd had a letter telling him so.

The Eve of St. Mark, a night of ghosts.

*

Gifford didn't know how long he drifted in and out of consciousness; he wasn't certain. Only that when he next woke, his senses were a little sharper. A smell of damp bricks and dust. Feathers. He ran his fingers over his chin, feeling the scratch of several days' stubble. He wondered what had happened to his hat. He was wearing his coat.

Filled with a sudden panic, he struggled to stand. Willing strength into his legs, pushing his shoulders into the bricks to lever himself up. He put his hand out and felt the cool dome of glass. His brief moment of courage died. Now he remembered.

Burning the letter in a panic, then staggering back downstairs. Taking the key off the hook and coming here. Hidden among the bell jars and treasures of his past. And the one newer glass case. The one piece of evidence he had of that night.

Gifford felt a moment of hope, then the spark died, to be replaced by terror. Remembering how he had stumbled on the steps and fallen down, down in the dark, hitting his head at the bottom.

In the depths of his deadened, drink-ruined mind, he realized he'd left Connie alone. No one was there to protect her if they came. *When* they came.

With a howl, he again tried to struggle upright, but he couldn't find the strength. He started to crawl toward where he thought the steps were. Slowly, closer to the door. To the light.

Pushing against it, except it wouldn't open.

Why wouldn't it open? He hadn't locked it after him, had he?

The door was a close fit to keep the exhibits at a steady temperature. No light or warmth from outside got in. Gifford pushed with his shoulder, using what little strength he had, and this time heard the padlock rattle over the latch.

Still, it refused to give. He was trapped.

Gifford shook his head, setting the world spinning. If they'd wanted rid of him, they'd have done it by now. They had no scruples. There were plenty of names carved in stone in the graveyard of those who'd been claimed by the treacherous mudflats. Easy to add one more to their number. No one any the wiser.

"But I told no one," he muttered into the darkness. "I kept my word . . ."

Chapter 9

"Miss Gifford?"

A man's voice calling, not one she recognized. Connie leaped up from the bed, for a moment forgetting where she was. Then she looked down at the half-burnt piece of paper in her hand and realized it had happened again. She had slipped out of time. How long had she been sitting here?

"Miss Gifford?"

She ran to the window and looked down. Mary was standing in the garden, her hands clutching at her apron. Beside her was a young man in his mid-twenties. In the slightest of moments between one breath and the next, she took in his appearance: medium height and build, brown moustache, starched collar, and a waistcoat, suit and tie each a different shade of blue. Cuffs on his trousers and a pair of polished Oxfords. Connie was certain she had never met him before.

"Are you there, miss?" Mary called.

"Here," she replied.

The stranger looked up and started to talk. Connie could see his lips were moving, but somehow she couldn't distinguish a word he was saying. "I'll come down," she called, "if you wouldn't mind waiting."

Why had Mary disregarded her instructions? Where was Dr. Evershed? There was no doctor's surgery in the village, so although he was retired—a well-respected amateur artist these days—he would know the correct procedures to follow. Who was this stranger Mary had brought instead?

Connie took a last look around and hurried out of her father's room, locking it behind her.

*

The back garden was now entirely in shadow. Connie recognized that she must have been upstairs for quite a bit longer than she'd thought.

Mary darted forward. "I'm sorry, miss, I—"

"That will do, Mary," she said, cutting off the girl's apology. She tried to behave as if everything was normal.

"I'm Constantia Gifford." She met the man's gaze. "And you are?"

"Harold Woolston." He raised his hat, then removed his gloves and held out his hand.

After a moment's hesitation, Connie took his hand and shook.

"I did what you said, miss," Mary gabbled. "The doctor wasn't there, but—"

"I was," Woolston said. "Your girl came flying out of nowhere, saying that she needed help. So here I am."

"Are you staying in the village, Mr. Woolston?"

"Just passing through."

Catching the hesitancy in his voice, Connie waited for him to say something further, but he did not. He had the most extraordinary color eyes, she noticed. Almost violet.

"Did Mary explain what has happened?" she asked.

"No. Only that she had been sent to fetch the doctor. Since I was on hand, I thought I might offer myself in his place."

"You are a friend of Dr. and Mrs. Evershed?"

His eyes widened. "Arthur Evershed?"

"Well, yes, but if—"

"I'd heard he lived near Chichester," Harry said. "He's the most remarkable artist, all while working as a doctor, too." He stopped, seeing the expression on her face. "Forgive me," he said quickly. "I'm apt to let my enthusiasm run away with me."

Connie stared at him. The habits of caution bred into her by watching over her father for years ran deep. On the other hand, she couldn't cope on her own and it would be an ugly business. Drownings always were. She'd witnessed that at first hand in January when the mill pond flooded and the body of an itinerant had been found in the reeds.

"It is rather unpleasant, I'm afraid," she said.

He gave a brief smile. "I'm sure I am equal to it."

"Can I go inside, miss?" Mary asked.

Connie hesitated. It would be easier with three of them. But though she forced herself to rise above the rumors and gossip that circulated about her father, she didn't want to be accused of causing distress to a young girl. Besides, she was genuinely fond of her.

"Yes. Mr. Woolston and I can manage."

Connie walked a few steps back toward the house with the girl.

"I don't suppose you saw Mr. Gifford, did you? On the path or in Fishbourne?"

Mary shook her head. "No, miss."

Connie held her gaze. "Thank you. I will call you when we're finished. Perhaps you could make some tea and take it out to the terrace for when . . . for later."

She took a deep breath, then turned back.

"So, how can I be of service?" Harry asked.

"I regret to say . . ." She paused, hating how stiff she sounded. "There's been a drowning. A young woman. Mary saw her in the stream and, of course, it gave her a fright."

He blanched. "A drowning?"

"I think so, yes."

"Is it common—" He stopped. "I'm sorry, I didn't mean *common* as such. Rather, is this something that happens at this part of the creek? Here, I mean. This spot. You're so close to the water."

Connie shook her head. "Not often. You see—"

"I'm sorry." Woolston jumped in, misunderstanding her hesitation. "Thoughtless of me to fire questions at you. I'm sure I can manage alone. If you'd rather. Not the sort of thing a lady should . . ."

"It will take two to bring her out, Mr. Woolston," she said quietly.

"Harry." He was awfully pale. "Harry is fine."

For a moment, the intimacy of his Christian name hung between them.

"Right," he said, his voice falsely bright. "Let's get this over with."

Chapter 10

Connie pointed to the far bank of the river.

"There," she said. "It—she—is on the far side."

Woolston removed his shoes and socks, then rolled his trousers up to just below his knees. He handed her his jacket, then folded back the sleeves of his shirt too.

It wasn't unusual for objects to be washed up into the creek and the little rills and streams. Flotsam, a torn coal sack or a child's fishing rod, seaweed when the spring tides coincided with a strong sou'westerly. But not a body.

Down on the coast, in the fishing creels of Selsey and Pagham and Littlehampton, drownings were a fact of life. This far up the estuary, accidents were more likely to occur on the marshes than in the sea itself. Men missing their footing in the dark, stumbling into the sinking black mud and unable to free themselves. Could the body have been swept all the way up here by the tide? Connie didn't think so.

"I think the best thing is for me to climb down," Woolston said. "See if I can pull the body—young lady—out without you having to get wet into the bargain."

"Thank you."

He stepped down into the water, then steadied himself in the current.

"How deep does it get?" he called up.

"Two feet, perhaps, in the middle. Less at the banks."

She watched him wade across, the incoming tide splashing up against him until the backs of his trouser legs were wet. When he drew level with the body, he hesitated, then reached out and took hold of the sodden shoulders of the woolen coat. The sudden movement caused the woman's head to loll to one side, her face breaking the surface of the water as if she was trying to breathe.

White face, blue lips, red hair.

Connie caught her breath. The sudden, sharp stab of memory. *Blood, skin, bone. Dust on bare floorboards, feathers.*

"But not water," she murmured. "Not drowned."

"She's caught on something," Woolston was saying. "There's some kind of a wire, all tangled up. Fishing line, perhaps? Do the lobster boats come this far?"

Connie forced herself to answer. "No. Not usually."

Harry put his hands beneath the woman's arms and tugged. At first, nothing happened. He pulled again, a little harder, and this time, the corpse came suddenly free. He staggered back, almost losing his footing in the water, but then adjusted his grip and slowly dragged the woman cross-current toward the near bank. As the water grew shallower, Connie saw how the woman became heavier in his arms.

She leaned down to help, grasping handfuls of wet wool and trying to pull the body up onto the bank. Such a dreadful way to die, struggling for breath. She shuddered and hoped that it had been quick.

Between them, they eventually hauled her up onto the grass. Breathless from the exertion, Harry rolled her over on her back, then stood up and walked a few steps away.

Connie looked down at the young woman. Her face was bruised and her features distended by her immersion in the water; she couldn't be sure whether or not this was the woman she'd seen watching the house, or, for that matter, the woman in the churchyard. The one face had been concealed by a veil, the second by the nighttime shadow and rain and the brim of her hat.

But it was the same coat. Connie didn't think there could be two such distinctive pieces.

She knelt and laid the cold arms across the chest, noticing how the backs of the woman's hands were scratched. Her skin was oddly pimpled, as if she had goose bumps from the cold, and there was a white foam in the corners of her lips and nose, tinged with blood. Her shirt had a pretty red embroidered pattern around the neck.

"Choked . . ."

The word slipped out of Connie's mouth. She felt her knees buckle, but she stayed upright. Woolston didn't notice. He was putting on his shoes and socks, rearranging his own clothes.

"Forgive me, I didn't hear what you said."

"I said nothing," she said. Her voice seemed to be coming from a long way away.

"A suicide, do you think?" Woolston said. "Though I can't understand how she got so badly caught up. Do you think she might have come off a boat? A fishing trawler, something of the sort?"

"No. Women don't go out on the boats," Connie said, trying to think.

She didn't know what to do, only that she had to get rid of him as quickly as she could. She walked to where the laundry still lay on the ground, picked up a sheet and laid it over the body.

"There's nothing more we can do," she said, keeping her voice level. "If you wouldn't mind, could you please go and tell Dr. Evershed what has happened? He will make arrangements. She—the body—will have to be taken to Chichester."

She felt his eyes on her, admiring how well she was taking things. Or disapproving, perhaps. Would he prefer her to be one of those frilly creatures forever collapsing in a haze of sal volatile and tears? If only he knew the turmoil she actually felt.

"I could do with that tea," he said. "Something stronger, even."

She met his gaze. "The sooner the right people are informed, the better. Don't you agree?"

"Well, yes. Of course," Harry said, realizing she was dismissing him. "May I at least wash my hands?"

Connie could see no possible way of denying him that. She led the way across the lawn and in through the front door, then escorted him along the corridor to the downstairs cloakroom. Did he think her callous? She was surprised by how much she would mind if he did.

"I really am very grateful and I'm sorry to ask you to go straightaway. I simply cannot bear the thought of being left here with . . . her for any longer than necessary."

He nodded. "Of course."

They were standing close to each other by the front door. Connie felt suddenly overwhelmed by his presence. She slipped past him and out onto the path. He stepped out to join her.

"Do you live here alone? It's awfully isolated."

"No. With my father."

He looked back into the house. "Is he here?"

Connie found a smile. "No, otherwise of course he would have dealt with all this . . . I am expecting him back at any moment."

"Maybe I should wait until he returns?"

"Thank you, but there's no need. I will feel better knowing the arrangements are in hand."

Harry tilted his head. "Thing is, I feel like I'm running out on you. In any case, you've hurt yourself."

"Hurt?"

He reached out and took her wrist, turned her hand over in his. Looking at the cuff of her shirt speckled with blood. Connie felt a charge shoot between them.

"It's nothing," she said, pulling her hand back.

"You should put a dab of iodine on it all the same."

"It's nothing, Mr. Woolston," she repeated, desperate for him to go.

"Harry. Please. Mr. Woolston is awfully formal after all this."

"I suppose it is." She paused. "Usually, I'm known as Connie. Not Constantia."

"Connie." He put on his hat. "I'll be as quick as I can. And I hope we will run into each other in less disagreeable circumstances. Perhaps I might call?"

"Perhaps," she said. "Thank you, Harry."

*

Connie listened to his footsteps on the gravel, the latch of the gate opening and shutting. She closed the front door, then sank down onto the hall chair.

Had he noticed?

The white in the woman's mouth, the specks of blood. The marks around her neck. Connie needed to examine her properly, but she was sure of what she had seen. The next thing was to send Mary away too. She had to think. Had to decide what to do for the best.

She found the maid sitting on an upturned milk churn in the scullery, twisting at her apron. Mary jumped to her feet.

"Sorry, miss, I'm all at sixes and sevens. I was just about to boil the water for some tea."

"That's all right, Mary, it won't be necessary. Mr. Woolston has gone to report what's happened to the authorities."

"Is she . . ." Mary cast nervous eyes in the direction of the garden.

"We have removed her from the water, yes. I'm going to wait for someone to come and take the body away. I came to say you may take the rest of the day off, Mary. You've had a nasty fright and you were brave."

"Are you sure, miss? Will you be safe here on your own, until the master gets back?"

"Do you know where he's gone, Mary?" she said quickly.

The girl frowned. "No, miss."

"Did you see him leave?"

"Leave, miss?" Mary said, becoming more puzzled with each question. "I just thought he was out same as usual, it being the afternoon."

Even though things had been different in the house over the past week, Mary clearly assumed Gifford had stuck to his usual routine and gone out after lunch. The girl couldn't have heard them talking on the terrace, or his fleeing upstairs.

"Of course, yes," Connie said.

If Mary believed Gifford had been away from Blackthorn House all afternoon, then that would make things easier in the long run. No need for any kind of explanation. She pulled herself up short, perturbed at the direction her thoughts were taking. There was no reason—no reason—to assume her father knew about the woman's death.

"Will that be all, Miss Gifford?"

Connie dragged her attention back. "Yes. Please keep what

has happened here to yourself, Mary. I don't want to encourage gossip."

"But what shall I say when Ma asks why I'm back early?"

"You can, of course, tell your mother, but no one else."

"And what about the washing, miss? It's still out there, all in the mud. It will spoil if it stays there."

"I will collect the washing while you get your things," Connie said, biting back her impatience. "You can drop it off with Miss Bailey at the laundry on your way home."

*

Connie set the linen basket down by the gate.

A few moments later, Mary came out of the back door and, taking care not to look in the direction where the body lay, walked quickly across the grass, picked up the laundry and went out onto the footpath. There was little hope of the girl holding her tongue for long, but Connie only needed half an hour's grace. After that, it rather depended on how observant Mr. Woolston had been and what he chose to say.

Connie rushed into the workshop, realizing with a sinking feeling that she had left the door open, as well as all of the windows. The dead jackdaw lay on the table beneath the newspaper, but was surrounded now by a haze of minuscule black flies. She flapped them away with the paper, then quickly took one of the glass bell-jar domes from the shelf adjacent to the counter. She placed it over the bird. If damage had been done, it would be clear by morning. She could not allow herself to mourn the waste of her labors yet.

She hurried to the rack where the tools hung on hooks. Hammers and files, flat- and round-blade forceps, cutters, scalpels, a pair of scissors. She grabbed the largest pincers and ran back outside. The garden was completely in shadow and a slight wind was blowing up from the creek. In the distance, she could hear the screeching of the gulls on the turn of the tide. The air felt brittle, sharp with anticipation.

She knelt beside the body, feeling the squelch and damp of the grass beneath her, and folded back the sheet. Fifteen minutes out of the water and already the skin seemed grayer. Connie was now almost completely certain it wasn't the woman who had been watching Blackthorn House. The hair was a similar color, a vivid chestnut, but there was no refinement in the features, and the body was stockier.

Despite being sodden with salt water, the quality of the coat was evident. An expensive and unusual design. Whereas the clothes underneath were cheap and threadbare.

Connie searched the pockets. There was nothing in them at all. Perhaps the coat was stolen, or someone had given it to her to wear. In the pocket of the plain green skirt there were a few damp seeds of grain, caught in the seams, as well as a black glass bead. She turned it over in her palm, while she steeled herself for what she had to do next.

It wasn't a red trim around the collar, but dried blood. An uneven pattern where the wound had heavily bled into the cotton, which had then been submerged in the water.

With care, Connie probed and maneuvered her hand around the distended flesh, feeling for the wire she knew must be there. At last she found it, deeply embedded in the woman's neck. She had to dig her fingernails into the spongy flesh to get purchase until she could position the pincers. She squeezed, felt the wire snip.

It was not a fishing line, caught up by accident, as Harry had supposed, but rather the sort of wire used by stuffers. Commonplace, the cheapest and most widely distributed make. In the old days, all the workshops along the south coast would have had it. Brighton, Worthing, Swayling, even Chichester twenty years ago. Now most of the old-timers had gone. The taxidermy studios closed for business. It was no longer something that could be bought on any high street.

Connie turned to see that the jackdaws had flown from the south garden to the north and were now lined up along the fence, their beaks up and their necks forward. They were calling to one another. A third pair flew down. They were carrion birds, after all.

Where was her father? The worry was there all the time, like a splinter under her skin.

As she hurried to finish the task of removing the garrotte from around the woman's neck, Connie tried to ignore the clattering, jabbering crescendo of the jackdaws. And she tried not to think about the empty hook on the wall in her father's workshop where the coil of wire should have been.

Chapter 11

The Old Salt Mill
Fishbourne Creek

Joseph's feet slipped off the sill. He woke with a jolt as the field glasses crashed to the ground.

"Let me alone," he bellowed, throwing a punch. For a moment, he was back in jail. Taking a beating, never properly sleeping, reaching for the stiletto of glass beneath his mattress. Then the sharp salt of the incoming tide penetrated his consciousness, the harsh shriek of the gulls overhead, and he remembered where he was.

Joseph had got into a brawl outside the Globe in January. Defending a lady's honor against a man with a foul mouth and a sharp right hook. The law hadn't seen it that way. Up again before the mayor and the bench, he'd been sentenced to the maximum judgment of three months' hard labor. Sergeant Pennicott had spoken against him and Joseph had no doubt that that interference had lost him his job at Howards, one of the butchers in Chichester. He wouldn't forget that in a hurry.

Joseph didn't want to find himself back in jail. At the same time, he couldn't deny he'd picked up some interesting information in there, all of which he was making the most of now. A man had to find a way to earn a decent living, if his livelihood was taken away from him.

He bent down and picked up the binoculars. Blackthorn House looked exactly the same, except the Gifford girl was no longer on the terrace. He put the glasses down again and yawned, wondering how late it was and whether anyone would come to relieve him. He could do with a drink.

There was a brisk wind coming off the water. Joseph began to close the window, then something caught his eye. He reached for the binoculars. Was someone on the move? He scanned the horizon, but all he saw was a flock of black birds fly up from the roof of the icehouse and float low over the chimneys toward the rear garden.

Joseph stretched, then stood up. In most matters, he was blessed with no conscience, though he prided himself on being honorable in others. He did what he was paid to do, no qualms about it and no questions asked. Within limits. The fact that he was being paid twice, for what was essentially the same thing, or so it seemed, only made the situation sweeter. He didn't care about the whys and wherefores, so long as the money kept coming.

Woolston didn't bother him. He was probably doing what he was told, as much as Joseph was. For a moment, Joseph allowed himself to be curious. He wondered who had such a hold over Woolston. He didn't look as if he could say boo to a goose. But then, the more respectable the man, the more he had to lose.

Joseph might ask. He might as well ask.

He lit the other of Woolston's cigarettes as he stared out at Blackthorn House. Still not a soul in sight. He could hear the waterwheel rumbling below, shaking the mill, as the tide came in.

Blackthorn House was completely still and silent.

Joseph started to think he might as well pack it in. Gifford had to be holed up inside. There were no signs of his making an appearance now, not if the day so far was anything to go by. It was possible, he supposed, that he had scarpered in the few minutes Joseph had been resting his eyes. A little longer. No reason to think that was the case. Joseph had been careful that neither the taxidermist nor his daughter should realize they were under surveillance. But if Gifford had, for the sake of argument, left Blackthorn House, the only place he'd be likely to go was the Bull's Head.

That being the case, Joseph concluded the debate with himself, wouldn't it make sense for him to go to the inn and check? The more he thought about it, the better an idea it seemed. He would wander over to the Bull's Head and see what gossip he could pick up. There was always something.

Didn't know how the world worked, men like Woolston. All that book learning and money, the law on their side, but not an ounce of common sense to rub between them.

Main Road
Fishbourne

"Mary, is that you?"

Mary hung up her coat and hat in the hall, then went through to the kitchen where her mother was shelling peas. The twins were sitting on the floor under the table. Maisie leaped up to hug her and show her that the peg doll had a new frock. Polly continued to dangle a piece of bacon rind on a string for the kitten to jump up at.

"You're early," Jennie Christie said, then stopped. "What's the matter, love? You look all somehow."

Mary glanced at her mother and, despite her intentions, burst into tears. A few minutes later, with the twins dispatched into the garden and a pot of steaming tea on the table, she was telling her mother everything.

"What a terrible thing. That poor, poor girl. And awful for you, Mary love." Mrs. Christie put her hand on her daughter's arm. "But at least Miss Gifford didn't expect you to help bring the wretched soul out."

"She sent me to fetch Dr. Evershed. He wasn't there, but there was a gentlemen staying. He came instead. Mr. Woolston, he was called."

The paring knife clattered into the bowl. "Woolston, did you say?"

"That's what he said. Ever so nicely dressed. Good quality. And such lovely eyes, almost purple they were. Matched his waistcoat and—"

"How old was this Mr. Woolston?"

"I don't know. Hard to say."

"Try, love."

"I don't know, Ma. Twenty-four or twenty-five, perhaps."

"Not older? Not in his fifties?"

"No." Mary paused. "Why do you ask?"

"No reason." Mrs. Christie carried on pushing the peas out into the bowl. "Is he a friend of Dr. Evershed's?"

"Must be, why?"

"It's not important."

"Obviously it is," Mary said, "or you wouldn't have asked. Do you think you might know him, Ma?"

"No." Mrs. Christie hesitated. "At least, that's to say I did run across a Woolston once, though I can't see why he—" She broke off. "Anyway, it can't have been him, not if he's as young as you say."

"I might be wrong."

"Did he have gray hair?"

"No."

Ma Christie smiled. "Well, it can't be the same person." She looked at her daughter. "What did Mr. Gifford have to say about all this?"

"He wasn't there."

Mrs. Christie shook her head. "Well, it's a dreadful shock you had, the pair of you. Good of Miss Gifford to let you off early. Didn't I tell you she'd be a nice lady to work for?"

Although her mother kept her distance from Blackthorn House, and appeared to disapprove of Mr. Gifford, she had been oddly insistent that Mary should accept the position when they moved to Fishbourne after Mr. Christie died. It suited Mary, being the only servant in a large house, for all its peculiarities. There was no one to boss her about or tell her she was doing things the wrong way, like in the bigger establishments. She had friends in service at the Rectory and Old Park, so she knew what superior servants could be like. Keeping everyone in their place. Mary could, give or take, please herself.

Mary nodded. "I dropped the laundry all in the mud and Miss Gifford didn't make a thing of that either. I left it with Miss Bailey, but forgot this." She looked down at the crumpled handkerchief. "Miss Gifford lent it me. I'll have to do it myself. Have we got any starch, Ma?"

"She's got a lovely hand," Mrs. Christie said, looking at the embroidered initials.

"Be surprised if Miss Gifford stitched it herself, Ma. I've never seen her pick up a needle, all the time I've been there. She never stops writing, that's more to her liking."

"Always was one for reading and writing," Mrs. Christie said. She paused. "Has she had any more of those turns?"

"Not that I've noticed."

"That's good. And Mr. Gifford?"

Mary looked at her mother in surprise at her interest. "Same as usual. Don't run into him much."

"Good, that's good," Mrs. Christie repeated, running on. "Keeping out of that workshop, I trust. Nasty old-fashioned business. Not hygienic."

"I heard Mr. Gifford was really famous once. Used to have his own museum over Lyminster way. People came from all over and—"

"That was a long time ago," Mrs. Christie said sharply. "No sense going on about it. All in the past."

"Did you go there then, Ma? Birds dressed up in little costumes, Archie said . . ."

Mrs. Christie got up and walked to the stove. "Can you clear up for me?"

". . . all posed in positions," Mary carried on, "little hymnbooks and what have you—"

"That's enough!"

Mary sat back as if she'd been slapped. Her mother rarely raised her voice, not even when the twins were playing up.

"I was only saying. There's no call to get sharp with me."

Mary started to wrap the empty pods in a sheet of paper. Mrs. Christie watched her, clearly already regretting her burst of temper.

"Here's a thing," she said in an emollient voice. "Do you remember Vera Barker? One that used to feed all the birds around Apuldram way?"

Mary shook her head, not willing to let it go straightaway.

"Yes, you do. Tommy Barker's eldest. Some people called her Birdie. Went a bit funny in the head. Had all that red hair and wore an odd black hat, flat like a pancake, with feathers sticking out around the rim. Gardener at Westfield House was always chasing her off."

Mary shrugged. "I never knew her. She was long gone by the time we came here."

"Well, be that as it may, it turns out no one's seen her for a week. There was all that flooding round Apuldram way and down-along, so nobody was thinking about poor Vera."

The two women stared at each other, as the same thought occurred to them both.

"Could it have been Birdie you found in the stream, love?" Mrs. Christie said slowly.

"I didn't get a proper look, Ma. I couldn't bring myself. I suppose so."

"Though now I come to think about it, don't see how it can have been," Mrs. Christie continued. "Tide wouldn't carry her up from Apuldram. She'd be taken out past Dell Quay." She looked down at the newspaper. "I might mention it all the same. Police asking folk to help with their inquiries. Someone wrote a letter to Tommy, anonymous, and he took it to the newspaper."

"But who'd do that, Ma? Who'd even notice she was missing?"

"Well, that I don't know," Mrs. Christie admitted. "They don't say. But there must have been something in it for them to put it in the paper."

"I suppose so."

Mrs. Christie's expression softened. "Anyhow, I'm sorry I snapped at you, love. All this weather, my nerves are in shreds. Why don't you hang up your things and call the girls in? Be nice to have you eating tea with us for a change."

Mary started to untie her apron, then her hand went to her pocket.

"Oh."

"What is it, love?"

Mary pulled out an envelope and put it on the table. "This was on the back mat. I picked it up, meaning to take it through to the hall, then forgot all about it. I had so much washing, making the most of the dry weather, wanting to get it pegged out."

The two women stared at the cream envelope with the black cursive lettering: MISS C. GIFFORD.

"Delivered to the back door, you say?"

"I thought that was odd too," Mary said. "What do you think I should do, Ma? Should I take it back now?"

"I wouldn't, if I were you."

"Lovely script, isn't it? Really pretty."

Mrs. Christie took the letter and put it behind the carriage clock.

"I dare say it'll keep until tomorrow. Probably nothing important," she said, though her expression gave the lie to her words. "Be one of those door-to-door insurance salesmen, likely as not."

Mary didn't notice that her mother's hand was shaking.

Chapter 12

The Bull's Head
Main Road
Fishbourne

Harry took out a cigarette to steady his nerves.

Above his head, the painted sign—THE BULL'S HEAD—creaked and swayed in the wind. His hands were shaking so much, it took several strikes before he got a light.

He couldn't get the image of the dead woman out of his mind: the bubbles at the corners of her mouth. Her puffy, swollen face. He'd never seen a dead body before. When his mother died, quickly and without warning when he was seven, he'd been away at school. Both sets of grandparents had passed away before he'd been born.

Harry drew breath deeply, letting the smoke settle in his chest. He felt he'd got himself into a devil of a mess. Somehow he had to organize a cart to go out to retrieve the body, as he'd promised, but not get drawn any further in himself. And he still had no idea what had happened to his father. Home, probably, by now.

"What a bloody awful business," he muttered.

He could hardly just walk up to Arthur Evershed's front door. The irony was not lost on him that one of the leading local artists—and a man who'd had a celebrated and distinguished medical career as well—lived in Fishbourne. In any other circumstance, Harry would jump at the chance to introduce himself. But if he hadn't actually lied to Connie, he certainly hadn't admitted that his presence outside what turned out to be Dr. Evershed's house was only a coincidence. When the maid had come flying around the corner, Harry had found himself somehow swept along by it. He felt he was rising to a challenge.

Ridiculous, though he couldn't say he regretted it.

Could he get away with going to Dr. Evershed and explaining the situation without giving his name? He thought for a moment, then dismissed the idea with great regret. It would be peculiar, and when Evershed spoke to Connie, it would still come out that Harry had been economical with the truth. The thought of her thinking badly of him made him sick to his boots.

Harry paused. She had taken the whole ghastly business in her stride. No fuss, a far stronger stomach than his. Formidable, though she hadn't been one of those hard girls. Such a striking profile; he'd love to paint her. Her pale skin and brown hair, those thinking eyes. She would be the most remarkable sitter, he knew it.

He ground his cigarette under his heel, dragging his thoughts back to the problem in question. The only option, so far as he could see, was to seek assistance from the landlord of the Bull's Head. It looked more respectable than the Woolpack and, given its position so close to the estuary, it was likely that they would have been called upon to perform this kind of task before now.

Such wonderful brown hair. Like Millais's muse and wife, Effie Gray. She sat for Thomas Richmond too, he remem-

bered. Then the unwelcome recollection of a different image—
Ophelia drowned—came into his mind.

Now he knew. In real life, there was no beauty in such a
death.

*

The Bull's Head was an old building, with a bar on either side
of the front door and a flight of stairs directly ahead.

Harry tried the private saloon first. An open-faced brick
and timber-beamed wall, a fire smoking in the grate. It was a
little too early for the end-of-day rush. Husbands who worked
in the banks and legal offices in Chichester coming in for a
quick drink and a game of cards before returning home. Young
professional men. Men like him, forced by their fathers to suf-
focate in shipping agencies and accountancy firms and property management.

Only two tables were occupied. At the first, three clerks in
black suits sat playing cards. At the other, an older, prosperous-
looking gentleman was smoking and reading the local newspaper. Aware of Harry's scrutiny, he looked up.

Harry nodded a greeting.

"If you're hoping for service, best go through," he said.
"More custom this time of day in the other bar."

"Thank you, Mr. . . ."

"Crowther," the man replied. "Charles Crowther."

*

The public bar was a mirror image of the private, except, as
Crowther said, it was busier and louder.

Most tables were occupied, and customers were two or three deep at the counter. Laborers, farm workers, shoeblacks, tanners, the workingmen of the village. One or two with the grime and dirt of the tannery or the forge on their hands. The air was thick with smoke, tobacco mixed with the damp scent of the applewood fire.

Everyone stared as he came in, taking in his appearance, then went back to their conversations.

Harry walked to the counter. "Is the landlord about?"

The barman put down the glass he was polishing. "Think you'd be more comfortable in the private bar, sir."

"I'm not here for a drink," Harry said, keeping his voice low. "There's a matter needing—"

"Not drinking?" laughed a man in a filthy long coat tied around the waist with string, propped up at the end of the bar. "Not much point coming in here then."

"That'll do," growled the barman.

"Not everyone's like you, Diddy," one of the laborers shouted from a table near the door. "Drowning your sorrows, is that it? Slow day?"

"Celebration more like," the man laughed again, holding up his sack. "Good haul."

Harry saw that the hessian seam was stained with blood.

"Two moles, a couple of rats," Diddy was saying. "Not bad for an afternoon's work, all told." He waved his empty glass. "In fact, I might drink to that."

Realizing he was getting nowhere, Harry fished a coin out of his pocket and slid it across the bar.

"Is the landlord about?" he asked again.

"And your name, sir?"

"It doesn't matter what my name is," he said impatiently.

"There's been an accident, house out on the marshes. Someone's in the water. Drowned."

"All right, sir, no need to take on."

Harry pushed another coin across the polished counter.

"There's a woman on her own out there. Someone needs to send a cart, a trap. Something. The path's narrow."

"Who is on her own, sir?"

"Miss Gifford. I don't know the name of the house."

Harry felt the atmosphere change. He glanced over his shoulder. No one seemed to be paying particular attention.

"Look, can you help or not?"

The barman held his gaze for a moment, then flicked his cloth across his shoulder. "Wait here."

Harry needed a drink. The shock was hitting home. He reached for another Dunhill. The packet slipped from his fingers, spilling the cigarettes over the floor.

"Let me, sir."

Harry looked up. "I can manage," he said.

"It's no bother," the man said, handing him the packet, holding on to it a fraction too long. "You said there'd been an accident at Blackthorn House?"

Harry stared blankly.

"The Gifford place."

"I don't know if I ought . . ."

The man smiled, though it didn't reach his eyes. "Didn't you say you needed help? Wasn't that what you were saying?"

Harry flushed. "Well, yes. But it's in hand."

"You got a connection with the Giffords, have you, sir?"

"I can't see what the devil it has to do with you," Harry said sharply.

"Good Samaritan, then?"

Harry met his gaze. "Something of the kind."

For a moment, the two men stared at each other. Harry was painfully aware that, even though the noise level hadn't appreciably dropped, every last man in the bar was listening to their conversation.

"You wouldn't happen to have one going spare, would you?"

Harry offered the packet. The man took two cigarettes, leaning forward for a light, then putting the other behind his ear.

"Odd place, Blackthorn House," he said, blowing a ring of smoke into the air.

"Odd?" Harry lit another cigarette for himself, appalled to see that his hands were still shaking.

"All sorts of things go on out there, so they say."

Harry looked to the door, willing the barman to return. What was taking so long? He'd given Connie his word; he wasn't prepared to leave until he was sure the matter was in hand. Still the man was hanging around.

"You're not from round here?"

"Fishbourne?" Harry leaned across the bar, trying to see into the back. "No."

"Chichester? It's just you remind me of someone. Older fellow. Similar features," the man continued, tracing a circle around his own face with his finger. "Same color eyes as you, though he wore spectacles. Short-sighted."

Harry spun around. "Today?"

The man gave a lazy shrug. "Might have been. Can't say I rightly remember."

"I would be grateful if you could try."

The coin was in the man's pocket before Harry had even seen his hand come out to take it.

"Today, I think it was. Two, two thirty, thereabouts."

That would fit, Harry thought. "And where did you see him?"

"Mill Lane, maybe it was. Or, on second thought, out on the marshes. Toward Blackthorn House, it might have been."

Harry turned cold. "Are you certain?"

"I don't forget a face."

To his intense frustration, the barman chose that moment to reappear.

"The guv'nor says you can leave it with him."

"What? Thank you," Harry said, then turned back to the man. He had rejoined his companions at the far end of the bar. "Damn," he muttered.

He considered going over, but decided against it. It was more than six hours since he'd overhead his father quarreling. Four hours since this fellow claimed to have seen a man resembling his father on the marshes.

He'd put things in hand, as Connie had asked him to do. There was no reason to hang about. The need for adventure that had set him hurtling after his father to Fishbourne, then offering himself as a knight in shining armor, had drained away. He felt foolish, and rather sick. Besides, wasn't it most likely that he'd arrive home and find his father there? Everything the same as usual.

He put his hat back on and headed for the door.

"Good evening to you, Mr. Woolston," the man called after him.

Harry stopped mid-stride, then carried on. The man's laughter followed him out into the street.

Chapter 13

Blackthorn House
Fishbourne Marshes

Connie pulled her cardigan tight around her shoulders.

An early-evening breeze was blowing off the water, damp, suggesting that the wet and windy weather would be back tomorrow. She could hear the whispering of the wind through the delicate tops of the reeds, like tiny fluttering silver flags, setting the long, thin stalks rattling and murmuring. She shivered, but she did not feel it would be right to go in and leave the body unattended.

As the light faded from the sky, more jackdaws had come. Their pale eyes and gray hooded heads, sentries keeping watch from the fence. Twenty of them, more. The noise they made was aggressive, threatening.

How long before someone arrived to take the body away? She'd had no idea Dr. Evershed was an artist of such repute. Harry clearly greatly admired his work. She'd noticed a smear of red oil paint on his shoe. Perhaps he was an artist too, given his interest in Arthur Evershed?

Connie glanced to the footpath.

Since she was the person who'd found her, on the edge of their property, might the coroner let her know in time what had happened to the woman?

Connie pulled herself up. Why should he? She had to keep telling herself it was nothing to do with her, nothing to do with her father, just a terrible accident of geography. If it ever came to it, she could honestly say it would have been simple enough for anyone to get into the workshop and steal the mounting wire. More than once she'd found little Davey Reedman skulking around and chased him off.

But with each passing hour, her concern for her father deepened. Her hand slipped again to her pocket, turning the fragment of burned paper over between her fingers.

She wished she knew the dead woman's name. She wished she knew who had given her the beautiful coat, and why. She glanced over to the shrouded body on the ground, then away again. She had laid a blanket over the sheet. In part, it was to restore to her some kind of dignity; the thin cotton clung too closely to the damp contours. It was also, she realized, to protect the cold flesh from the birds.

The sky turned from a pale blue to white.

Connie became increasingly aware of the dark corridors of Blackthorn House stretching out behind her. All those echoing and empty rooms. She had told the truth when she said she wasn't scared of being left with the body. But at the same time, she did not want to be here alone when darkness finally fell.

"The sleeping and the dead are but as pictures."

Again, that same soft voice from the past, speaking lines from a play this time, not a poem.

Connie held her hands out in front of her, like her father had done earlier on the terrace. There were traces of blood still under her fingernails, from the business of removing the wire embedded deep in the woman's neck. She'd scrubbed and scrubbed with carbolic soap, but blood was the hardest stain to shift.

Shakespeare, of course. Lady Macbeth. A young woman's voice, reading aloud. Connie suddenly saw her younger self, her memory clear for once. A hot summer's day, elbows on the table, hair loose over her shoulders, listening. Captivated by the story.

By the voice.

Chapter 14

The West Sussex County Asylum
Chichester

Dr. John Woolston leaned forward and tapped the cab driver on the arm.

"This will do," he said. "I can walk from here."

The Dunnaways man pulled up his horses, then turned around on his seat. "Are you sure, guv'nor? It's ever so dirty underfoot after all the rain."

"Quite sure," Woolston said. He fished a note from his pocketbook, paid the agreed fare and added a generous tip.

There was no reason for Brook to drag him all the way up to Graylingwell, given that they were due to meet tomorrow morning anyway. Only the thought of his son kept Woolston going. He was worried for Harold's future and didn't want him to lose his position, even though he was well aware the boy hated the work and despised Brook. Rightly so, as it turned out, though Woolston couldn't tell him that. More than anything, he did not want Harold to find out his father was not the man he believed him to be. He did not want to lose his son's respect.

The sun grazed the tops of the trees in the parkland, the beauty of the afternoon at odds with Dr. Woolston's state of mind. He stood at the boundary of the West Sussex County

Asylum, and for one glorious moment toyed with the idea of not going in.

Woolston served on the Committee of Visitors, a group of gentlemen responsible for visiting all such establishments throughout the county to ensure they were being run properly. He never met the patients or came into contact with any but the most senior of the medical staff. The committee's job was to inspect the records and verify that each patient was receiving the treatment appropriate to their condition. Even so, Woolston was particularly proud of what was being pioneered at Graylingwell, and his small contribution to it. No forbidding walls, no iron gates to keep the patients in, no use of restraints. They treated all forms of mental illness—acute mania, melancholia, epilepsy, hereditary feeblemindedness and genetic alcoholism—in modern, humane ways. There were some patients who would never leave, but many would, in time, be relieved of their symptoms and returned to their families. From time to time he would stroll through the grounds and wonder about the lives that the patients led. More often, when walking up North Street or through the Pallants, he wondered if any of the people he encountered had ever passed through his hands as names on a piece of paper.

Now, because of this damnable business, all this was at risk. It had robbed him of any pride or pleasure in what he had achieved. His entire world had been stripped back to that one night ten years ago.

Woolston took a deep breath and walked in through the gates. The distinctive outline of the water tower loomed ahead of him, constructed like most of the buildings in a warm red brick. The hospital was almost entirely self-sufficient, with two working farms, substantial vegetable gardens and a meat herd. There were separate wards for men and women, as well as accommodation for private patients and an isolation hospital. At the heart of the site were the administration buildings and a theater, which was where Brook's instructions said he was to go.

Woolston followed the graveled path beneath the chestnut trees with their pink and white blossom. Wednesday afternoon was visiting time and, due to the clement weather, there were several patients walking in the grounds with their families or sitting in one of the pleasant wooden shelters in the airing courts. At a discreet distance, attendants and nurse probationers kept a close eye on their charges.

It was rare for a patient to escape, though just before Easter a private patient had managed to slip into the gardens and make it out of the grounds. Even though the fee-paying inmates stayed in what had been the Graylingwell farmhouse, away from the public wards, the security was as stringent there as in the rest of the hospital. It was clear that someone must have helped in the escape. The nurse on duty had denied any complicity, but she'd been dismissed all the same.

There were regulations governing everything. All patients, having been certified as insane, were committed to the asylum in the first instance by a justice of the peace and could only be released on the order of a doctor. However, if someone did escape, and succeeded in remaining at large for the statutory period of fourteen days, it was considered evidence enough that they were capable of surviving outside of the hospital. Woolston didn't know the precise details of the recent case, but so far as he was aware, the patient had not been apprehended.

*

Woolston reached the administration buildings without meeting anyone he knew. With relief, he stepped into the corridor and walked quickly to the entrance to the theater and through the double doors.

The auditorium was empty. For a moment, he stood still in the shadow of the overhang of the gallery. The dominant colors in the room were cream and beige. Everything was designed to be soothing to troubled spirits. A pleasing repeat-pattern wallpaper, brown and cream, below the dado rail. Small pillars set on pale painted plinths supported the balcony. It was modern and clean and light. Dr. Woolston admired the interior of Blomfield's design as much as the exterior. He had once nursed similar ambitions, and had it not been for his father's insistence that he should follow in his footsteps as an army doctor, he might have trained as an architect. Harold had inherited his artistic inclinations, though he too had been forced to accept a position with good financial prospects. If he was serious about painting, he would keep it up all the same. That chap in Fishbourne—Arthur Evershed—managed it, after all.

Woolston became aware of a knocking sound, like the branch of a tree tapping on a window. He looked up to the high mullioned windows, but could see nothing. Then he realized it was coming from the far end of the room, close to the stage. The stage itself was hidden by the heavy curtains, which were closed.

He walked out from under the balcony into the open space of the auditorium at the same time as a gray-haired woman in cap and apron appeared from behind the stage. The char put down her pail, dipped her mop into the water, tapped the wood on the edge to shake off the excess, then continued her cleaning.

"Room's not in use," she said when he drew level.

"I see that." He paused. "I have an appointment. I'm meeting someone here at six o'clock."

"Gentleman?"

He hesitated. He assumed so, since the note had come from Brook, though it was true it hadn't said as much. He asked a question instead.

"Has anybody come in while you've been working?"

"Room's not in use," she repeated.

The woman clearly knew nothing about the matter. Woolston suddenly felt oddly hopeful. He had followed the instructions to the letter. If Brook had changed his mind, although it was a nuisance and a waste of his time, then he was off the hook. He looked at his pocket watch. It was already ten past six. He could be home by six thirty, enjoying his whisky and soda. His hand went to his breast pocket. No need for heroics. He would take a quick look backstage, to be sure, then call it a day.

"I'll have a look around all the same."

The woman shrugged. "Suit yourself."

Woolston walked to the stage and slowly climbed the steps, the sound of his shoes echoing through the auditorium. His hand fumbled blindly, until he found the gap in the curtains, and he stepped carefully through onto the hushed stage.

"Brook?"

The smell of sawdust and mothballs. All the theater paraphernalia; a rail of costumes, still holding the imprint of the last person to wear the skirts and jackets. He looked up into the flies, the ropes hanging down, a chandelier suspended high above. On a wooden table in the prompt corner was a precarious stack of straw boaters. Fans and headdresses. Feathers.

Black feathers, lots of them, scattered over everything. Always reminding him, always taking him back.

Woolston felt his legs turn to water. Purple-black, ink-blue feathers, the scene returning as clear as day. The cases, the candlelight reflected in the domes of glass, the shock of the moment. The blood.

Then from the wings, a voice. "Hello, Jack."

It wasn't possible. Woolston recognized the soft tones that haunted his nightmares, getting fainter with each year that passed, but always there. Suddenly he realized that it was one of the things that had most upset him about the man who'd come to his consulting rooms earlier. The man who seemed to know everything about that night ten years ago. His voice had reminded Woolston of hers, although he knew it couldn't be. The girl had had no family, they'd made sure of that.

"Or do you go by the name of John these days? I think I might, were I in your shoes. So much more respectable."

Woolston spun around, almost losing his balance, but was unable to work out where the sound was coming from. The light was extinguished and he found himself instantly disorientated on the bare stage. He took a few blind steps toward the prompt corner, reaching out his hand but finding nothing but air.

"Who are you?" he shouted. "What do you want?"

He heard the intake of breath.

"Jack," she said, gently coaxing. "I gave you a chance. Don't pretend you can't remember . . ."

Woolston panicked. He turned on his heel and tried to run, but pain exploded in the side of his head. The ground rushed up to meet him. His ribs cracked as they hit the wooden surround of the trapdoor, then he dropped, like a stone, down through the stage to the cellar fourteen feet below.

Chapter 15

Blackthorn House
Fishbourne Marshes

Connie went to the gate at the sound of voices. She raised her hand as a group of men came into view, recognizing Pine, the barman from the Bull's Head, and Mr. Crowther. She knew little about him, other than that he was said to be enormously wealthy from investing in the copper mines of the Transvaal. His main residence was somewhere in Surrey—Guildford, she thought—but he spent much of the summer at his weekend cottage in Fishbourne.

There were two other men with Crowther, carrying a wide wooden board. Dr. Evershed wasn't there, and neither was Harry.

Connie was surprised to realize she was disappointed.

The party crossed the last of the three bridges over the creek, and stopped on the path outside Blackthorn House.

"Evening, Miss Gifford," Pine said, touching his hat.

"It's kind of you to come."

"You know Mr. Crowther?"

"I do," she said, inclining her head.

"And this is Gregory Joseph and Archie Lintott."

She nodded a greeting. "Is Dr. Evershed not with you, Mr. Joseph?"

"Were you expecting him to be, Miss Gifford?"

"I had thought Mr. Woolston had gone to fetch him."

"Woolston, was it?" said Pine. "That's what you thought, wasn't it, Gregory?"

"That's right," Joseph replied, though he was looking at Connie.

"Came into the bar and said there was trouble. Don't know what he did after that. Perhaps he's gone on to Eversfield?"

"Dr. and Mrs. Evershed went up to London a couple of days ago," Crowther said. "He has a few pieces in an exhibition, I believe."

Connie looked from one man to another. "I don't suppose it matters," she said quickly. Now that the moment had come, she was nervous. Harry had taken the situation at face value. She had buttoned up the woman's blouse high around her neck, to hide the marks left by the wire, but anyone would see she hadn't drowned if they looked closely. The coroner, of course, would notice the marks immediately. All at once, her attempts to conceal the injuries seemed ridiculous. But she had acted on instinct.

"Your father keeping all right, Miss Gifford?" the barman asked.

"Should he not be?" she replied, more sharply than she had intended.

"It's only that we haven't seen him in for a few days."

"Most times you can set your watch by Gifford."

"That'll do, Joseph," Crowther said.

Connie took a deep breath. "Thank you for asking. In point of fact, my father has been unwell." She hesitated. "He is staying with friends, in fact."

"If you would pass on my regards," Pine said. "Tell him

we're looking forward to welcoming him back once he's on his feet again."

"I will."

Connie noticed Joseph glance straightaway up to her father's window, and she wondered how—if—he knew it was his room.

"Nothing serious, I hope?" Crowther said.

"No."

For a moment, everyone stood in silence. No one moved.

"The body, Miss Gifford . . . ?" Crowther asked eventually.

"I'm sorry, yes," Connie said. "It—she—is through here."

Joseph and Lintott picked up the makeshift stretcher and followed Connie into the kitchen garden. The jackdaws were watching, silhouetted against the dusk sky.

"Heck of a lot of them about this year," Lintott said, "excuse my French, miss. And so late in the day. It's odd, that."

Crowther gestured that they should put the board down.

"What will happen next?" Connie asked, suddenly reluctant to let them take the body.

"We'll take her to the Bull's Head overnight."

"And then?"

Crowther met her gaze. "It depends. A doctor will ascertain cause of death and discover her next of kin, then decide what should be done." He paused. "Do you know who she is, Miss Gifford?"

"No."

"I'll have a look in her pockets," Joseph said. "There's usually something, though it depends how long she was in the water."

"There's nothing—" Connie began, then bit her tongue. She didn't want anyone to know she had searched already.

Crowther bent down and removed the blanket. She felt the atmosphere sharpen. Not simply shock, but something else.

Surprise? She glanced around, and fancied she saw a look pass from Joseph to Crowther.

Frowning, Joseph checked the woman's pockets. "Nothing," he said, straightening up.

Connie shivered. In the dying light, the woman's skin looked translucent. Her face had lost all color now, though her lips were chalk-blue.

"I think I know her," Archie said. "I can't be sure, not when she's been in the water, but her red hair . . . I think it's the girl they're talking about going missing, isn't it?"

Connie suddenly felt dizzy. Four men, a woman lying motionless on the ground. No one speaking. She wrapped her arms tightly around her waist to disguise her shaking hands.

"Vera Barker—everyone called her Birdie. Used to feed the birds over Apuldram way." He turned to Gregory Joseph. "You knew her too, didn't you?"

"I think you're right," Pine said. "One of Tommy Barker's daughters. There was some kind of falling-out—she was always a bit soft in the head, and of course, a man like Tommy couldn't be doing with that. She was in Graylingwell for a while, or so I heard." He frowned. "Funny place for her to choose."

Connie realized that Pine, like Joseph, like Harry earlier, assumed it was a suicide.

"Poor old Vera," Archie muttered, taking off his hat.

"At this point," Crowther cut in, "it doesn't matter how the unfortunate girl got here or what she was doing. We need to take her away and leave Miss Gifford in peace."

Connie nodded gratefully.

"We'll take good care of her, Miss Gifford, don't worry."

"Steady," said Pine, as the men tried to slide the wooden board beneath the body. "On my count."

The two men put their hands beneath the wood and lifted the body up. One of Vera's hands came loose, out from under the blanket. In the purple evening light, there were marks on her palm that looked like stigmata. She must have tried to protect herself from the wire. Connie felt the ground lurch beneath her feet.

"Are you all right, Miss Gifford?" Crowther asked.

"It's been a distressing afternoon, but yes."

"Would you like me to find someone to sit with you, given that your father is indisposed? Mrs. Pine, I'm sure, would be more than happy to oblige."

Connie was grateful for his concern, but she didn't want a stranger in the house. She wanted to be left alone to think.

"A good night's sleep is all I need."

The solemn procession moved forward. Joseph and Lintott maneuvered the makeshift stretcher through the gate, then continued in silence along the path. Connie could hear the squelch of their boots in the mud.

She pressed a coin into the barman's hand. "Thank you, Pine. All of you. And thank you, Mr. Crowther, you've been most kind."

Crowther raised his hat. "Good evening, Miss Gifford."

*

Connie waited until the last echoes of their voices had died away, then turned back to the house.

The birds began their dusk chorus. A hen blackbird and her mate, collared doves and wood pigeons, the sweet trill of a chiffchaff. But the elegy for the dying day was overshadowed by the shrieking of the gulls out over the creek.

Connie was chilled to the bone, terrified not of the coming dark or the solitude of the empty house, but of something larger and nameless and more malevolent.

Gifford's rambling conversation, then disappearance; the dead woman and the borrowed coat, too big for her, the threadbare clothes beneath. Joseph searching through Vera's pockets as if he was looking for something in particular. Mr. Crowther had noticed too, she was sure of it.

Vera's hands. What had Archie Lintott said? That she was known for feeding the wild birds. Scratches all over the tops of her hands and cuts on the palms. Connie hugged her arms around herself. Could Vera have been responsible for letting loose the birds in the church? And if so, why? Who would have persuaded her to do something so cruel?

Across the estuary, midway between Fishbourne church and Apuldram, Connie saw a light. In the woods near Dell Quay. A single lamp burning in the dark. Someone making their way home across the fields? She watched for a moment, then it vanished.

Feeling suddenly very vulnerable out on the marshes alone, Connie quickly went inside. She locked and bolted the scullery door, then the side and front doors, before going through to the drawing room to check the terrace was also secure. She didn't want her father, if he came home, to find himself locked out, but she was too scared to leave the house open. If Gifford did return during the night, she'd no doubt he'd make noise enough for her to hear him.

Connie lit the lamps, then poured herself a generous measure of her father's brandy. She took the glass and the tartan carriage rug to the large window on the half-landing. She sat down and wrapped the blanket around her legs. She had a hard lump in her chest, a fist tightening around her heart.

Last night, her father had kept watch from this spot. Now

he'd disappeared. She didn't know what he feared, or where he was, only that she felt some malice in the darkness too. Felt that someone was out there. Watching, waiting.

She looked at the fragment of burnt paper and the single legible word: ASYLUM. Did it take on a new significance now she knew that Vera—if the dead woman was Vera—had been a patient there? And was the glass bead she'd taken from her pocket a match to the bead she'd picked up in the churchyard a week ago? Two black glass beads. It had not seemed important at the time, so she'd thrown it away. Another decision she regretted.

She took a sip of brandy. Also, Gregory Joseph, Mr. Pine and Archie Lintott had all been in the graveyard a week ago, along with her father and—now she was sure of it—poor Vera Barker in her borrowed coat.

Had Mr. Crowther also been there?

Connie's hand stole to the scar on the right side of her head, hidden beneath her hair. And with it, the fear came seeping through her bones, like ink through blotting paper, that what was happening now had its roots not in the gathering in a village churchyard last week—nor even in the fact that an unknown woman had stood watching the house a few days before that—but further back still.

In the vanished days.

This naturalist [Schoeffer], after skinning them, contented himself by cutting the birds longitudinally in two, and filling one half with plaster; fixing the skin properly at the back of a box, of a depth proportionate to the size of the bird, he stuck in an eye, and replaced or represented the beak and claws by painting; he then carefully fixed a glass on this frame, to protect the object from insects.

TAXIDERMY: OR, THE ART OF COLLECTING, PREPARING, AND MOUNTING OBJECTS OF NATURAL HISTORY

Mrs. R. Lee
Longman & Co., Paternoster Row, London, 1820

It is not a question of guilt or innocence, but of the punishment being equal to the crime.

I gave him a chance to redeem himself. To confess to what he—what they—had done. To make it known. But the habit of concealment ran too deep in him and he did not listen. He could not see that his old respectable life was built on sand. That it was already lost.

Jackdaw lay still. He was already dead, I showed him that kindness. His was a crime of omission, not commission. He deserved a different kind of reckoning. He was a coward and a hypocrite, but he was less guilty than the others. But he did not stop them and he held his tongue.

I am certain that your conscience will be troubled. Not so much by the act itself, but rather by the method of it. You will wonder if I felt shock or revulsion. But, though I know these words damn me further, I did not.

What else can I tell you?

I can tell you how I placed a handkerchief over his face to hide his cloudy, unseeing eyes. How I undid the buttons, one by one by one, and folded the shirt back from the body. How I lined up the blade at the top of the breastbone, then maneuvered the tip into place, separating sinew and muscle and vein, until I found the best point of entry.

I did hesitate then. For a moment, I looked up and out of the windows onto the darkening night, and thought of you. And from that came courage.

I lined up the scalpel, put the weight of my body behind the blade, and pushed. At first, nothing. A moment of suspension. Then the tip pierced the skin. A hiss of air and a sigh as the flesh unfolded, as if

Jackdaw too was relieved the waiting was over. A leaking of liquid and the distinctive coppery smell of souring blood. Then, with my knife and untutored fingers, I began to peel the skin back from his shattered bones.

It was difficult work, dirty. I felt the struggle of it in my shoulders and in my hands, the handle cutting into my palm. I labored for hours, finishing only as the night had robbed the sky of all color and the light returned.

When it was finished, I thought again of you.

Then of the next destined to die.

PART II

Thursday

Chapter 16

Blackthorn House
Fishbourne Marshes
Thursday, May 2nd

Connie was woken by the harsh chattering of a bird. She lifted her head from the glass of the window with a jolt, and looked out into a gray dawn.

A single magpie sat on the gate at the end of the path. *Pica pica.* Glossy black and white. Wing feathers of purple blue, the long green sheen of his tail. Connie saluted.

"One for sorrow."

Her neck was stiff and she was cold, exhausted as much by relief that the night had passed without incident as by her lack of sleep. The anxiety that had led her to spend the midnight hours watching from the stairs had faded with the coming of the day, damp and miserable as it was.

Outside the window, the marshes were calm and flat in the strengthening morning light. Farther out, the surface of the mill pond was choppy. Connie opened the window and smelled the rain in the air, felt the wind on her face.

She folded the tartan blanket and stretched. A sleeping house and an empty house had different atmospheres, in the quality of silence and stillness. Though she knew in her bones her father had not come back, she went to check all the same.

She unlocked his bedroom and went inside. The same undercurrent of despair hung in the stale air. This morning, she noticed a glass she'd missed on his bedside table, a hardened sediment at the bottom. She sniffed it. Brandy and ash. Her eyes flickered around the room, just in case she had overlooked a note or some other clue, but there was nothing remarkable. She wondered where her father had spent the night, and if he was all right.

The truth was, Gifford often took himself off without explanation or warning. No mystery to it, only a dark and self-destructive impulse that led him to drink until he had blotted out all the black thoughts in his head. It had scared her when she was younger. Now, more than anything, she hated how helpless she was to prevent it from happening.

The magpie continued to rattle its warning from the gate. Connie lingered a little longer in the room, hearing a faint echo of Gifford's voice in her head.

*

A new memory. Or, rather, an old memory retrieved.

Once, her father had conjured such clever stories. He'd been a salesman, as well as a skilled stuffer, and his business thrived because of the way he could talk and talk. A showman. Connie could see him now, standing at the counter of a large, well-appointed workshop—not here at Blackthorn House, but before—so proud of a piece he had created. A magpie mounted in a wooden box, the sky a painted forget-me-not blue. Its tail touching the sides of the glass. Her father's card affixed to the back: PRESERVED BY MR. CROWLEY GIFFORD—STUFFER OF BIRDS.

There had been a customer, and Connie had been listening from behind the door that led from the workshop into the museum. The color of the magpie, her father was saying, was symbolic of creation. The void, the mystery of that which had not yet taken form. Black and white, he said. Presence and absence.

The woman was hanging on his every word, and Connie felt pride at that. Watching the client trying to resist his patter, but being drawn in all the same. Of course, the magpie's a trickster too, he was saying, and the woman was nodding with his description of the bird, the powdered face and wide eyes just visible beneath the brim of her wide summer hat. Gray gloves stained black at the seams, brought to mind with complete clarity. The smart clothes and careful manner, but gloves that had not been washed.

The woman did not know Gifford was playing her. Connie remembered seeing his expression, as he turned around for a moment: a mixture of avarice and cunning. Then, for an instant, realizing how others might consider her father a charlatan. A spinner of tales.

Such a very watchful bird, the magpie, he carried on, fearless and manipulative. An excellent piece for a domestic setting, a sentinel to guard the house. It died naturally, madam, yes, of course. Struck by a hansom cab. Shame to waste such a beautiful specimen. When there was a group of them, it was called a tiding. A tiding of magpies, wasn't that something?

All the time he was talking, her father was rubbing a soft cloth over the surface of the glass. He made the woman feel a sadness for the bird. Connie remembered how she had dabbed at her eyes with a handkerchief.

Connie tried to change the view, to see herself rather than the scene, but found she could not. She remembered how her father had called to her to fetch brown paper and string, to wrap the magpie. She carried it out to a landau waiting at the curb. A pair and two, a chestnut and a bay.

She frowned, trying to work out how old she might have been. Old enough to bear the weight of the case, or had someone helped her? Four hands on the box, not two.

She remembered how proud she had been to be asked to write out the rhyme affixed to the back of the case. Small, neat letters.

One for sorrow, two for joy.
Three for a girl, four for a boy.
Five for silver, six for gold . . .

She had admired her father once. Been proud of him. When had that changed?

*

A knocking brought Connie back to the present. She went to the window and looked down to see Mary waiting patiently at the kitchen door.

For a moment, Connie did not move. She was becalmed, like a boat out on the creek with no wind. Caught halfway between remembering it all and forgetting.

With a great effort of will, she tore herself away from her father's room, and her memories and his secrets, and went to let Mary in. The words of the child's rhyme continued to go around and around in her head.

Seven for a secret never to be told.

Chapter 17

North Street
Chichester

"You're certain his bed hasn't been slept in, Lewis?"

"Quite certain, sir."

Harry threw *The Times* onto the breakfast table. "And he didn't return home for dinner?"

"As I said, sir," the butler replied in his toneless voice, "he did not."

Harry glanced at Lewis, but his face gave nothing away. The whole conversation had been a struggle, and his headache was getting worse. "And no message?"

"No, sir. No message."

Harry waved a hand to encourage the butler to go on.

"At nine thirty, when neither Dr. Woolston nor yourself had returned," Lewis continued, "Mrs. Lewis and I cleared the dining room and prepared a cold supper instead." He paused. "I trust you found it satisfactory, sir?"

"Yes, thank you," Harry said uncomfortably. For the second night in a row, he had been glad of the plate of food when he staggered home in the small hours, having missed dinner.

Rattled by his experiences at Blackthorn House, the maelstrom of conflicting emotions, Harry had walked back to Chichester from Fishbourne to clear his head. The familiar lights of the Castle Inn in West Street were hard to resist, so he had gone in, intending to have a shot of gin, a glass of Dutch courage to prepare himself for the conversation with his father. He'd somehow persuaded himself by then that not only would the old man be waiting at home as usual—with a perfectly ordinary, dull explanation for his unscheduled visit to Fishbourne—but also that he would prove sympathetic to Harry's desire to chuck in working for Brook and dedicate himself to a career in art instead. Even his father could see that he had no commercial skill for selling or brokering deals.

In truth, Harry was struggling to forget the face of the drowned woman. The pallor of her skin. As the hours had passed, he'd found himself more shaken by what he'd witnessed rather than less.

One glass became two, became three. Harry grew boisterous. The regulars were a welcoming crowd, lots of them stuck in the same dead-end situations as he was. After sharing horror stories about fathers who were holding them back, who didn't understand the new generation, and several more rounds of drinks, the talk had turned to the ghosts supposed to haunt the inn. A Roman centurion had been sighted several times, not surprising given its position backing onto the old flint walls of the city. Harry wondered if there was a tavern in Chichester without a specter.

All thoughts of tackling his father slipped into the background. And, finally, so did the horror of the swollen face and hands, the memory of dragging the corpse across the tide and onto the bank.

By the time Harry left the Castle Inn, it was after midnight. The night air, far from sobering him up, seemed to do the opposite. He found it a challenge to put one foot in front of the other. Staggering past the cathedral green, clinging to the railings to keep his balance, he saw Sergeant Pennicott standing at the Market Cross. He'd run into him once before. The sergeant was a teetotaller and took a dim view of public insobriety. Harry had also discovered, to his embarrassment, that he was incorruptible. It was only thanks to his father that he had been let off with a caution.

To avoid the policeman, Harry ducked into the Rifleman for a nightcap, the only place in Chichester that stayed open into the small hours. All in all, having taken a roundabout route— by mistake rather than design—he hadn't made it home until well after one o'clock. His concern, then, was not to wake his father up.

Stumbling up the stairs, he dropped his Oxfords outside his bedroom door to be cleaned, then fell fully clothed into bed and slept until five, dreaming of Connie sitting in his studio, inspiring him to paint the most astonishing portrait of his career. Raging thirst had woken him and driven him to the kitchen, where he found the plate of cut meats. He wolfed it down with what seemed like a gallon of water, then returned to bed to try to beat his hangover—without success.

"And no word from my father this morning, Lewis? A telegram? Message from his office?"

"No, sir."

It was extraordinary. Even if there had been some sort of accident, his father would have found a way of letting him know. Of letting Lewis know, at least. He didn't like the servants to be inconvenienced.

Harry frowned, which sent a new wave of pain rolling around in his head. He wondered if a mustard poultice might help. He couldn't remember ever feeling quite so dreadful. Not since coming down from Oxford. End of Trinity Term, 1907. That had been an evening to remember, up all night after the

Coronation Ball. Champagne and dancing in the streets. He'd kissed that pretty brown-haired sister of the chap on the staircase next to his.

Not a patch on Miss Gifford—Connie. He wondered how she was this morning, and if she was recovered from their shared ordeal yesterday. On reflection, he was sure she would be fine. She had backbone.

"If you don't mind me saying, sir," Lewis added, cutting into Harry's reflections, "I am certain there will be a rational explanation for Dr. Woolston's absence."

Harry looked up, disconcerted by the fact that the old servant was trying to reassure him. It somehow made the situation more alarming.

"Absolutely," he said, injecting confidence into his voice. "Some miscommunication or other, I'm sure. In fact, I'll go to his consulting rooms now, to see how things stand. See what Pearce has to say."

Lewis cleared his throat. "Or . . . and forgive me for suggesting it, sir, but perhaps also a visit to the West Sussex County Asylum? Dr. Woolston's colleagues there might be expecting him."

Harry nodded, then regretted it. "Good idea."

"Will you be home for lunch as usual, sir?"

Harry dropped his napkin on the table and pushed his chair back. If he had no luck in finding out where his father was in Chichester, he was thinking he might go back to Fishbourne. Not least, he could call on Connie at Blackthorn House to see how she was. No one, not even his father, could consider that inappropriate. He could introduce himself to her father at the same time. He was rather interested to know what kind of man he was.

He stood up. "No, I'll be out all day."

Harry walked down North Street.

After the brief promise of summer yesterday, the weather had sunk back into another damp, gray spring morning. Harry was glad of his mackintosh and boots. The cool air was helping his hangover and he was starting to feel rather less ill.

The glazier was replacing the glass in the butcher's window. Harry tried to remember if he'd passed this way on his route home last night. Inside, he could see people moving about, including Pennicott, so he increased his pace.

He turned right at the Market Cross into West Street. Was he making too much of his father's absence? There was bound to be some dull-as-ditchwater explanation. On the other hand, even though Lewis was unaware of the scene in his father's consulting rooms, and his father's dash out of town, he was also worried.

Harry hesitated outside for a moment, then, telling himself everything was bound to be back to normal, he pushed open the door.

Today, his father's assistant was sitting behind his leather-topped writing desk as usual. Every pen, his blotter, each sheet of paper in perfect and symmetrical order. Harry gave a sigh of relief.

"Morning, Pearce," he said. "Another glorious day."

Pearce looked at him over the top of his spectacles. "Do you think so?" he said. "I thought it rather overcast."

Harry stared at him. "It was a joke."

"I see."

"Is the old man in?"

Pearce frowned. "As a matter of fact, he is not."

Harry felt his stomach lurch. "But you are expecting him?"

"When I arrived this morning, I found the door unlocked. Most irregular. I assumed that Dr. Woolston had been called away and, though this is most unlike him, had omitted to secure the building."

Harry frowned. "He didn't leave a note, I suppose, saying where he was going?"

"He did not." Pearce sniffed, dabbing at his red nose with a handkerchief. "Which is most unusual. Whenever Dr. Woolston is intending to be away from the office, he makes sure I am aware of it. Very methodical."

"Have you checked his appointments diary? Perhaps that will give some clue as to where he is?"

Pearce looked scandalized. "I couldn't possibly do that without Dr. Woolston's express permission. It's private."

"I'm sure he won't object to me having a look," Harry said, bounding up the stairs two at a time.

"I don't advise—"

"Tell him I bullied you into it, Pearce."

*

Harry's unease deepened when he saw the chair on its side.

He bent down and picked it up, then cast an eye around to see if anything else struck a false note. He glanced out of the high Georgian window, which looked out over rooftops to St. Peter's Church, then back to the room. His father's desk was not untidy, but it was not in the pristine state Harry knew the old man left things in at the end of each working day. It was evident his father had not come back after the quarrel Harry had overheard. He glanced at the carriage clock on the mantelpiece. Each evening, before he left the office, his father wound it. It was already running slow.

Harry checked the desk diary, scrupulously maintained in his father's neat handwriting. An hour-by-hour record of meetings and commitments. It was entirely free of appointments yesterday and today.

He felt shabby going through his father's private possessions, but opened the desk drawer all the same. There was nothing unusual, except for a small silver snuffbox. Harry smiled, feeling rather touched at this sign of a normal—though unexpected—human vice. A second glass of claret at dinner was the closest to indulgence he had known his father to get.

"Is there anything noted in the diary?" Pearce said.

Harry turned around to see the clerk standing in the doorway.

"Nothing," he said, closing the drawer. "You haven't been in here this morning, Pearce?"

"Of course not." The clerk was shocked. "I never come into Dr. Woolston's rooms without invitation."

"I dare say," Harry muttered. "As it happens, I popped in yesterday lunchtime, but I didn't see you. Were you here in the afternoon?"

"The exceptional warm weather yesterday brought on, I regret to say, a disabling attack of hay fever. Dr. Woolston was quite concerned and suggested I should go home. I demurred, of course, but your father insisted upon it."

Harry thought for a moment, then fell back on the same reassurance that Lewis had tried to give him.

"I'm sure there's a rational explanation for my father's absence," he said. "All the same, would you send a telegram to the chap at the asylum. What's the fellow's name?"

"Dr. Kidd."

'Kidd, that's right. Ask him . . ." He stopped. What, in fact, was he asking? "If there was perhaps an emergency meeting called of the committee yesterday afternoon, a last-minute arrangement. You know better than me the sort of thing that goes on up there, Pearce, you decide what to put. But don't break the bank."

Harry walked past the clerk and down the stairs. "Oh, and while you're at it, would you mind popping across the road and explaining that I was called away on family business yesterday afternoon. Won't make it in today, either."

"I couldn't possibly—" Pearce began, but Harry had already left.

*

Harry went back to the railway station first, thinking he might be able to find the driver who'd taken his father to Fishbourne.

Even at ten o'clock in the morning, there was a crowd of men outside the Globe Inn. Smoking, caps pushed back on their heads, eyes blurred and watchful.

A row of black pair-and-two Dunnaways taxis were waiting at the stand outside the station building, the horses still in the damp air. Some were wearing nosebags, and there was a smell of straw and the stable.

"Taxi, sir?"

"I'm looking for a driver."

Someone laughed. "Come to the right place."

Harry ignored him. "I'm looking for the driver who took a gentleman to Fishbourne yesterday lunchtime. Possibly brought him back, too."

The cabman shrugged. "Not me."

"In his fifties, well turned out, middle-aged. Wears spectacles."

Since this could have served as a description for half the professional men within the city limits, it didn't get Harry far. He worked his way down the row all the same, right to the end.

"I think Bert might have taken a fare out Fishbourne way yesterday," the last cabbie said, accepting a cigarette.

"And which one is Bert?"

"He's off Thursdays."

Harry scowled. "But he took a gentleman to Fishbourne?"

"I said I thought he might have done," the driver corrected him. "Only remember because he was going on about a big tip."

Harry sighed. "Will Bert be here tomorrow?"

"Should be."

*

Harry decided to go to Fishbourne next rather than tramp all the way up to Graylingwell. He was better leaving that to Pearce. He knew the ropes up there.

Having waited so long yesterday for a train, he opted to walk. Blackthorn House was on the Chichester side of the village, so it would take much the same amount of time to get there under his own steam as it would to take the train and have the walk from Fishbourne Halt at the other end. He would go into the Woolpack, ask if anyone had seen his father, then possibly go to the Bull's Head and check that the barman had arranged things with the removal of the body. It would give him a reason to pay a visit to Blackthorn House if he had something to tell Connie. And when he'd suggested he might call on her again, although she hadn't encouraged him, she hadn't forbidden him either.

He headed out of the city through Westgate, past the back of the theological college, and toward the old turnpike. Houses soon gave way to fields. He passed a homespun memorial at the side of the road at the junction with Apuldram Lane, marking the place where a carriage had overturned in the March storms, killing a husband, wife and three young children.

Harry was attempting to remain calm, trying not to assume the worst, but something new was niggling at the back of his mind. Something he'd noticed but whose significance he had not registered. He ran through everything he'd done so far this morning, retracing his steps in his mind: Lewis's concern, his father sending Pearce home yesterday and leaving the office unattended, the chair lying on its side in his rooms, his father's desk.

He pulled himself up. That was it. An absence, not a presence. The one thing he should have seen in his father's desk drawer—his old service revolver—had not been there.

It began to rain.

Chapter 18

Blackthorn House
Fishbourne Marshes

Connie looked out at the first drops of rain.

The promise of heat had come and gone in a single day. Everything had returned to the endless gray. Black clouds were bumping across the surface of the estuary, and a gusty squall was chopping, slicing the water. Even though the tide was at its lowest, the streams were still full and puddles of salt water dotted the path.

Since the weather looked as if it was setting in, Connie decided to go to Fishbourne straightaway. The jackdaw, waiting for her beneath the glass bell jar, would have to wait a while longer. She wanted to make discreet inquiries as to whether anyone had seen her father. Also, since the news of the discovery of a body near to Blackthorn House was bound to have spread by now, she thought she'd rather know what was being said and face it head on than be ignorant of what stories were circulating.

She put on her coat. "I'm going into Fishbourne, Mary," she called out. "There are things we need."

The girl rushed into the hall. "Are you sure you don't want me to go, Miss Gifford? The rain's just coming on."

"I'll take an umbrella."

"If you're sure, miss," the girl said, twisting the tea towel in her hands.

"I'm not expecting visitors, Mary. However, should anyone call—in connection with yesterday's events, perhaps—please give my apologies and say I will be at home this afternoon."

"Shall I ask them to wait, miss?"

Connie paused. There was no reason to think the woman she'd seen watching the house might return, but she didn't want to lose a second chance of talking to her.

"In fact, yes. I shan't be away long."

"Very good, miss. And the master?"

"I don't want my father disturbed," she replied, hoping it wouldn't come to light that he wasn't in the house.

Mary pulled anxiously at her apron. "May I ask you something, miss?"

Connie reached for her latchkey from the hook, then noticed that the key to the icehouse wasn't in its usual place on the row.

"Did you have reason to go out to Mr. Gifford's storeroom, Mary?"

"No, miss, but—"

"The key appears to be missing."

Mary wasn't listening. "It's going round that it was Vera Barker we found in the river," she blurted out. "It wasn't me, Miss Gifford. I promise I didn't tell a soul. At least, Ma got it out of me, but I didn't say nothing to anyone else." She took another deep breath. "My friend Archie was one of the boys who came out with Mr. Pine last night. He wouldn't tell me anything, he's good like that, but then when I went to collect the laundry from Miss Bailey on my way here this morning, she said her friend Mrs. Goslin—Kate Goslin, whose sister is married to Mr. Pine . . ."

Connie held up her hands to try to stem the tide of words. "Mary, I—"

"... said, according to Miss Bailey that is, they'd laid her out in the barn. Then old Tommy came bellowing to be allowed to see his daughter, but Mr. Crowther had—"

"Mary," Connie said loudly, "please, stop."

The girl came to a halt. "But is it true? Was it Vera Barker? Ma thought it might be—there was something in the paper about her having gone missing. I never knew her. She was long gone from Fishbourne before we came to live here, but Ma always knows—"

"Mary, all I can tell you is that one of the young men who came with Mr. Crowther last evening said it was Vera Barker and the others appeared to concur."

"Archie." Mary blushed. "As I said, he's by way of being a friend of mine. Not that he told me. Mr. Crowther said they were all to keep it quiet. I didn't tell a soul."

Connie pictured the knot of men in the dusk.

"It's all right, Mary. Don't worry. All the same, I think it's best if we don't talk about it. You know how rumors spread. Let's wait until we know something for certain."

"Yes, miss."

Connie put on her hat, pushed the pin through to hold it firm, then took her gloves from her coat pocket.

"About the key, Mary."

"Miss?"

"To the icehouse," Connie said, as patiently as she could.

"I don't know anything about the key, miss, but the padlock was lying on the ground last night."

"What did you do with it?"

"Locked it right back up. Someone must have left it open."

"Was the door open?"

"No. It was all shut up like always."

Connie wondered if her father might have gone to the storeroom for some reason, then dismissed the idea. He usually avoided the place, saying it reminded him too much of the loss of their old life. But then again, nothing about the last few days had been as usual.

"There's a spare key somewhere, Mary, probably in one of the drawers in the kitchen. Could you look for it while I'm in Fishbourne?"

*

Connie glanced toward the icehouse as she left, but everything looked secure enough for the time being.

Once Mary found the spare key, she would take a lamp and go and make sure everything was as it should be. She couldn't remember the last time she'd gone into the storeroom, there was never any need. But it couldn't hurt to check.

She glanced up at the sky and realized she needed to hurry. The rain was already steady, and black clouds were massing over Dell Quay, suggesting worse to come.

Light-headed from lack of sleep, Connie made her way along the footpath, already a patchwork of puddles and standing seawater. She trod carefully, trying not to slip in the mud. The sluice gates by Fishbourne Mill were open and the water was surging through. The mill pond was lapping at the edge of the road and inching closer to the front garden of Slay Lodge and Pendrills. It would be too bad if Mr. Crowther was flooded again. There had been enough damage in April, sandbags and straw stacked up against all the doors. Rugs and furniture set in the road to dry.

Connie heard the sound of wings, then the rattling cawing

of magpies. She looked up, to see a pair of black-and-whites perched on the thatched roof of the cottage. No reason to think they were the same birds from the garden, but she felt a sudden, inexplicable surge of anger. There was the familiar building of pressure in her temples, and though she tried to fight it again, this time she felt herself falling out of time.

*

All at once, Connie was no longer aware of the wind worrying at her hat and tugging the pins from her hair. She was no longer standing in Mill Lane, but instead looking down through the bars of a wooden cage.

A room of glass, candlelight flickering and reflecting. The scent of perfume and desire. Cigars. Men's voices, loud and quarreling.

Jackdaw. Magpie. Rook. Crow.

Connie remembered the feeling of menace, of threat. She was scared, woken by ugly sounds she didn't understand. Masks, glittering reflections and sequins. Feathers, and the scent of whisky and sherry spilling on the old wooden floor.

Fear becoming anger. Then pain. Her bare feet sticky, slippery. A sensation of falling, spinning, flying through the air.

Then, nothing.

"Get away," she shouted, clapping her hands to ward off the feathers overwhelming her, trying to save herself from the vicious sharp beaks.

*

Connie realized her feet were wet. She looked down and saw she was standing in water.

She was back in the present. In Fishbourne, with rain streaming down the back of her collar and the pond now seeping across Mill Lane. Still disorientated, she clapped her hands again to scare the birds away. But when she looked up, the magpies were nowhere to be seen.

Chapter 19

West Street
Chichester

"I have a message for Mr. Brook," Pearce told the clerk, Sutton. "Mr. Woolston has, regrettably, been called away on an urgent family matter. Utterly unavoidable. He asked me to pass on his apologies." He hurriedly thrust his handkerchief to his nose to cover a sneeze. "And to say that, of course it goes without saying, he will make up the time at Mr. Brook's convenience."

The temperature in the tiled entrance hall seemed to drop.

"It would be much better if you waited to deliver the message yourself," Sutton said. "Mr. Brook has been waiting for Dr. Woolston for some time. He is most displeased."

Pearce fixed him with a cold stare. "You misunderstand me. The message is from *Mr.* Woolston, not *Dr.* Woolston."

"Well, that's part of the difficulty. Mr. Brook was already very much put out by young Mr. Woolston's failure to arrive for work yesterday afternoon—having generously allowed him to take the morning—so when Dr. Woolston also failed to arrive for their meeting . . . well, you can imagine."

"You must be mistaken," Pearce said coldly, resenting the clerk's attempts to draw him into his confidence. "Dr. Woolston does not have an appointment with Mr. Brook today."

"I don't wish to disagree, but I can assure you—"

A door opened at the far end of the corridor. The smell of shipping lists and dust and cigar smoke seeped out on the coat-tails of the two men who emerged from the room.

"Here is Mr. Brook," Sutton said quickly. "You can tell him yourself."

The two men were both in their early fifties. The first was tall and slim, black hair and moustache, wearing a well-cut gray office suit and a bowler hat. Pearce recognized him as working for one of the largest property agents in Chichester. The other, Brook himself, was built on an altogether different scale. He filled the space, every part of him oversized: his ears, his hands, his nose, moustache, even the shock of black hair, too uniform to be entirely natural. A Donegal tweed waistcoat beneath a shooting jacket strained to contain his stomach. As he drew closer, the clerk seemed to shrink into his cheap black suit. Pearce, realizing he could not slip away, took off his hat and pressed himself closer to the wall.

"Get an umbrella for Mr. White!" Brook bellowed in his strong Staffordshire accent. "Hurry up, man."

The clerk scuttled out from behind his desk, rushed to the hat stand and fumbled at the base until he'd found something suitable.

"Stupid of me to forget mine," White was saying. "Awful weather. Still, should be used to it by now."

"Sure you won't join me for the shooting up at Goodwood?"

White shook his head. "I have an appointment with a client in Apuldram." He smiled. "I have high hopes."

Brook nodded. "You can always join us later. Thinking of trying the Kursaal in Bognor."

"I might do that," said White, then lowered his voice. "On the other matter, you'll speak to Charles?"

Brook nodded. "Leave it with me."

"Good." White put on his hat and gloves. "Good. Well, let me know if there's anything you need me to do. Otherwise, wish me luck!"

*

Brook closed the door and strode back into the hall. For so large a man, he moved with surprising grace.

Sutton scuttled around from behind his desk.

"Mr. Pearce has brought a message from Mr. Woolston, sir," he said quickly.

Brook strode up to Pearce and stood right in front of him. Pearce had to force himself not to take a step back.

"Well? What's his excuse?"

Pearce cleared his throat. "There appears to be some misunderstanding," he said. "I am *Dr.* Woolston's private secretary; however, I was asked to bring a message from Harold Woolston. He was called away on an urgent family matter yesterday afternoon."

"I am more concerned, at this precise point, as to why Dr. Woolston failed to turn up this morning."

In his own domain, Pearce was master. Here, he felt diminished.

"I was unaware that Dr. Woolston had arranged a meeting with you, sir," he said, with as much dignity as he could manage. "Mr. Harold Woolston paid a visit to his father's rooms this morning, so when news came of the . . . the family crisis, I volunteered to walk across to pass on the message to you, in person."

Brook poked Pearce in the chest. "Very well. What's

Dr. Woolston got to say about his son?" he demanded. "I only took the boy on as a favor to him. If he doesn't measure up, he'll be out on his ear. Claimed he was ill. I warned him."

"I couldn't say, Mr. Brook. I'm not privy to . . ."

"To what?"

It went against all Pearce's principles to reveal anything about Dr. Woolston, but he felt himself wilting.

"I'm waiting, Pearce. What is this 'family crisis' that allows Dr. Woolston to send his son off and then not bother to turn up himself? Is that how he thinks business is done?"

"Not at all." Pearce cleared his throat. "It is just that Dr. Woolston is also, unexpectedly, away from the office."

"Because of this same crisis?"

"No," Pearce said, making a last-ditch effort in support of his employer.

"Then where is he? Stop talking in riddles, man."

"The fact is, sir, I am not currently aware of Dr. Woolston's whereabouts."

Brook's eyes narrowed. "What do you mean?"

"Dr. Woolston has not arrived at the office this morning. His son was concerned and so asked me—"

"Are there reasons for concern?"

"I couldn't say, sir."

"You damn well will say!"

"I don't know," Pearce stammered. "Only, when I arrived this morning, the door was unlocked. I got the impression from Mr. Woolston that his father had not been home. In fact, that no one has seen Dr. Woolston since yesterday morning."

Brook stared at him. His silence was, if anything, more threatening than shouting. Pearce dropped his head. All he could think about was how displeased Dr. Woolston would be at his indiscretion, yet what else could he have done?

Sutton was cowering in his chair, moving papers around the desk.

"Get after Mr. White," said Brook. "Ask if he might spare me a couple more minutes."

"What, now?" Sutton stuttered.

"Of course now!"

The clerk ran to the front door, slipping on the polished tiles, and out into the street. Moments later, he came back and stood cringing, like a dog expecting to be beaten.

"I'm sorry, sir. I was too late. I saw Mr. White getting into a hansom at the corner of Tower Street."

Pearce pressed himself back into the bookshelves, praying that Brook wouldn't turn on him again.

"Well then, get over to his offices instead and tell them to pass on the message. I need to speak to him urgently the moment he gets back. Do you hear? Immediately!"

"Yes, sir."

Brook swept Pearce out of the way as he strode back into his office, slamming the door with such force that three books fell from a shelf.

For a moment, the two clerks stood frozen. Then Pearce reached for his hat and Sutton picked up the books and put them on his desk.

"Good day," Pearce said, trying to recover his composure.

Sutton did not meet his eye.

*

Outside, in the damp street, Pearce stood shaking.

It was too bad, really it was too bad to have been put in so invidious a position. Not only had Dr. Woolston made a business appointment without informing him, but on top of that, he had not honored it. A muddle of that kind reflected badly on Pearce, even though he'd known nothing. As for being expected to run errands for the doctor's idle son, as if he was some kind of office boy, it wouldn't do. He would have words with Dr. Woolston.

All the same, beneath his affront at the slur on his own reputation, Pearce was worried. It was out of character. In all the years he had worked for Dr. Woolston, he'd never known him to behave in so thoughtless or unprofessional a manner. Brook was not a Chichester man, of course. He was a tradesman, when all was said and done, and from the Midlands. His manner was most unfortunate, vulgar even. Having never met the man before today, it surprised Pearce hugely that Dr. Woolston would have put his son to work for such a person.

But Dr. Woolston knew how to behave. He did the right thing.

Out of the corner of his eye, Pearce noticed Sergeant Pennicott standing at the Cross. He hesitated, then, rather than going back to the consulting rooms, walked quickly past the bell tower up West Street to speak to the policeman instead.

Chapter 20

Main Road
Fishbourne

Connie shook the rain off her umbrella, then went into the post office and general stores. The women queuing at the counter turned, saw her and fell silent.

"Ladies," she said, wiping her feet on the mat.

One of Levi Nutbeem's sons was behind the counter. "I'll be right with you, Miss Gifford."

"Thank you."

Connie felt the customer at the front of the queue glance over at her, then away. There was something familiar about the woman, but she couldn't bring to mind where she had run into her.

The tiny shop was stacked floor to ceiling, every square inch accounted for. At the back, next to the post office window, were pails, packets of pins, drums of Zebra blacking and Seidlitz powders. Shelves of tins filled the side wall, and on the long wooden counter, Coburgs and flat tin loaves; a marble slab with blocks of butter, lard and cheese ready to be cut; a brick of salt too. On the floor, hessian bags filled with sugar, loose tea and flour.

Connie watched as Nutbeem twisted a sheet of blue paper to

form a cone, turned over the point, then filled it with candied peel, raisins and sultanas.

"There you go, Polly," he said, handing the cone to a little girl hiding shyly in her mother's skirts.

"And what about you, Maisie?"

Maisie pointed at the currant buns, displayed in a wooden tray. He nodded, picked one up with his fingers, shook the sugar off, and dropped it into a brown paper bag.

"Say thank you to the nice man."

"Thank you."

"It's my pleasure, little lady. Will there be anything else, Mrs. Christie?"

Connie paid more attention now she realized the woman must be Mary's mother. No wonder she'd thought she recognized her. She had the same pretty, open expression as her daughter.

"Five rashers of bacon."

He cut thick slabs from the haunch with a long-blade knife, then wrapped the meat in greaseproof paper and put it straight into Mrs. Christie's shopping bag.

He pushed the chit across the counter, and Mrs. Christie counted out the coins.

"Thank you," she said, taking her change. She glanced again at Connie. This time, Connie smiled back.

"Good morning, Mrs. Christie."

"Morning, Miss Gifford." She held Connie's gaze for a moment, then turned back to the twins and shooed them out of the shop.

Connie passed her list across the counter. "There's not much."

Nutbeem's was mostly used by village families, rather than the private houses who tended to patronize Blake's, so the customers queuing at the post office counter remained silent. But as Nutbeem worked his way down Connie's list and the minutes ticked by, the women forgot she was there and went back to their interrupted conversations.

Connie listened with half an ear for any mention of Vera, but they had moved on to parish matters.

"There's a lot to carry, Miss Gifford," Nutbeem said. "I've got a deliveryman out this afternoon. We could add you into the round, if you like."

Connie smiled at him. Previously, Nutbeem's and Blake's had both said that Blackthorn House was too inaccessible for their delivery cart. "I'd be very grateful, Mr. Nutbeem, it would be a help. I am rather wet already."

"My pleasure, miss," he said.

She realized that his generosity was probably a reaction to yesterday; that he felt sorry for her. Connie didn't want to encourage gossip, but it seemed too good an opportunity to miss. She risked a question.

"You heard of the tragedy yesterday?"

She felt the atmosphere in the tiny shop shift. And though she didn't turn around, she sensed that every set of eyes was fixed on her back.

"I did, Miss Gifford," Nutbeem said quietly. "Most unpleasant for you, miss. And of course for the young lady herself."

"I would like to send some mark of condolence to her family," she said.

"That's very decent of you, Miss Gifford. I am sure that would be appreciated." He tapped a box on the counter. "We've got a collection going, for the flowers. Funeral's set for Saturday."

"So soon?" The words were out of her mouth before she could check them. "Has the coroner released the body already?"

"Coroner? Don't know about any coroner, but Mr. Crowther's

organizing the service. Vera's body will be released to her father this morning, so I heard."

Connie stared. It was not possible that a doctor would have thought Vera's death an accident, surely?

"Did Dr. Evershed do the examination?"

"No, Miss Gifford. Dr. and Mrs. Evershed are away. They had to get some chap from Chichester to come out. Dr. Woolston, I think Mr. Crowther said he was called." He shook his head. "None of those Barker girls were taught to swim; Tommy didn't hold with it. With tragic consequences."

"Woolston . . ."

She and Harry hadn't really talked much yesterday afternoon, so she didn't know if it might be someone connected with him. Surely, if a father or brother had been in the village too, he would have mentioned it? It was possible there was no relation, but Woolston was hardly a common surname.

"Will there be anything else, Miss Gifford?"

Connie looked up. "No. That's all, thank you."

"On account, or are you settling?"

"Account, please."

He ran his finger down the ledger. "Will three o'clock be convenient for the delivery? Weather permitting. Otherwise, first thing tomorrow."

"Either will be fine," she said. "And really, I'm most grateful."

*

Connie put up her umbrella and stepped out of the cover of the porch, her head spinning.

She had intended to go to the Bull's Head to check that arrangements were in hand, but given what she had heard, she now wasn't sure. Vera's funeral was taking place on Saturday? How could that be?

The fact was that the barman, Pine, had been present last night, as had Charles Crowther. If Nutbeem was correct, a Dr. Woolston had signed a death certificate for a verdict of accidental death, even though he must have known it was no such thing. The gash around her neck where the wire had cut in, the bubbles of blood at the corner of her mouth . . .

Connie couldn't deny that part of her was relieved. If Vera's death was seen as an accident, then there was no reason for Blackthorn House—or her father—to be drawn any further into the matter.

But deep down, she railed against the injustice. A young woman had been murdered and her death was being covered up. Just because she was poor, or thought to be a little strange, it didn't mean her life should count for nothing. It was wrong.

"Miss Gifford?"

Connie's heart leaped. "Mrs. Christie, you startled me!"

"I wonder if I might have a word, Miss Gifford."

"Of course."

"Girls, go and play with Pip," Mrs. Christie said, pointing at the black-and-tan terrier sitting outside the Woolpack.

Connie suddenly feared Mrs. Christie might be about to give notice on her daughter's behalf.

"Mary was so brave yesterday," she said quickly. "I couldn't have managed without her."

"She's fond of you too, miss."

Connie found herself surprisingly touched. "Well, I consider myself lucky to have her. She's a credit to you."

She glanced up at the sky. A new bank of black rain clouds was rolling in from the southwest, skimming the tops of the red roofs and the chimney pots. On the opposite side of the road, she saw Mr. Crowther, who raised his hat. Three of the women came out of the post office, hesitated when they saw Connie, then nodded and went on their way too. Everyone wanted to get home before the next downpour.

Mrs. Christie looked her straight in the eye. "Do you recognize me, miss?"

Given that they had exchanged pleasantries less than five minutes ago, it seemed a peculiar thing to ask.

"Well, yes. Of course. You're Mary's mother."

Mrs. Christie held her gaze, and for an instant, Connie saw something more in her eyes. Disappointment, perhaps?

"Forgive me, Mrs. Christie, have I misunderstood your question?"

The older woman dropped her eyes. "No, Miss Gifford."

Connie was confused. "I can truly say I did take every care to spare Mary any unpleasantness yesterday, Mrs. Christie. I would hate to lose her."

"That's not why I wanted to speak to you, miss, at least not directly. But when I heard about Mr. Woolston and what happened last evening . . ."

She took an envelope from her pocket. "It wasn't Mary's fault, she was that upset."

Connie saw the name on the cream envelope. "I don't understand, Mrs. Christie. Why do you have a letter addressed to me?"

"Mary found it on the mat yesterday morning and picked it up, meaning to bring it to you. Then, what with everything, she forgot."

Connie held out her hand. "Give it to me, please."

"Will you open it?" Mrs. Christie said quietly. Her behavior and interference were wholly inappropriate, yet there was something about her Connie felt she could trust. A genuine concern.

Connie took the letter. "Why didn't Mary simply bring it with her when she came to work this morning?"

"I didn't want you alarmed, miss. It's just I thought I recognized the handwriting."

"Alarmed? Why should I be alarmed?" Connie stared at the worried, pretty face—familiar, almost—realizing for the first time how similar mother and daughter were.

"Please open it," Mrs. Christie repeated. The request was so extraordinary that rather than object, Connie found herself doing what she was asked.

She looked down at the envelope in her hand. The elegant block letters in black ink. A flicker of memory. Was it possible that she too recognized the handwriting? She ran her finger along the join, pulled out the single sheet and read what was written.

"What does it say?" Mrs. Christie asked in a low, taut voice.

"'Do not be afraid,'" Connie read. "'I am watching you.'"

We then unite the skin by sewing it as we have said before, separating the feathers at each stitch: we furnish the orbits with chopped cotton, which we introduce with small forceps, rounding the eyelids well, we then place the eyes, introducing them under the eyelids, and when a part of the nictating membrane appears below, we must push it in with the point of the needle; that the eye may remain in place.

TAXIDERMY: OR, THE ART OF COLLECTING, PREPARING, AND MOUNTING OBJECTS OF NATURAL HISTORY

Mrs. R. Lee
Longman & Co., Paternoster Row, London, 1820

The knife sits well in my untaught hand.

What shall I tell you next? Perhaps that it is so simple, after the event, to identify the moment when our eyes are opened and we see the world as it is. A sequence of tiny, inconsequential events—unremarkable except when taken all together—or a blow delivered once too often. The realization that the laws and principles of justice apply to some and not others. That the truth can be bought.

Four fine gentlemen.

You will wonder how I managed. It was not difficult to put everything in place. I picked my associates well, blind to anything but their own advantage. If one has money, anything can be done in time.

You will ask if I have any regrets, and I do. I regret having to cause distress to those I care for, though I had no choice in the matter. In time, my reasons for acting as I did will be clear. Also, that in the pursuit of my retribution, someone innocent had to die. That death, unnecessary and unwarranted, only served to convince me of the justice of my cause and my chosen course of action.

The punishment must suit the crime.

Chapter 21

Blackthorn House
Fishbourne Marshes

Connie battled home against the wind and slanting, sharp rain.

The moment she'd handed Mrs. Christie the note to read for herself, the heavens had opened. The little girls had come squealing back to their mother, abruptly cutting short the conversation. Connie had invited her to Blackthorn House at five o'clock so they could talk further.

She instinctively liked Mrs. Christie, who seemed honest and decent. She hoped she would keep the appointment.

*

Arriving home, drenched to the skin, Connie unpinned her hat and dropped her wet coat and boots on the floor, then went straight to the parlor in her stockinged feet and poured herself a measure of her father's brandy.

She downed it in one, then emptied the bottle into the glass and sat down in the armchair next to the fire.

Mary appeared cautiously in the doorway. Connie felt the girl's gaze take in the glass.

"Are you all right, Miss Gifford?"

"I'm cold," she said, considering whether to raise the subject of the letter with Mary. She took another sip of brandy. She didn't want Mary to think she was in trouble, and besides, Connie was disturbed by the note herself and wanted time to think about it privately. She decided to wait.

"Has anything happened?"

"No, miss."

"Any visitors?"

"No, miss, and not a sound from upstairs either."

Connie glanced up. Her conversation with Mrs. Christie had momentarily pushed thoughts of her father out of her mind. Now, it seemed more important than ever that she talk to him about the past. To ask him if he knew who might have delivered such a note to Blackthorn House. If he knew of anyone who might have reason to watch the house.

"Do you want me to lay a fire, miss? It's awful damp in here and you've been out in the wet. A rug, at least?"

Connie smiled at the girl's concern. "A rug would be very welcome, and my slippers too. And if you could fetch my journal, that would be helpful."

"Of course, miss. Where is it?"

Connie tried to remember what she'd done with it when she came in from the terrace yesterday afternoon. Had she taken it into the workshop? She didn't think she had.

"Perhaps in the drawing room? I was writing at the table on the terrace."

Connie felt the heat of the brandy seeping into her bloodstream. She tilted the glass, and the last drop slid down her throat. She looked to the sideboard to see if there was something else she might drink, then decided better of it.

She took off her stockings and rubbed her cold feet, then

tucked them up under her in the armchair and leaned back against the headrest.

She did not mean to sleep.

*

Connie was looking out of the window of a train at hips and haws, ground ivy and blue-eyed speedwell. A yellowhammer and a robin redbreast, commonplace garden birds.

She was accompanied by a vivacious, smiling girl, eight or nine years older than herself. A ruffled blouse with a lace collar, a long black skirt. Chestnut hair beneath a plain straw hat, decorated with yellow flowers around the rim.

They bought a lunch basket at one of the stations along the line. Connie could remember how greasy the chicken leg was between her fingers. Some cold beef too, and a little bread and butter. Remembered laughing and playing word games like Cupid's Coming and Taboo. It was a dull day, she remembered that too. The guard came to light the lamps in their carriage. Or was that another journey altogether?

On her lap, a book of nursery rhymes. Too young for her. Feet skimming the floor of the carriage, backward and forward as the train rattled on. In sleep, the colors and sights and sounds of that day were coming back to her.

They changed at Shoreham-by-Sea to the Steyning line. Waiting on the damp platform for their connection, the day still overcast with a sea mist slipping in from the harbor. A small carriage, the drag of the motor engine, the fireman on the plate stoking the fire. Crossing the River Adur on an old wooden bridge and disembarking at Bramber, the name picked out in large white letters on a black-painted board on the platform.

A single, narrow main street. A steep hill and the remains of a ruined castle, along the dusty road to a small flint building with a pitched roof. Outside, an old man—in black suit and bow tie, a straw boater—sitting on a bench. Whiskers. Affixed to the front of the building, the sign read MUSEUM: OPEN DAILY. Someone, that same guardian, told her the man was Mr. Walter Potter himself, the owner of the museum. In the pretty courtyard garden, lots of visitors waiting their turn to be admitted to the displays.

Connie had no memory of waiting or of purchasing a ticket; only that the front door had stained-glass panels, glinting like a kaleidoscope in the weak afternoon sunlight, and led into an antechamber. A wooden cash desk, polished and surrounded by photographs and a vase of fresh meadow flowers. A glass jar containing Siamese twin pigs, their features squashed and gentle in the confined space. Trotters and tiny snouts and ears. Connie had thought they looked as if they were smiling. At the base of the jar, a sign explaining that the deformed animals had been a gift to the museum some twenty years earlier and were believed to have been formed by witchcraft.

What else? A suspended wooden seat for weighing jockeys, and an iron mantrap, its metal teeth clutched and browned by the blood of victims long dead. A clapper from a Sussex church bell.

Holding hands, walking forward into a room so full of treasures it was impossible to know where to look first. Birds' nests suspended from the ceiling, a jumble of glass and feather and furs, pelts hanging from the rafters. And everywhere, waist-high display cases—at eye level for her—with a spine of glass domes along the middle of the room containing stuffed birds: an owl, a robin nesting in a kettle, a duckling with four legs. A fox and her cubs, a two-headed kitten. A mummified hand, charred and blackened and sticky; withered flowers from a plundered grave. Grotesque and chillingly beautiful.

But her clearest memories of the day were the tableaux. Large glass cases filled with stuffed animals and birds, each telling a story. All of them the work of Mr. Potter, the owner and proprietor of the museum. The guinea pigs' cricket match, the accompanying band holding precise instruments, silver trumpets and a slide trombone. The score frozen at 189 for 7. A kittens' tea party, complete with doll's house chairs, blue-and-white porcelain cups and saucers and a silver teapot. Chicken and cake on the table molded from paste and glue. And around each tiny feline neck, blue ribbons or red, a copper necklace.

In only one tableau were the animals fully dressed. The kitten minister in his cassock, holding a prayer book between his claws. The veiled kitten bride in her wedding dress, her groom in black. Pearl and tulle, a posy of orange blossom, the female guests hung about with strings of red beads and blue, earrings clipped to their ears.

Connie moved slowly from case to case, her fingers pressed upon the glass. The smell of dust and overheated air, the lingering aroma of tobacco on men's coats, and camphor. A magical world of imagination. Life captured and preserved forever.

But what mattered most about that day, what had imprinted itself on Connie's pliant memory, was one of the largest of the tableaux, a polished metal plate affixed to the case: THE ORIGINAL DEATH AND BURIAL OF COCK ROBIN. Nearly one hundred birds—had someone told her this?—with glass-beaded eyes: bullfinch and robin, red-backed shrike, hawfinch and bunting, the sparrow with his bow and arrow. Old tombstones and disinterred bones, sepulchers and a tiny blue coffin, a dish of blood. Every verse from the nursery rhyme portrayed inside the case. An owl with white-and-gold feathers digging the grave with a pick and shovel. A grieving lark with a black sash around its neck. The rook who served as the parson holding a prayer book in its claw.

Staring into the case, imagining the noise of the cawing in the trees surrounding the house. The tolling of the bell. And in the middle of such delight, the slow realization, and her world shattering into pieces. Even though she was young, Connie understood that her father's museum—GIFFORD'S WORLD-FAMOUS HOUSE OF AVIAN CURIOSITIES—was based on this one. A few of the cases all but identical.

All those telegrams and words overheard. Court cases and summonses. An auction to sell off their possessions, a cart arriving to take the boxes and packing crates away. For a couple of days, just the three of them left in the almost empty museum with the few displays yet to be sold.

Her, Gifford and Cassie.

*

In her armchair in Blackthorn House, Connie stirred. Hearing a woman's voice, close at hand.

"Miss?"

She jerked awake, and saw a pretty face looking down at her.

"Cassie?"

"It's Mary, miss."

Connie blinked, then registered the girl standing in front of her chair clutching a blanket and a pair of slippers. Disorientated and embarrassed, she sat up.

"I'm sorry, of course. I must have fallen asleep."

Mary handed Connie her slippers and the rug. "I didn't mean to disturb you."

"No, it's better I wake up. Did I tell you Nutbeem's will deliver at three o'clock."

Mary's eyes widened. "That's good, miss."

"It is." Connie nodded. "Did you fetch my journal?"

"That's what I was coming to say, miss. I've looked everywhere, and I can't find it."

Chapter 22

"It must be somewhere."

"Your ink and pen were in the drawing room, like you said, but I looked all over the house for the journal and can't find it."

"My father's room?"

"Not there," the maid admitted. "Not in the workshop either. But everywhere else. I'm sorry, miss."

Connie folded the blanket back from her legs and stood up. She felt light-headed from the after-effects of the brandy and her short sleep.

"Don't worry, I'll look for it myself. I'm sure it will turn up. If you could bring me my pen and ink, and some loose writing paper, that will do for now."

"Shall I bring you something to eat? Some bread and butter, perhaps? It's gone one o'clock."

Connie wasn't the slightest bit hungry, but realized it would be sensible. "Some buttered toast would be nice."

"Perhaps a little paste, too? There's a new jar, and some pickled egg left from yesterday's lunch as well."

Connie was touched by the girl's determination to care for her.

"That's a good idea, thank you. I'll have a tray in here."

"Do you want me to prepare a tray for the master, too?"

Connie felt the tightening in her chest. As the hours went

on without her father coming back, she was no longer sure why she was continuing with the pretense. It would come out soon enough. On the other hand, she didn't feel she had the will to explain.

"We'll leave him be."

Mary nodded. "One more thing, miss. I don't like to bother you with it, not really, but he won't take no for an answer. Dave Reedman's boy is at the back door. He says he's got something to tell you. Bound to be nothing. He'd lie as soon as spit." Mary broke off, blushing.

"Did he say what it was?"

"No. I told him to hop it, but he's stood standing there all the same. Says he won't speak anything to anyone but you." Mary pursed her lips. "Shall I send him away?"

Connie was about to agree when it occurred to her that the boy might know something about her father's whereabouts. Davey was on the marshes day in, day out, when he should have been in school, fishing for eels and scavenging for jam jars, which he'd sell for a farthing or two. If anyone had seen Gifford, it would be him.

"No, show him in," she said. "Let's hear what he has to say."

*

Moments later, Mary ushered the grubby child into the drawing room. He was sporting a fine pair of binoculars around his neck.

Connie had no idea how old Davey Reedman might be—small boys were a mystery to her—but she guessed ten or eleven. His bare knees were a patchwork of scabs and cuts. His face looked as if it hadn't been washed in weeks, and there was a gray line of dirt around his moth-eaten collar. All the same, his eyes were bright and he looked intelligent.

"Take your cap off," Mary said, clipping the boy around the ear. "Show some respect."

Davey did what he was told, but Connie saw a flash of cheek in his coal-black eyes, and rather liked him for it.

"Hello, Davey," she said. "I gather you have something to tell me."

"In private," he said, throwing a glance at Mary. "Not speaking while she's here."

Mary raised her hand, but the boy dodged a step back.

"Thank you, Mary," Connie said swiftly. "I'll call when I need you."

The maid shot daggers at the boy, then picked up her skirts and flounced from the room, shutting the door theatrically behind her.

"Well, Davey, what is it?"

"Can I sit down, miss?"

Connie hid a smile. "You may sit on that chair there," she said, pointing to a ladder-back chair.

Davey grabbed it, swung it around and placed it right in front of her.

"So I'm wondering what's in it for me, miss?"

Connie tried to look stern. "That rather depends on what it is you have to say."

"Suppose that's fair enough," he said, crossing his left leg over his right knee. "How's about we talk, then we have a bit of a . . ." He wagged his hand back and forth.

"Negotiation?"

Davey nodded. "That's the johnny. Negotiation. So, here's how we do it. I tell you what I saw, you decide what it's worth, then we negotiate and settle." He spat on his hand and held it out. "All right?"

"All right," said Connie. "I shall assume you're a man of your word, Master Reedman, so there is no need to shake hands. Go ahead. The floor is yours."

It gave Connie pleasure to see the boy sit up straighter.

"So here's the thing," he began. "Yesterday, I was out on the marshes. I wasn't looking for birds' eggs or anything, just minding my own business . . ."

For five minutes, Davey talked without drawing breath and Connie let him. Despite his peculiar grandiloquent turns of phrase, and attempts to justify himself at every twist and turn, the boy told his story clearly and well. She only interrupted at one point, to ask him to pass her the pen, paper and ink that Mary had brought in. Davey obliged, and from that point on, Connie made notes of what he was saying.

"So, that's the long and the short of it," Davey concluded. "I mean, he looked like a workingman, clothes and all, but small bloke, ever so tidy. Hat all but covered his face." He leaned forward in the chair. "What d'you think, miss? Worth something?"

"Just to be absolutely clear, Davey. You are certain you saw a man watching Blackthorn House yesterday morning?"

"Sure as we're sitting here."

"He wasn't simply, I don't know, walking on the footpath? Going about his business?"

"No, miss. He was standing dead set in the middle of the cattails, off the path, just looking this way."

Connie frowned. "And this was yesterday morning? You're sure of that? You're not muddling up the days?"

Davey shook his head. "Don't know the time, but early. After eight, before eleven. Sun hadn't come round." He paused. "So, what do you think it's worth, miss?"

Connie put down her pen. "How much do *you* think it's worth?"

For the first time, the boy was lost for words. "Well, I don't rightly know." He looked at her from beneath his dark, unkempt hair. "I'm thinking, well—maybe a penny?"

"I think that's most reasonable. But I tell you what. If you could agree to let me know if, on your travels, you catch sight of my father, I think I could run to tuppence."

"Gone missing again, has he, miss?"

Connie tried to look stern. "*If* you see him and let me know," she said firmly, not answering the question.

Davey made a poor job of hiding his delight. "It's my civic duty as I see it, miss."

"Is that so?" Connie reached into her purse and pulled out a coin. "Though this is on the understanding that it is a one-off payment. I won't expect to see you back."

The boy flushed. "Of course not, miss. I'm not like Gregory Joseph, cross my heart." He offered his hand. "Though he's all right at the bottom of it."

Connie smiled. "I am prepared to take your word for it."

The boy put the chair back where he'd found it, then sauntered across the room and opened the door.

"Miss Gifford and me have finished our negotiations," he called down the corridor, putting his cap on his head. "And seeing as how you've dealt with me so far, miss," he said, "I'll tell you something for nothing."

Connie raised her eyebrows. "And what's that?"

"There's a copper grubbing around the top of your garden."

Chapter 23

The Bull's Head
Main Road
Fishbourne

Harry stood with Charles Crowther under the porch of the Bull's Head, sheltering from the rain. He'd run into him by chance and remembered him from the private bar the previous evening.

"It is a relief to know the matter is resolved," Harry said, when Crowther had finished explaining how he and others had identified and retrieved Vera Barker's body.

"The poor creature had been estranged from her father for some time," Crowther concluded. "She had a reputation for being not quite there and, of course, they found that rather difficult. A pity."

"Barker lives in Fishbourne?"

"All his life, and his father before him. His wife passed away some years back. There are two married daughters, both local."

"What about Vera?"

"She seems to have spent most of her time recently in Apuldram, though no one's sure where she actually lived. She'd certainly been detained once or twice, for causing a public nuisance, that kind of thing. Known for feeding the birds, which didn't make her popular with the farmers. I gather she has been in and out of the county asylum."

"I wonder if her name would be familiar to my father?" Harry said.

"I wouldn't have thought the committee members came into contact with individual patients."

"No, probably not."

"Barker was sent some kind of anonymous letter; he took it to the *Chichester Observer* when it emerged that no one had seen Vera for a week. The newspaper reported on it yesterday."

"Did the doctor think she'd been in the water that long?"

"I don't know."

"You weren't present at the postmortem?"

Crowther shook his head. "Leave that kind of thing to the professionals."

Harry looked at him. "Forgive me, I realize I never asked what line of business you were in, Mr. Crowther."

"Been lucky with investments, mining and the like, all rather dull," Crowther said lightly. "But what brings you back to Fishbourne so soon, Mr. Woolston?"

Harry considered how much he ought to say. Crowther seemed pleasant enough, and had been very decent about the unpleasant business of helping with the drowned girl, yet he hesitated. He still didn't know where his father was, or what he was doing; he felt he should be circumspect. On the other hand, since he'd come back to Fishbourne in search of information, there was little point in being too discreet. No one in the Woolpack had seen his father or knew his name. If he didn't ask some more questions, he wasn't going to get anywhere.

"Do you know Fishbourne well, Mr. Crowther?"

"Quite well," Crowther replied. "I have a weekend cottage

here. Slay Lodge, at the bottom of Mill Lane. During the late spring and early summer, I spend much of my time here. It's a lovely spot, even in this dismal weather."

Harry offered Crowther a cigarette, which he refused, then lit one for himself.

"This will sound rather peculiar . . ."

"Shall we perhaps go inside? We'll be more comfortable."

They sat at a corner table in the private bar. Crowther was a good listener, and Harry found it helpful to lay out the few facts in his possession.

"So, to summarize," Crowther said when Harry finished, "the only link between your father and Fishbourne is the word of a Dunnaways man? Not the driver who apparently took the fare, but someone listening behind him in the line."

Harry nodded. "When you put it like that, I admit it sounds rather weak, though he did go somewhere in a rush."

"But no certainty that he came to Fishbourne."

Harry paused, deciding how much further to confide in Crowther. "No, though when I went through to the public bar last evening, a fellow there claimed he'd seen someone fitting my father's description near Blackthorn House. And taken with the fact that I overheard my father quarreling with someone in his offices yesterday lunchtime—which is utterly out of character—well, I started to wonder if it might have been the same man."

"Is there any reason to think it was?"

Harry glanced up at Crowther's sharp tone. "Well, no. I suppose not, other than that he seemed the type."

"The type?"

"The type who might threaten someone, I suppose," Harry said, not exactly sure what he did mean.

"Did you see the man who was rowing with your father?"

"No, I only saw the back of his head and his boots as he came down the stairs. Slight chap."

"And the man in the Bull's Head?"

"I admit he was bigger built," Harry conceded, with ill grace. "He had a local voice, coarse." He paused. "Not the same man, no."

Crowther smiled. "Forgive me, I'm playing devil's advocate."

Harry raised his hand. "Don't apologize. It helps to see things from all angles." He stubbed out his cigarette in the ashtray. "The thing is, Crowther, my father never does anything on the spur of the moment. A place for everything and everything in its place, you know. I'm worried."

"Your concern does you credit," Crowther said in the same, steady voice. "Have you informed anyone he's missing?"

"What, do you mean the police?"

Crowther shrugged. "The police, or colleagues, anyone?"

"Pearce, his private assistant, knows there's something up. I spoke to him this morning and asked him to make inquires at Graylingwell, in case my father was called up there for some reason without our knowledge. But otherwise, no." Harry gave a short laugh. "He's not even missing, as such. It's just so . . ."

"Out of character, yes, you said."

Harry took a sip of his whisky. "Do you think I ought to speak to the police?"

Crowther put his own glass back on the table. "I don't know your father, Woolston, but I wouldn't if I were you. I'm not sure he would thank you for it."

Harry looked at Crowther and suddenly guessed what he was getting at.

"I'm sure it's nothing like that. Since my mother died, I've not known him to pay any attention to the fairer sex at all. He's not that kind of chap."

"You might be surprised," Crowther said mildly.

Harry blushed, not wanting to imagine the idea of his father in some kind of liaison. "Of course, I wouldn't want to embarrass the old man, though I'm sure . . ." He drained his whisky and stood up.

"Thanks for the drink, Crowther. You've been more than generous with your time. May I leave my card with you? If you do hear anything, gossip around the village or what have you, I'd be obliged if you'd let me know."

Crowther also got to his feet. "My pleasure. Are you returning to Chichester now?"

"Actually, I thought I might go out to Blackthorn House. See if Miss Gifford has recovered from her ordeal."

Harry saw a spark of new interest flicker in Crowther's eyes.

"I didn't realize you were acquainted with the Giffords," he said. The words were innocuous enough, but all the same, Harry suddenly felt he had said too much. He liked the man, but he didn't want to discuss Connie with him or anyone.

He held out his hand. "Thanks for the advice, Crowther. So fortunate I happened to run into you."

Crowther put the card in his pocket. "If I hear anything, I'll be in touch."

*

The two men came out of the Bull's Head together.

Crowther watched Harry walk down Mill Lane until he was out of sight, then his expression changed. He headed to the long single-story barn that stood at the back of the inn, unlocked the door and went inside. He paid no attention to the body lying beneath the tarpaulin.

He sat at the table and wrote two identical notes. He put

each in an envelope, addressed them, then went back into the inn.

"Has Joseph been in yet, Pine?"

"I haven't seen him all day, come to think of it. There's a first."

"Is there anyone else who might deliver these to Chichester?"

Pine took the envelopes. "Leave it with me."

Chapter 24

Blackthorn House
Fishbourne Marshes

Connie adjusted the field glasses.

"It stinks in here."

"If you can't be quiet, Davey, I'll send you away."

"It does, though," the boy said, ostentatiously holding his nose. "Awful it is."

Connie continued to train her gaze out of her father's bedroom window at the policeman who was methodically working his way through the cattail beds that stretched all the way from the stream at the end of their garden to the backs of the houses on the main road. From time to time, he'd bob down out of sight, his black cape flapping in the gusty wind like the sail of a little dinghy, then reappear a few feet farther along the bank.

"What's he looking for, miss, d'you reckon? Do you think there's another girl got drowned?"

Connie didn't answer. If Nutbeem had been right that Vera's body was being released to her father for a Saturday funeral, wasn't it rather odd that the police were sniffing around now?

"Or maybe she was done in and he's looking for clues?"

"Sssh," she said sharply.

"He can't hear us all the way up here," Davey said.

"That's true, but Mary can."

The boy shrugged. "So what? You can do what you want in your own house, can't you?"

Connie couldn't decide. If she went out and spoke to the policeman, would that look suspicious? He wasn't on their property, after all. Or would it seem more peculiar if she *didn't* go out? She handed the binoculars to the boy. "Do you recognize him?"

"Why should I?" he said belligerently, confirming her suspicion that he'd run into trouble with a fair few of the local officers in his short life.

"Do you?"

Davey made a show of looking. "Reckon it's Pennicott. Sergeant Pennicott, to give him his proper name." He handed the glasses back. "Yes, reckon it is. Fancies himself a detective."

"What do you know about him?"

The boy shoved his hands into his pockets. "Why should I know anything about him?"

"You are, as you told me yourself, a noticing sort of a boy. I don't imagine you miss much."

The boy pulled himself up. "Fair point. Pennicott's the one what testified against Gregory Joseph. Pennicott's fault he was sent down for three months, so he says."

Connie thought back to the way Joseph had stared at her in the garden. His calculating eyes and the determined way he had searched Vera's pockets as she lay on the damp grass. She wasn't the least bit surprised to know he'd been in prison.

"When was he released?"

"Few weeks back."

"When we were talking just now, you said you weren't like him, Davey. What did you mean?"

The boy scuffed the floor with the toe of his unlaced boot.

"I never."

"Yes you did. You said you weren't like him, then crossed your heart."

Davey flushed. "He's always listening. He knows stuff, holds stuff over people, though he's all right in his way. Not so free with his hands as some."

"What else?"

"He's signed the pledge. Won't let a drop of alcohol pass his lips. Looks hard down on any who does."

"Gregory Joseph?" she said in surprise.

Davey laughed. "Thought you wanted to know about Pennicott. No, Joseph spends almost as much time in the Bull's Head as your old man."

Connie gave him a stern look.

"Sorry, miss," the boy said quickly. "Didn't mean to be disrespectful. Always let my tongue run away with me. Old Ma Christie pulls me up for it. She says it'll be the undoing of me."

Connie smiled. "You know Mrs. Christie well, do you?"

"She's kind. You know how it is, if I'm passing and there's something needing doing, she'll give me a hot oatcake or a glass of milk. Now and then, nothing regular."

Connie looked at the scrawny, determined boy and realized that, though she was accustomed to seeing him about, she knew nothing about his life. Where he lived, who looked after him. If anyone did.

"And she fixed these for me," he said, pulling at his tattered short trousers. "Split all up the back last week." He sighed. "Yes, she's all right, Mrs. Christie."

"I thought the same," Connie said, putting her hand on his shoulder and noticing how thin he was. "Before you leave, Davey, we'll go to the kitchen and ask Mary to give you something to set you on your way. We have some Shippam's meat paste, if you like that."

For a moment their eyes met. Connie saw the wariness fade for a moment. He nodded, then his gaze sharpened and he went back to his cheerful, guarded self.

"That would be mighty decent of you," he said, in his strange formal way. "A little bread and paste would do me the world of good."

Connie held out the binoculars. "Where did you get these?"

It was obvious they were far too good to be his. She could feel him struggling to tell the truth, rather than lie, and it suddenly came to her how much he and her father would enjoy each other's company.

"As a matter of fact, they're not mine as such."

"They're not?"

"I didn't nick them. I found them."

"Found them?"

"Honest, I did. Over in the Old Salt Mill, there's a little room up the top, above the wheel. They were on the window-sill, looking out. Facing this way, pretty good view of this house, as it happens."

They were far too good to be left lying about. It was probably someone birdwatching, but Connie remembered the glint she'd noticed near the Old Salt Mill yesterday, and wondered.

"Do you ever talk to my father, Davey, when you're out and about on the marshes?"

"From time to time, miss."

"What about yesterday? Today, even?"

The boy shook his head. "Last few days, been noticeable by his absence, so to speak. Pennicott's coming this way now, miss."

Connie raised the glasses again, then caught her breath. Not because Sergeant Pennicott was opening the black wrought-iron gate and walking along the path toward the front door, but rather because there was someone else half hidden on the path behind him.

Three loud raps of the door knocker echoed through the house.

"The copper's here," Davey said unnecessarily. "I might make myself scarce, miss, if it's all the same to you."

Chapter 25

Themis Cottage
Apuldram

On the eastern side of the creek, a little way outside the cluster of houses that made up the hamlet of Apuldram, a small cottage stood on its own patch of land beside the water.

Gerald White knocked on a door, then stepped back to wait.

The cottage was pleasant enough, he supposed. A squat red-brick building, thatched roof, the paintwork in need of a little attention. It was not to his taste—he thought it rather a desolate spot, stuck out here, miles from anywhere, nothing but sea all around—but he accepted that some people preferred solitude. He noticed a new sign above the door: THEMIS COTTAGE. An odd name, but clients often had the strangest ways of putting their stamp on a property. He made a note to tell the office to change it on the lettings agreement.

White looked down the side of the cottage to the garden. The tide was lapping over the edge of the grass. It would only need one more cloudburst or a particularly high spring tide, and the lawn would be underwater.

After leaving Brook's offices, he'd visited one of the firm's other properties, then had a pleasant lunch in the Anchor Bleu in Bosham, leaving him with the right amount of time to be in Apuldram for three o'clock. It was days like these that reminded him what a good decision he'd made moving from Croydon to Chichester ten years ago.

Over coffee in the inn, White had gone over the discussion in Brook's offices earlier. They'd found themselves in complete agreement that it boded badly that Woolston had flunked the meeting. He wondered if Woolston had panicked after that business in the graveyard. Was he losing his nerve? If so, what were they going to do about it?

The only point of difference between them was the source of the blackmail. Brook was certain it was Gifford. White wasn't sure. He couldn't see why the man would suddenly turn on them, having held his peace for so long. He also couldn't see him arranging or pulling off the ridiculous stunt with the birds. The man was a drunk.

White knocked again.

Two eyes peered through the narrow gap. "Yes?"

"Gerald White," he said, passing his card through the crack between the door and the frame. "I am expected."

The door closed. He waited, half amused and half put out by the caution. His firm had a department that dealt with the appointment of domestic and outdoors staff. He might suggest to his client that they could help in that area too. A little more commission, nothing significant. A moment or two later, the rattle of the chain being slipped and he was admitted.

"Wait here."

The man vanished, without taking his hat and coat. White hesitated, then hung his bowler on the stand, shook out his umbrella and stood it against the wall. He had been fortunate to pick up a hansom on the corner of Tower Street immediately after he came out of Brook's office, otherwise he would have been soaked.

He brushed the few drips of rain from his collar and sleeves, then looked around the hall. The property had been on their books for many years, long before he'd joined the firm. The owner had never lived in it, and it had been rented out for most of the time. It was the first occasion White had visited, but as he looked around, he was pleased to see that the description on the particulars seemed accurately to represent the cottage.

A red-tiled entrance hall, a low ceiling, and a narrow flight of stairs immediately ahead leading to two upstairs bedrooms. Two wooden latched doors opened off to left and right, the parlor and the drawing room, if he remembered rightly. A door at the end of the corridor led to the kitchen. A little damp, but a perfectly sized property.

He had never met the owner and had no idea why they suddenly wanted to take back possession of the cottage now. All business was conducted by letter, so White had no clue to the sort of person he was expecting to meet, other than that they knew their mind and there was clearly no shortage of funds. When the client had said there had been a change of circumstances, there was already a tenant in the cottage. But White had found a loophole in the original tenancy agreement and, though it had taken a certain amount of doing, had managed to have the tenant evicted.

He put his hand into his inside breast pocket and pulled out the cream envelope. Elegant handwriting, italic letters and good-quality black ink. He didn't even know if his client was a man or a woman, though the writing suggested the distaff side.

A long-case clock marked time.

In any other circumstances, White would have postponed such an appointment as this and accepted Brook's invitation— he always enjoyed an afternoon's shoot at the Goodwood Estate, even out of Season—but he was intrigued to meet this client.

He could always join Brook later. From past experience, things would go on well into the early hours.

White glanced at the clock again. Almost three o'clock. Perhaps he would be invited to stay for tea. He was looking forward to the next hour or two. He checked his collar and cuffs, picked a speck of dust from his sleeve and continued to wait.

*

Joseph stared at the visitor through the bowed wooden jamb of the kitchen door. Having brought news of Vera Barker's death and seen the reaction, Joseph had found his curiosity piqued. So he'd asked what this man—and what Dr. Woolston before him—had done, and been told.

The answer had sickened him.

Joseph had been told to leave White standing for fifteen minutes and watch to see what he did. Then, to teach him a lesson. Nothing too much, but enough. After that, it wasn't his business. He cracked his fingers, thinking how he'd kill for a cigarette, if only to help the next quarter of an hour pass more quickly. He wasn't complaining. The whole setup was odd, no doubt about it, but he'd done well out of it so far. And men like Woolston, like White, deserved everything coming to them.

He picked at his teeth with a broad thumbnail, then pressed his eye to the door again and continued to watch until the hands of the clock had marked their fifteen minutes. Without making a sound, he pushed the door open and slipped out into the hall.

"I was starting to think you'd forgotten about me," White began, then stopped when he saw it was only the hired man.

His face hardened. "Am I to be kept waiting much longer?" he demanded.

"This way, sir."

White walked past him, confirmed in his resolution to offer help with the appointment of appropriate domestic staff. The man stood back to let him go through the door first.

At the last moment, something caught White's attention and he turned, just in time to see the blur of the man's fist. The side of his head seemed to explode in pain. He staggered sideways. He heard the sound of the hand breaking the air again, connecting with the back of his skull, then a deep burrowing sensation at the nape of his neck. Stunned, he felt himself grabbed by the collar. His forehead smashed into the sharp, pointed edge of the wooden door frame, sending shock waves through his entire body.

The world turned red.

White slumped to the ground. He didn't understand what was happening, or why, only that he had to get away. He tried to struggle up onto all fours, but his hands slipped in the blood on the ground and he couldn't find purchase. The toe of a heavy boot crashed into his side.

He heard one of his ribs snap, and he passed out.

Chapter 26

Blackthorn House
Fishbourne Marshes

Pennicott knocked again. Connie came down the stairs, at the same time as Mary appeared from the back of the house.

"Mary," she said quietly, "can you take Davey into the kitchen and find him something to eat. He has an errand to run for me, but he'll come straight back."

Mary's eyes narrowed. "An errand?"

Connie turned to the boy. "You remember what to say, Davey? The exact words?"

"I do, miss."

"Come back and tell me, quick as you can, but not until Sergeant Pennicott has gone. You understand?"

He gave a mock salute.

Mary's eyes widened in alarm. "The police are here?"

"There's nothing to be concerned about," Connie said, knowing that the girl would have the usual village horror of being caught up with official business.

"Shall I answer it, miss?"

"I'll do so myself."

Mary hesitated, then gave Davey a gentle push. "Come on with you then, though you needn't think I'm going to be waiting on you."

Connie waited until they were out of sight, then checked her hair in the hall mirror, pinning a loose strand back into place. She straightened her pale gray skirt and striped blouse, both of which were creased from having fallen asleep in the armchair, then glanced at the clock. Would he detect the smell of brandy on her breath? She hoped not. She was surprised to see it was already four o'clock. Had Nutbeem's delivered, or had the rain stopped them from coming out? Whatever happened, she had to make sure Sergeant Pennicott had gone by the time Mrs. Christie was due to arrive.

She straightened her shoulders, then opened the door.

The policeman removed his helmet. "Good afternoon. Miss Gifford, is it?"

"It is."

"Is your father at home? Mr. Crowley Gifford?"

Connie sighed with relief. If Pennicott was asking, he couldn't be bringing bad news about him.

"I regret to say my father is not here. Might I help instead?"

Sergeant Pennicott frowned slightly. Connie wondered if he was good at his job. He looked a rather unthinking sort of a man.

"Perhaps you can, Miss Gifford. May I come in?"

*

Davey crept around the back of the workshop and through the hole in the hawthorn hedge to the fields. From there, there was a path that ran down to the stream where Vera had been found.

Vera was peculiar, no doubt about it, but Davey was sad she'd gone. All that ginger hair flying loose all over the place. But she was kind to him too, and from time to time, when he ventured across to the fields on the Apuldram side of the creek, she'd let him watch her feed the birds from her hand. Bramblings, chaffinches, siskins, greenfinches, linnets. Vera loved songbirds best, disliked the crows and gulls. Bullies, she called them. Her pockets were always full of seeds.

As Davey tramped through the sodden marsh, balancing on branches or flattened reeds to keep the mud from going over the tops of his boots, he wondered what had brought her over this side of the creek. She was scared of her father so mostly kept away from Fishbourne. If the rumors were right that she had drowned, Davey couldn't see how she could have been washed up from Apuldram to here, not even on a high spring tide. Her body would have caught on something farther downstream. It was all peculiar, no doubt about it.

There was an overgrown path that ran around the side of Blackthorn House and came out farther upstream. When the tide was low, it was possible to cut across and get up into the village without having to go all the way around to Mill Lane. There was a small open clearing, surrounded by reeds, then another trail through a patch of bulrushes and up toward the road. It was all private land, of course, but Davey had no idea who owned it and took no notice of signs warning trespassers to keep out. It was here he'd seen the odd fellow spying on Blackthorn House.

Davey crouched low, taking care not to be seen. Miss Gifford had been particular that when he passed the message on, no one else was around to hear it. He crept forward, ignoring the spray of black tidal mud splashing up his bare calves and the way in which the reeds covered his sleeves with raindrops as he pushed his way through.

Finally, he had the man in his sights. He was smoking a cigarette. Davey watched for a while, until he was certain the man was on his own, then he whistled.

"Mister."

The man spun around.

"Over here," Davey said, whistling again. "Miss Gifford sent me. Got a message for you."

"Miss Gifford?"

The man turned again and was peering into the reeds, trying to work out where he was. He looked so confused, Davey could have laughed, if he wasn't so bothered about doing the right thing.

He stood up straight. "She says to come with me. Pennicott's in with her. She says you should come in around the back and wait until he's gone."

Now the man looked alarmed, so much so that Davey had a moment of doubt.

"You are Harry, aren't you? Because if you're not . . ."

"I am," the man said quickly.

Davey looked dubiously at him. "Harry who?"

"What?"

"Harry who?"

"Woolston," the man replied impatiently. "Harold Woolston, Harry to my friends. That good enough?"

The boy nodded. "If you don't want no one to see you, you best hurry up."

*

"Shall we go through to the dining room, Sergeant?" Connie said. Her eyes dropped to the policeman's mud-encased feet. "I wonder if you would mind leaving your boots in the hall? Perhaps your cape, as well? You do appear to be rather wet."

Sergeant Pennicott blushed brick red, and Connie was glad. It made him seem less threatening.

The dining room was barely used, so it felt damp and gloomy. Connie took her time lighting the lamps, wanting to create an impression of unhurried calm. The fact was, her pulse was racing.

"Please," she said, waving the policeman to a chair and sitting down opposite him. "Now, Sergeant . . . ?"

"Sergeant Pennicott."

"Sergeant Pennicott," she said, folding her hands in her lap. "How might I be of assistance?"

Pennicott perched on the edge of the chair and got out a notebook. Connie's pulse tripped again.

"As I said, miss, it was really your father I wanted to speak to. Would you mind telling me where he is?"

"Would you mind telling me why you are asking, Detective Sergeant?" she said, playing for time. If Gifford appeared while they were talking, it would be awkward. But if he didn't, it was wisest to keep to the same explanation she'd given to Pine and Mr. Crowther last evening. It was possible the policeman had already talked to them.

"If you wouldn't mind answering the question, Miss Gifford?"

"His health is not good, Sergeant, so he is currently staying with friends. For a few days, to recover his strength. The climate here, so close to the water, is damp and it's been such a dreadful spring."

Connie realized she was letting her tongue run away with her. Do not embroider, do not explain more than absolutely necessary.

"I'll bother you for the address of those friends before I go, if I may, Miss Gifford."

"Is that really necessary?" she said quickly. "I'd rather he was not disturbed."

"Very natural, miss." Pennicott looked at his notebook. "I wonder if you happen to know if your father is acquainted with a Frederick Brook?"

"I don't, I'm afraid."

"What about a Dr. John Woolston, Miss Gifford?"

"I don't believe he's ever mentioned someone of that name either," she said slowly. "It's possible."

The policeman looked her in the eye. "What about you, Miss Gifford? Are you acquainted with Dr. Woolston?"

"I'm afraid this is rather muddling me, Sergeant. I assumed that you were here in connection with the matter of that unfortunate girl yesterday afternoon."

"Excuse me?"

"Vera Barker."

"My concern is to ascertain if your father is acquainted with Dr. Woolston and"—Pennicott looked back down at his notes—"other individuals. So, if you would not mind answering the question, miss, do you or do you not know Dr. Woolston?"

Connie matched him with a cold stare. "I do not."

The policeman wrote something in his book. Connie had to stop herself straining across the table to see what it was.

"And what about his son?"

Connie was at a loss as to how to respond. Since it appeared to have nothing to do with the discovery of the body in the stream, she had no idea what information the police officer was actually after, or why. She was loath to say anything at all.

"His son?" she replied weakly.

"Mr. Harold Woolston. The son of Dr. John Woolston."

"I was not aware of that."

"So you admit that you know Mr. Harold Woolston."

"'Admit' is a rather singular choice of word," Connie said, keeping her voice level. "But if you are asking if I am acquainted with Harold Woolston, then, yes. I met him for the first time yesterday and he was extremely kind in what, as you can imagine, were distressing circumstances. He is a friend of Dr. and Mrs. Evershed, I believe. He helped me with Vera Barker's body."

"Vera Barker?" he said sharply.

"Yes," she said impatiently. "I told you, Detective Sergeant Pennicott. The woman reported missing in the newspaper this week; she was the person I found in the river at the top of the garden yesterday. Harry—Mr. Woolston—helped me bring her body out of the water. I was under the impression, from what I have heard in the village, that Dr. Woolston signed the death certificate yesterday evening. Mr. Crowther could tell you more."

"This is the first I've heard of any body being found in Fishbourne."

It took Connie some time to go through the events surrounding the recovery of Vera's body. Pennicott wanted every name, every address, every variance of timing, and several times asked, again, for the details of where her father was staying.

"I still don't understand why you want to know if my father is acquainted with Dr. Woolston. I can't see how it is relevant at all."

Pennicott put his book down on the table. "I am here, Miss Gifford, in connection with the unexplained absence of Dr. Woolston."

Connie didn't know what to think. Her head was spinning; all these half-connected stories.

"Absence?" she echoed.

Pennicott glanced at his notes. "A Mr. Pearce, who is employed by Dr. Woolston in his offices in West Street, Chichester, has expressed concern about his employer"s whereabouts. I hesitate to call it, at this early stage, a disappearance as such."

"Does Mr. Woolston know of this?"

"I have not yet had the opportunity to speak to Mr. Woolston," he said. "But your father's name has come up in the course of my inquiries."

"That's ridiculous to imply—"

Pennicott kept going. "According to Pearce, it appears your father and Dr. Woolston were acquainted some years ago and have recently renewed contact with each other."

Feeling suddenly overwhelmed, Connie decided the only thing she could do was to bring the conversation to a close and give herself time to think.

"Forgive me, Sergeant, I cannot say for certain whether or not your information is correct, but since my father is not here—and I have never met Dr. Woolston—I don't believe there is anything further I can do to help you." She stood up, taking Pennicott by surprise. "I will, of course, inform my father of your visit and ask him to be in contact with you as soon as his health and circumstances permit."

Without giving him a chance to object, Connie opened the door and walked out into the hall. "I am sorry you have had a wasted journey, Sergeant."

Pennicott reluctantly stood up. "I must trouble you for the address of the friends with whom your father is staying, Miss Gifford."

"I will have to look it up."

"I am prepared to wait."

Connie pretended not to hear. "Mary," she called along the corridor, "Sergeant Pennicott is leaving, if you could show him out."

"Coming, miss."

"The address, miss?"

"The maid will bring it to the station in Chichester, as soon as convenient. Good day, Sergeant."

As Mary hurried along the corridor toward the front door, Connie walked in the opposite direction. She didn't trust herself to speak. She heard the front door close and felt a gust of wet air come in, but she kept going and let her feet take her to a place of refuge.

"I found your Mr. Woolston, miss."

Connie heard Davey's cheerful voice calling from the kitchen, but she didn't stop. She went into the workshop, closed the door behind her and sank down on a chair.

Chapter 27

Themis Cottage
Apuldram

Gerald White tried to open his eyes.

Found he could not. He tried again. The right lid remained firmly shut, but he managed to half open his left. It was crusted and sore with blood. His entire face was swollen. He could feel the skin straining as he tried to see.

Something was digging into his back, as if he was lying on a branch or the spine of a book. Something sharp. He attempted to shift, but a violent jab of pain snaked along his flank, winding him. He struggled to get air into his lungs, taking short, shallow breaths, each one as agonizing as the last.

The face of the hired man flashed into his mind. The look of pleasure as his fist came down, the flash of retribution in his eyes as his boot connected with White's ribs.

He lay still, uncomprehending as to why he had fallen victim to such an attack. Had he been robbed? He tried to feel his jacket, to see if his pocketbook was still there, but now realized his hands were strapped. Even in his pain-confused state, he could feel the restraints on his wrists cutting into his skin. He sent a message from his brain down to his feet and realized his ankles, too, were tied.

And something else. That he was very cold. That there was

no protection of cloth between his bruised back and the surface of whatever he was lying on. While he had been unconscious, someone had removed his waistcoat, shirt and vest. Would a thief go to such trouble?

A wave of panic washed through him, an animal instinct to get free, overriding the pain of his wounds and the raw open cuts in his skin.

But he was already too late.

As White fell back, gasping against the wooden boards, the sound of his own blood pulsing in his head gave way to the realization that he was not alone. He became completely still. He perceived there was someone else with him, motionless but close at hand.

Then the lightest of touches on his bare chest, like feathers being gently stroked across his skin. Despite everything, White felt himself react. Even now, the memories of that night ten years ago excited him, stimulated him, more than they appalled him.

Feathers, his black-and-white mask, the glittering candles. The cotton and lace trim above her knees. The girl begging them to stop. Someone stopped her talking. Not Brook and not him. A stab of longing shot through his bruised body. Pleasure and pain, a contradiction he knew well.

As his various senses started to come back to him, White detected a strange smell. A perfume, but overlaid with a chemical tint of alcohol or sterilizing fluid. Like an operating theater. And the same gentle rising and falling of someone breathing in, breathing out.

"Who's here?"

The panic started to return, fear igniting his desire to get free. Struggling, again, against his restraints. Not leather or ribbon, but something sharp. Wire? Each time he moved, a tiny slice of skin was peeled back.

White focused every ounce of energy he possessed on trying to open his eyes. If only he could see, then he would know what was happening.

Now, to his horror, he realized it was not his injuries stopping his eyes from opening, but that his eyelids were sewn shut. He could feel the thin stitches pulling against the skin each time he tried to force himself to see.

"I have been waiting for you to wake up."

It wasn't possible. At the same time, it was the voice he expected. Calm as it sounded, it brought back to him, with extraordinary clarity, the terrified tones that pleasured his nightmares. But it was not possible.

"I don't understand," he managed to say through cracked lips. "What are you doing?"

That same, soft laugh from a decade ago. No fear in it now. The power, this time, was on her side.

"The punishment must fit the crime, don't you think?"

White thrashed on the table, desperately trying to loosen his bonds. Then the lightest of touches, downy, as feathers seemed to be covering his chest, and again he felt himself respond.

"Your tastes don't appear to have altered," she said, her mouth close to his ear. "I shall finish this. Then we can 'move on to more enjoyable matters.' What do you say?"

In the depths of his memory, White recognized something he himself had said.

"What do you want?" he cried. "Whatever you want, I have—"

His words were stolen by his scream as the needle pierced

his eyelid, the point splitting the membrane, the pain of the thread being pulled through and back.

"Now, now," she murmured, "what was it you said? 'Don't be silly'; do you remember saying that? And 'don't make a fuss'?"

Beneath his bloodied and torn eyelids, White felt tears begin to flow. Another roar of pain as the needle pushed through his septum and the thread began to draw his nostrils together.

The ache in his chest later, when the knife cut him open and the blade was drawn lovingly down his breastbone, came as a relief.

Chapter 28

Blackthorn House
Fishbourne Marshes

For a moment, Connie emptied her mind of everything. Then, gradually, the familiar outline of the workshop came back to her—the wooden counter and the silver tools, the glass jars, the paint—and she sighed. Here, at least, she felt safe.

"Miss Gifford?"

Connie turned in her chair to see Harry standing in the doorway.

"May I come in?"

She exhaled. "Yes, do."

"A boy claimed you'd sent him to fetch me," he said, inching farther into the room. "But I won't stay if I'm intruding. If you'd rather I went, just say."

"Davey," she smiled. "No, I'm pleased you're here. Come in."

Harry stepped tentatively into the room. "Are you all right?"

She nodded. "I slept badly last night, as you might imagine, then the policeman . . ." She stopped, reliving the wave of panic that had swept through her. "It was all rather too much."

She looked at Harry's face and realized he was struggling not to stare at the skinned inside-out jackdaw beneath its protective glass dome. With regret, she saw she would probably have to let this one go. She had left it untended for too long.

"I saw you from the window," she said, taking pity on him and throwing a cloth across the glass. "I thought it might be better if you didn't come to the house while Sergeant Pennicott was here."

"I must have looked very peculiar out there."

"Given that you were standing in among the reeds, rather than on the footpath, you did rather."

"I was on my way to see you, to make sure you were quite recovered from your ordeal yesterday. Then I saw Pennicott, and I thought I had better stay out of sight . . ."

Connie raised her eyebrows. Harry flushed.

"The thing is, there have been one or two occasions when high spirits got the better of me—Christmas and the like, you know—and he comes down hard on . . ."

"He's a teetotaler. Davey told me."

Harry nodded. "I was knocked off my stride to find Pennicott skulking around—all the way out here—and I suppose I thought it would be awkward if he saw me. Require all sorts of explanations I'd be disinclined to give."

"So you hid," she said bluntly.

Harry reddened. "Well, yes."

"Not very well."

"Evidently not."

For a moment, they held each other's glance. Then they both started to smile, his expression mirroring hers, transforming their anxious faces. An instant of uncomplicated camaraderie. Harry broke contact first, looking around the workshop with naked curiosity. Connie watched his changing expressions and was surprised at how reluctant she was to spoil things by telling him what Pennicott had said. Why he'd come to Blackthorn House.

"What an extraordinary place," he said.

Connie gave a sigh of relief, grateful that he was not plunging straight in either. He had passed a test she had been unaware of setting him. If he had tried immediately to question her, she would have seen it as a lack of good faith.

"It's one of the reasons we took the house. Plenty of space for our needs. There is also a disused icehouse in the garden that we—my father and I—use for storage."

He gestured to the rack of tools on the wall.

"And what are all these things for? Rather grisly, some of them."

Connie realized that Harry, too, wanted to keep away from the topic that had first brought them together for as long as possible. She liked him the more for it.

"No more grisly than medical instruments," she said, setting another trap for him. "You must have seen things like these before?"

Harry caught her gaze, but chose not to question how she knew what his father did.

"He's not that kind of doctor," he said, and tapped his head. "Strictly up here. Paperwork and policy these days, not patients." He pointed to the forceps. "What are these used for?"

Connie led him along the row, pointing out each tool in turn. How the pincers were used to break bones, the scissors to cut tendons and muscle. She kept glancing at his face, trying to work out his reaction to her, a woman, talking in such detail. He looked fascinated, not a hint of disapproval or distaste in his expression.

"Taxidermy is a craft. More than anything, it is about beauty. Preserving beauty, representing beauty, about finding a way to capture the essence of a bird or an animal."

Harry was nodding. "I'm a painter. At least, it's not how I earn my living, but I will. So I feel the same when I'm working on a piece, that it's about everything that lies behind the portrait as much as the paint on the canvas itself." He slid the cloth off the jackdaw in its glass sepulcher. "But, this. This is so much harder. How do you manage not to damage the very thing you're trying to save?"

Connie was delighted at how completely he seemed to understand.

"In the first instance, the key is a sharp scalpel. If the blade is blunt, the skin will tear and won't be usable."

"Does your father work only with birds?"

"Mostly. In his younger days, he was one of the best bird taxidermists in Sussex."

Harry glanced at the jackdaw, then at the things Connie had got ready to use: wood wool and a dish of cleaning solution, a pile of cotton torn into strips, newspaper and paint.

"He lays out his workbench with admirable precision. My father would approve. The old man's a stickler for things being in their proper place."

At the mention of his father, Connie felt a shadow fall over the conversation. She had to tell him about Pennicott eventually—should already have done so—but she was enjoying the discussion too much to bring it to an end. She wasn't usually conscious of feeling lonely, except at times like this, when she was reminded of how rare such congenial company was. Just a few minutes more.

"If not preserved properly," she said swiftly, "exhibits can easily be destroyed. Maggots, moths. It's why most craftsmen, like my father, set their work in glass cases or display boxes."

She reached up to the bookshelf and ran her finger along the spines, though failing to find the book she wanted.

"I was going to show you my father's bible, if that isn't too blasphemous a way in which to refer to it, but it doesn't appear to be here. It's by Mrs. R. Lee. Gifford swears by it."

"An authoress?"

Connie waited, again so much hoping that Harry would not fall at this hurdle. Even men who professed themselves to be modern in their views sometimes fell prey to a prejudice that women shouldn't even write books on taxidermy, let alone practice it.

"How interesting" was all he added.

Connie smiled. "Although it is rumored that her husband wrote it, the reason my father values Mrs. Lee's book is because it concentrates on how the techniques of preserving animals and birds have developed, from Réaumur—who pickled birds in alcohol to try to prevent them from rotting—to Bécoeur, who invented arsenical soap." She stopped, realizing she was going into too much detail. "I'm sorry, I'm boring you."

"Not in the slightest," he said, perching on the counter. "As I said, I know what it's like to be transported by something."

"Well, as you can see, Gifford has built up quite a library. There's a reference in Shakespeare's *Romeo and Juliet*, so for a while, he kept a copy of that play on display here too." She pointed at another book. "There are writings dating back to the late seventeenth century—this is a copy, of course—describing how the Dutch were the first to bring live specimens and skins of cassowary and other exotic birds into Europe. The first manual, such as it was, was published even earlier than that, in the mid–sixteenth century."

She came to a halt again. She looked across and saw Harry was staring at her.

"What is it?" she said quickly.

"Nothing. At least, I was thinking perhaps you should write

a book. You're very knowledgeable and you explain it all so clearly." He traced her name in block capitals in the air: MISS CONSTANTIA GIFFORD, THE TAXIDERMIST'S DAUGHTER. It has a good ring to it, wouldn't you say?"

She blushed. "It does rather."

"Are you a practitioner too?" he asked, clearly unaware that it was rare indeed for women to work in the field.

"I help my father from time to time." She looked and saw nothing but interest in his eyes. "He was a wonderful teacher. Although I called him a taxidermist, he himself would use the old terminology. A stuffer of birds is how he would introduce himself. He thought 'taxidermist' was too fancy. We looked up the origins of the word once, to try to persuade him."

"Which are?"

"It comes from the Greek: *taxis*, to arrange, and *derma*, skin."

"Nothing to offend there, I'd have thought."

"I agree, though if anything it put him off even more. He said it took it away from what he was doing."

Harry folded his arms. "Which was?"

"Telling stories," she said simply.

He nodded. "When I'm working on a portrait, I'm always thinking about everything that made my sitter the person they are, not just what's visible on the canvas."

"That's it," Connie replied. "It's the sense that if the bird—jackdaw, magpie, rook, whatever—could talk, it would tell you its life story."

"So," he said quietly, "we understand each other."

"It appears we do," she said, realizing that a conversation such as this was as rare for him as it was for her. For a moment, there was a companionable silence between them. Connie caught Harry's eye.

He let out a deep breath. "You were saying your father rejected the 'fancy' word, as he saw it."

"'Stuffer' is a more modern word, he maintains, not dating back to antiquity. From the French *émpailler*, to stuff with straw. All very simple."

"Does it matter what he calls himself? It's the end result that counts, isn't it?"

Connie thought of the days and days at the museum when no one came. Remembered the grief of understanding that something had changed. Saw his skill and his craft and imagination turn to dust until he became bitter and desperate, a drinker. A man brought low.

"Everything matters," she said quietly. "We had a small museum once. Gifford created beautiful tableaux. Nursery rhymes, folklore, songs. Used the birds he found, or that were given to him, to create stories. Whole cases filled with hundreds of birds: 'Cendrillon,' 'Snow White,' 'The Sorry Tale of Cock Robin.'"

He smiled. "Like Mr. Potter's museum in Bramber."

"You've heard of it," Connie said.

"Loved the place when I was a boy. I'm sorry to say I never heard of your father's museum, though. Why did he give it up?"

Connie paused. For once, she was tempted to share something of herself. She looked at Harry's honest, attractive face, and made her decision.

"He gave it up because . . ." She took a deep breath. "Because it appears that some of our tableaux were direct copies of Mr. Potter's exhibits. Not all, but enough. I was too young to understand at the time, but there was a court case—brought by my father, not Mr. Potter, I should say—and we lost. Gifford was forced to sell up and close the museum."

"I'm sorry," he said simply. "That must have been hard for him. To lose everything he'd worked to build up."

Connie remembered the auctioneer appointed by the court. His nose red and pickled, his breath sour with self-importance. Walking around the museum, tapping his cane on the floor like Blind Pew, issuing orders to his men to take note of everything for the inventory. Which things were salable, which weren't worth the effort. Not just her father's tableaux and display cases, but the assets too: the ticket machine, the wooden sign above the door, all her father's treasures reduced to black squiggles in an accounting column.

"It broke his heart. He was never the same after that."

"May I ask you something? I hope you won't think it impertinent."

"Yes."

"I wondered why you call him Gifford?"

Connie became still. It was so obvious a question and yet she could not remember anyone having asked her before. She herself had wondered the same thing, why 'Gifford' often came more easily to her lips and why her father often reacted better when it did.

Harry took her hand. "I mean, you say 'my father' too, but just as often 'Gifford.'"

"Because that's what Cassie called him."

The words were out of her mouth before Connie was even conscious of having thought them.

Chapter 29

Connie felt a wave of affection rush through her, then something crueler. Loss. Grief.

She withdrew her hand from Harry's clasp.

"Is Cassie the same person you mentioned earlier?"

Connie was reeling. "Earlier?" she said, hearing the echo of her own voice in her head.

"You said 'we' looked up the word 'taxidermist' to try to persuade Gifford to think better of it. Was that Cassie?"

She got to her feet and strode to the opposite side of the room, unable to sit still, arms folded across her chest as if to hold all her emotions tight inside.

She felt Harry come to stand beside her. "I'm sorry, I didn't mean to pry."

"It's not that."

Harry put his hands on her shoulders. She felt the heat of his palms through the material of her shirt, and a pulse of attraction swept through her. They were so close, she could smell the perfume of the shaving soap he had used and the pomade on his moustache, the sweet fragrance of tobacco on his skin and the underlying hint of oil paint.

"So who is Cassie?" he asked.

Connie heard, behind the simple words, his genuine concern and interest. She raised her eyes to his and saw him looking at her—properly, seeing her as she was—wanting to know what she was thinking, wanting to know about her. At that moment, all they should have been discussing and had been avoiding, everything that had brought them together, seemed to melt away. All utterly unimportant compared to this moment of connection.

"I don't know," she admitted.

"You don't know?"

She shook her head, unable to bring herself to speak. For a few, long moments they stood in silence, connected by everything they did not know about each other, then Connie took a step away. As if they had come to some kind of agreement, she sat back at the counter. Harry fetched himself a chair too and set it down opposite.

"Miss Gifford—Connie—you can trust me."

She looked at his concerned, gentle expression and felt that she could.

"The vanished days," she said.

*

"Any more of that paste?" Davey asked. He was enjoying himself.

Mary turned around from the sink. "Greedy little scrap, aren't you?"

He grinned. "Growing boy, me."

Mary wiped her hands, then walked into the larder, took a jar of Shippam's meat paste, and put it on the table beside a loaf of fresh bread sitting on a wooden breadboard, with a square of butter on a Willow-pattern plate. Davey reached to help himself.

"I'll do it," Mary said, snatching the bread knife out of his hand. "As if I'd let you go at it all heavy-handed. The master's not made of money."

"What, a great big house like this?"

"Eat your tea," she said, flicking him with the tea towel, "then I can get on. Having you here's putting my day right out."

Davey had helped her carry the Nutbeem's delivery from the gate, and she'd given him a glass of shandy. They got on well enough, him and Mary, when there was no one around to see. When there was, she put on superior airs and talked harshly to him. He didn't mind.

"Do you like working here, Mary?"

Mary went to the dresser at the side of the kitchen and started to look through the drawer.

"I do, as it happens. No one to tell me what to do."

"Miss Gifford a good mistress?"

"Lovely to work for. Never takes advantage, leaves me to my own devices. As long as everything gets done." She shut the first drawer and moved on to the next. "Mind you, she's too much on her own—Ma thinks so too, but Miss Gifford doesn't seem to mind."

Davey jerked his head toward the workshop.

"What's all that about, then? This Harry bloke?"

"It's nothing to do with you, that's what that's about."

Davey took another large mouthful of bread spread liberally with paste.

"She keeps herself busy. Helps the master out. Does more than he does, if truth be told. And always scribbling in that notebook of hers."

Mary paused for a moment, remembering that she'd failed

to find the current journal. Not that it mattered in the long run. When Miss Gifford had used up one, she put it away and started another.

She shut the second drawer and moved to the third.

"A couple of months back, we had a bit of trouble," she said. "Stones being thrown at the windows of the master's workshop, knocks on the door and running away . . . You wouldn't happen to know anything about that?"

"Me?"

"You," she said firmly. "It's only that I notice we haven't had any trouble for a few weeks now."

"Well, as it happens, I might." He tapped the side of his nose. "All I can say is, I had a word and no one won't be bothering you anymore."

Mary grinned. "So you're not such a wicked boy as they say."

"Who says I'm a wicked boy?"

"Half of Fishbourne," she teased, continuing to search through the drawer.

"What are you looking for?"

Mary shut the last drawer and stood up. "Key to the padlock for the storehouse," she said. "It's gone missing. Mistress asked me to fetch the spare for her, but I can't find that either."

"Do you want me to have a gander?"

"Go on then," she said, stepping back. "Fresh pair of eyes might do the trick. It's about so big, silver. I reckon a magpie took it; they've been hanging about the house for days."

*

"The vanished days," Connie repeated. "At least, that's how I think of them."

She paused to gather her thoughts, realizing she had never told the story to anyone before. But then, who would she have told?

"I had an accident when I was a child. The spring of 1902. I was twelve. My father was working late in the museum, finishing a last few things before we were to leave. I know now that it had already been sold. I didn't know that then. I woke in the night, was frightened and so went to find him. In the dark, I fell down the stairs and hit my head. I only survived thanks to the good fortune that a doctor was visiting a patient in a neighboring house and he helped. My father never knew his name."

Harry frowned.

"I remember being in bed for such a long time. Months and months. Hearing adults talking over me, not realizing I could hear. I wasn't expected to recover."

"Who looked after you? Your mother?"

"No, she died when I was born. I never knew her. There was a nurse, I think. Someone kind."

"What about this Cassie? Was she there?"

"This was someone older," she said. "I don't remember being scared. Detached, if anything. I have a sense of kindness and care, but I can't remember."

"What about your father?"

"He was there, but not there, if you see what I mean." She took a deep breath. "In time, I recovered. A year, perhaps, and I was back on my feet. Physically, there was nothing at all the matter with me, but I'd lost my memory. Everything from the first twelve years of my life had gone, wiped clean. No memory of people or places, the child I'd been. Nothing. The only person I remembered from before was Gifford."

"And Cassie?"

"No, not even her. It's only recently that I have started to remember her. It's as if my mind is full of ghosts. People I know. They are there inside me, yet I can't see them or remember them."

"What does your father say?"

"He refuses to speak of it. Apart from telling me about the accident itself. My questions distress him. He never got over losing the museum, everything he had worked so hard to achieve, though he claimed he'd sold it because he was unable to bear the constant reminder of how close he'd come to losing me."

"Which you now know to be false?"

Connie nodded. "As I got older, I realized there was much about my father's account—the authorized version, as I came to think of it—that didn't make sense. It was both plausible, and yet somehow a bit pat."

She sighed. "When I was eighteen, and without telling Gifford, I went back to Lyminster—where the museum had been—to see if I could jolt my memory."

Harry leaned forward. "And?"

"Our old house and attached building were gone, burnt down in a fire."

"Deliberate?"

"I don't know. I could find nobody who remembered us, the little girl and her father who'd lived there. Then, two years ago, I discovered my father had been declared bankrupt in March 1902—a few weeks *before* the accident. At that point, realizing that the explanation Gifford had given for the sale of the museum was untrue—or at least, only partially true—I started to question how much else of what he'd told me was false, and . . . and why even now he will still not talk about the past."

Harry lifted his hand and rested it gently against her cheek. Connie felt, for the slightest fraction of a second, that her heart had stopped.

"Isn't there anyone you can ask? About Cassie, I mean?"

"Who could I ask? No one knows us from back then."

At least, that was what she had believed. Given what Pennicott had claimed, Connie realized it might not be true.

"And you don't remember anything before the accident, nothing at all?" Harry asked.

"For years, nothing. Just impressions, the memory of emotions, I suppose, more than events or people. I suffered—I still do occasionally—from petit mal, where I lose track of my surroundings for a moment. The strangest thing is that as these episodes have become less frequent, I've started to remember things more clearly. Things I've not thought of before, snapshots of my life. Only glimpses, not the whole picture."

"Well, that's a good thing, isn't it?"

Connie thought of the dread that flooded through her with each recent recollection. The twist in the pit of her stomach, the fear that there was some black secret hidden within her clouded memories.

"I'm not sure." She met his gaze. "I think something else happened back then—not only my accident, but something more. The consequences of which are coming back to haunt us now."

"Us?"

"My father and I, Cassie—wherever she now is—and . . ."

Connie stopped. The conversation had finally come around,

of its own volition, to the subject she had been avoiding. She could no longer put off telling him about Sergeant Pennicott's questions.

"And you, Harry."

"Me?"

Connie nodded. "You and your father. That's why Sergeant Pennicott was here."

Chapter 30

Harry listened in silence as Connie told him about the man Davey had seen watching the house, about the peculiar note Mrs. Christie had given her; how she believed Vera had been murdered and how she had recognized the coat, first from the woman she'd noticed outside Blackthorn House, then a week later in the graveyard of Fishbourne church on the Eve of St. Mark.

"I knew I shouldn't have left you here alone," Harry said, furious with himself.

"I gave you no choice," she said, smiling.

"No, I suppose you didn't. I thought I'd done something to offend you, to be sent packing so suddenly."

"Not at all."

"It's odd, though," Harry said after a moment. "The old man went out that night. He came back after midnight, soaking wet. Went straight to his study."

Connie frowned. "How can you be so sure it was that night?"

"April the twenty-fourth is my birthday, so I'd been expecting him home for dinner to mark the occasion. He's big on that kind of thing."

"Is he a large man? Broad-shouldered?"

"Not particularly, why?"

"There were several gentlemen there that night. They stood out, among the local people from the village."

"Were there women too?"

"A few."

Harry thought. "Do you think the woman you saw watching the house was Vera?"

"I did at first, but no. I think they are two different people. The first woman was tall and slender, elegant. The coat was a perfect fit. Vera was shorter and stockier. Also, as the bells finished tolling, a flock of songbirds came flying out of the church and—"

"Vera was known for feeding the birds—it was the one thing people knew about her—so it would make sense she had been involved in setting that up."

Connie looked surprised. "How do you know that?"

"Crowther told me," he said. "I ran into him earlier in the village. Why did you go to the churchyard that night? I hadn't imagined you to be a superstitious person."

"I'm not," she said. She met Harry's gaze. "I was there because I'd followed my father from the Bull's Head. He is inclined, from time to time, to drink more than is good for him. On those occasions, it's unwise for him to make his way home, unattended, across the marshes. As you can imagine."

"I can indeed," Harry said formally, and she was grateful he made no other comment.

"You didn't recognize any of the gentlemen there?"

"No. But I think someone must have invited them to be there. I can't see how they might have stumbled on such a local tradition by chance. They were so out of place."

"Invited by whom?"

Connie shook her head. "I don't know."

"Or why?"

"For the past week, I've tried and failed to come up with any plausible explanation," she said.

"What does your father say about it?"

Connie took a deep breath, deciding to make a clean breast of it. "The truth is that, having been in a rather terrible condition this past week, my father went out sometime during the course of the afternoon yesterday. I don't know when and I don't know where he is. I'm sorry I didn't tell you."

"No apology is necessary," he said quickly. "You had no reason to trust me. Forgive me for asking, but is this something that happens often?"

Connie chose her words carefully. "It's not unusual, in certain situations, for him to take himself off—though this is longer than usual. When Sergeant Pennicott came this afternoon . . ." She stopped, to gather her thoughts. "I assumed he had come to take a statement from me about Vera Barker. In fact, it transpired he knew nothing about the fact that her body had been found."

Harry frowned. "Then why was he here?"

"He had come to speak to my father. He wanted to know if he was acquainted with a Dr. John Woolston."

Harry's face expressed open bewilderment. "*My* father? But why?"

"Pennicott claims that your father and mine have a prior acquaintance."

"What?"

"I know. I was able to say, with complete candor, that Gifford had never once mentioned your father's name."

"I can confirm the same."

"He mentioned another man too. A Frederick Brook."

Harry slumped back. "What the devil . . ."

Connie's eyes widened. "You know him?"

"Worse than that, I work for him. My father fixed it up. A favor from an old friend, as he put it, though it's more like a life sentence. Shipping china from one end of the country to another." He stopped, his eyes glinting. "Brook is a very substantial man . . ."

"Like the gentleman in the graveyard," Connie said, finishing his thought for him.

"I still don't understand why Pennicott was here," Harry said eventually. "Even if the old man does know your father, what of it? There's no crime in that."

Connie took his hand.

"Harry, there are two things that came out in the course of my awful interview with Pennicott. I should have told you sooner, I admit, I just didn't know the best way to do so."

She felt him squeeze her fingers tightly.

"First . . ." She hesitated. "The gossip in the village—and I'm sure it is only gossip—is that it was your father who signed Vera's death certificate."

"But that's absurd," Harry flushed. "If what you say about the ligature around the woman's neck is right, he'd never miss something like that."

"That's what I thought too. The second thing is that Pennicott claims someone—a Mr. Pearce—has reported your father missing. Or rather, as Pennicott put it, that there were concerns for his absence. That's why he had come to speak to Gifford."

"Pearce! He's my father's clerk, though what the hell gave him the right to go to the police, I can't imagine," Harry said angrily.

Connie turned cold. "Are you telling me it's true? Your father is also missing?"

He raised his eyes, and this time she saw such despair in

them, such confusion, that it was as much as she could do not to take him in her arms.

He nodded. "It's true. No one's seen him since yesterday lunchtime. That's why I was in Fishbourne yesterday in the first place."

"Tell me," she said, their roles now quite reversed.

Chapter 31

Main Road
Fishbourne

Charles Crowther stood in the narrow hall of Mrs. Christie's small cottage beside the laundry on the main road.

"It's lucky you came when you did, sir," she was saying. "Five minutes and I'd have been gone."

"I was concerned about you, Mrs. Christie. You looked distressed when I saw you talking to Miss Gifford outside the post office. Since I happened to be in Salthill Road, I thought I would check that nothing was the matter."

"It's very decent of you to come in person, sir."

"Nonsense." Crowther waved his hand. "I don't keep a large staff at Slay Lodge, in any case. A couple of manservants, a gardener, a cook. It didn't seem appropriate to send any of them."

"There's not many gentlemen as would be so thoughtful, Mr. Crowther. In my time, I've worked in a number of houses—large and small—and you learn to appreciate things. Maybe it's different abroad, I dare say."

Crowther frowned. "Abroad?"

Mrs. Christie flushed. "Sorry, sir. I'd heard you were out in Africa."

"Ah. Well, yes, I was. Transvaal, though it's a long time ago now." He smiled. "I wonder who told you that, Mrs. Christie?"

"I don't rightly think I can remember," she said. "It was all round the village when you took the Lodge, sir. It had stood empty for such a long time. Always prone to flooding, you see."

"How long have you lived in Fishbourne, Mrs. Christie?"

"Only since my husband died, sir. Two years now."

"And before that?"

"I was married before. Mr. Wickens—he's Mary's father—died young. Then I met Mr. Christie and he took us both on, me and Mary. I was in service to make ends meet, though I never lived in. Always a daily, could come and go. A few places around Boxgrove and up-along. Then Mr. Christie inherited a little money from his aunt and I didn't have to work anymore. We settled in Lavant. Very happy there."

"I'm glad to hear it."

Mrs. Christie's face clouded. "So you don't think I should worry?"

"It sounds as if you did all the right things already. You talked to Miss Gifford and told her about the note."

"I didn't know who else to ask. It's not been easy since Mr. Christie passed away."

Crowther smiled. "I'm more than happy to be a listening ear."

"But you don't think I should take it further?"

"I wouldn't, if I were you. There's no call to distress Miss Gifford. She had an unpleasant shock yesterday—as indeed, of course, did your Mary."

"But if something happens to Miss Gifford and I . . ."

He smiled kindly. "Nothing will happen to Miss Gifford."

"Begging your pardon, Mr. Crowther, but how can you be

sure? Who's to say where the note came from? It's a threat, that's what it is."

"Remind me what it said," he asked.

"'Do not be afraid. I am watching you.' That's all."

"That doesn't sound like a threat to me. If anything, the opposite. A Bible quotation, even?" He paused. "There was no signature on the note, initials? No indication where it had come from?"

"Nothing."

"And left on the mat at Blackthorn House on Wednesday morning?"

"The backdoor mat, so Mary says."

"As I said, I'm sure it's nothing more than some kind of unpleasant prank."

"Nasty sort of a prank."

"I regret to say Blackthorn House attracts more than its fair share of such things, does it not?"

"That's true enough, sir. Mary says she's more than once had to chase boys from the village off. Throwing stones and what have you."

"They are scared of what they don't understand. Ignorant souls respond in the only way they know how."

She frowned. "The thing is, I saw the handwriting and it brought a lot of nasty things back, sir. Things I thought were over and done with."

Crowther was still smiling, but his eyes sharpened. "What sort of things, Mrs. Christie?"

Immediately, she clammed up. "I couldn't possibly say."

"It will remain between ourselves, if it would help to talk about it further."

She shook her head. "I've never been a one for gossip, Mr. Crowther."

"Very well."

"I've held my tongue for ten years, sir. I'm not going to let him down now."

"Him, Mrs. Christie?"

She blushed brick-red. "No one. In any case," she went on quickly, "now I've had time to think, I realize I must have been mistaken. One person's handwriting's much like the next. This business with Vera Barker has got me all somehow."

Crowther thought. "Did you tell Miss Gifford why you were so shaken?"

She looked scandalized. "No, sir, I wouldn't want to upset her. She's so much better now and I wouldn't want to stir things up. In any case, the rain came on ever so heavy just then—you remember, Mr. Crowther, you were caught in it too. That's why she invited me to Blackthorn House." She looked anxious again. "But you don't think I should keep the appointment? I don't want Miss Gifford thinking badly of me."

"It seems to me, Mrs. Christie, that talking about it more might achieve the opposite to your intention. She's a rather troubled young woman."

"I wouldn't say she was troubled, as such."

"I'm sorry, I heard that she was sometimes ill."

"When she was younger. That's all in the past now."

Mr. Crowther stared. "Well, that is good, good. Even so, let me put it another way. I'm sure it would be better not to add to her difficulties."

"How do you mean, sir?"

"If you go to talk to her, especially in this dreadful weather, don't you think it suggests you *do* think there is some cause for concern?"

Mrs. Christie frowned, then nodded. "I see that it might."

Crowther peered through the small cottage window. "And the weather is deteriorating as we speak."

"But I don't like the idea of her waiting and me not arriving, not without any explanation."

Crowther nodded. "I tell you what, since I'm going back that way—almost halfway there, in fact—why don't I go and see Miss Gifford and give your apologies?"

Mrs. Christie's face flooded with relief. "Would you?"

"It would be my pleasure to help. You stay dry. Keep an eye on those charming little girls of yours. You can always go to Blackthorn House tomorrow, if the weather lifts."

"So you will explain, Mr. Crowther? That on reflection, there didn't seem the need?"

"Leave it to me, Mrs. Christie."

"It's funny though, isn't it, that she can't remember a thing about when she was little?"

"Nothing?"

"Not a thing." Mrs. Christie shook her head. "A wonderful thing how the mind protects itself."

The Bull's Head
Main Road
Fishbourne

Crowther strode back to the Bull's Head.

"Any messages for me, Pine?" he asked.

The barman jumped. "You startled me, Mr. Crowther."

"Sorry, Pine. Any word?"

"No," he said, sliding a glass of whisky across the bar. "Very quiet."

Crowther nodded his thanks. "What do you know about the Christie family?"

"Nice, respectable woman," the barman replied. "Nursed her husband through a long illness."

"Did you know Christie?"

Pine shook his head. "I knew of him. She moved here after she was widowed. For the second time, I heard. From Lavant, I think it was. She doesn't come from round here, though."

"Oh?"

"I have a mind she originally came from Slindon or Crossbush, somewhere Arundel way. Maybe it was Lyminster?"

"Are you sure?"

Pine flicked his cloth over his shoulder. "Just something I heard, but it might be wrong. Before my time."

Crowther carried his drink to the window and looked out. The trees on the far side of the road were plunging in the wind, and the gables of Fishbourne House and Willow Cottage were shrouded in mist and rain.

The moment Brook had told him of the summons to the churchyard, Crowther had worked out what was happening. But now he was starting to wonder if he'd been mistaken. The note concerned him, though since Mrs. Christie had handed it back to Connie Gifford, there was no way of Crowther learning anything for himself from that quarter.

Where was Dr. Woolston? It had seemed a perfect solution to use his name on the death certificate. Two birds with one stone. But now the man had disappeared. Had he seen or heard something in the Old Salt Mill that had caused him to bolt?

In the background, Crowther registered the sound of everyday conversation from the public bar. Men coming in to shelter from the rain. Drowning their sorrows for an hour or two.

He looked down at the amber liquid, then downed it in one. He'd promised to pass on Mrs. Christie's apologies to Miss Gifford. Perhaps Gifford himself would be back.

Crowther put the glass on the counter and set off for Blackthorn House.

We pass a needleful of thread across the nostrils, tie it underneath the inferior mandible, having the thread the length of the bird, to prevent the blood from coming out of the beak during the operation. We stretch the bird on the table, the head turned towards the left of the operator; we divide the feathers of the belly right and left with small forceps, put out the down which covers the belly, make an incision in the skin from the commencement of the sternum or breast-bone until beyond the middle of the belly, raise the skin on one side by the forceps, separate it from the muscles with a scalpel, approaching as near as possible to the wings; this done, we put a little floured or powdered cotton on the skin and flesh.

TAXIDERMY: OR, THE ART OF COLLECTING, PREPARING, AND MOUNTING OBJECTS OF NATURAL HISTORY

Mrs. R. Lee
Longman & Co., Paternoster Row, London, 1820

I have no doubt I shall be judged harshly. By those who fill the pews on a Sunday, by those who fill the pages of the newspapers with their hypocritical cant. The respectable citizen will demand I should hang. An eye for an eye.

In the myriad ways in which men condemn women.

But can you see, now, how it was inevitable? How they were architects of their own misfortune, not I?

There must be justice in retribution. No wild reckoning or a half-hearted calling to account, but rather a measured recompense. They did not choose to make amends. They did not seek forgiveness or redemption. They did not seek to atone.

Neither do I. And since there is no recourse under the law, what else could I have done? And though I know there is no possibility of clemency in this world—what I am doing is beyond any acceptable bounds—there will surely be some who praise me for it.

As for those who helped me in good faith, I here set it down that they did not know what I intended. They, as much as you, will be horrified when they learn what I have done.

The decision to kill was mine. The act and method mine alone.

Do not be afraid.

Chapter 32

Blackthorn House
Fishbourne Marshes

Connie and Harry were sitting close together in the fading light of the day. Outside, Connie heard a noise and glanced up at the window of the workshop.

"Did you hear something?"

"No," he said. "Nothing."

"Probably only the magpies."

Connie looked around the workshop in the gray shadow of dusk. Everything had taken on strange silhouettes, elongated black shadows and distorted, sharp shapes. The glass dome, with the jackdaw within, caught the last slivers of the damp, dying day and sent refracted glints of light across the wooden surface of the bench. Connie knew the bird had been left for far too long now. She would have to give it up—bury it—once Harry had gone. So beautiful, but already the process of decay had begun.

She stood up. "I was expecting Mrs. Christie to have come by now. It must be well after five o'clock."

Harry looked at his pocket watch. "It's half past six."

"So late already."

"Did you expect her to keep the appointment?"

Connie sighed. "Not really, no. She was worried talking to

me this morning; once she'd read the note, even more so. I had to persuade her to come. Perhaps I should go to her instead?"

"Do you want me to go with you?"

"I think that would make Mrs. Christie more anxious, not less." She sighed again. "No, I think we should stick to what we agreed. I'll come to Chichester tomorrow morning at ten o'clock. If your father still hasn't turned up by then, we will go to Sergeant Pennicott together. After that, let's see."

Harry nodded. "And *your* father?"

The smile faded from Connie's face. "I'll continue to wait. Hope he comes back under his own volition."

Harry hesitated. "You don't think something might have happened to him?"

"No. At least, I can't be sure."

At that moment, they heard a knocking at the front door.

"There you are," Harry said. "Mrs. Christie's come after all."

"I don't think she would come so late, and not to the front door, in any case." Connie went out into the hall, listening for the sound of Mary's footsteps in the hallway. None came.

"That's odd," she said.

"What time does she go home at the end of the day?"

"Seven o'clock, but she always tells me when she's leaving."

"Perhaps the kitchen door is shut and she didn't hear. Would you like me to go in her stead?"

Connie shook her head, liking the fact that they had become so comfortable in each other's company this past hour that Harry had forgotten how quickly gossip would spread if he answered the door.

"I think it's better if I do," she said.

Everything in this long afternoon had been so strange. The world seemed both the same and yet utterly transformed. Connie didn't think she'd talked so much—or so much about herself—for years. Ever, perhaps. Then she realized that Harry didn't want to remain alone in the darkening workshop.

"Why don't you go through to the drawing room? It's the last room on the left, at the end of the corridor. I'm sure it isn't Pennicott back again, but it's best if you stay out of sight just in case."

*

Davey Reedman couldn't put off going home any longer. He'd spun out his tea for as long as he could, but Mary was getting impatient.

He flipped his cap onto his head, hooked the purloined binoculars back around his neck, then surprised Mary by giving her a quick peck on the cheek.

"The sauce of it," she scolded, though she was smiling.

"Thanking you, Mary."

The boy sauntered out of the kitchen and through the scullery to the back door.

"Stay out of trouble," she called after him, "or Ma will have something to say about it."

"She will, will she?"

"Yes, and so will I!"

For a moment, Davey stood outside in the garden, admiring the mackerel sky and enjoying the rare sensation of a full belly. He yawned. It had been a good day, one of the best. He'd earned tuppence, dined like a king and no one had shown him the wrong side of their hand.

He looked at the clouds, wondering how soon it was going to start raining again. He was reluctant to go home. He didn't want to get wet if he slept out, though it was nonetheless still a more attractive option.

Then he remembered the icehouse. There was a little brick porch that would give a bit of shelter, provided the wind didn't come around. He couldn't see why anyone would bother him there. Mary hadn't been able to lay her hands on the missing padlock key, though she'd spent half the afternoon looking for it. Davey hadn't pinched it, but he wondered if he might shelter there for tonight. He didn't think Miss Gifford would mind, and Mary knew how it was for him at home.

He crept along the side of the workshop. Miss Gifford and Harry's voices were audible through the open high windows and Davey gave a low whistle. Still talking after all this time. He was pleased. She deserved a bit of company her own age from time to time, just like Mrs. Christie said.

He rounded the corner into the south garden, then stopped, taken aback by the large number of birds massed on the roof of the icehouse. Magpies, but mostly rooks. The distinctive harsh sound. As Davey got closer, he noticed there was a pair of crows too, sitting apart from the others on the fence. Glossy black carrion scavengers. Funny, he thought. They normally kept to themselves.

He went on cautiously, keeping close to the boundary fence and taking care not to alarm the birds. He didn't want to scare them off. That many taking flight, they'd make one heck of an almighty racket.

He reached the door of the disused icehouse, checked over his shoulder, then reached out and examined the padlock. It was locked. He hesitated, then suddenly decided he'd better not actually break in. He didn't want Miss Gifford, or Mary, come to that, to think badly of him.

Davey curled himself up against the door, folded his arms, pulled his cap over his face. Ten minutes' shut-eye wouldn't hurt.

Connie opened the front door herself.

"Mr. Crowther," she said with surprise.

"I'm sorry to disturb you at this hour, Miss Gifford," he said. "I wonder if I might beg a few minutes of your time?"

"Of course, do come in."

As Connie stepped back, she noticed there were muddy footprints from the policeman's boots on the parquet flooring.

"I regret my father is still away, Mr. Crowther," she said, sticking to the same story. "Were you hoping to see him?"

He removed his hat. "Not at all. I had intended to come after yesterday's tragic event, to make sure you were quite secure in your father's continued absence, but the day got away from me in the way things can."

Connie smiled. "Yes, indeed."

"Then I met Mrs. Christie. The poor woman is worried about having been unable to keep her appointment with you—she couldn't find anyone to mind the girls and she didn't feel it appropriate to bring them with her—so I promised I would pass on her apologies, since I was coming this way in any case. She didn't want you to worry."

"I wouldn't have minded. Mary could have watched them."

"I don't imagine Mrs. Christie wanted to impose," he said lightly. "And of course it's an unpleasant walk with two young children in this weather."

She nodded. "It's very kind of you to pass on the message, Mr. Crowther."

They both turned at a sound from the drawing room.

"I'm so sorry, Miss Gifford, I didn't realize you had guests. I don't wish to intrude."

"You're not intruding in the slightest," Connie said, opening the door and leading him in. "You know Mr. Woolston, I believe."

Connie saw a look of interest flicker in Crowther's eyes, though quickly hidden.

"Twice in the space of as many hours," he said, holding out his hand. "Good evening again to you, Mr. Woolston."

"Evening, Crowther."

"I thought you were returning to Chichester to see if there was further news about your father."

"That's right, though I believe I mentioned I intended to visit Blackthorn House first."

"So you did, so you did."

Connie was puzzled. Harry had spoken warmly of Crowther's kindness earlier, but now he seemed belligerent. She looked between the two men, wondering why they were behaving so cautiously.

"Mr. Crowther has come with Mrs. Christie's apologies," she explained. "May I offer you a drink?"

Crowther held up his hand. "No, thank you. I'm not staying. I don't wish to impose."

"Really, it's the least I can do, since you have come all the way out here."

Remembering she had finished the brandy earlier, she poured both men a shot of whisky.

"Thank you, Miss Gifford," Crowther said, accepting the glass. "Is Mary not with you this afternoon?"

"I don't want to take her away from her other duties," she said, catching Harry's eye. "As it happens, I've had a number of unexpected visitors this afternoon."

"The bottom of Mill Lane is flooding," Crowther said. "More than likely, the trap can't get through." He took a sip of whisky. "As for anyone else, I'm impressed at their fortitude. It's very wet. Who, I wonder, would risk their boots?"

Connie smiled, then gestured that they should all sit down.

"Thank you," Crowther said, settling himself in one of the armchairs beside the fire. "You said you had a number of unexpected visitors?"

"Sergeant Pennicott, for one."

"Indeed? What on earth did he want?"

Connie glanced at Harry, then back to Mr. Crowther.

"I know that Harry—Mr. Woolston—confided in you about his concerns for his father. As it turns out, he was right to do so. Pennicott came on the same errand. He asserted—and I have no way of knowing if this is true or not—that my father and Dr. Woolston were acquaintances."

"And are they?" Crowther asked. His tone was light, but Connie could hear the determination underneath.

"Not to my knowledge, no," she replied. "I've never heard my father mention Dr. Woolston, certainly. I explained that Harry and I had met yesterday for the first time. I fear he did not believe me. He kept asking if I knew where Dr. Woolston had gone and pressed for the address of the friends with whom my father is staying."

"Did you give it to him?"

Connie shook her head. "I do not want my father disturbed while he is convalescing."

"Quite right." Crowther pressed the tips of his fingers together. "I am still of the opinion—if you'll forgive me repeating myself, Woolston—that it's premature to assume that something has happened to Dr. Woolston. He's only been missing for twenty-four hours, after all. If, indeed, he is missing at all." He fixed Harry with a stare. "But of course, if you felt it wise to speak to the police, then . . ."

"It wasn't me, Crowther," Harry said. "My father's clerk, Pearce, reported him missing."

Crowther's eyebrows shot up. "His clerk?" He stared at Harry. "Forgive me, but why on earth would he take it upon himself to do such a thing? That's surely overstepping his responsibilities?"

"It is."

"What does the man say?"

"It's only just come to light, so I haven't had the chance to ask him."

"But you intend to?"

"Of course," Harry said.

Connie spoke quickly, unable to bear the look of dejection that had come over Harry once more. "Though as I've said to Harry, Mr. Crowther, I'm sure it's just as likely he will find his father waiting for him at home."

"Your good spirits are an example to us all," Crowther said.

Chapter 33

West Street
Chichester

Pearce took a final look around the office, then stepped out into West Street and closed the door behind him. He took off his spectacles, cleaned them with his handkerchief, then put them back on his sore nose. His hay fever was still troubling him, despite the damp.

He heard the cathedral bells strike a quarter to seven, the familiar notes echoing between the buildings and through the quiet early-evening streets. Usually, it was a reassuring sound. All afternoon, he'd regretted the impulse that had sent him from Brook's offices to the Market Cross to speak to Pennicott. The policeman clearly thought he was making a fuss about nothing, and Pearce had spent the remainder of the day caught between hoping for the sound of Dr. Woolston's footsteps and dreading them. He feared his employer would chastise him for speaking out of turn. Perhaps even dismiss him without a reference. Then where would he be?

He looked down at the telegram in his hand. The reply from the county asylum was unequivocal. There had been no emergency meeting of the committee called; no one had seen or heard from Dr. Woolston.

Deeply troubled, Pearce turned the key in the lock and

pulled the door toward him to make sure it was firmly shut. He looked up at the sky as the first drops of rain began to fall, then put up his umbrella and began the long walk home to Portfield, on the eastern side of Chichester.

North Street
Chichester

In the elegant Georgian house at the top of North Street, Lewis straightened a soup spoon for the third time. He hesitated, then moved the linen napkin on the side plate a little to the left.

Two identical place settings, at either end of the polished mahogany dining table. A glass for white wine and one for red. The butcher had delivered lamb instead of chicken this morning—there had been some difficulty, the shop had been broken into yesterday, which had affected the orders. Lewis didn't think Dr. Woolston would mind, but he had taken the precaution of searching out a good claret all the same.

He glanced out of the dining room to the checkerboard-tiled entrance hall, then into the drawing room on the opposite side of the house. Dr. Woolston's tray was ready beside his chair. A heavy glass tumbler with an inch of whisky and a small jug of water. Everything was as it should be, except for the fact that his master was not present. Lewis had received no word from Mr. Harold either, though Mrs. Lewis claimed that was encouraging. If there had been bad news, then someone would have informed them.

Lewis wasn't sure. He had worked for Dr. Woolston for twenty-five years. First in the army, in the stifling heat and horror of the Transvaal, the Boer Wars and the desperate waste of life. In 1902, they had returned home to Chichester and settled into a quieter, more ordered kind of life. Lewis would no more assume to know what his master thought or felt than Dr. Woolston would have dreamed of asking Lewis for an opinion on anything other than the smooth running of the household. All the same, they knew one another well. Each knew where they stood.

Mrs. Lewis told him not to fret, that there would be a rational explanation, seeking to reassure him, just as he had attempted to reassure Mr. Harold the previous day. Lewis didn't know if his wife believed what she was saying, any more than he himself had when talking to the boy. For all his faults, Harold was fond of his father. Lewis didn't want him to worry until—unless—there was something to worry about.

He saw the first spots of rain strike the glass. He went to the window and looked out, but the street was still empty.

West Street
Chichester

Frederick Brook stumbled out of his room, leaving an erotic art book open on his desk, and along the corridor.

His large, ruddy face glistened with sweat from the whisky he'd been drinking, and his pupils were tiny black points in his bloodshot eyes. Ash from his cigar fell unnoticed to the ground.

After a disappointing afternoon's shooting, Brook had discovered he was wrong to assume that he would be invited to stay for dinner. It was all very politely done, circumstances beyond the host's control and all that, but Brook suspected it meant that some bigwig staying at West Dean Estate had arrived unexpectedly and elbowed the local men out. Or, rather, that despite his influence and the money he brought into

Chichester, he was not considered local enough. He'd had it often enough in the past. His accent, and the fact that he was a self-made man, had not inherited his fortune, meant he wasn't one of them. They looked down on him because he made his living in "trade."

Knotted with rage, Brook had turned down an invitation to the Dolphin, returned to his office and opened a new bottle of Usher's. Three-quarters of the whisky was now gone, and he was in a fighting mood.

"Damn the lot of them," he slurred, "bloody disgrace. Shouldn't . . ."

The rest of his complaint was lost in a fit of coughing and cigar smoke. Where the devil was Sutton? He'd been calling for half an hour, and still the man hadn't come.

Brook came to a halt in the entrance hall. The lamp was not lit and the clerk wasn't there. His desk was tidy, no papers or pens, though there were three books balanced on the corner. Brook swayed. He hadn't given the man permission to leave, so where the hell was he?

He flung out a large hand to steady himself against the bookcase, realizing he was very drunk and the hour was evidently later than he'd thought. He'd come out to tell the clerk to go to his house to pick up his evening clothes, but the man had clearly gone home. Brook had taken off his Norfolk jacket, but he was still wearing his breeches, gaiters and worsted waistcoat, and he could hardly go out to dine dressed like that. He'd intended to change here, in the office, then take a hansom to Bognor. He fancied trying the Kursaal, the new entertainment palace on the pier. After that, who could say? Any kind of taste might be indulged, provided one had the money to pay for it and knew who to ask.

Damnable weather; everything smelled of mold. Brook took a step forward in the dark and banged his shin on the portable heater set in the hall to take the edge off the damp. The floor seemed to lurch beneath his feet. Cursing Sutton, and Woolston's idiot son, Brook edged his way toward the front door, thinking he might find a boy in the street to run the errand for him. There were usually a fair few hanging around the yard of the Dolphin Hotel.

Light from the gas streetlamp shone through the glass above his office door, illuminating a cream envelope on the mat. Damning the clerk for having failed to deal with it before going home—another black mark against him—Brook braced his knees, bent over and picked it up.

The bells of the cathedral struck the quarter hour. As he tried to straighten, Brook wondered if it had gone seven o'clock, or even eight. The whisky had blunted his sense of time. Perspiring heavily, he tore open the envelope. It contained a handwritten invitation. He brought it close to his face and away again, making sure he'd read it correctly, then he smiled.

"Well done, White," he muttered. "Bloody well done."

Abruptly his evening had taken on an entirely different character. One that he wouldn't have to subsidize out of his own pocket either. Even better, because it was a private house, his lack of appropriate clothing wouldn't matter so much. It wasn't quite the thing, but he'd be among friends, and once the evening really got going, what he was wearing would be the last thing on anyone's mind.

Awfully short notice, though.

Brook screwed up the paper and dropped it on the floor, then lurched back to his office to fetch his cigars and lighter. He put away the book and locked the drawer, for a moment wondering how on earth White had managed to organize such a party so quickly. He wasn't always so resourceful and the man had been working all day. Not that Brook was complaining.

Fifteen minutes later, he was flying down the Stockbridge Road in a two-and-pair, heading toward Apuldram. He had a few hours to kill before the gathering was due to begin, but the Crown and Anchor at Dell Quay seemed as good a place as anywhere to spend the time.

Chapter 34

Blackthorn House
Fishbourne Marshes

Connie glanced at the clock, then at the pained expression on Harry's face.

Mr. Crowther was cordial and pleasant, but after the intimacy of their shared time in the workshop, Connie could see that Harry was finding his presence trying. Answering polite inquiries about his job with Brook, or how he spent his time in Chichester, when she could see that all he could think about was his father. It truth, the conversation had lasted no more than ten minutes, but it felt endless, and it was a relief when Crowther announced he was leaving.

"Thank you very much for your company, Miss Gifford," he said, putting down his glass. "Yours too, Woolston. I'm sure there's nothing to worry about. In fact, I'll go so far as to guess that your father will be there waiting for you when you arrive home."

"I hope so, sir," Harry said with feeling.

"How are you getting back to Chichester?"

Harry shot Connie a glance, though he knew he would have to leave.

"I hadn't thought about it, I'm afraid."

Crowther smiled. "I'm more than happy to lend you my

trap, if that would help? Unless, of course, you've already made arrangements."

Harry flushed. "I couldn't possibly accept, Mr. Crowther. I wouldn't dream of putting you out."

"Nonsense. I'm not going anywhere this evening, and you won't pick up a taxi in Fishbourne, I'm afraid."

"I shall be fine walking to the station," he said.

"I'm afraid the railway service at Fishbourne Halt is poor in the evenings," Connie said.

"And I don't wish to be a Cassandra," Crowther said, "but the rain's about to start up again, and Mill Lane is already flooding."

"Well, if you are sure, Crowther. I don't mind admitting it will make things far easier. It's very decent of you."

"It's my pleasure." Crowther put on his hat and coat. "Are you all right, Miss Gifford? You are awfully pale."

Connie blinked. "Yes, I'm fine. It was just you said something that . . ." She gave a brief shake of her head, then smiled at the two men. "Nothing. It's gone."

Harry put on his coat and hat too, and together they all three walked along the corridor to the front door.

"Good night, Mr. Crowther. Mr. Woolston."

Crowther stepped outside.

"You will come to Chichester tomorrow, as agreed?" Harry whispered to Connie. "Promise you will."

Connie nodded. "I will."

"Good night, then."

The two men walked down the footpath together and through the latched gate onto the path. Connie watched until they were out of sight, then went back indoors, still trying to work out what it was Crowther had said that had set a new memory chasing in her mind.

The sound of a door slamming close by woke Davey.

He was on his feet before he knew it, expecting trouble, then he realized where he was. He turned up the collar of the jacket. He could feel that the wind had come around, and though it wasn't raining yet, he could smell it in the air. If he was going to get off home, now was the time to do it.

Then, at his back, he heard a noise.

The boy froze. He spent most of his time outdoors, listening to the strange sounds of the marshes, the calls of the owl and the fox, the way in which ordinary noises distorted at dusk, at night, at dawn into mysterious and threatening things. But this was something different. A kind of low keening, like an animal caught in the iron teeth of a trap, and it was coming from inside the icehouse.

"Please . . ."

He pressed his ear against the wooden door, trying to identify what he could hear. Everyone knew old Gifford had got monstrosities hidden down there. Skeletons and furless animals and birds with no heads.

A barely human voice. "Someone . . ."

Davey didn't wait to hear any more. He turned tail and ran, back to the house, now not caring who heard him. The birds flew up in a startled mass.

"Mary," he cried. "Mary, come quick."

Main Road
Fishbourne

Gregory Joseph walked past the Rectory Gardens, crossed over Clay Lane and into the fields on the outskirts of the village.

His foot knocked against a shard of red clay tile. He picked it up, examined it, then decided it was worthless so flung it into the bushes. Odd bits and pieces of pottery were always turning up hereabouts.

It had been a long round trip and his feet were tired and wet. From Fishbourne to Apuldram, Apuldram to Chichester—to deliver a letter to premises in West Street—and he was now finally on his way back to Fishbourne.

He gave a raw smile. What wouldn't he give to be a fly on the wall when Gerald White turned up for work tomorrow and tried to explain his black eye and broken nose. He wouldn't be so pleased with himself then. It was always a pleasure taking men like that down a peg or two.

Joseph walked past Fishbourne Lodge. He flexed his fingers. His knuckles were sore too. He hadn't gone to town on White; his orders had been clear: teach him a lesson, then take him into the kitchen to leave him to come around on his own. Left to himself, he would have done, given what he was guilty of. In Joseph's opinion, men like that, who interfered with women, deserved everything coming to them.

Joseph drew level with the Woolpack. Not his local. There were lads in there it was better to avoid, so he kept walking. He hoped White wouldn't cause trouble when he came around. Joseph would have been happier staying put, until the matter was concluded and White was off the premises. But it wasn't what he'd been told to do and, as he kept reminding himself, he wasn't being paid to ask questions.

Poor old Birdie. He'd passed that news on, at least.

These past forty-eight hours had been strange, no denying it. He wasn't afraid of hard work, but having the Sayers Removals men deliver the belongings so late at night was peculiar. Carrying the big trunk on his own had nearly put his back out. He wasn't even sure how many people were staying at the cottage. It was hard to tell.

Ahead, he saw the lights of the Bull's Head and quickened his stride.

Blackthorn House
Fishbourne Marshes

Davey and Mary stood beneath the lowering sky in the far southwest corner of the garden, staring at the brick icehouse in the gloom.

It was no longer day, and not yet night, but the rising moon was throwing a peculiar cold light over everything.

"What if it's a ghost?" he said.

"No such thing."

"Why won't you come with me, then?"

Mary pointed at the roof of the icehouse, now covered with black birds. It looked as if every tile had been replaced by black feathers.

"Look at them, there's so many of them."

"Come on," Davey pleaded.

"It's just the birds you heard," she said.

"It wasn't a bird. Besides, they won't harm us," he added, with more courage than he felt. "More scared of us than we are of them."

"Listen to them," Mary whispered. "Horrible sound. And why are there so many of them? It's not natural, not this time of night."

"I'm not fibbing," Davey said, pulling at her sleeve. "I heard a voice. Someone's in there, I'm telling you."

"There can't be," she said. "I told you, it's locked and we can't find the key."

"What about if someone *took* the key?" he reasoned.

Mary stopped staring at the birds and looked at him.

"Who'd do a thing like that?"

Davey shrugged. "I'm just saying."

At that moment, the distinct cry of a human voice was heard in between the calls of the jackdaws, magpies, rooks and crows.

"There," he hissed in triumph. "What did I tell you?"

"We should get someone," Mary whispered.

"I did," he said. "I got you. Anyway, who else is there? You can't be asking Miss Gifford to come out here," he added gallantly, "not when we don't know what's down there." He paused, seeing he was making it worse rather than better. "It's probably nobody. More than likely a fox got caught. They sound half human when they want to."

He stared at Mary, certain she wouldn't really let a ten-year-old boy go down there on his own. "Look, are you coming or not?"

"All right then," she said.

Mary moved out of the lea of the building. They took short, careful steps across the garden, all the time watched by the birds, until they were standing in front of the wooden door.

They both heard the unmistakable sound of someone groaning.

"There *is* someone down there," Mary said, in disbelief.

"Haven't I been telling you that? Now, have you got a pin?"

"You can't do that!"

"Got a better idea?" asked Davey, holding the padlock.

Mary hesitated, then took a pin from her hair. Davey expertly picked the lock and took it off.

He put his hand on the doorknob.

"You ready?" he said.

His heart was going nineteen to the dozen, but he wasn't going to let her know that. He counted to three under his breath, then slowly turned the handle and pulled the door toward them.

A half-conscious, collapsed figure fell forward and slumped on the step, like a sack of coal. Davey jumped back. Mary screamed. Some of the birds, startled by the noise, took flight.

The man was barely moving, but Davey could hear him breathing. He took a deep breath, then crouched down beside the emaciated shape. He didn't want to touch him, but he lifted a strand of dank hair away from the face, and saw a mass of bruises.

"It's the guv'nor," he said. "Half dead by the looks of it."

At that moment, Gifford shifted position. Davey jerked back.

"Save your strength, sir."

Gifford tried to push himself up from the ground with his arms, but seemed incapable of supporting his own weight.

"How long's he been in there, do you reckon?" Davey whispered.

Mary shook her head. "I don't know."

"Miss Gifford asked me to look out for him. I got the impression he was missing. When did you last see him?"

"Tuesday, maybe," she said after a while. "He was out yesterday afternoon, like usual, but Miss Gifford gave me to believe he was in his room this morning."

"All a bit off, isn't it?"

Gifford's weak voice interrupted their speculations. "Boy . . ."

"I'm here, sir. Don't you worry."

Between them, Mary and Davey managed to roll him

onto his back, half supported against the brick wall. Gifford smelled sour, his clothes stiff with dried sweat, and his skin was clammy.

"Stay here with him," Mary hissed. "I'll fetch Miss Gifford."

"Bring him something to drink. He's all dried out."

*

Davey sat watching over Gifford. He was drifting in and out of consciousness, mumbling and remonstrating with himself, unaware of where he was, or what had happened. Davey was no stranger to the effects of drink, from keeping out of the way of his own father and grandfather often enough; he thought Gifford would be all right in the long run. His lips were cracked and his right eye was swollen shut. There was a trail of dried blood and dirt on his cheek. The tops of his fingers were damaged too, but Davey couldn't see any other serious injuries. He reckoned he'd fallen down the steps in a stupor and been unable to get himself out again.

Gifford's eyes suddenly popped open. "Who's there . . . who . . ."

Davey edged closer, caught between a horrified fascination and pity.

"It's me, sir. Davey Reedman."

Gifford didn't seem to hear him. His eyes rolled back in his head, and for a moment, in the pool of light from the main house, Davey saw the whites of his eyes alive with fear.

"Got to get her away, boy. Got to save her."

Davey hesitated, then put his hand on Gifford's shoulder, felt how his jacket was thick with dust and straw, and wondered what he'd been up to down in the sunken icehouse. He wanted to go and look. He was nervous of what might be down there; curious, too. But he didn't think he ought to leave.

"These things pass," he said, repeating the words Mrs. Christie said to him when things were especially bad for him at home. Davey didn't know if he believed it. Not much in his short life had led him to think that tomorrow would be better than today, but he'd been comforted by her, and how it made him feel safe for an hour or two.

"Won't seem so bad tomorrow. These things pass."

"What else . . ."

"Mary's gone to fetch Miss Gifford," he said, hoping the old man could hear him.

Gifford suddenly tried to sit up. "Got to tell her . . . warn her. Mustn't trust anyone." His muscles were shaking with the effort and he fell back. "Keep her safe. Get away . . ."

Davey increased the pressure on Gifford's shoulder. "Don't get yourself worked up, sir. Miss Gifford's all right, don't you worry about her."

*

Connie came flying out of the side door, with Mary following behind holding a lantern and a glass of water.

She saw the little boy sitting beside her father on the ground. He leaped up as she approached.

"I don't know how long he's been in there, miss."

She was horrified by the look of him, emaciated and filthy, but she held her voice steady. She didn't want to alarm him.

"Father, can you hear me?" she said calmly, talking to him as if he was the child and she the parent. "It's me, Connie."

The effort of speaking had taken what little strength Gifford had remaining. He was now lying slumped on the wet brick steps with his eyes closed.

"He looks worse than he is," Davey said. "That's what I think."

Connie took the cup from Mary and, holding Gifford's head up, poured a little water into his parched mouth. He coughed and choked, but finally managed to swallow. She kept going until the cup was empty.

"Father, we're going to try to take you inside. Do you think you can stand up?"

He made no answer, so Connie put her hand beneath his head to encourage him to sit up. Another torrent of words fell from his mouth.

"Get Jennie to take her away. Keep the girl safe."

Connie looked at Davey.

"Has he said what happened?"

Davey shook his head. "Can't make head nor tail of it, to be honest, miss. No offense."

Gifford suddenly fell onto his side. "Don't trust him . . . Worst of all . . ."

"Father," Connie said in a firm, clear voice. "Gifford? Can you stand? We must get you inside."

Davey felt the dew on the grass and the dampness in the soil. There was a sharp salt tang in the air.

"Best be quick. More rain is on the way."

Connie straightened. "Mary, you put your arm under his left shoulder, I'll do this side, and let's see if we can't get him up."

Gifford was bone thin from a fortnight of barely eating and the past twenty-four hours trapped in the icehouse, but even so, he was too heavy for the two women to carry. They tried, several times, Connie encouraging her father, but it didn't work.

"I got an idea, miss," Davey said. "If we got him onto a blanket or something, we could drag him back to the house. Might be easier to get him on his feet once there's something for him to lean on."

"That's a sensible idea. Mary, there's a tarpaulin inside the scullery door. Can you fetch that?"

Mary rushed back toward the house.

"How did you find him, Davey?"

"I'm sorry, I never done it before, cross my heart, but the rain was coming on and I thought I'd shelter, and—"

"It's all right, Davey, it's good you did."

Mary returned, out of breath, holding a large square of brown tarpaulin in her arms. It smelled damp and musty. Between them, they managed to slide Gifford onto it and settle him in place.

The first drops of rain began to fall. The two women—with Davey in the middle—pulled Gifford across the slick grass toward the house. He was a deadweight and seemingly unaware of what was happening to him, but slowly they succeeded in covering the distance between the icehouse and the side door.

In the distance, Connie heard a rumble of thunder. There was a pause, as if the night itself was holding its breath, then the familiar sound of the rain falling harder, as if a tap had been turned on. Striking the leaves and the roof of the storeroom, the chimneys and red tiles of the house.

A combination of the rain on his face and the light from the lamp above the door jolted Gifford back to consciousness. Without warning, he flung his arm across his eyes, then, in part of the same movement, propelled himself into a sitting position. He looked like a puppet without strings, all folded in on himself. Connie felt the familiar mixture of pity and disappointment that he had come to this.

"All the money, but no need of it now. No need. She's dead."

"Don't try to talk," Connie said. "Save your strength. I need you to stand up. Mary, Davey and I are going to help you to walk. Just into the drawing room. Not far."

Gifford blinked at her through blurred eyes, but seemed to have understood the instruction. He put his hand out to steady himself on the jamb, his skin gray and sickly in the yellow cast of the light above the door. With their help, he heaved himself up onto his feet. Davey positioned himself behind, in case he fell backward. Though his legs trembled, Gifford held his ground.

"Proof," he said, gesturing wildly. "I kept it. Keep her safe." He peered at Connie. "Jennie will help. You can trust Jennie."

"He's been talking like this the whole time, miss," Davey said. "About keeping you safe. Seems to upset him worse than anything."

Connie didn't respond. She wasn't certain her father was thinking of her. Or at least, not only of her.

PART III

Friday

Chapter 35

Themis Cottage
Apuldram

Frederick Brook stared at the narrow track leading from Apuldram Lane to Themis Cottage.

For a moment, he wondered if he was in the wrong place. He understood the need for discretion—to be away from prying eyes and ears—but this was very remote even by those standards. Then again, these select gatherings were often arranged in unusual locations, and White's directions on the invitation had been clear. And there were ruts in the lane, suggesting a cart or carriage had recently come this way.

Brook set off, unsteady after several hours' drinking in the Crown and Anchor, picking his way carefully along the muddy track sodden with rain and seawater. He felt light-headed with expectation and whisky and ale. He was grateful, now, that he hadn't changed out of his shooting clothes. In the dark of the Sussex night, with the promise of enjoyment ahead, Brook felt as if he was going hunting. A pulse of desire surged up in him, cutting through the effects of the whisky, as he allowed himself to imagine the evening that was waiting behind the closed door. What kind of girls might White have rounded up?

It began to rain again, harder this time.

In the dark beneath the canopy of branches, Brook took his

lighter from his pocket and held it in front of him. A gift from a grateful client, to whom Brook had given favorable terms in return for one or two pieces of information about his rival suppliers. The flame guttered, so he kept his thumb on the wheel to keep sparking the flint.

The beech trees loomed above him as he staggered on, his weight sending him deep into the mud with each heavy footstep. He could hear the wind in the highest branches and, just audible now, the suck and pull of shingle and the sea. The flame went out again. This time, it refused to be revived.

Finally, after it seemed he had walked about half a mile, Brook rounded a bend in the track and saw, to his relief, a single light burning in the window of a cottage ahead, set in a large garden. So far as he could see, there were no other houses anywhere close by. From the sound of the waves on the shore, he realized he was now right down at the water's edge.

He stepped off the muddy lane onto a paved path, ghostly in the moonlight, that led to the front door of the cottage. He immediately felt reassured. He put his dead lighter in his pocket and got the worst of the mud off his boots on the scraper, then knocked with mounting anticipation. He wondered what tantalizing surprises the evening might have in store.

Blackthorn House
Fishbourne Marshes

"He is going to be all right, isn't he, miss?"

Connie put her hand on Davey's shoulder. "I think so."

It was just after midnight. Connie was in her usual armchair, with the boy sitting cross-legged on the carpet beside her. Mary had also refused to go home, despite already having stayed on many hours past her regular time, and Connie was grateful. And although it was ridiculous—she had known him for less than forty-eight hours—Connie wished Harry could be here also.

She felt guilty. All afternoon she'd sat chatting with Harry, instead of keeping to her original plan to check the storeroom as soon as she came back from the village. If she had done so, she would have spared her father several hours of distress.

"You weren't to know, miss," Davey said, seeing the expression return to her face.

"It is lucky you were here, Davey."

"It's all right, miss. Glad to help."

Between them, they had managed to help Gifford out of his dirty clothes. Connie had washed and treated his injuries, which—as Davey had said—weren't as bad as they'd looked at first sight. They'd settled him for the night in the drawing room, the stairs being too much for him to cope with. He had drunk a cup of beef tea and eaten a little bread, and now was sleeping on the daybed with a blanket over him. Mary sat on a chair beside him, struggling to keep her eyes open.

"You don't have to stay, Davey," Connie said. "Mary and I will manage between us."

"I'm all right. Don't like to think of you out here on your own."

"I'm used to it," she said, rubbing her eyes.

"Different now, though, isn't it? Things have changed."

Connie stared at him with interest. "Why do you say that?"

"Didn't mean to be impertinent. That's what Ma Christie says."

"You shouldn't be passing on what one person says to another," Mary put in. "Not if it's private."

"That's not private, it's learning. Increasing my vocabulary, that's what your ma says."

"Don't be cheeky in front of Miss Gifford."

"I don't mind," Connie smiled. "I'd like to hear what he thinks. Go on, Davey."

The boy shifted position. "Well, the police for one. Then, poor Birdie being found here."

"Birdie?" Connie said.

"Vera. That's what we all called her. I mean, I know she wasn't on your property as such, miss, but near enough. And Gregory Joseph's up to something, strutting around, cock of the walk, pleased with himself." He hesitated. "Then there's the guv'nor. I know he's partial to a drop, but it seems to me something set him off. More than the usual."

"Go on," she said, genuinely interested.

"Mary said—she wasn't talking out of turn, just ordinary chat—that Mr. Gifford never goes to the storeroom. So, my question is, why now?"

Even in her exhausted state, the boy's words struck a chord. Davey was right. She'd been so busy trying to work out how long her father had been trapped in the storeroom that she had failed to consider why he'd gone there in the first place. He must have had a very compelling reason, given the state he had been in. What triggered him to come downstairs, locate the key on the hooks, make his way to the icehouse and go inside?

"Did you go in, Davey?"

Davey shook his head.

"I wouldn't mind if you had."

"I didn't think you'd want me to, miss, not without an invitation. If you see what I mean."

"Davey," Mary warned.

He flushed. "All right, I might've taken a peek," he admitted, "but it was dark and I couldn't see nothing. I didn't go down."

Connie glanced over at her father. The rage and the shame that characterized his expression when he was awake had fallen away. For now, he was sleeping peacefully. Bruised, tired, but set free for a moment from the secrets that tormented him. Victim or the architect of his own misfortunes, Connie still didn't know. But, as Davey said, it was different.

Why now?

Had Gifford been looking for something in there? Or concealing something?

Connie stood up. "Would you like to see inside properly?"

The boy's eyes flared wide. "Now?"

"My father won't wake for a few hours at least. Mary will keep an eye on him."

"What if he wakes, miss?" Mary said anxiously.

"We won't be long."

"Won't it be ever so dark, this time of night?" Davey said.

Connie smiled. "We'll take the lantern. You don't have to come, if you'd rather not. You can stay here if you like."

Davey scrambled up from the floor. "No, I'll come. What do you think you're going to find, miss? What are you looking for?"

"I don't know," she said again. "But I hope I'll recognize it when I see it. As you said, Davey, there must have been a reason for my father to go there."

"I'll fetch the lamp."

Themis Cottage
Apuldram

Brook knocked. No one answered or acknowledged him. No one asked for his name, but the door opened all the same.

He shut it quickly behind him, then stepped face first into a black curtain draped immediately in front of him. Irritated, he pushed it aside and went through into the small entrance hall.

He frowned. Odd that there was still no one to greet him. He was surprised that White hadn't arranged things better, that he wasn't here himself. At the same time, Brook felt his senses—sight, smell, touch—starting to come under pleasurable assault.

Hundreds, it seemed, of tiny flames from candles set on every surface. Reflecting in the red floor tiles and the mirror, dancing up the walls and across the low ceiling. A scent of incense from two burners on the window ledge, and the hiss and crack of gramophone music playing in another room. The air was hot and dry. His skin prickled with anticipation.

There was a narrow flight of stairs immediately ahead, a twist of red velvet brocade across the bottom, leading to the dark upstairs. Two wooden latched doors to left and right, both closed. Straight ahead there was another heavy black drape, the sort of thing you'd find backstage at a theater, partially covering another door.

Then, from somewhere, Brook heard the sound of a woman's voice. He caught his breath. His heart seemed to be keeping time with the ticking of the long-case clock. Though he couldn't see anyone, now he felt sure there were other people close by. He smiled, wondering where White was hiding himself, though he didn't call out. He didn't want to spoil things. He had hoped there might be a game to begin proceedings— perhaps a series of tasks, or questions to answer, before he was admitted—and this met all his expectations.

He liked to earn his reward.

Standing in the bedazzling hall, Brook identified other smells beneath the incense. The heady, familiar scent of perfume and desire, women's potions and powders. A Parisian boudoir, as he imagined one might look, created in the wood-lands of Apuldram.

As his eyes adapted to the shifting light, he noticed that there was a silver tray set on a wooden table near the foot of the stairs. He removed his hat and, after a moment's hesitation, his mud-caked boots and jacket, and loosened his collar. He was constrained by his outdoor clothes and he didn't expect to be leaving for some time.

He stepped forward. On the tray was a single sherry glass, filled to the top with a rich, dark liquid. He picked it up and sniffed it, took a sip. It wasn't unpleasant, a concoction of something akin to port mixed with black currant, not like a cocktail, more the consistency of a tincture or fortified wine. He assumed it was intended for him. There was also, beside the tray, an eye mask. Black velvet with a twist of feathers for the strap. He rubbed the material between his forefinger and thumb as he read the instructions on the accompanying card telling him what he was to do next. He remembered wearing a mask much like this once before.

Expectation building, Brook drained the last of his aperitif and felt the heat of the liquid hit his stomach. Then, with the mask in his hand, he walked toward the door at the end of the corridor and through into the room beyond.

Chapter 36

Blackthorn House
Fishbourne Marshes

"Shall I take it?" Connie said, as they stood at the door of the icehouse.

Davey was insisting on holding the lantern and going in first, but from the jerking of the flame, Connie realized he was terrified.

"It's not heavy, miss. I can manage."

"I know," she said, not wanting to embarrass the boy. "But since I'm the taller of the two of us, it makes more sense for me to hold it. We'll be able to see more that way."

"Well, when you put it like that . . ."

They swapped positions.

"Ready?" she said in a firm voice, despite the fact that she was equally nervous about what they were going to find down there in the dark.

"As I'll ever be, miss."

Holding the light high above her head, Connie slowly started to walk down the narrow brick steps, with Davey following behind.

A smell of blood and damp straw wafted up to meet her, the musty odor of underground air rarely disturbed. She hung the lantern on the iron hook set in the roof at the bottom of the stairs. The pale yellow light sent distorted shadows scattering through the long, narrow space. She tried to remember when she had last come to the storeroom.

Years ago, possibly. Not since they had first moved in.

*

It had been another wet spring. April 1905.

All the packing crates and trunks and the heavy coats of the moving men dripping with rain as they trudged backward and forward along the footpath between Blackthorn House and the Sayers Removals cart waiting at the end of Mill Lane. It took so long, the horses became restless.

Gifford had taken the house furnished, so there had been no large pieces to move. A few cases of books—not considered valuable enough to include in the forced liquidation sale—and two or three trunks of clothes, with her father's tools hidden inside to save them from the bailiff. Then the wooden cases, sealed to keep the moths and parasites from getting in, containing the remaining exhibits. All the best tableaux of posed birds had been sold to pay their debts, and, she later realized, her medical bills. Only a few individual cases—the more commonplace birds no one wanted to furnish their homes with anymore—had survived the auction and come with them to Fishbourne.

Not the swan, though. Someone had purchased that.

Sayers' men had carried the wooden crates down into the icehouse; Gifford had made it ready by covering the dirt floor in straw, to absorb the moisture in the air, and set paraffin heaters burning to settle the temperature. When the men were gone, sent on their way with a glass of beer each and a packet of cigarettes to share among the three of them, he had looked at the crates stacked disconsolately against the wall—what was left of his once-successful business—then turned his back and walked away, saying they could be dealt with at a later date.

He had never mentioned it again. He had never asked for her help. The look of defeat in his eyes, the ruin of his ambition and reputation, had haunted Connie ever since.

*

Davey's awed voice brought her back to the present.

"It's like Aladdin's cave in here."

Connie looked around, seeing what the boy was seeing, and found it hard to believe her eyes. It was no longer a sad store-room for crates too painful to open. All the contents had been removed, polished and put on display. Had Gifford done this? All alone? Lining each of the walls of the long rectangular brick room were the birds: partridges, wood pigeons and a pair of collared doves, a hen blackbird and her mate, the display cases set on top of the packing crates. Domed bell jars and square boxes with her father's distinctive label clearly stuck on the side: PRESERVED BY MR. CROWLEY GIFFORD—STUFFER OF BIRDS.

Tears came to her eyes. At some point, without her knowing, her father had unpacked his treasures and tried to re-create his museum with the few pieces remaining to him. Even the sign that had once sat above the door was here: GIFFORD'S WORLD-FAMOUS HOUSE OF AVIAN CURIOSITIES. No one had wanted that.

She reached out and touched the case closest to her, an oystercatcher, another black-and-white bird, with its long red bill standing against a painted shoreline. The label was peeling away from the wood, crumbling to dust.

"Didn't think it'd be like this, miss," Davey said in a hushed voice. "It's amazing. Look at that." He pointed at a tiny preserved blue tit. "And what about that up there!"

Connie looked up to a nest suspended from the ceiling. "It must have been wonderful, miss."

"It was," she said, wiping a tear from her eye. "There was ten times as much then. People came from all over Sussex."

Almost straightaway, her thoughts started to darken. Why had her father re-created the museum in secret? To remember the glory days of his past? Or was it some kind of macabre shrine? Evidence of a guilty conscience, of something he had done?

"And look at this, miss," Davey said. "I reckon they knew, that lot out there. Reckon that's why they came. So many of them."

In the dim light, Connie could see that the far end of the store was occupied by a single large case. Even from this distance, she knew it was a display she had never seen before.

She unhooked the lantern and walked slowly toward it. This was not a piece Gifford had brought from the museum, but something he had created here. Something else he had done without her knowledge.

She put the lamp on the case and stood beside Davey to look at the preserved birds. A large label was pinned to the top of the case: THE CORVIDAE CLUB. Her father's handwriting.

She could see marks in the dust where the display had recently been opened. She looked closer, and saw something protruding from beneath the base.

"Can you get that out for me, Davey?"

He pushed his small fingers between the rim and the base, and pulled out a folded piece of paper. As he handed it to Connie, something fell into her hand.

"Villainous-looking creatures," Davey said.

Connie looked at the scrap of yellow ribbon, then at the four beautiful, glossy birds: first, a gray-hooded jackdaw; next, a magpie in its evening-dress plumage and iridescent tail feathers; third, a sooty rook with sharp eyes and thick, wooded beak. *Corvus frugilegus.*

"A storytelling of rooks."

She was suddenly struck by a memory of how she'd learned all those whimsical collective nouns, reciting them by rote until they were fixed in her head: a colony of jackdaws, a tiding of magpies, a parliament or a clamor or a storytelling of rooks. It was Cassie who had taught her.

"Cassie," she said. "Cassandra."

"Who's she?" Davey asked.

"My friend," Connie heard herself say.

Finally, after ten years missing, Cassie stepped out from the shadows of Connie's fragile memory and back into the light. Now Connie could see her clearly. The tall, spirited young woman with the chestnut hair and the bright eyes, the woman with the lilting voice, teaching Connie poetry and plays and rhymes. Employed as a governess, a companion, an older sister for a motherless child. Cassie, who called her father Gifford, a habit Connie had copied. Eight years older than Connie, a girl herself when she first arrived.

A girl with a red ribbon in her hair.

She and Connie had written all the Latin labels for the museum for Gifford, some in Greek too for the story displays, giving each bird a character: Athena, the goddess of reason and wisdom, for a tawny owl, commissioned as a gift for a wedding anniversary; Themis, the goddess of divine justice, for a kestrel presented to a man called to the bar.

Connie put her hand over her mouth to stop herself from

shouting out. To stop herself from being overwhelmed by the deluge of memories flooding into her mind. She and Cassie growing up together. Cassie, who had cared for her and loved her and taught her the value of friendship. Connie had to force herself to stay on her feet as Davey kept talking and talking beside her.

"Mind you," he said, tapping the glass in front of the fourth bird, "I wouldn't want to be on the wrong side of him."

"*Corvus corone*," she said automatically, as she unfolded the scrap of paper she was still clutching and read what was written: JACKDAW, MAGPIE, ROOK, CROW.

Four names. Four birds.

"Anything interesting?" Davey asked, peering at the sheet.

"I don't know," Connie replied honestly.

For a moment, the boy held his tongue.

"A storytelling of rooks, I like that one," he said. "So what about crows? I know crows don't go about in groups so much, but if there was to be a whole lot of them together, then what?"

Connie looked back to the display case: four birds, representing four men? The members of the Corvidae Club?

"A murder," she said. "It's a murder of crows."

Chapter 37

The Bull's Head
Fishbourne

It was two o'clock in the morning. The last of the customers had long gone and Gregory Joseph had the place to himself.

Knowing that Vera was laid out in the barn didn't bother him. He'd help take the coffin to the church tomorrow and then it would be over. He didn't have any idea who'd killed her—he'd seen the marks around her neck—but he reckoned it had to have been someone in the graveyard. He'd seen her carry the cages into the church. She'd been alive and kicking at eleven o'clock when she'd put on the coat, but after that, he'd lost sight of her.

He was sorry it had happened. Birdie had always been funny in the head, though the spell in Graylingwell had sorted her out for a while, but there'd never been any harm in her.

He looked down at his grazed knuckles. Could White have had something to do with it? He'd been there in the rain that night. Given what Joseph now knew about him, it was in his character. Gifford had been there too, and that made more sense. Vera hadn't been in the water for a week, that much was obvious, so if she'd been done for that night, where had the body been kept? And if it wasn't something to do with Gifford, why had she turned up so close to Blackthorn House? He couldn't make head nor tail of it.

He blew a final smoke ring in the air and stubbed out his cigarette. Then he sat back in the chair, folded his arms across his chest and tried to sleep.

Seconds later, his eyes snapped open.

Someone was moving about in the private bar downstairs. Straightaway, he was on his feet. He wasn't paid as a watchman, but Pine let him sleep here in return for keeping an eye on things until he found another job.

Now he heard the unmistakable sound of a glass being taken down from the shelf above the pumps. A burglar was hardly likely to hang about for a drink. He crept across the floorboards and down in his bare feet, carrying his boots, pausing only to put them on at the foot of the stairs.

In the light coming in from the moon, Joseph saw that the front door showed no sign of having been tampered with. All the windows were closed; nothing seemed to be broken or damaged. The only sound he could hear was a smattering of rain against the glass, like pebbles being thrown.

He reached out his right hand and, without revealing himself, pushed open the door. Nothing. He straightened up, then peered into the room.

A single figure was standing at the bar, cupping a glass in his hands.

Joseph gave a sigh of relief, then stepped into the saloon.

"Everything all right, sir?"

Crowther didn't look around. "Where've you been all day, Joseph?"

"I'm sorry," he said, surprised by Crowther's hostile tone. "I didn't know you needed me."

"Important work?"

"Paid work. Apuldram way," Joseph said, not seeing any need to hold that back. "Helping a lady out moving into a new cottage."

"A lady? What was her name?"

"I don't know," he replied, meeting Crowther's gaze. "It didn't come up, and I didn't ask."

He watched Crowther drain his drink, go around behind the bar and refill his glass.

"Why you, Joseph? How did she get to hear about you?"

Joseph paused. "I don't rightly know, Mr. Crowther. Private recommendation, I suppose." He narrowed his eyes, not sure what was going on. Not sure why Crowther, who was usually cordial, appeared to be so angry. "Is there a problem with my work, Mr. Crowther?" he said. "Everything you asked me to do, I did."

Crowther swilled the liquid in his glass. "Do you know where Dr. Woolston is? Have you found out anything?"

"No one knows. Not his man, that clerk of his, no one."

Crowther continued in the same weary voice, as if Joseph hadn't spoken.

"And you don't know why our friend Pennicott's sniffing around?"

"Pennicott?" Joseph said, genuinely surprised.

"Yes, Pennicott. He was at Blackthorn House this afternoon. Which, if you had been watching, rather than robbing some mysterious lady in Apuldram, you would have seen." He paused. "Inquiring into the whereabouts of Dr. Woolston, it appears. Pearce reported him missing."

Joseph's heart was in his mouth, though he kept his voice steady.

"Oh?"

"Is that all you've got to say, man?" In the half-light of the bar, Joseph felt the full force of Crowther's anger. "I advise you to tell me the truth. Do you know where Dr. Woolston has gone to ground, Joseph?"

Joseph managed to hold his gaze.

"No, sir. Haven't seen him since he left the Old Salt Mill on Wednesday afternoon."

"Did he say where he was going?"

"No."

"And what about Gifford? Picked up anything about where he is?"

Joseph frowned. "Didn't his daughter say he was convalescing with friends?"

Crowther laughed. "And you believe that? The fact is, despite your very generous remuneration, you have failed to find out anything."

Joseph felt his temper spike, but he managed to hold his tongue.

Crowther carefully placed his glass down on the counter. "I want to know where Woolston is. I want to know where Gifford is. Do you understand?"

"Yes, sir."

Crowther turned and walked out of the room. Joseph heard the front door to the inn open, then close again. He let out a long sigh of relief. For the first time, a sense of foreboding swept through him and made him question whether he was doing the right thing. What *was* the right thing?

Gregory Joseph thought for a moment longer, then pushed his conscience aside. The right thing was what gave him an advantage. It was the philosophy he'd lived by for long enough, and mostly it had served him well. Look after number one, let the others look after themselves.

But as he went back upstairs, he knew something had changed.

Chapter 38

Blackthorn House
Fishbourne Marshes

Three o'clock in the morning.

Connie was sitting in the same armchair, listening to the rain battering against the window. Heavy and relentless and steady. The wind howled and gusted, chased down the chimney, bringing cold, damp air into the drawing room. A half-moon, silver, cast its ghostly light over the rough waters surging into the creek in the rising of the tide.

She looked around the room. Davey was asleep, curled up on the settee with his thin arms across his face. Mary was dozing on an upright chair set beside the daybed, where Gifford lay peacefully and quietly. For the time being at least, he was free of his troubled, tormented past.

Connie removed the pins from her hair and let it fall loose. She wanted to rest, but her agitated thoughts would not leave her in peace. She was cold, too, though she suspected it came from within rather than because of the temperature in the room. Mary had lit a fire, but it had long since burned out.

She listened, and heard a growl of thunder in the distance. The rain grew heavier and a violent gust of wind hit the corner of the house, making the building seem to creak and sigh around her. In the distance, out at sea, a flash of lightning.

Connie was waiting for the night to reveal itself. She was listening for the truth of whatever was hiding in the darkness.

*

Half dozing, she'd suffered the nightmare she'd had once or twice in the past. Except now she knew it wasn't a nightmare. Not imagination. It was true, a memory of something awful and real that she had witnessed.

White skin, blue lips, hair the color of autumn fanned across the wooden floor.

Blood, skin, bone.

A room of glass, candlelight flickering, reflected and refracted. The scent of perfume and male desire and cigar smoke.

Black masks; one black and white: jackdaw, magpie, rook, crow. A place of glittering glass and sequins, feathers and beads and the scent of sherry spilling on the old wooden floor.

Something else too, a crescendo of noise and smells and wildness.

The heat and the slip of blood on the polished wood. A possession. Flesh on flesh. Forced and brutal, violent.

Connie could remember her twelve-year-old self, understanding yet not understanding. Looking down through the banisters at a dark crescent, a semicircle of coats and men's backs. Dress shoes and patent leather. Cassie shouting, her hands hitting against the air, trying to stop them doing what they were doing.

The violent, sudden silence of a life extinguished. Choked. A red ribbon in a man's hands.

Fear becoming anger. Connie knowing it was wrong, that

she had to help. Had to save her friend from the black brows and the beaks and the red ribbon pulled tight around Cassie's neck.

Skin, bone, blood.

Shouting and running. In the darkness, falling and falling and falling through the air. Free, for an instant, flying and flying. Weightless.

Her head hitting the stone floor at the foot of the stairs. Nothing. Everything gone in an instant.

Innocence, love, home, safety. All gone.

*

Connie found herself on her feet. Without warning, she was doubled over by grief. Crippled by the memory of Cassie, her friend and teacher. The knowledge that she had once been cared for and cherished and looked after. An understanding, now, of what she had lost. What had been taken.

After light, darkness. After love, silence. Only the beating of her child's heart left alone. She hugged her arms tight around her. These feelings of loss were habitual. Often they crept up on her in the small hours, taunting her with a vision of what life might have been. She had always thought that it was, perhaps, because she had never known her mother.

Now she knew it was Cassie she grieved for.

How cruel it was, after all these years, to finally remember. To remember, only to understand how much she had lost.

Cassie was dead. Murdered in front of Connie's eyes. Had been dead for ten years.

"Are you there?"

She jumped at the sound of Gifford's voice, loud in the

sleeping room. Outside, the storm was gathering force. Cracking and pushing at the house, surrounding them and rattling the windows. Connie went immediately to his side.

"It's me, Gifford," she said quietly. "It's only me."

His vague eyes danced around the moonlit room, then came to rest on her. To her horror, she saw tears.

"You're safe," he said, breathing out the words with a sigh. "You're a good girl, Connie. A good girl. You look after your poor old dad. You never left me."

Connie wanted to remain in the past for a while longer. To stay with Cassie. To remember more of their shared life, without giving in to grief. But, as she had done so many times before, she locked her private emotions away, the better to tend to her father instead.

"Can you remember what happened? You went into the storeroom to look for something and perhaps you fell? Hit your head? Do you remember?"

"Proof," he said, tapping the side of his nose. "Names, evidence. I kept my word, girl. I didn't talk."

"The Corvidae Club. That's right, isn't it? You made a display case. It's beautiful, I saw it. Is that why you went into the storeroom?"

But Gifford was lost in his own thoughts, not hearing hers. He started to shake his head.

"Made no difference in the end. She's dead. All of it for nothing; she died all the same." He suddenly raised his head and looked her in the eye. "Cassie's dead, you see."

She nodded, both of them grieving, finally acknowledging the loss that had kept them separate from each other for ten years.

"I know, I remember now. I remember her."

"All these years." He was shaking his head from side to side.

"All these years, I kept my word. Said nothing. Tried to do right by her. And now?" He gave a shrug, arms and hands flapping at the air. "Dead. They haven't even told me about the funeral. Why won't they tell me? Don't I have the right to know when they're putting her in the ground?"

Mary suddenly woke up, sitting bolt upright on the hard chair. Davey stirred too. Without speaking, Connie gestured to them both to slip away. Looking anxious, Mary gathered the boy to her and guided him out of the room.

Connie put her hand on Gifford's arm. "Don't distress yourself."

"I thought I saw her. In the churchyard. Her hair, blue coat, thought it was her." He let out a long sigh. "A ghost."

He suddenly howled. The sound, so full of pain, chilled Connie to the bone.

"It wasn't a ghost," she tried to explain. "It was a real woman. Vera Barker, she looked like Cassie. At least, I think she did."

"Ghost," he said. "Knew it couldn't have been. They told me. Wrote to me. Been dead a week."

"Cassie's been dead longer than that, Father," she said as gently as she could.

"April it was, just when we were ready. Prepared." Again, in the midst of his muddled ramblings, he suddenly looked Connie clearly in the eye. "Influenza, the letter said. Why won't they tell me when she's to be buried? I have the right, don't I, Connie? I've got the right to know."

She could see Gifford was working himself into another state. If that happened, nothing she could say or do would get through to him.

"Of course you have the right," she said, trying to pick her way through his incoherent comments. "I'll tell them."

He nodded. "You do that, you do that. All these years wait-ing. I paid the bills. Hospital has to tell me. I have a right."

Connie turned cold. "Graylingwell Hospital?"

Gifford suddenly gave a bark of laughter, then put his finger to his lips and shushed. "We kept it secret," he said, leaning toward her. "It's what they had to believe, to keep her safe. We kept it to ourselves." He reached across and put his finger on Connie's lips instead. "Not even Jennie knew."

"Jennie?"

But his eyes were clouding in confusion. The moment of clarity, of transparency, had gone. He dropped his thin hand on Connie's shoulder.

"Had to keep you safe too."

Chapter 39

North Street
Chichester

Four o'clock.

The rain was drumming on the roofs of the houses in North Street, ricocheting off the red tiles and the gray slate, washing everything clean. The Pallants and Little London, Lion Street and Chapel Street.

Harry couldn't sleep. For hours, since he returned home, he'd been pacing up and down, listening for the sound of his father's latchkey in the lock. Wondering where he was, if he was all right, what tomorrow might bring. The sight of Lewis's face when he'd arrived home, the way it seemed to collapse in upon itself when he saw it was only Harry, not the old man, had been heartbreaking in itself. The butler had heard nothing, seen no one. The only thing that had happened was that a personal note for Dr. Woolston had been delivered.

Harry lit another cigarette, letting his thoughts return to Connie. It had been awful to leave, though he could hardly have stayed. His presence in the house at night would certainly have attracted comment.

Then to have been obliged to keep up a stilted conversation with Crowther as they rushed along the sodden footpath toward Mill Lane, when all Harry could think about was what had happened to his father. That had been difficult too. A decent man, Crowther—and very charitable of him to send Harry back to Chichester in his own carriage—but at the same time, there was something about him that made Harry think he was always observing from the outside, rather than being part of it.

He stared blankly at the canvas again. Then, unable to face the evidence of his failure any longer, he went to his easel and turned the picture to face the wall. He'd start something new in the morning.

He shook his head.

No, not tomorrow. Today. Today he and Connie would meet and share what new information they had garnered. Harry had nothing to offer, but perhaps she would. He would speak to Pearce. Ask him what the devil he was playing at speaking to Pennicott.

But then, if there was still no sign of his father—of Connie's, either—they would go to Pennicott themselves. Lay everything before him and ask for his help. Neither he nor Connie wanted to involve the police, but with each hour that passed, the knot of cold fear in his stomach grew stronger.

Harry looked at the rain streaming down the windowpanes and, in the distance, heard a first rumble of thunder. He wondered what Connie was doing. Was she sleeping? Was she awake and anxious like him?

Would she come? Or in the gray light of day would she think better of it? Would she think his fears were ridiculous? These sorts of things simply didn't happen in a place like Chichester. It was absurd, all of it. Or would be, except for the fact that two men were missing and a young woman was dead. Murdered, if Connie was right.

Harry poured himself a nightcap. The bells of the cathedral struck the quarter hour. Then, suddenly, he realized what he had to do. There was only one way to fill the hours until Connie arrived at ten o'clock.

He found a blank canvas, about ten inches by eight, and flung the old one onto the armchair. Not even stopping to put on his painting smock, he took a brush from the jar, wiped it on a cloth, then prepared his palette. He didn't need a sketch, he didn't need her sitting in front of him. In his mind's eye, he could picture every inch, every shade of her changing expression, the way she held her head. He closed his eyes, remembering how her brows furrowed when she was thinking, bringing to mind the color of her hair, the tint of her skin.

Her image clear, he opened his eyes and began to paint.

Little by little, Connie's features began to emerge. Soon, she was looking straight out of the painting at him, with the jackdaw held gently in her hands.

He [Bécoeur] opened his bird in the usual manner, that is to say by the middle of the belly, he easily took out the body by this opening, without cutting off the extremities, he then removed the flesh by the aid of a scalpel, taking the precaution to preserve all the ligaments; he anointed the skin, and put the skeleton in its place, carefully dispersing the feathers on each side. He ran the head through with an iron wire, in which he had formed a little ring at nearly the third of its length; the smallest side passed into the rump, in such a manner that the ring of the iron wire united to pass into the little ring; he bent these extremities within, and fixed them with a string to the iron in the middle of the vertebral column. He replaced the flesh by flax or chopped cotton, sewed up the bird, placed it on a foot or support of wood, and gave it a suitable attitude, of which he was always sure, for a bird thus mounted could only bend in its natural position.

TAXIDERMY: OR, THE ART OF COLLECTING, PREPARING,
AND MOUNTING OBJECTS OF NATURAL HISTORY

Mrs. R. Lee
Longman & Co., Paternoster Row, London, 1820

He was my greatest challenge.

Such a large man, cumbersome, I knew that the only way was for him to come to me of his own volition. That was not difficult. A message too clear to misunderstand, an invitation that he would find impossible to resist.

I killed him alone. Others helped with the purchasing of candles and drapes. The tincture was easy to make, using Birdie's recipe. She knew every plant, every extract, had laid out everything I might need. I waited for her to come back. I know, now, she is dead. Though I do not know which of them is responsible, I know they murdered her. Vera was simple and kindhearted, she helped care for me once. Then, I cared for her.

Her death is on my conscience.

*

I am listening for the sound of men's boots on the path, men's fists at the door. I do not think I will survive much longer. I feel them circling, like the gulls overhead, closing in on me.

I wanted Brook to know what was happening to him. A man so violent, so cruel. To watch the knife slicing him open, and be unable to stop me. Fair retribution. I wanted him to see the way his fat and flesh fell from the blade. But he was too strong, too hard to restrain, so I knew I could not take the risk.

Belladonna in his drink. A pleasing touch, don't you think?

I removed his heart first, red and still beating, still pumping. Watching it slow, and slow, stutter and die. Next his lungs and his stomach, the endless gray rope of intestines, the texture of uncooked dough. Peeling back his skin, layer after layer, my hands paddling in his chest.

When the knife was no longer equal to the task, I used the saw stolen from the butcher's shop. Kneading and scraping out and pressing down, until I'd made a cavity large enough for my purposes. When it does not matter what damage is done, little skill is required.

The rain started to fall harder as I positioned the hooks. Striking off the roof and the paved path leading to the door. Even now, I hear the suck and roar of the sea, pulling at the shingle with the turn of each wave. Higher and higher, until it sounds as if it is lapping against the walls.

I heard the first warning rumbles of thunder out at sea and knew the storm was beginning as I pushed the first of the wires into place. Jabbing under his skin, hardening against my caresses. Forcing the wire into his shoulders and his wrists, into the gaping flesh of his stomach and his neck. Two separate twists of wire on either side.

The candles burned low, and still I worked.

Next, the wood wool and the feathers, filling out the cavities as if stuffing a mattress with straw. A different sort of life, like one of Madame Tussaud's waxworks, but better. All around me on the floor, stained strips of bloodied cotton, the coppery smell, both sharp and sweet at the back of my throat.

Finally, I took up the trussing needle, and with fingers sore from the hours of working, I began to sew. Pushing the needle through the cooling flesh and drawing it out again, picking up tattered threads of skin. I always did have a delicate hand for embroidery.

Finally, the moon slipped back to earth and I was done. Exhausted, barely able to stand or to think, but satisfied with my work.

Now morning is here, though the sky remains dark. Great black banks of cloud are rolling up the estuary, bringing with them harder and heavier rain. On an instant, a fork of lightning illuminates the outline of the Old Salt Mill in the center of the channel, and the houses around the edge of Fishbourne Creek.

I think of both of you. Are you sleeping?

The tide is continuing to rise. I can see the swell crashing against the defenses and wonder if the sluice gates will hold for a little while longer. I want to rest, but my thoughts will not let me go.

Soon, now. Soon it will be over.

One more to be brought to account. Then, at last, I shall be at peace.

Chapter 40

Blackthorn House
Fishbourne Marshes

Connie looked out on the drowning world. The purple sky, the black sea, the trees and spartina grasses, the wych elm and the weeping willows: everything seemed to have merged into one. The waves were hitting the sluice gates and throwing angry white foam high up into the air. Even with the windows shut, she could hear the frantic rattling of the wheel in the Old Salt Mill, turning, rumbling, faster and faster.

"When's the next high tide?" she asked, looking out over the marshes. Rain was streaming down the windowpanes, obscuring the view.

Davey came to stand beside her. "Five o'clock, give or take. It's going out now, though there's barely any difference between low and high water." He paused. "Do you think the gates will hold, miss?"

"The miller will do what's necessary," she said, with more confidence than she felt. The boy knew as well as she did that the combination of the full moon, the high spring tides and heavy rain was dangerous. "He'll open the gates. Send the water back out to the sea."

"They couldn't keep back the floods in January," Davey said. "Water even got as far as the bottom of Salthill Road. Mary said Ma Christie had to rush the little ones upstairs to keep them safe when the water came in under the door. None of them can swim, not even Jennie. Had to wait for a boat to come and rescue them from the first-floor window."

"We're better prepared this time," Connie said only half believing her own words. "We know what to expect. Fishbourne has stood firm against the sea for hundreds, maybe thousands of years. The land is designed to cope with such extremes."

At the head of the creek, she could see the tide washing against the brick wall of the garden of Salt Mill House. The sea was taking back the land. Already the fields closest to the shore were half submerged. And it would only get worse.

"Shall I stay here with you, to keep an eye, until Mary comes back?" Davey asked.

"Thank you," Connie said, realizing that the boy was frightened. Something he'd said had lodged itself in her mind, but she couldn't work out what it was.

"Blackthorn House survived the storms of March and April," she continued. "This is no different. We just have to pray the rain doesn't get heavier."

"It'll be worse later with the next high tide, come what may."

She feared he was right. Another front was threatening out at sea. And even if the rain stopped now, which it showed no signs of doing, the next few hours were critical.

She glanced over at the daybed, where her father lay sleeping. Their long conversation in the middle of the night had worn him out.

Connie had remained awake, waiting for the dawn. Thinking and wondering and trying to remember.

When Gifford woke again, they would talk more. However painful it might be for her father, the truth had to be acknowledged. There was no other way to bring the story to an end.

And to understand what was happening now. Connie didn't know what she feared, only that she knew in her bones there was something more to come.

She looked, again, at her father. Gifford might sleep for many hours more, long enough to give Connie the chance to get to Chichester and back. Despite the threat of flooding, she was determined to keep to the arrangement she and Harry had made to meet at ten o'clock. She had so much more to tell him now, though she dreaded the hurt it might cause. He clearly loved his father, as she loved Gifford.

She kept telling herself that when she arrived at the house in North Street, she would discover Dr. Woolston was there. That it had all been a misunderstanding. In truth, she knew this was wishful thinking.

She looked at the clock, working out how long she might be gone. The only possible moment to attempt the journey was now, in the brief break in the clouds. The rain had eased a little and the wind, though strong, had softened. There would be a few hours' respite before the tide turned and the next storm blew in with the rising waters.

Davey could hold the fort until Mary returned. She had sent the girl home at six o'clock. Mrs. Christie would have been worried sick when her daughter hadn't come home last night. Connie wouldn't be in Chichester for more than an hour or two. Besides, the thought of Harry looking out of the window on North Street, waiting for her and losing heart when he realized she wasn't coming, was too much to bear.

"I'm going to have to go to Chichester for a while," she said. "Can I leave you in charge?"

Davey's eyes widened with alarm. "But the footpath's all but underwater already, Miss Gifford. Even if you get through, what about if you can't get home to us?"

"While I'm gone, can you stack sandbags against the doors," she said, touched by the boy referring to Blackthorn House as home. "Mary will be back soon, and she should check the pails in the attic straightaway. Start with the icehouse first, it's the most vulnerable, then the side door and the back door." She looked at him, wondering if he knew the word. "That's to say, the most likely to let the water in."

"I know what 'vulnerable' means," he said proudly. "Ma Christie told me."

Suddenly Connie realized what had snagged her attention. In the January floods, Davey had said, Mrs. Christie had had to get the twins upstairs because none of them could swim— "not even Jennie."

Jennie.

Last night, Gifford had said that Jennie could be trusted. Then, later, that "not even Jennie knew." Connie had registered the name and stored it in her memory.

"What are Mary's little sisters called?" she asked quickly.

"Maisie and Polly. Twins, though they don't look the same."

"Not Jennie?"

Davey looked at his boots. "I didn't mean any disrespect by saying that."

Connie put her hand under Davey's chin and tilted his face up.

"Disrespect to whom?"

"Mrs. Christie," he said, still looking awkward. "Given she's a grown-up, and everything. Calling her by her Christian name."

A memory of a round, comfortable-looking face looking down on her, nursing her through her illness. Not Cassie, an older woman.

Jennie Christie?

No, that wasn't right. A different surname. Not Christie.

Connie thought back to their meeting at the post office. Mrs. Christie's odd question, and how she had seemed familiar, though they'd never met before.

North Street
Chichester

Harry stood back and looked at the canvas.

His hands were shaking from the repeated cups of coffee laced with whisky he'd had to keep him going through the night. His clothes, and the room, were impregnated with cigarette smoke, one lit from the tip of the one before. The only way to withstand the bleak, nighttime fears for his father was to drink and smoke and to paint.

Not think.

He hadn't shaved and he was still in his clothes from last night, but he had finished. She—the portrait—was beautiful. A perfect picture of Connie. He tilted his head to one side. Her hair was the right mixture of autumn browns. Had he caught her direct, clever stare? He thought so. The texture of her skin? The only fault, if he was pressed to find one, was the bird. The jackdaw's feathers were a little too black, its eyes too dull. It didn't matter. Connie was perfect.

He put down the brush, wiped his hands and walked to the window.

What if she didn't come?

He placed his hands on the frame and, for a moment, rested his forehead against the cold, steam-slicked glass. Rainwater was streaming down North Street, lapping at the steps of the

Wheatsheaf Hotel. From time to time, a carriage went past, its wheels sending a spray up onto the sidewalks, like sparks from an anvil.

Harry's thoughts spiraled, tying his stomach in knots. Each worry drove out the one before. Trying not to despair, hoping his father would return of his own accord led him back to Connie's father, then from Gifford back to Connie herself. The whole cycle beginning all over again.

How could she possibly get through? How could he be so selfish as to want her to attempt it? He couldn't expect her to venture out in weather like this, it would be madness.

"Do you think it would be wise to eat something, sir?"

Startled, Harry turned to see Lewis standing in the doorway. The old servant looked gray, as if he also hadn't slept.

"Any news, Lewis?"

"No, sir." He paused. "Mrs. Lewis could prepare some eggs."

"My stomach's not up to it."

"Perhaps some dry toast and tea?"

Harry shook his head. "What time is it?" he asked.

"A quarter to seven, sir."

Harry let his head rest back against the window. So early, too early. Nearly three hours before Connie came. If she came at all.

"I will ask Mrs. Lewis to lay breakfast in the dining room," Lewis said.

Harry was about to argue, then realized that Lewis also needed something to do to keep his worries at bay. Routine, keeping up appearances, what else could he do while they waited for news?

"Thank you, Lewis," he said. "Quarter to seven, did you say?"

"Yes, sir."

Harry lit another cigarette and smoked it to the very end,

wedged between the second and third fingers of his right hand, then went through to the dining room.

The letter addressed to his father lay untouched on the salver on the hall table.

Harry stopped. In normal circumstances, he wouldn't dream of opening the old man's private correspondence. But these weren't normal circumstances.

He tore open the envelope. Dated yesterday morning, it was a terse, clear request that his father should immediately be in touch. His eyes jumped to the signature at the bottom of the page. He read the name, and turned cold.

This couldn't be right.

He checked the time scrawled in a rushed hand at the top of the letter. Twelve o'clock on Thursday, the second of May. Before Harry had returned to Fishbourne, before his conversation in the Bull's Head, before Sergeant Pennicott had paid his visit to Blackthorn House.

How could this letter have been written before that?

Harry gasped as the reality hit him. They had been seeing everything from the wrong point of view. He'd been taken in; they all had. He grabbed his hat and mackintosh.

"Lewis," he shouted.

He and Connie had wanted to avoid talking to Pennicott yesterday until they were sure of what they knew. Now, there was no time to lose. The policeman was honest, Harry had evidence of that. With Pennicott, right was right and wrong was wrong. He would pursue the truth, regardless of how unpalatable that truth might turn out to be.

He pushed from his mind the question of why his father came to be receiving such a summons in the first instance.

"Lewis!"

The butler came running into the hall. "Is there news, sir?"

"Soon, I hope," Harry said urgently. "A Miss Gifford is due to arrive at ten. I should be back long before then. But if not, ask her to please wait. She *must* wait."

Whyke Road
Chichester

Ten minutes later, the rain streaming off his hat and coat, Harry was standing beneath the blue light of the modest police house off St. Pancras.

"Pennicott?" he yelled, out of breath from running across town. He banged on the door again, not caring who he disturbed.

The policeman answered the door in his shirt sleeves. "Mr. Woolston?"

"Sergeant, we weren't completely frank with you yesterday."

Pennicott wiped the last of the shaving soap from his chin, then flicked the flannel over his shoulder.

"Who might 'we' be, sir?"

"Miss Gifford and I. We . . ."

Harry stopped, not sure where to begin. Connie was protective of her father, mindful of his poor reputation. He felt Pennicott's cool, appraising eyes on him, but he could see there was sympathy, too.

"I was at Blackthorn House yesterday afternoon when you called. Miss Gifford told me of your conversation, and I think . . ." He stopped again. If he confided in Pennicott now, there would be no going back. He looked at the policeman's honest face. "There are things we need to tell you."

Pennicott peered out into the rain-drenched street. "Is Miss Gifford with you?"

"Not yet. She and I arranged to meet at ten. It's just . . ." He thrust the letter at Pennicott. "When I saw from whom this had come, I had to come at once. Don't you see? He can't have known. When he wrote this letter to my father, he can't have known. Not unless he was responsible."

Pennicott scanned the letter, saw the signature at the foot of the page, then stood back.

"You had better come in, Mr. Woolston."

Chapter 41

Mill Lane
Fishbourne

Connie walked as fast as she dared, her boots sliding in the mud. Despite what she'd said to Davey, she couldn't remember conditions as terrible as this. Water was lapping over the first of the bridges across the creek. It was impossible to know if it was the sheer volume of fresh water making its way from the chalk downs to the sea, or the powerful tides forcing salt water up and over the land.

The stream where Vera's body had been found was now a river, swollen by the overnight rain and the surge of the neap tide. Only the tops of the cattails were visible; the rest was hidden beneath the angry surface of the sea. With each pulse of the current, more of the brackish, swirling water came up over the banks and onto the grass.

The wooden handrail on the second of the bridges was slippery, green beneath her glove, and Connie almost fell, but she held firm and carefully made her way over. The third bridge was covered by leaves and broken branches.

Water was roaring through the sluice gate by Fishbourne Mill. The driveway to Salt Mill House was already under an inch of water. It wouldn't take much for Slay Lodge to flood too. She looked at Pendrills, where yesterday she had seen the magpies. Today, the roof was empty. The birds had taken shelter.

For the third time, Connie stopped and looked back in the direction she'd come. Should she turn around? If Blackthorn House was cut off, what would happen to Gifford in his fragile condition? Then she strengthened her resolve once more. She hoped she could trust Davey. She wasn't going to be long, after all. This was her only chance, before the next high tide.

She peered through the mist and rain and thought of Harry, waiting for her. She had to tell him what she had found out.

Slay Lodge
Fishbourne

From an upstairs window in Slay Lodge, Charles Crowther caught a glimpse of Connie Gifford's back, before she turned the corner onto the main road and disappeared from view.

He was worried about the young woman. She was carrying a great deal on her shoulders, and he wondered what could possibly have brought her out in such dreadful conditions. News about her father?

Crowther went quickly downstairs and followed her out into Mill Lane, holding his mackintosh over his bare head.

"Miss Gifford," he shouted, but his voice was lost in the cracking of the wind.

West Street
Chichester

The bells of the cathedral were striking eight as Sutton fumbled with the keys, struggling to open the front door. Rain dripped down the inside of his collar, and his fingers were cold and stiff.

He stumbled into the entrance hall. He stamped his feet on the mat, turned his umbrella into West Street before propping it open to dry. The same familiar sinking feeling came over him at the thought of another day's work. Being shouted at, menaced, pushed and prodded, made to feel foolish.

Hanging his sodden coat on the hatstand, hoping it wouldn't drip too badly—Mr. Brook wouldn't take kindly to that— he picked up a crumpled ball of wastepaper from the floor. He wondered how he'd missed it when he'd gone home last evening.

He opened the glass doors and walked into the vestibule. He wrinkled his nose, detecting whisky and cigar smoke, and his heart sank further. The smell, held in the damp air, gave away the fact that Mr. Brook had returned to the office from Goodwood. Sutton had left at his usual time, not a minute before, but Brook nonetheless would have been furious to find the office unattended.

Sutton sighed. The best he could hope for was that Harold Woolston took it upon himself to turn up today. If he did, having been absent for two days without permission, then Mr. Brook might take his anger out on Woolston instead and leave his clerk alone.

He dropped the screwed-up letter in the rubbish bin, got out the appointments diary and ledger and arranged his pen, ink and pencils. Whatever time Mr. Brook did arrive, he wanted to be ready and waiting.

Main Road
Fishbourne

"I don't need you to come with me, Ma," Mary argued. "I only nipped back to let you know I was all right. What will Miss Gifford think if I turn up with my mother in tow? It makes me look half-witted."

"No, it doesn't," Mrs. Christie said. "And if even part of what you tell me happened last night is true, then Miss Gifford will be glad to see me. I should have gone yesterday, but I let myself be talked out of it." She shrugged her arms into her coat. "As for him, someone's got to take him in hand."

"Him?" Mary stared at her mother in disbelief. "But you don't hold with Mr. Gifford. Neither use nor ornament, that's what you said."

"And I'm sure it's not right for me to turn my back on a fellow Christian in time of need," she said tartly, adjusting her hat in the mirror. "Well, are you coming, or am I to go on my own?"

"What about the twins?" Mary said, making a last-ditch attempt to stop her. "You can't leave them on their own."

"Kate Boys is going to mind them." Mrs. Christie pushed a hatpin through her hair. "There. Now, are you ready?"

"Ready." Mary conceded defeat.

The truth of the matter was, for all her complaining, she was glad of her mother's company. After the events of last night, Mary was nervous about what else might have happened at Blackthorn House in the hours she'd been gone, and what she might find when she returned.

Chapter 42

South Street
Chichester

Connie rushed out of Chichester railway station.

Because of the atrocious weather, there were only a couple of hansom cabs waiting at the Dunnaways rank. The horses were restless, jittery in the wind.

"Taxi, miss?"

"Reasonable rate," said the next. "Anywhere you want to go. Save your boots."

Connie shook her head. "I'm not going far."

Only nine o'clock, but there was already a handful of men outside the Globe Inn, huddled tight against the wall, sheltering from the squall. It seemed quiet, though every week in the local newspaper a list was published of men up before the bench for brawling and bound over to keep the peace. If Davey was right, this was where Gregory Joseph had got caught up in the fight that had seen him sent to prison. Defending a lady, Davey had added with a touch of admiration. Got sent away for three months all the same.

Connie hurried by, ignoring the mumbled compliments or insults—they sounded the same—and up into South Street. Past the Regnum Club and the main post office, the tobacconist and fishmonger. All familiar landmarks but she barely noticed them.

A flower seller and Joe Faro, nursing his pie oven, sheltered from the rain under the Market Cross. One or two black-suited juniors from Chichester businesses—law firms, doctors, property managers—who met each morning under the clock to exchange letters by hand. She knew Sergeant Pennicott often stationed himself there, hoping to pick up gossip.

Not today.

She glanced up at the clock and saw she was early, though she didn't think Harry would mind. And the sooner they talked and decided what to do for the best, the sooner Connie could be on her way back to Fishbourne and her father. Away from Blackthorn House, her sense of foreboding had increased. More than ever, she regretted not seeing last night's conversation through to its conclusion. But her father had been so confused and exhausted, she couldn't possibly have bullied him.

She arrived at the Georgian house at the top of North Street. She was cold and very wet, yet she felt her pulse accelerate.

A tall, gray-haired servant answered the door and stood back to let her step under the porch and out of the rain. He looked worn, tired.

"I'm Constantia Gifford," she said. "Could you tell Mr. Woolston I am here?"

"He is expecting you, miss," he said. "Mr. Woolston has gone out, but asked if you might wait."

Connie looked back down the street. "I don't suppose you know where he has gone . . ." She broke off. "I'm sorry, I don't know your name."

"Lewis, miss. Mr. Woolston didn't say. Only that he would be back soon."

It obviously made sense to wait. They had an arrangement for ten o'clock. Of course, Harry would keep to it. Perhaps he'd decided to go to Graylingwell to see what he could find out.

"Has there been any news, Lewis? About Dr. Woolston?"

She saw the old servant's expression waver. "No, miss, I regret to say there has not."

"I'm sorry to hear that."

Connie looked down at the rain running off her coat onto the floor and, suddenly, was overcome with fatigue. The succession of revelations, her recovered memories, the lack of sleep—she felt it had stripped every bit of flesh from her bones. She was completely exhausted.

The butler gestured to the drawing room. "If you would like to make yourself at home, Miss Gifford, I could bring you a tray of coffee?"

She pulled herself together. She couldn't allow her resolve to fail now.

"Thank you, Lewis," she said, handing him her hat and coat. "I will wait."

Blackthorn House
Fishbourne Marshes

Gifford was turning his bedroom inside out. Checking everything, his hands pulling at his bedsheets, shaking out every book, searching the pockets of his clothes in the wardrobe.

Someone—Connie most likely—had tidied the room, he could see that. All the bottles had gone and the ashtrays emptied. But she wouldn't have taken the letter, would she? He stamped from one side of the room to the other. Despite his ordeal, he was steady on his feet. The letter had to be somewhere. He needed to check exactly what it said. The postmark and the address, all the details he'd barely registered before.

He forced himself to stand still. For a moment, all he heard was the howling of the wind down the chimney. It was so dark, though it was past nine o'clock in the morning. He checked his trouser pockets again, trying to piece together the sequence of events.

Where had he put it?

The letter from the asylum had arrived in April. A Wednesday. Was that right? Who had brought it? He couldn't recall that either. Only that from the second he had read the words on the page, he'd felt as if his chest had been sliced open and his heart torn out.

Then what? Drinking. Attempting to drown his grief, a grief he could share with no one. Not even his daughter.

Gifford paused. Jennie would have understood. For a moment, he allowed himself to remember the woman of whom he'd been so fond, then he shook his head and continued to search.

The remainder of April, drinking to forget, drinking until he couldn't remember who he was or what he had become. The pain came crawling back in the end, every time. Whisky, ale, brandy, nothing strong enough to obliterate the bleak fact that Cassie was dead.

A week later, another note. Block capitals. Unsigned. Inviting him—ordering him—to the graveyard on the Eve of St. Mark. Horrified to see them—three of them, at least—there as well. Distressed by the death of all the tiny birds, battered against the tombstones and trampled underfoot.

And seeing her.

A ghost, he'd thought then. Wearing Cassie's blue coat. Later, looking out of his bedroom window and seeing her sepulchral image in the stream as well. Everywhere Gifford looked, he saw visions of Cassie. A spirit, an echo. But last night, Connie had said she was a real person. A girl called Vera. And during the night, as the dark gave way to the dawn, he had remembered that Cassie had known a girl called Vera in Graylingwell. A girl with the same color hair.

Who else—other than Cassie—could have given Vera the coat?

What if the letter hadn't come from the asylum at all?

Gifford lifted the mattress, hunting between the cracks of the bed frame and the floorboards. Had it been written on the usual headed notepaper?

If Cassie had died three weeks ago—influenza, the letter had said—why hadn't they told him about the funeral yet? Once a month, Gifford collected mail from the poste restante at the main post office in Chichester and settled the monthly account with the hospital. Connie didn't know. No one knew. Could information about the burial be waiting for him there instead?

He had to find the letter. Find the envelope. Had to be sure.

Gifford lifted the glass ashtray. Then, in a rush, he remembered. He had burned the letter. He pictured himself, standing in the middle of the room, his shaking hands struggling to light a match. Holding it to the corner of the paper and watching the words go up in smoke.

He walked to the window, hardly daring to trust the direction his thoughts were taking. He knew how remorse and grief played tricks on a man. How the mind would protect itself from truths too painful to accept. He rubbed the damp from the glass with his sleeve.

Out in the creek, the wind was whipping the water ever higher, ever more fiercely against the foundations of the Old

Salt Mill. The black clouds were so low, separating Fishbourne from Apuldram, that Gifford couldn't see across to the far side of the estuary.

He couldn't see the cottage.

But he knew it was there. And if he was right—he prayed that he was right and Cassie was not dead—where else would she go but there?

North Street
Chichester

Connie stood in front of the portrait.

Light-headed from lack of sleep, she felt as if she was looking at herself in a mirror. She recognized herself in the direct stare and the tilt of her head. She wondered when Harry had painted it.

"Here you are," said Lewis, appearing in the doorway carrying a tray.

"I found I couldn't sit still. Since the door was ajar, I came in here. I don't think Mr. Woolston will mind."

"No, miss." Lewis glanced at the easel. "If I might make so bold as to say, it is a good likeness."

Connie smiled. "It is. I don't know much about art, but I think he has a real eye. For what matters."

Lewis nodded. "Dr. Woolston is proud of him," he said, "even though—"

The butler stopped, clearly horrified to have forgotten himself so far as to express an opinion.

"I haven't yet had the pleasure of meeting Dr. Woolston." Connie paused. "I assume there is still no word from Mr. Woolston?"

Lewis shook his head. Connie glanced at the clock on the mantelpiece, then toward the window.

"The weather is getting worse," she said, looking at the rain. "I'd hoped it might ease."

If the storm came in quicker than predicted, she ran the risk of not being able to get to the village, let alone Blackthorn House.

"Mr. Woolston was very insistent that I should impress upon you how much he hoped you would wait until he returned, Miss Gifford."

Connie nodded. She heard another rumble of thunder, still some way off. She would give him another half an hour. But if he hadn't arrived by ten thirty, however desperate she was to see him—and she was, even more so now she'd seen the painting—she would have no choice but to leave.

The butler put down the tray on a side table and left her alone.

"Come on, Harry," she murmured, looking again at the hands of the clock. "Hurry up, come on."

Chapter 43

Blackthorn House
Fishbourne Marshes

"Davey," said Mary, "what are you playing at?" She shook his shoulder. "Wake up."

The boy was awake and up on his feet, fists in front of him, before Mary had the chance to shake him again.

"It's all right, boy," Mrs. Christie said softly. "Nothing to be scared of."

Davey looked at her, then at Mary, with bleary eyes. He remembered where he was and lowered his hands.

"Sorry, Mrs. Christie. For a moment . . ."

She put her arm around him. "I know, lad. No one's going to hurt you here."

Davey put his hands in his pockets. "What time is it?"

"Nearly ten o'clock," Mary replied, "though you wouldn't think it. It's as black as pitch outside."

"Ten!" he said. "Miss Gifford told me to put out the sandbags, but I must've nodded off. And she wanted me to tell you to check the pails in the attic."

Mary raised her eyebrows. "And since when do I take my orders from you? I'll wait until Miss Gifford tells me herself."

"It's good she's still asleep. It'll do her the world of good."

Davey shook his head. "She's not sleeping, Mrs. Christie. She went to town."

"What in the name of heaven possessed her to do that?"

Davey glanced at Mary, not sure how much she might have told her mother about what had taken place at Blackthorn House. He had a healthy suspicion of all adults, but Mary was half-and-half.

"I told Ma about what happened last night," Mary said.

"All of it?" Davey asked.

"Most of it."

"What didn't you tell me?"

"Nothing, Ma."

Mrs. Christie looked from one to the other.

"Honest," Davey said, crossing his fingers over his chest.

"Why's she gone out in this weather? Something her father said?"

Davey shook his head. "None of what he was saying made sense."

"Don't be cheeky," Mary scolded.

"I'm just saying it as it is."

"Why has Miss Gifford gone to Chichester?" Mrs. Christie repeated.

"She arranged it before. To meet Harry."

Mrs. Christie was silent for a moment, then she looked at the rumpled daybed. "And what about Mr. Gifford? Is he all right?"

"Seems to be," Davey said. "Took himself upstairs a couple of hours ago. He woke up about eight, give or take. Asked where Miss Gifford was. I told him. Then he wanted to know if anyone had come to the house. I said they hadn't, except for Mr. Crowther, who came to inquire after Miss Gifford first thing. That was that. The master went back upstairs. Haven't seen hide nor hair since."

"I wonder if I should take him up a tray," Mary said.

"I wouldn't if I were you, love," Mrs. Christie said quietly.

Mary folded her arms. "You've got an opinion on everything now, Ma."

"I'll tell you something else for nothing," Davey said, turning to Mrs. Christie. "Miss Gifford made quite a palaver about your name."

"Oh? And why might my name be of the slightest interest to anyone?"

Her voice was calm, but Davey and Mary both heard the strain in it.

"Don't ask me," Davey said. "I was talking about the floods back in January and said your Christian name—I didn't mean any disrespect by it—and Miss Gifford got all somehow. Wanted to know who 'Jennie' was, and when I told her, she went all quiet. I think Mr. Gifford mentioned someone called Jennie earlier, so I reckon it struck a chord."

"Did he now?" Mrs. Christie said softly.

"And it's funny," said Davey, running on, "because before— not that I was listening, mind—he came out with a different name when he was talking to Miss Gifford." He frowned. "Cassie, I think it was."

Mrs. Christie turned white. "I knew it."

To her daughter's astonishment, she sank down in one of the armchairs.

"Ma," Mary said urgently. "Get up! What if the master comes down?"

"Let him," she said. "It's high time. By the sounds of things, he won't be surprised to see me."

"What are you saying?"

Mrs. Christie gave a deep sigh, then pulled up another chair and patted the seat. Mary glanced at Davey, and sat down beside her mother.

"Me and Crowley Gifford go way back," Mrs. Christie said.

"He's never said so," Mary said, looking even more confused.

"No reason for him to know," said her mother, half smiling. "It was a long time ago. I was Jennie Wickens then."

Davey sat down cross-legged on the floor to listen too, the sandbags quite forgotten.

North Street
Chichester

A loud crack of thunder overhead shook the cup and coffee pot on the tray.

It was ten forty-five. Harry still wasn't back. Connie went out into the hall again, hoping to find Lewis, but the butler was nowhere to be seen.

In her sleep-starved state, she felt as though time and space, all the hours and minutes, were rolling into one continuous present. Now that the wall in her mind had been breached—the wall that for ten years had divided her present from her past—reminiscences, scenes from her childhood, sights and sounds and smells were coming back to her.

Most of all, Connie remembered Cassie.

She had arrived at the age of twelve, when Connie was four. Cassie had been brought up by an aunt, then come to Lyminster when her aunt died. Bright and spirited, everyone loved her. Connie's father had employed Cassie as a tutor, a big sister *manquée*, a friend to look after Connie while Gifford worked in the museum.

It was Cassie who taught her to write and read, to quote poems and learn plays off by heart. Cassie who told her about how swans mated for life, she remembered now, and Cassie who'd tied a red ribbon around the neck of the preserved cob in the entrance hall of the museum to show Connie how pretty it was, not frightening at all. Was it the same red ribbon Gifford had been hiding in the icehouse all these years?

She saw flickering images of the years passing, as they both grew up. Cassie wearing a smart ruffled shirt and a long black skirt, her hair pinned up. They were happy then. Her father, for all his salesman's patter, his charlatan ways and lapses of judgment, had been a good man. He was going to pay for Cassie to train to be a teacher, as soon as Connie was grown up enough to manage without her.

The smile faded from Connie's face. She didn't believe Gifford would have harmed a hair on Cassie's head. But if her recollection of the night in the museum was accurate, then at the very least, he had colluded in covering up her death?

Would he have done that?

Connie didn't think so. He would have done anything in his power to bring her attackers to justice.

Piecing together her father's comments, his terrible collapse over the past few weeks, and the ways in which secrets were leaking out now, though he'd held his peace for all of these years, everything pointed to the same conclusion.

The bells of the cathedral started to chime eleven.

Connie rushed through to Harry's studio. She scribbled a brief message on a scrap of rough paper, asking him to join her at Blackthorn House as soon as possible, then charged back into the hall. She feared for Dr. Woolston and she feared for Harry. Most of all, she felt sick with fear for her father.

"Lewis?"

The butler still did not appear. Connie dropped the note on the salver on the hall table, grabbed her hat and coat from the stand and rushed out into the storm.

The rain was flooding in torrents down North Street. Men were hauling sandbags and propping pieces of timber and board in front of the doorways. Even so, the rainwater was sweeping up against the stone steps of the Georgian houses and over the lower thresholds of the shops and hotels. She hoped Davey had done what she'd asked of him.

Was her father's life in danger? If he saw no reason to keep quiet any longer, then what was to stop them silencing him? Someone had killed Vera Barker and covered up her death. Connie was certain it was a member—members—of the Corvidae Club. The four preserved birds, each seemingly representing the men there that night. They were murderers. Witnesses to a murder.

She started to run, not caring who saw her.

Chapter 44

The West Sussex County Asylum
Chichester

"I told you," the cleaning woman repeated. "Dr. Woolston came in when I was cleaning the theater. Said he had an appointment with a gentleman at six o'clock. 'Room's not in use,' I told him. He went up the steps, through the curtain onto the stage. That was the last I saw of him. I don't know nothing more."

Pennicott wrote another methodical note in his pad. Harry looked from the policeman to the medical superintendent and back again. He wished he could ask his own questions, but the superintendent had only agreed to allow him to be present at the interview on the understanding that he did not speak or interfere in any way.

"When you say 'gentleman,'" Pennicott said carefully, "did Dr. Woolston say as much?"

"Not in so many words," she admitted.

"So he could have been meeting a man or a woman?"

She shrugged. "Could've been."

"And he gave no indication as to whether this person was a patient or a visitor?"

"It don't matter how many times you keep on at me, I've told you all I know already."

"No need to take that tone," Dr. Kidd said.

"It's as wise to be clear." Pennicott looked back to his notes. "So Dr. Woolston went onto the backstage area, and you left the theater and began work in the corridor. Is that correct?"

"Correct," she said sullenly.

"You heard nothing more?"

"No."

"And you did not see Dr. Woolston come out again?"

"No." She turned to the medical superintendent. "Can I get off now, sir? Some of us have got work to do."

"Sergeant?" Kidd asked.

Pennicott nodded. "You can go. Thank you."

He returned to his notes. Dr. Kidd waited patiently.

Harry was impressed with how helpful the medical superintendent was being. Having received the telegram Pearce had sent on Harry's behalf asking if Dr. Woolston had been summoned to the hospital on Wednesday, Kidd had already made discreet inquiries, so he had been able to answer many of their questions.

Because of the fine weather, he explained, more patients and visitors had been on the grounds during Wednesday afternoon than usual. One of the senior attendants, who knew Dr. Woolston by sight, had noticed him heading toward the administration buildings. Further inquiries revealed that the cleaners had been working in the theater at about the same time. So far, though, no one had seen him leave the premises.

Pennicott turned to a fresh page.

"You've examined the backstage area?" Kidd asked.

The policeman nodded. "We did."

Harry had searched everywhere. Costumes and painted flats, a few loose feathers from a headdress, but nothing to suggest his father had been there.

There was a knock at the door.

"Come in," Kidd called.

A servant handed him a piece of paper, and withdrew. The doctor quickly scanned the page.

"You were right, Pennicott," Kidd said. "Vera Barker was here, some years ago. During that time, she made the acquaintance of one of our private patients, though I can't imagine how. The fee-paying patients are housed separately, well away from the main women's wards. The lady in question was one of our longer-term patients. Very charming, but delusional. Unable to separate truth from falsehood. The kind who makes all kinds of accusations."

"What kind of accusations?"

Kidd waved his hand. "I'm afraid that is confidential information, Sergeant."

"May I have her name, sir?"

Kidd looked back to the note. "Miss Cassandra Crowley."

"Crowley," Pennicott muttered. Harry glanced at him, but his face gave nothing away. "Might it be possible to talk to her? Or does her . . . illness make that difficult?"

Harry noticed Dr. Kidd's expression alter.

"I'm afraid to report that Miss Crowley is one of our rare escapees, Sergeant," he said.

Harry couldn't help himself. "She got away?"

"That is not how we care to think of it, Mr. Woolston," Kidd reproved him. "This is a not a prison facility."

"No. I'm sorry. But she's no longer here?"

"She is not." Dr. Kidd looked down at the piece of paper. "I wanted to be sure of the details before I spoke to you. Miss Crowley came here ten years ago. Admitted having made an attempt on her own life, she was diagnosed with general delusional mania. Her health is good and she is—was—popular with the other patients."

"Who pays the bills?" Harry asked.

Dr. Kidd checked his notes again. "An anonymous benefactor."

"Is that usual?" Harry put in again.

"It's not unusual," Kidd replied carefully. "Even these days, there is a stigma attached to having an association here. Some, therefore, choose to conceal their involvement. In this case, in fact, there is no family. To my knowledge, she never had any visitors."

"When did Miss Crowley abscond?" Pennicott asked.

"At the beginning of April. Before Easter weekend. Our rules are very clear. If a patient succeeds in getting out, and remains at large for a period of fourteen days, then they are automatically discharged from our books."

"How often does such an occurrence take place?"

"It's very rare," Kidd replied. "Very rare indeed."

"How easy would it be?" Harry asked. "When we came in, I noticed there weren't the kind of high fences or gates I was expecting."

Kidd smiled. "It is part of our philosophy to create a natural, calming environment. We pride ourselves on our modern approach. But, to answer your question, it is difficult. I would go so far as to say that someone must have helped Miss Crowley, though no one has admitted to doing so. And as I said, she was popular. Helped those who could not read or write. Wrote letters for them, and suchlike. If other patients or even nurses knew of her intentions, they kept it to themselves."

Pennicott shut his notebook. "Thank you, sir. We won't take up any more of your time. You've been very helpful."

Kidd showed them to the door. "I'm sure there's nothing to worry about, Woolston," he said, holding out his hand to Harry. "All the same, you will let me know if there's any news?"

Harry and Pennicott got back into the carriage.

"When Kidd came out with the woman's name," Harry said immediately, "you frowned. Why?"

"Didn't you notice, sir?"

"Notice what?"

"Her surname. Crowley. It's Mr. Gifford's Christian name." Harry felt the policeman's eyes on him. "Odd coincidence, don't you think?"

*

Gregory Joseph was not the only person sheltering from the storm beneath the Market Cross.

Sooner or later, it was said, if you stood at the Cross, everyone in Chichester would walk past. Joseph turned his collar up. All well and good, if you were prepared to wait long enough.

His patience had been rewarded. He'd seen Constantia Gifford rush from North Street into South Street. Coming from Woolston's house, he supposed. He tailed her as far as the station, where she picked up a taxicab and he lost track of her.

He had returned to his post at the Cross in time to see Sergeant Pennicott and Harold Woolston come out of Gerald White's offices. He'd loved to have been a fly on the wall while White tried to explain away his black eye and broken nose.

Pennicott and Woolston then leaped into a carriage waiting at the curb and headed for Frederick Brook's offices in West Street. Joseph had known, then, that Crowther's concerns were justified. The police officer had put two and two together. Had worked out that Brook, White and Woolston were connected.

He quickly slipped from his hiding place at the Cross and

rushed down West Street, to keep a better eye on what they were doing. He found shelter in the doorway of St. Peter's Church, almost opposite Brook's front door, and waited.

Gregory Joseph had no illusions about the sort of man he was. A brawler, a petty thief, a man not averse to making the most of information that came his way. Free with his fists from time to time, but only with those who had it coming. He was prepared to take his chances when standing at the Pearly Gates.

But this? This was different. When she'd asked for his help—told him what they had done—for the first time in his life Joseph believed himself to be on the side of the angels. Administering justice when the law was blind. One rule for the rich, one for the poor; always been the same way. He'd no doubt Pennicott wouldn't see it like that, but it was natural justice.

He was proud to help. Proud to be righting a wrong.

He stamped his feet and shook the water from his shoes. What was starting to bother him, though, was Gifford's place in the scheme of things. He had assumed that Gifford was involved with Brook and the others and had for some reason fallen out with them. That was why he'd been set to spy on him from the Old Salt Mill.

But was that right?

And how did Connie Gifford and Harry Woolston fit into things?

Suddenly he realized that Woolston and Pennicott were back out on the street and heading toward him. He shot across the street and threw himself into the doorway of the Bell Tower. He heard their raised voices, shouting to be heard over the noise of the wind. He gave it a couple of seconds, then stepped out and followed them back up West Street.

"Well?" Harry demanded. "What did he say?"

They had agreed it was better if Harry—given his relationship with Brook—stayed out of sight.

"Mr. Brook has not come in today either," Pennicott said. "The clerk found a letter lying on the hall floor this morning. He swears it wasn't there when he went home last night."

"Sutton would know. He never leaves anything to chance."

Pennicott held out the sheet of paper. The wind nearly ripped it out of his fingers.

Harry took it, then frowned. "Isn't this the same address that White's office said was in his appointments diary for yesterday?"

"It is."

"What are we going to do? Go there, or wait for reinforcements?"

"There's no evidence that any crime has been committed," Pennicott said.

"Don't be ridiculous," Harry said fiercely. "Four men are missing, Pennicott. And what about Vera Barker?"

"I only have your word for that, at present."

"Someone forged my father's name on her death certificate," Harry plowed on. "It must be possible to find out who."

The bells of the cathedral began to strike twelve. Suprised, Harry looked up at the time.

"Damn," he said, "I had no idea it was so late. Miss Gifford will have been waiting for hours. I've got to go to my house and tell her, if she's still there—God, I hope she's still there— what we've discovered. Will you wait for me? For us? I want to come with you. If there's any chance my father might be . . . I want to be there."

Pennicott put his heavy hand on Harry's shoulder.

"Best to leave it to me from here on in, sir," he said firmly. "You've been helpful, I don't deny it, but this is an official police matter. As you say, four men are missing, all it appears with a connection to one another."

"You can't do this, Pennicott," Harry said in disbelief. "I have the right to be present."

"With respect, Mr. Woolston, you do not."

"Pennicott, I insist."

"Get out of the storm and into the dry. Talk to your Miss Gifford. Tell her as much as you think is appropriate, without giving her further cause for alarm."

"For the last time, I'm coming with you."

"I'm sorry, sir."

Harry suddenly realized that Pennicott was as much trying to protect him as wanting to stick to the rules.

"You think my father's on the wrong side of this, don't you?"

Pennicott held his gaze. "It's a police matter now, sir."

"My father wouldn't be caught up in . . ." Harry heard his voice rising. "How dare you even consider that a man like him would in—"

"Go home," Pennicott said, this time with a touch of steel in his voice. "Look after Miss Gifford."

"You must report this, Pennicott. You can't do this on your own."

"Mr. Woolston, given what we know now—the sort of men who appear to be involved in this business—don't you think it's better for us to keep it to ourselves for as long as possible? As soon as I have the evidence I need, I will act."

"But—"

"Go home, Mr. Woolston."

Chapter 45

Blackthorn House
Fishbourne Marshes

"It's getting worse," Davey said, running back into the room. "Are there any more sandbags I can use, Mary? A flour bag we could fill?"

"In the pantry," Mary said, though she didn't turn to look at him. Mrs. Christie said nothing.

The boy stared, then turned on his heel. "All right, I'll do it all on my own. Even if the rain's coming down in stair rods."

"I'll be with you in a minute," Mary said.

She folded her hands on her lap, then unfolded them again. She was restless, didn't know what to do. Only now, after listening to her mother's story, did Mary realize she'd never before asked herself what sort of woman her mother was, or what she'd been like when she was young.

"I don't regret it for an instant," Mrs. Christie said. "If I had my time over, I'd do the same again."

Mary had no memory of her real father. Her earliest memories were of living in Lavant, with her mother and her new father. A few years later, the twins coming along. Then Mr. Christie becoming ill, and moving to Fishbourne when he died. By the age of forty, her mother had buried two husbands.

Mary glanced at her mother and saw the strain on her face.

She couldn't take in that her mother and Mr. Gifford had been friends—fond friends, by the sound of it—but that she had never mentioned it until now.

"Are you going to tell him?"

"We'll see," Mrs. Christie said. "Ten years is a long time."

Mary crossed the room and put her arms around her mother. "I'm proud of you, Ma," she said. "Having the wits to get her proper care." She paused. "Does Miss Gifford not remember you?"

"No." Mrs. Christie shook her head, then reconsidered. "At least, I think she knew we'd met before, but no more than that."

"But you saved her life, Ma."

"And the doctor," she said. "He did just enough to keep her going. Very anxious his name wasn't mentioned."

"Why?"

"I don't know, love." She gave a weak smile. "That's why it gave me a turn when you came home talking about a Mr. Woolston. It brought it all back." She sighed. "Poor little scrap. Ill for such a long time, and then, when she was better, her memory gone. No bad thing, as it turned out."

"Why do you say that?"

"Gifford took on this young woman to teach Miss Gifford. Nothing as fancy as a governess, just basic teaching. More like part of the family, a big sister to Connie. He was very good to the girl. But when he lost the museum, then with Miss Gifford being ill, she moved on. Left them in the lurch."

"Was she the ungrateful type?" Mary asked.

Her mother frowned. "To be fair, Cassie was a lovely girl." She pursed her lips. "But she upped and left them. It would have broken Connie's heart, if she'd have remembered. So it was for the best in one way."

"Did you say Cassie?"

"That's right. Short for Cassandra; silly name I always thought." She hesitated. "What is it, love? You look like you've seen a ghost."

"The master kept talking about her last night, Ma. I was half asleep, not listening or anything, but hearing, if you know what I mean? Mr. Gifford said she was dead."

"Dead?"

"That's what he said."

"When? Did he say when?"

Mary frowned. "No, but he mentioned not knowing about the funeral, so recently, I suppose."

Mary watched her mother take a deep breath, then suddenly begin to sob.

"It's all right, Ma," she said quickly. "No need to take on."

Mrs. Christie took a handkerchief from her sleeve. They both looked up at a noise from the doorway.

"Sorry to, and all that," Davey said from the threshold, "but these sandbags isn't going to be enough. Look."

Mary squeezed her mother's hand, then went to the window and wiped the glass with her sleeve.

Black clouds were rushing across the fields and over the creek, blown by the ferocious sou'westerly wind. There was no longer a difference between the land and the sea. The spit in the middle of the creek had vanished and the water had breached the wall of the garden of Salt Mill House. The mill itself looked as if it might buckle and collapse and be swept away at any moment.

"Much more of this and we'll be cut off," Davey said.

Mary ran to the side window, noticing how the seawater was already surging up against the banks of hawthorn and blackthorn. Sometimes it was covering the footpath and draining back, but soon it would be into the lowest-lying reaches of the garden.

"Did Miss Gifford say how long she'd be, Davey?" Mrs. Christie said.

He shook his head. "Only that she'd be quick as she could. Back before the tide started to come in." He paused. "She's late."

"Just look at it," Mary whispered.

Mrs. Christie walked to the door. "I'm going to wake the master," she said firmly. "It's Gifford's house. It's up to him to tell us what he wants done."

Mary felt Davey's thin fingers grasp her arm.

"Look," he said, pointing through the glass. "Someone's out on the marshes."

Mary rubbed the glass again, then, when she couldn't see properly, ran up the stairs to the large window on the half-landing for a better look. Davey followed. Through the driving rain, and across the water, a small, dark figure could just be seen battling his way along the sea wall on the Apuldram side of the creek.

"Ma," she called. "Ma! It's him."

Mrs. Christie joined them. Her hands flew to her mouth.

"Didn't you tell me Gifford hadn't the strength hardly to stand, let alone get himself downstairs and all the way over there?"

As they watched, Gifford suddenly changed direction and headed inland, disappearing from their view in the rain and spray.

"Miss Gifford asked me to hold the fort," Davey wailed. "To keep an eye on him."

Mary put her hand on his shoulder. "You're not to blame."

"I am. She left me in charge."

Mrs. Christie turned to Davey. "Here's your chance to make

amends. You've got to go after him, lad. Stop him. Can you do that?"

"Stop him doing what, Ma?"

"I don't know, I don't know," she said, her voice rising in panic. "Only, I want him back safe here. He shouldn't be out there, not with the tide coming in. Not with all this going on."

"What do you mean? Do you think he's in danger?"

Mrs. Christie didn't answer. "Can you get to him, boy? Bring him home?"

Davey looked to Mary, who nodded.

A few minutes later, he was racing down the treacherous footpath toward Mill Lane. The water was lapping up to his ankles, but he knew the safest tracks over the dips and folds of the unstable ground. He knew where the mud was deepest, most dangerous.

"Bring him back in one piece," Mary called after him. "But you take care of yourself, too. Do you hear me, Davey?"

Mill Lane
Fishbourne

The rain beat down on Davey's face and the wind boxed his ears. Over the creek, the break and crack of thunder. He glanced up the road and saw, on the corner by the Bull's Head, Gregory Joseph come out of the tavern. Looking back the other way, he saw a trap approaching, slowing down. Recognizing the driver, Davey nodded but didn't stop, anxious nothing should delay him.

"Sir."

"You shouldn't be out in such weather. A new storm is coming in; you should be inside."

"But it's Mr. Gifford, sir," Davey said, struggling to catch his breath. "He's out on the sea wall. Mrs. Christie's sent me to fetch him home. She's worried for him."

Davey wiped his nose on his sleeve. The rain was streaming down his face, and every moment he stood talking, he felt Mr. Gifford getting farther away. He'd failed in his duty once. He didn't want to fail again. "So I need to get on. I gave my word."

"What about I take you in the trap?" the man said.

Davey's eyes widened. "Would you?"

"Climb in the back, young man. We'll be there in no time."

This method of passing the central wire through the neck after it is stuffed, is preferable to all others, not only because it is easier, but because it preserves the neck in its cylindrical form: we even stuff the neck of a swan before we introduce the wire.

TAXIDERMY: OR, THE ART OF COLLECTING, PREPARING,
AND MOUNTING OBJECTS OF NATURAL HISTORY

Mrs. R. Lee
Longman & Co., Paternoster Row, London, 1820

These are the last words I will write. My last instruction is for your journal to be returned to you.

It is almost over.

The rain continues to fall and the wind to howl over the estuary. If he does not arrive soon—the last of my four guests—I fear the track from the road to the sea will be impassable.

I have lost my appetite for this game. The preparations and the planning and the execution. The end is all that matters.

Have I said there are things I regret? Poor, dear Birdie, lost through this sorry business. The fact that you and I did not, could not, meet. The fact that I caused profound grief to one who tried only to do his best by me. Had he known my intentions, though, he would have tried to stop me and I could not allow that.

I knew, long before he did, that there was no comfort to be had. All those years of talking cures, of kindness, the sunlit terraces and pink and white horse chestnut trees in the park. Everything designed to soothe a troubled mind. None of it made any difference in the end.

Then I saw one of them—Jackdaw—in a crowd of men in top hats and tails, the men of the committee come to sit in judgment. Rage, anger such as I had never experienced before, and I understood.

I could not forget and I would not forgive while they walked free. Crime, punishment, justice.

*

Do I hear something above the noise of the storm? In the thundering of the tides? The sound of boots on the path? The drumming of fists on the door? Or is it not yet time?

Chapter 46

Apuldram Lane
Fishbourne

The top of Apuldram Lane was completely flooded, Connie could see the swirling brown water covering the road and surging around the foundations of the houses. The small homespun shrine to the family killed in the March floods when their trap overturned was completely submerged. Bedraggled flowers clung to the memorial, their petals ripped off by the strength of the current.

The cabman pulled up and twisted around on his seat.

"I'm sorry, miss," he shouted over the wind, "I can't get any farther. I can't risk my horse. Even if it's not too deep, there's no guarantee I'll get back."

Holding her hat on with one hand, and fumbling in her purse, Connie pulled out a coin and pressed it into the driver's hand. He touched his cap.

"Good luck, miss."

She watched him turn the carriage, then snap his whip and set his horse back toward Chichester.

Overhead, a clap of thunder. Closer this time.

Connie quickly took stock. A lake had formed at the bottom of Clay Lane, and as the driver had said, it was impossible to know how deep the water was ahead. She walked fast, to the path that ran down the side of Clayton Cottage into the water meadows. Those fields had never completely recovered from the devastating spring floods, but at least they were designed to flood. On the road, there was nowhere for the water to go and she feared Mill Lane might be impassable.

Heading down against the wind, she pressed forward, desperate for a first sight of Blackthorn House on the far side of the creek. She had a cold, sick feeling in the pit of her stomach. Fear for her father; worrying about why Harry had not kept their appointment.

However many times she tried not to read something dark into his absence, it made no difference.

She plowed on. Her face was soaking and the brim of her hat, lifted by the wind, flapped around her head like a huge bird. After a moment, she took it off and put it in her bag, then struggled on.

Vera, Dr. Woolston, her father, Cassie.

Then, some way ahead, Connie noticed she wasn't the only person foolhardy enough to be out of doors. About half a mile away, closer to the water, someone else was battling the storm and the tides. She saw him fall, then heave himself up and keep going, stumbling along the vanishing shoreline toward Apuldram, regardless of the obstacles in his way.

The man fell again, got up again.

Now, something about the motion and the way he staggered through the mud triggered a recognition. A spark of relief followed quickly by fear and panic. What was he doing?

"Father!" she shouted, but her voice was carried away by the wind. "Gifford!"

Abandoning all thoughts of her own safety, Connie struck out across the marshes after her father.

Davey sat up and spat the straw from his mouth. He had no idea what had happened.

Last thing he remembered, he was in the trap. Sitting huddled on the floor, to keep out of the wind, and seeing something beneath the bench. A large floppy black hat, with feathers pinned all over it. Wondering how Vera Barker's hat came to be in there.

Then, nothing.

He put his hand to the back of his head, wincing at the touch of a lump the size of an egg. He rolled his shoulders, then stood up. He was in some kind of stable or animal pen. There were old rags on the ground, bird dropping everywhere, and a stack of wooden birdcages. On an upturned packing crate, a single candle in a plain brass holder.

Where was he? How had he ended up here?

*

"Father!" Connie shouted.

She was astonished at how quickly her father was covering the ground. Despite his fragile condition, if anything he seemed to be drawing away from her. He clearly had a fixed destination in his mind.

Connie's heavy skirts were clinging to her legs, her saturated coat weighing her down. She could barely feel her feet, and with each heavy step, she seemed to be sinking lower into the mud as the seawater rose higher and higher over the ground.

Then, to her relief, she saw Apuldram Woods ahead. She hoped that Gifford would take shelter there.

"Father!"

There was no answer. Connie ran into the cluster of trees. The branches were plunging forward and back, like untamed horses, but the canopy of leaves provided some protection from the rain. She exhaled, letting the ringing in her ears die away. She still couldn't see Gifford.

She traced her way through the trunks of the ash trees and the oaks. She had lost all track of time, but she could see the tide was terribly high. She kept going until she saw the outline of a small, single-story cottage in the distance through the trees. The grass at the end of the garden had been reclaimed by the estuary, but the path was passable still.

She made a dash into the open, onto the path and up to the front door. The sign read: THEMIS COTTAGE. Connie frowned, another memory of Cassie coming back to her. The handwritten label. Themis, the goddess of justice.

She rapped on the door. "Hello? Let me in. Please."

Another gust of wind at her back slammed into her, all but knocked her off her feet. She hammered harder.

"Is there anyone here? Father?"

When no one answered. Connie tried the latch and found the door was unlocked.

She stepped inside.

Chapter 47

Themis Cottage
Apuldram

Davey heard the sound of someone rattling the latch. He was about to shout for help when it occurred to him that it might be whoever had thumped him, coming back to finish him off.

Gregory Joseph? Davey shook his head; he'd been too far away up Mill Lane. Had the trap gone over? Had he been thrown out, bashing his head in the process? If that was the case, how had he ended up locked in here? Where was Mr. Crowther? Was he hurt too?

Davey had no idea what he'd done to deserve this, but when had that ever made any difference? He stood his ground. In his short life, he'd learned how to be knocked down and get back on his feet again. He'd also discovered that sometimes it was better to keep out of the way. Live to fight another day.

This was one of those days.

He looked around for a place to hide. The only possibility was to climb up into the rafters and hope they didn't look up. Whoever "they" might be. When the door opened, he'd have a chance to jump down and run. He reckoned he could outrun most people.

There was a metal manger on the wall. Davey hauled himself up onto it, regained his balance, and reached up to the lowest beam. His hands slipped. He tried again, this time gaining purchase and swinging himself upright. There was just enough height. Panting with exertion, he pressed himself back against the wall and tried not to breathe too loudly.

Apuldram Lane
Fishbourne

Harry stared at the narrow waterlogged track that led from Apuldram Lane toward the sea. He flinched at another clap of thunder overhead, pulled his hat down over his ears, and set off.

Immediately, he went down into deep mud. Black estuary water flooded over the top of his boots. Was he going in the right direction for Themis Cottage? The Dunnaways man said he'd taken a fare out to Apuldram the previous night.

Harry plowed on. He couldn't understand why the hell there was no sign of Pennicott. No sign of police activity at all. The sergeant had said he needed more evidence, but surely that wouldn't prevent him coming to Apuldram to make inquiries. Both White and Brook had a connection to the cottage, Pennicott already knew that.

A fork of lightning split the sky, followed a few seconds later by another roar of thunder. Harry glanced up, wondering if he was safer under the trees or if he'd be better off out in the open.

When he'd left Pennicott and returned home to North Street, he'd discovered Connie had left, having waited for over an hour. Then he'd seen the note she'd left him on the salver in the hall, asking him to come to Blackthorn House as soon as possible. That she had things to tell him. At the bottom of the scribbled letter, a postscript that, even in the midst of such darkness, had made him smile.

"It is beautiful. No doubt, you are an artist." Then, beneath, the words "Thank you. CG."

He'd set off intending to do what she'd asked, but when he got to the outskirts of Fishbourne, he realized it made more sense to go to Themis Cottage first. He desperately wanted to see Connie, but Themis Cottage was the only lead they had, and if Pennicott wasn't going to act, then Harry would. Harry couldn't abandon the old man now.

He knew Connie would understand. She loved her father too.

To his surprise, he saw a trap with no driver plowing up the track toward him. Crowther's trap? He could see the whites of the horse's eyes, crazed by the thunder and the sound of the wind, and tried to grab for the reins. The horse reared, but Harry kept hold and fumbled with the harness until he'd got the animal free of the carriage. How the devil had the horse got all the way here without harming itself? Harry was no good with animals, so he didn't know if it would be better to tether the horse until he could find someone to deal with it, or set it free. There was another clap of thunder, directly over-head, and the decision was taken out of his hands. The horse reared up again, ripping the reins from his hands. He couldn't stop it. All he could hope was that it would find its own way back to Fishbourne.

Harry slipped in the mud and almost went over. He continued to battle his way down the track, his boots sinking deeper with each step. Finally, to his relief, he saw a small building ahead at the end, set in a large plot of land. To the right, an area of woodland; directly ahead was the sea. He supposed this must be Themis Cottage, though it seemed a peculiarly ornate name for so modest a house.

He had convinced himself his father was inside. Now that

he was here, he wasn't sure what to do for the best. If the old man *was* here and being held against his will—despite Pennicott's unspoken insinuations, it was the only explanation Harry was prepared to accept—the last thing he should do was rush in and run the risk of messing things up. He realized it was possible that Pennicott, though he'd not seen any sign of him, was here already.

A strong gust of wind nearly lifted him off his feet. His clothes were soaking, heavy against his legs and arms. He didn't think he could stay outside for much longer. He looked around for a place from which to watch the house. He pulled his collar up, then crouched low and ran to what looked like a coal cellar at the back of the cottage. That would do for the time being.

As he took shelter, he thought again of Connie. He hoped that, whatever revelations did emerge about her father, she would be strong enough to cope. Whatever the situation was, Harry was determined to stick by her.

Mill Lane
Fishbourne

The mill pond had burst its banks. Water was flooding across the road, up and over the steps to the low-lying properties, streaming through the gaps between the doors and the stone thresholds of Pendrills and Salt Mill House.

Pennicott's cape flapped in the wind as he raised his hand and rapped again on the door to Slay Lodge.

"Sir?" he shouted. "Open the door, please. This is the police."

The house seemed to stare back at him. Every window was tight shut; there was no sign of life. Pennicott was cursing the time it had taken to get the evidence he needed. You couldn't make mistakes with these kinds of men, whose wealth and standing in society protected them, so Pennicott had done it by the book. He glanced at his watch. His colleagues should have arrived at Themis Cottage by now, so long as Apuldram Lane was passable.

"Sir?" he shouted again.

This time, when there was still no answer, Pennicott stood back. He summoned the young officer waiting behind him.

"We're going to have to break it down," he said. "On my count."

He and the lad jammed their shoulders against the door.

"And again," Pennicott ordered. "Again."

Little by little, the hinges started to splinter and crack. Finally, after one last attempt, the door came away from the frame and they were in.

Pennicott rushed inside and found himself staring at a huge preserved swan standing in the hallway.

He knew, immediately, that his man had gone. The house felt empty.

"Check upstairs," he ordered.

Pennicott himself went through the study and the drawing room, noticing that all the drawers of the desk were open. He hoped the others would have better luck at Themis Cottage.

"Found anything?" he asked, as the boy reappeared.

"Only this," the boy said, holding out a coil of taxidermist's wire.

Chapter 48

Themis Cottage
Apuldram

Connie staggered into the entrance hall, out of the storm, then struggled to close the door in the teeth of the wind.

Her first sensation was relief. Her skin was thick with salt water carried off the sea. The cottage was utterly and completely quiet.

"Father?"

There was an odd concoction of perfumes. Candles, with incense and something unpleasantly sweet underneath. An old and familiar scent that she knew well from the workshop.

Blood.

"Gifford?"

Had he taken shelter here? Where else could he have gone?

Two doors led off the hall, with a third directly ahead at the end of the corridor. They were all closed. Connie tried the right-hand room first. A small parlor; it was empty, although there were signs of recent occupation. A plate and a knife, a stack of newspapers and a couple of books on a low side table. She was on the point of going back into the hall when she noticed the title of the book on the top of the pile. She picked it up.

"*Taxidermy: or, the art of collecting, preparing, and mounting objects of natural history,*" she read. "Mrs. R. Lee."

The same Longman edition, by the looks of it, as her father owned. Then she remembered how, when she and Harry were in the workshop, she hadn't been able to lay her hands on it. She opened the flyleaf and saw her father's bookplate on the inside cover: MR. CROWLEY GIFFORD, STUFFER OF BIRDS.

Had her father brought the book here? Lent it to someone?

She looked down at the volume beneath Mrs. Lee's manual. Not another book, but her journal. The current one, missing since Wednesday afternoon. Could her father have taken that too? Brought it here too? She didn't think so. He had been in a dreadful condition that day, almost unconscious with drink.

She flicked through the leaves, not sure what she was looking for, pages and pages of her own familiar handwriting. A sheaf of loose paper fell out; then, in the journal, she saw the color of the ink change. Black ink, not blue.

Distinctive handwriting, but not hers.

Connie shook her head. It wasn't possible. Cassie was dead. She could not have written these entries.

She thought again of her father's distress. He was confused and his thoughts had gone around in circles, but he had admitted that Cassie was dead. When Connie had talked of the Corvidae Club, trying to get him to confess that he knew they had murdered Cassie ten years ago, he hadn't corrected her.

The same chink of doubt.

Connie thought of the woman she'd seen watching Blackthorn House, about the man Davey had seen in the same spot. Ever such a small chap, Davey had said, something not quite right about him. The same thing Harry had said about the man he'd heard quarreling with his father. She thought of the letter Mrs. Christie had given her—hand-delivered to the house, that script familiar—and the strength of Gifford's grief. A fresh, raw emotion, not something a decade old.

"Cassie?" she heard herself say.

Still no one answered. No one came.

Her heart thumping, Connie took the journal and walked across the hall to the room opposite. It was empty apart from a heap of black drapes, like curtains from a theater, and a selection of butcher's tools on the ground. There were brown stains on the teeth of the saw.

Blood, skin, bone.

There was only one room left. Still holding her journal in front of her like a shield, she walked slowly down the corridor to the end.

Was her father here? Was Cassie? Someone pretending to be Cassie?

Every muscle in her body told her not to go on, but she had come too far to turn back. For a decade she'd lived with secrets poisoning everything. It was better to face the truth, whatever it was and however difficult it turned out to be. It was better to know than to spend the rest of her life, like the past ten years, wondering.

Connie put down the journal on the hall table, then walked forward toward the closed door at the end of the corridor.

*

Davey dropped down from the beam onto the straw, landing behind the figure standing in the doorway. He tried to make a run for it, but Joseph lunged for him, grabbing his jacket, threw the boy back onto the straw and blocked the door with his body.

Davey flew at him. Joseph put his arms around the boy and lifted him off the ground.

"Shut this row. He'll hear us," he hissed.

"Where's Mr. Gifford? What have you done with him? If you've harmed him . . ."

"Gifford?"

The surprise in Joseph's voice was so obvious that Davey stopped fighting.

"Look, I'll put you down, but I swear, if you start that racket up again, I'll swing for you. Clear?"

Davey nodded. Joseph dropped him.

"Where are we?"

"Don't you know?"

"No. Ma Christie sent me after Mr. Gifford. He was heading this way, but I . . . To be honest, I'm not sure."

Joseph shook his head. "Why's Gifford here? What's he playing at?"

"The trap must have gone over," Davey said, thinking aloud. He looked at Joseph. "Was it you who slung me in here?"

"Course not. I'd hardly be letting you out if I had."

Davey thought and decided that made sense. "Who was it then?"

For a moment, their eyes met, and Davey remembered. "Vera's hat," he said. "I found it in Crowther's carriage."

*

Connie couldn't take in what she was seeing. Not at first.

The room was dark, with the exception of three candles

burning behind three chairs, which threw the shadows forward to meet her. She waited. Allowed her eyes to adjust to the semi-light. She looked again.

Three life-sized mannequins had been positioned in Louis Quatorze chairs. Like Pierrots, though wearing black robes instead of white, and decorated with different embroidered patterns. Each wore a beautiful mask in the shape of a bird's head: a jackdaw, with its silky gray hood; a magpie with the glinting purple-and-green of its tail feathers; the third with the woody beak and sooty black feathers of a rook.

It was a macabre re-creation of the display case her father had made and hidden in the icehouse: jackdaw, magpie, rook. The fourth space was unoccupied.

Crow was missing.

Connie weakened, as she started to realize what she was actually seeing. She refused to let herself look away. She had to learn the truth. She took shallow breaths, trying not to let the overheated, sickly air of the room get into her nose and throat, waiting for her pulse to steady. Finally, the last missing memories of the night Cassie died came back to her.

*

Four men sitting in the museum on chairs that, to her child's eyes, seemed like thrones. Peering down into the room from above, hiding behind the wooden banisters on the first-floor landing.

The candles and the smoke, the feathers. Noise, men's voices.

Her father and Cassie arguing in the hall. Was that what had woken her? Gifford pleading with Cassie to keep the visitors well oiled while he went into the village to see what was keeping them.

Cassie folding her arms. "Them?"

"A bit of dancing," he said, looking away. Not able to meet her eye. "Professional entertainment, no harm in it. He gave me his word."

"Dancing!" she said contemptuously. "Working girls, more like. Shame on you, Gifford, with your daughter in the house."

"All above board, he gave me his word as a gentleman," he said. "I'll only be five minutes, Cassie. He arranged it all, only they should have been here by now. I've got to go and check where they are. Lost their way, near as like. I'm only asking you to hold the fort for five minutes. Keep their glasses topped up. That's all."

Connie watching and waiting, then Cassie nodding. "Five minutes. No longer."

The sound of the side door closing.

Connie pushing herself back into the shadows, knowing that she would be in trouble if Cassie knew she was out of bed. Hearing the voices of the men getting louder and more impatient. Listening for the sound of her father coming back, but he didn't return.

Cassie pausing in the hall, holding a tray of drinks. She looked cross, not worried. Then she fixed a smile on her face and walked into the room. The door stayed open. Connie clutched at the spindles, pressing her cheeks against the wood to see.

Cassie still smiling, trying to keep smiling as hands pulled at her. Pushing her and pulling at her clothes, and Connie realizing Cassie was angry.

Then frightened.

Glass breaking. Dropping the tray. The smell of brandy and whisky. The noise getting louder, and the shouting. One of the largest display cases tipped over and shattered, the songbirds thrown out, as if they had come back to life. All the tiny birds, the brambling and chaffinch, the siskin, greenfinch, linnet, her father's beautiful handiwork trampled underfoot.

Black feathers of the masks. Four men in masks.

One of them telling Cassie not to be a silly girl, not to make a fuss. It was just a bit of fun. He seemed to think it was funny when she struck him. Made him pull at her skirts more, roughly now. Holding her wrists now, trying to kiss her.

Cassie tried to get away. The man in the jackdaw mask took no part, but he didn't stop them. She ran for the door, but the man in the magpie mask blocked her way and put his hand on her throat. The sound of material and a flash of bare skin. Cassie fighting, trying to twist away, then the man in the rook mask hit her and she fell down, screaming now, as he hit her again. And him lying over her and doing something that made her shout, anger and then pain. Hurting her. Cursing her. Blood on Cassie's face.

But she didn't stop fighting, kept screaming.

The man in the crow mask had watched, his arms folded, but finally he stepped forward and grabbed Cassie by the hair. He dragged the red ribbon, turned it in his hands, then crouched down and pulled. Pulled again.

Connie didn't understand what they were doing or why, didn't know why her father hadn't come back.

Then, abruptly, there was silence.

Cassie wasn't screaming anymore. She wasn't making a sound. She was lying on the floor.

White face, blue lips.

"Pity," said the man with the crow mask, standing looking down at her with the length of red ribbon in his hand. "Get rid of her."

Connie caught her breath at the sharp stab of memory. Dust on bare floorboards, feathers.

Cassie was dead. She had seen her die.

And Connie not understanding, except she knew it was wrong. That it was bad. And not caring if her father told her off, or if Cassie told her off, but she couldn't stay silent anymore. Shouting at the top of her lungs, hurling herself down the stairs to try to get to Cassie.

Flying through the air. Falling, her shoulders and elbows and arms hitting the wall, the tread of the stairs, her head striking the stone floor at the bottom. The cold of the night air on her face, the sensation of being carried in someone's arms.

She had never seen Cassie again.

Chapter 49

Connie put her hands up to her face and realized she was weeping. Her mind was retreating from what she'd witnessed in the past, preparing her to face the terrible present.

She heard a clock ticking, keeping pace with the beating of her heart. Gradually she found herself back in the airless cottage room and forced herself to look again at the macabre tableau. At the chairs, and the mannequins posed on each, the decorated robes and the masks.

Jackdaw, magpie, rook. The empty fourth chair.

The pattern on the first costume was the plainest. Black and gray feathers, but no jewels or glass. The second piece was more elaborate. An exquisite fan of black-and-white plumes, iridescent magpie tail feathers, long and exotic, sewn into the fabric. The third was the most extravagant of all: a riot of feathers of all colors, red and white, black, gray, brown, all exploding out of the center of the mannequin's costume like a firework.

Finally, Connie's conscious mind forced her to accept what her unconscious mind had known all along. She had identified the smell the second she stepped into the cottage, but tried to pretend it wasn't there. The sickly sweet smell of flesh beginning to rot.

These were not mannequins. They were not intended for

another kind of life. The process of decay, in the airless room, had already begun.

Not mannequins, but men.

Not exquisitely decorated costumes, but rather feathers stuffed into the chest cavities, between the bones, under the skin. Their eye sockets, visible through the slits in the velvet, not encrusted with rubies or jet. Rather, dried seams of blood around openings filled now with glass and enamel.

She clamped her hand over her mouth as the floor seemed to lurch and slide. She refused to let herself fall. Not this time. Not ever again. She feared that if she slipped out of time now, she might find herself trapped in the horror forever.

She stepped forward and removed the mask from the first man's face: Jackdaw. His skin was gray. She closed his eyes. Even in death, she could see the likeness between his features and Harry's.

Her hand shaking, she took the mask from the second man: Magpie. Shiny black hair. His eyelids had been sewn shut, the blood encrusting his lids. Ugly black stitching pinched his nostrils together. She did not know him.

She recognized the bulk and size of the man in the third seat from the graveyard. Frederick Brook, Harry's employer. Slowly, she removed his mask.

Brook's mouth was sewn shut and he had black marbles in the bloodied eye sockets. A piece of carved wood, like the semblance of a rook's beak, had been forced into the space where his nose should have been. It was congealed with blood. And protruding from his neck and his throat were twists of wire, holding him upright against the back of the chair. He, too, had been stuffed with feathers, but unlike Magpie, Connie could see that his torso had been gutted, the ribs sawn away.

The Corvidae Club. The noms de guerre of the members,

nicknames chosen to represent each. Jack, a common abbreviation for John, the name of Harry's father; Magpie, she didn't know; Brook was obvious, the name of the bird contained within his surname. For a brief moment, Connie thought of Harry and how she would do anything to spare him this sight. But how could she? His world was about to come crashing down and there was nothing anyone could do to prevent that.

She forced Harry out of her mind and thought, instead, about the fourth man. A crow mask was ready, waiting on the last chair. The man who had watched while two men attacked a defenseless young woman, the man who had put a ribbon around her neck and choked the life out of her to stop her screaming, dispassionate and indifferent. The murderer's seat was empty.

Connie's thoughts slipped from Harry's father to her own. She shuddered, her belief in his innocence challenged once more. Crowley.

She shook her head. Gifford had not been there when Cassie was murdered. Connie had heard him leave the museum and he had not come back. But had she remembered everything? What remained lost to her, suppressed by shock and fear? Her unconscious mind had blocked out so much. This too?

Finally, she felt her knees buckle. She staggered back, suddenly unable to remain for a second longer in this living tomb. She ran to the door. Her hands were shaking and she couldn't catch hold of the handle to get free.

To her horror, she heard a noise in the hall outside. She looked around desperately for somewhere to conceal herself, somewhere the bloodied and sewn eyes of the dead men would not be looking at her, but there was nowhere.

The footsteps came closer. She stepped back behind the door. If he walked far enough into the room—perhaps bringing a fourth victim with him—might she be able to run around and out before he caught her?

He? Who was she expecting to see?

She heard the sound of her own blood pulsing in her ears.

The footsteps stopped short.

Connie stared at the handle, willing it not to turn, but it did. The door began to open. Then she heard with relief a voice she recognized, whispering through the gap.

*

"What the hell are you doing?" Davey demanded.

"Shut your trap," Joseph hissed. "Do you want him to hear us?"

"Who?"

"Who do you think?" Joseph said, trying to hold the door ajar in the gale. "I thought it was Gifford who put Vera up to it, then killed her to stop her talking."

Davey stared. "Mr. Gifford kill Vera? Don't be daft."

"What do you know? I thought he was blackmailing the rest of them, that's what I was told. It made sense. He had to be part of it."

"Blackmail?"

Joseph wasn't listening. Just carried on as if Davey hadn't spoken.

"Of course, I realize now he did for Vera, then put her body near Blackthorn House to throw suspicion back on Mr. Gifford. Been looking at it upside down all along."

"I haven't a clue what you're talking about."

"Didn't she take on when I told her," Joseph said. "Kept saying she had innocent blood on her hands. How it wasn't meant to happen."

"But Miss Gifford didn't even know Birdie," Davey interrupted. "How was it anything to do with her?"

"I'm not talking about Miss Gifford."

"Then what the heck?"

"Quiet!" Joseph hissed, dropping a warning hand on Davey's shoulder. "Someone's out there."

Davey tried to peer through the gap in the wooded slats, but the rain blotted out anything beyond a few feet away. Joseph shoved him out of the way.

"Did you see where Mr. Gifford went? Did he go in the house?"

"I don't even know if he's here or not," Davey shot back. He came to a halt. "Hang about, how come you're here so quick? I saw you in Mill Lane before."

Joseph spun around and Davey instinctively nipped back, out of harm's reach.

"Stop asking stupid questions and do as you're told."

Davey frowned. He'd always been scared of Joseph. Had taken care to stay out of his way. But now? He didn't know. He seemed different.

"You been down this way before, Joseph?" he said slowly. "That how you knew where to come?"

Joseph hesitated, then nodded.

Davey held his gaze. "D'you know who lives here?"

"A lady," he said finally. "Not been here long. She's suffered, if you know what I mean. I've helped her a bit, here and there."

Davey didn't know what to think, only that this was a side of Gregory Joseph he'd never seen.

"What about Mr. Gifford? He been here before?"

"Not so far as I know."

"But he's here now."

Joseph nodded. "I got him wrong. I don't deny it. Want to put it right. Are you going to help or not?"

Davey hesitated a moment longer, then spat in his hand and held it out to Joseph. He saw temper flare briefly in Joseph's eyes, but he thought better of it.

"All right," he said, shaking Davey's hand.

Davey nodded. "What d'you want me to do?"

*

"Harry," she said, slipping into the hall and closing the door behind her.

"Connie, my God."

She saw shock and delight, confusion, relief all rush across his face, before his violet eyes darkened with concern.

She put her finger to her lips. "Sssh."

"Are you all right?" Harry said, dropping his voice to a whisper. "You shouldn't be here, it's not safe. How do you come to be here? Is it your father?"

"We found Gifford last night. He'd been trapped in the storeroom, an accident all along. Nothing to do with . . ." She broke off. "I don't know why he left Blackthorn House to come here. I saw him across the water meadows and followed him, but I can't find him anywhere."

Connie saw the light go out of his eyes. "What is it?"

"I'm afraid, that . . ." He stopped, clearly reconsidering what he was going to say. "Have you seen Sergeant Pennicott?"

Connie frowned. "No."

"This address came up in connection with Brook and a man called Gerald White."

"White," she repeated. "Of course."

The occupant of the second chair, the combination of his

surname and his glossy black hair earning him the nickname Magpie. Connie forced herself not to let her eyes go to the door behind her. She was certain Harry would notice and want to go in.

Harry was looking puzzled. "I only heard about White today," he said. "Do you know the name?"

Connie flushed. "Perhaps Sergeant Pennicott mentioned him."

"Pennicott didn't want me to come. He tried to put me off. I thought he was worried I'd be in the way, official business and all that, though he let me tag along to Graylingwell this morning."

Connie grew still. "What did you find out?"

"That my father did go to the asylum on Wednesday afternoon, after he'd been to Fishbourne. There was no meeting, but he was seen going into the theater. No one saw him leave."

"To meet someone?"

Harry nodded. "Yes, though we don't know if the meeting took place or not. Or with whom. The medical superintendent was very helpful. He thinks a great deal of my father, he made that clear. Kidd also told us of a private patient who had been friends with Vera when they were there together. No family, all bills paid by an anonymous fund."

"Harry," Connie interrupted, raising her voice over the howling of the wind. She was desperate to get him to move away from the room. "Will you help me look for Gifford? I've searched downstairs, but don't want to go up alone."

Harry stared at her. "What's wrong?" he said. "What's happened?"

"I'm worried about my father," she said quickly. "You know that."

"Of course, but there's something else. I can see it in your eyes." He looked over her shoulder at the closed door. "What's through there?"

Connie felt the color drain from her face and knew he'd noticed. And all the time they were talking, the likelihood of the owner of the cottage coming back—of someone coming back—grew stronger.

"Please, don't."

He gently removed her hand from his arm. "Have you looked in here?" He stepped around her.

"You mustn't go in there."

"Why not?"

"It's best that you don't," she said, her voice rising in desperation.

"Is my father in there, Connie?" He looked so very pale.

"Please, Harry. Don't go in," she said again.

Harry looked into her eyes, then turned the handle and walked in.

Connie wrapped her arms tightly around her body, steeling herself for what was to come.

At first, there was silence. She imagined him looking but not yet able to take in what he was seeing, just as she had done. Then, as the grotesque tableau revealed itself for what it was, she heard a single wild howl of grief, of horror.

She raised her head as Harry walked back into the hall, shutting the door behind him. The deliberate, considered movements of a man struggling to keep control. He was gray; the shock had drained all life from his face. His eyes were glazed.

Connie reached forward and lifted his fingers from the handle.

"Who did this?" he said in a low voice. "Your father?"

"No!"

"Are you sure?"

"Yes. He wouldn't—could not . . ."

Connie broke off. Harry was only voicing her own unspoken fears. She did not blame him. And soon, he would discover why his father had been murdered in such a way, and he would grieve again for that.

"Not Gifford," she said firmly.

Harry stood dazed, looking straight through her. Then suddenly, as if a switch had been flicked, he rubbed his eyes and seemed to come back to himself.

"God, Connie, no. Forgive me. I didn't mean to accuse your father. But who . . . who would do such a thing? Such a vile, unspeakable . . ."

"Harry, listen to me" She took his hands, trying to get him to hear her voice. "Did Dr. Kidd tell you and Sergeant Pennicott the name of the patient who was friends with Vera in Graylingwell?"

"He did," he replied, so quietly Connie could hardly hear him. "It was a coincidence, but I can't remember what. Connie. My father! What did they do to him?"

She had to force herself not to put her arms around him but to keep trying to make him think.

"What was the patient's name?" she said. "You must remember."

Harry closed his eyes. Connie waited.

"Her name was Cassandra Crowley."

Connie's hands began to shake. "Cassie."

"She escaped," he said in a dead voice. "Kidd told us. In April. She was never caught. No one knows where she went to ground . . ." He broke off, registering what Connie had said. "Did you say Cassie?"

She looked at the journal lying on the hall table, filled now with someone else's words, written in black ink. And finally accepted what she had dreaded to believe. Quickly, she picked it up and put it in her pocket.

"I think she's here, Harry." She glanced at the room. "And she hasn't finished. There's one more chair to be filled."

Their eyes met, both suddenly thinking the same thing.

"Where's Gifford?" Harry said.

Chapter 50

Apuldram Woods

Crouched in the undergrowth between the oak trees, Gifford struggled to catch his breath. As the tide rose higher and higher, it brought with it greater gusts of wind. He had a partial view of the front of the cottage, though he hadn't gone in.

After struggling over the marshes, he'd made it as far as the path before he heard the sound of hooves and wheels on the sodden ground and stepped back, not knowing who it might be. He'd seen a trap pull up and a man in a heavy country coat and hat lift something out of the back and stow it in the outhouse.

Gifford had moved and the man had turned and seen him. Without waiting to think, he'd run back into the woods and hidden.

Now he heard the crack of the undergrowth beneath the howling of the wind and turned in the direction of the sound. He saw the muzzle of the gun as the man scoured the untended paths through the wood. He had pulled a black scarf, a muffler, over his jaw and nose now as well, so his face was almost completely obscured.

It seemed Gifford's instincts to hide had been correct.

"Gifford? I know you're here."

How long had it been? Half an hour? Longer? Gifford's

muscles still ached from the desperate dash across the drowned fields, and his hands were shaking, though from exertion or from the cold, he wasn't sure.

Where was Cassie? Was she inside? It was torture to be so close but not able to see her.

Methodical, backward and forward, searching for him. Gifford had managed to evade him so far, but wasn't sure how much longer it would be before the man found him. He recognized the voice, but couldn't yet put a face or a name to it.

In ten years, Gifford had never come to the cottage. He'd settled the bills and had liked knowing it was there, on the far side of the water from Blackthorn House, ready for when Cassie was well enough to come out.

Was he right? Was Cassie here?

"I saw you. I know you're here."

To his relief, the man was moving farther away. All the same, Gifford pushed himself back deeper into the protective shadows of the drowned wood.

For ten years, Gifford had been haunted by the memories of the night at the museum. Leaving Cassie for a few minutes, never imagining for a moment that she would be in any danger. They were gentleman. They were waiting for the dancers to arrive, girls well used to looking out for themselves. He wasn't gone for long. Waiting at the end for the entertainers, who never came, then seeing a carriage careering at breakneck speed through Lyminster and having a premonition of disaster. Filled with unnamed dread, he ran back to the museum to find all but one of the men gone and Cassie lying dead on the floor. Over time, he'd identified three of the four men present that night: John Woolston, Gerald White, Frederick Brook. But the fourth had never removed his mask, not even at the end.

An accident, he'd been told. Most unfortunate.

The situation was, the man continued, simple. He— Gifford—was in an invidious position. People would assume he was responsible for the girl's death. After all, no one knew of the impromptu party. The girl worked for him. However, if Gifford was prepared to come to some sort of arrangement, then there would be no problem.

Too late, Gifford understood the sort of men he was dealing with. Men with no conscience, no respect for life. The fact that Cassie was dead meant nothing to them. Their only concern was for their own skins.

But even as the vile terms were being proposed, he realized there was a chance Cassie's life might still be saved. He was accustomed to death. He knew the way in which skin changed its color as life drained away. The slipping from pink to white to blue. He'd picked up birds—stunned by being hit by a carriage or flying into a window—who'd appeared dead but had come back to life beneath his hands in the workshop. It wasn't the same, of course, but as his eyes darted to Cassie's body on the floor, then back to the man in the mask, Gifford realized that she might survive. If he could only get her away, he might still be able to save her.

Quickly, he agreed with the man. He promised cooperation, knowing that every second counted.

It seemed like an age before the man turned and left, without even glancing at the body on the floor. Gifford rushed Cassie to a doctor in Arundel who was prepared to accept his story that his niece, Miss Cassandra Crowley—the first name that had come into his mind—had attempted to kill herself. She needed care and understanding. Her reputation had to be protected; no one could know she was there.

The country doctor, a regular visitor to the museum, did not question Gifford. He proved willing to commit Cassie to the county asylum, where, Gifford knew, she would be cared for. She would become invisible for a while, protected by a false name. Safe from harm.

Gifford had kept his word. He realized that the only way to keep Cassie out of danger—to stop the men coming after her again—was to continue to pretend she had died that night. For ten years, he'd settled the hospital bills from the money paid to him to keep his mouth shut about what had taken place in the museum. A rash promise—though he'd had no choice but to make it—and one that cast a shadow over his soul. It was years before Gifford knew how badly hurt Cassie had been that night. The violation by one man, as others watched, the violence of it. The horror of the birds' masks and the feathers. Not a harmless drinking club, but men of venial and depraved tastes. But, by then, Gifford was committed to his course of action and he needed the money for her treatment.

Everything was done through Brook, though Gifford had always known that the man was simply following instructions.

Hidden within the wood, Gifford wiped the rain from his face with the sleeve of his coat. He had saved Cassie then, though at what cost? Physically she grew stronger, but her spirits were troubled. The lighthearted, cheerful girl was quite gone. Lost in the violence of that night. The fiction of her melancholia and need for solitude became, in time, a reality.

Gifford dropped his head in his hands as he thought of his daughter, only twelve years old at the time. He hadn't even known Connie wasn't safe in her bed until the following morning, when Jennie Wickens, their nearest neighbor, came with news of the accident and to reassure him that his daughter was expected to survive. It was Jennie who'd told him how Woolston had found Connie lying unconscious at the foot of the stairs, rushed her out of the house and sought

Jennie's help. Gifford was unaware of how much Jennie knew, or what she suspected, but their friendship was another casualty of that night. She nursed Connie back to health while he was wounded by grief and silent guilt. In preserving the secret of Cassie's disappearance, he lost another chance of happiness. The last he'd heard, she had married and moved away.

"I know you're there."

Gifford's head snapped up. The man was very close. And he recognized the voice, even after so many years. The man who thought he'd killed Cassie and paid Gifford to cover up the murder.

Blood money.

"Gifford!" he shouted again.

Gifford pressed himself back into the shelter of the trees, relying on the storm to cover the sound of his breathing. The man was bluffing. He was trying to flush him out. In the cracking of the wind and the rain, Gifford didn't believe he could see much through the mist and haze hanging between the oaks.

In April, Gifford had believed Cassie was dead. In his grief and self-pity, he'd failed to see what was under his nose. Who else but Cassie would have sent the letter from Graylingwell? Who else but Cassie would have summoned those who had harmed her to the graveyard? Gifford frowned. Had it been a warning of what was to come, or to give them a chance to make reparation?

Why had Cassie not confided in him? Why had she sent him a letter telling him she had died?

Now all he wanted was to ask her why she had turned her back on him after ten years. He had to reassure her that he would look after her. He and Connie would look after her. He wouldn't let any harm come to her this time.

Was she here?

He heard the snap of a branch underfoot. The man was closer still, pushing his way through the sodden undergrowth.

"Everyone knows what you've done. You won't get away with it."

Gifford didn't know what he meant, only that it was time to bring things to an end. The secrets and lies had eaten away at him, poisoned everything that had ever been dear to him. It was only a matter of time until the man also realized Cassie wasn't dead and tried to silence her too.

Gifford thought of the crow mask, the sharp black beak and sequinned eyes. He remembered the way the man had threaded Cassie's red hair ribbon through his fingers, as if it was a thing of no consequence. As if *she*—the girl lying dead at his feet—was a thing of no consequence. He could see only one way to end this, and with that acceptance came a quiet kind of peace that had eluded him all these years.

In the final moments, Gifford thought of his courageous, principled, kind daughter. Connie had cared for him and loved him, even though he'd done everything to drive her away. He was proud of her, her character and patience, her skill and dexterity. He had known, from the first time he allowed her into his workshop, that her skill would far outstrip his. His preserved birds were accurate, but Connie had the rare gift of capturing the living essence of a creature. In the set of a bird's wing, the tilt of a head, she hinted at a more beautiful life to come. Perfection, not an echo of death. All these years, Connie had stood by him. Now, it was time to bring the story to a close and let her—let Cassie—be free of the past.

Gifford looked down and saw that his hands were no longer shaking. He drew in his breath and smiled. His salesman's smile, just like the old days. Getting ready to charm a customer.

"I'm here," he said, breaking his cover.

*

Crime, punishment, justice.

Everything was done. The last part of her plan was ready. Nothing left to chance, and with that, the courage to finish what she had started.

Then peace. Silence.

Her confession—her testimony—was finished, explaining what she had done and how and why. In the end, it was simple. That while they continued to live, showing no remorse or contrition, she would find no rest. Knowing that the memory of the violence of what had been done to her that night would never let her go. With each passing year, her spirits grew worse, not better. She suffered more, not less, at the thought of their lives continuing without consequence for what they had done.

There was only one course of action. She had taken it.

Nothing now remained other than to bring the last of them—the worst of them—to account. He had enjoyed watching them destroy her, like animals, then taken his pleasure in killing her. Taken her life as if she was no more than a bird or a fly beneath his boot. She'd never doubted he would come, any more than believing the others would not. The seeds of their undoing lay in their own characters. To each according to their desires: reputation, appetite, violence, power.

Gregory Joseph had proved steadfast, a good and loyal servant. He had delivered this last invitation to Mill Lane this afternoon, battling through the wind and the storm. Joseph had no idea of what horrors he had set in motion, any more than did Gifford.

Gifford had never recovered from the guilt of having left her alone that night with such men. She did not blame him, but he blamed himself for trusting their word, for his naïvety, for letting his need for money cloud his judgment.

She had tried hard to spare Gifford, even writing of her death on stolen asylum notepaper, though she knew it would break his heart. There had been no choice. He would have tried to stop her. He would not have understood that she could have no life after the asylum while they were free in the world. After ten years, no one would have believed her. A woman, with no income or support, a former hospital patient. And she wanted no blame to be attached to him. Nor to Connie. Joseph's final act would be to return Connie's journal to Blackthorn House for her to read what Cassie had written.

Everything was ready. The sight of her macabre tableau was intended for the eyes of her final victim only. She wanted him to see how his partners had suffered, to see the empty chair and the mask set upon it, and understand.

She knew she could not take any risks with him. He was cleverer than the others. There could be nothing persuasive or subtle about this last act of killing. She intended to use John Woolston's revolver to disable him, and then begin her work.

But as the storm came in, things had started to go wrong.

She saw his carriage arrive, but rather than coming to the cottage as he was supposed to do, he had dragged something from the back of the trap and gone to the outhouse instead. He turned, as if something had suddenly caught his eye, then ran toward the woods that separated the end of the gardens of Themis Cottage from the marshes.

She waited. He did not reappear, so she had no choice but to go and look for him. She could not let him escape. His associates awaited him. He was the last.

Time passed, though she did not know how long. She slipped through the woods, from tree to tree, shrouded in the mist and rain, until she saw him in an opening between two lines of oaks. Fifty yards away, perhaps more. He had a gun in his hand and she realized that he was hunting someone he knew was sheltering in the woods.

His head turned to left and right, unaware that she was there. He turned again to face her in the distance. She shuddered at the sight of a black scarf pulled up over his face. A narrow strip of bare skin around his eyes. She wanted him to suffer, as she had suffered. The crow mask was waiting for him, the tips of the feathers still warm with blood. She could not rest until he was dead.

From time to time, she heard him shout out. His words were stolen by the wind, smothered by the roar of the sea. She moved closer.

*

"I'm here," Gifford said again.

He stepped out from behind the trees. The man was a few paces in front of him. There was barely anything visible between the brim of his hat and the top of a dark scarf. Did Gifford know him?

"You're a fool, Gifford," he said, pointing the gun at his chest. "Turn round and walk straight ahead. Put your hands on your head."

Gifford did as he was told. "Where are we going?"

"Just walk."

The wind was racing through the trees, shaking the trunks

and bringing down branches. Gifford glanced back toward Themis Cottage. The garden was now mostly underwater. They'd be cut off if they didn't get to higher ground. Yet the man was driving him in the opposite direction, toward the seawall.

"You've been paid well enough for your silence; what changed?"

"She died."

"That was ten years ago," the man said impatiently.

Gifford had no answer. Could he have been so little touched by what he'd done that night?

"Where are they?"

They? Gifford didn't know what the man meant, so he said nothing. He simply wanted to lead him away from the cottage. Away from Cassie, if she was there. Beyond that, he hadn't considered.

"Where's White? Where are Brook and Woolston?"

Gifford frowned, but didn't dare turn around. He stumbled forward into the wind, his tired shoulders aching from keeping his hands high. He felt the jab of the gun in his back.

"Where is Woolston?" the man demanded again. "Answer me!"

"I don't know what you're talking about."

"You're lying."

Genuinely confused, Gifford tried to reason with him. "I haven't spoken to Woolston for ten years."

"White and Brook are missing too. You invited them to the churchyard and a week later they've all vanished. I don't believe in coincidences, Gifford."

Gifford was thinking furiously. He was sure it was Cassie who had lured them to the graveyard, but this man was accusing him instead.

"You were there, Gifford. I'm giving you one chance to tell me what's happened to them."

Gifford half turned, but a blow from the muzzle of the gun to the side of his head forced him on. His ears were ringing, but he managed to reply.

"I don't know. I swear, I don't know."

"I don't believe you."

Gifford paused. The man had obviously been at the church too. Gifford must have seen him, but not associated him with his past.

"Did you kill Vera?" he said.

"She wouldn't tell me why she did it. All those birds. Someone set her up to it."

"That's it?" Gifford said, failing to keep the contempt from his voice. He felt his interlocked fingers tighten.

"Keep walking."

He could feel a trail of blood running down his cheek. There was another sharp jab in his back.

They stumbled on, farther out toward the exposed sea wall.

"What about your daughter? What does she know?"

"She's got nothing to do with this. Leave her alone."

"Another coincidence, then, that she's spent most of the past few days with Woolston's son?"

Was it true that Connie knew Woolston's son? She'd never mentioned him. But then perhaps she had. For so much of the time Gifford couldn't remember what he'd been told or who people were. Hours, days sometimes, blacked out as if they'd never been. Drink had stripped away his memory, his grasp of everyday things.

He breathed a deep sigh. Every choice he'd made had been wrong. He raised his head as a blast of wind hit him, and saw they were out of the shelter of the woods and approaching the sea wall. Far enough away from Themis Cottage. He could see it clearly, around the curve of the wall, the lowest levels of the garden underwater.

He guessed where he was being taken and he knew he wouldn't survive. The only question was could he bring this man down with him? The waters had broken through the sluice gates, a thundering torrent sweeping everything away.

If he could, Cassie would be safe. His daughter would be safe. Perhaps they could care for each other, once he was gone.

"Does she know where the money comes from, Gifford? That you've been happy to be paid to keep your mouth shut? That you covered up a murder?"

Ten years of rage surged up, giving Gifford the strength he needed to launch his attack. With a bellow, he turned and hurled himself into the rain and the wind. The first bullet went wide. Gifford kicked out, then tried to get his arms around the man's legs and bring him down. They both fell to the ground, shoulders splashing into the black marsh mud. Gifford shot his arm out and snatched at the scarf covering the man's face, stripping it away.

"You! Crow—"

The gun was fired again.

Chapter 51

Themis Cottage
Apuldram

Connie and Harry threw open the door.

"There," she shouted. "There, on the seawall."

They ran out together into the storm. The torrent poured over the step and flooded the hall. Unstoppable black sea, silt and mud, racing under the ill-fitting doors, over the bloody cracks of the tiles, sweeping away the books from the table in the parlor and tipping over the table. All the way through the hall to the room at the end where the dead men sat.

"Hurry," she cried, pointing at the two figures just visible through the driving rain. Then she saw a third, slightly built man, moving quickly, breaking cover from the woods. Another gust of wind swept up through the estuary and he lost his footing, falling forward onto his hands and knees. His hat was ripped half from his head by the wind, briefly releasing a cloud of chestnut hair.

Cassie. Not a man at all.

"They're going to be swept into the sea," she cried. "We've got to get to them."

The wooden wheel of the Old Salt Mill in the center of Fishbourne Creek was shuddering and cracking, loud enough to be heard even over the bluster and rumble of the thunder.

Suddenly, there was a terrible groaning. Connie watched in horror as the mill wheel was ripped from its moorings by the surge of the tide and sent racing into the current as if it was no more than a child's spinning top.

"There are steps up to the eastern seawall a few yards to the north," she shouted. "If we can get to them, we have a chance."

She led him through the woods, knee-deep in the heaving water. The boles of the trees were now all submerged and the fields beyond the wood had disappeared under the swirling, surging sea. On the far side, Blackthorn House had become an island. Mile after mile of water. The rivers and streams that dotted the landscape had all burst their banks, each joining with the next until the creek and the marshes were one enormous lake.

The roof of the Old Salt Mill was still just visible, though the waves were crashing up and over it, ripping away the tiles and the exterior wooden stairs. Finally, the structure surrendered and it, too, was carried away on the surge of the tide.

Connie cupped her hands over her mouth. "Come down," she screamed. "The wall's going to give way."

It was impossible that Cassie could have heard her over the cracking of the wind, but she stopped and turned. For an instant, she seemed to look straight at Connie.

"Cassie," cried Connie. "It's me. Please . . ."

She reached out her hand. Cassie held her glance for a moment longer, but then she turned and continued running toward the two men on the seawall. Her father sank to his knees.

Connie ran too.

Behind her, she heard Harry cry out. She spun back. He'd fallen badly into the mud. The more he struggled, the deeper he sank.

"Don't move," she said, kneeling at the edge of the marsh

and putting her hands beneath Harry's arms. "It will drag you down quicker. Stay still."

She cast around for something to use. She found a branch blown free and held it out. Harry grabbed hold of it and she pulled. It was hard to keep a grip, with her wet, cold hands. She hauled again, until he was close enough for her to grasp his coat. With his remaining strength, he propelled himself up and onto firm ground.

"My ankle's bust," he said. "Leave me. Help Gifford."

Connie hesitated, then went. Head down, splashing over the drowned land and up onto the stone steps. Hand over hand, she scrambled up onto the seawall, fighting to keep her balance in the wind. She doubled over for a moment, to catch her breath, then drove herself on for the last few yards.

Finally, she could see the storm-blasted group clearly. Five people now, she realized, not three. Cassie, tall and beautiful in her man's suit, her hair flying loose. She took a step closer.

"Davey?" she said in disbelief.

The boy had flung himself down beside Gifford, who was slumped on the ground, clutching his side. To her astonishment, Gregory Joseph was now somehow standing next to Cassie, shielding her from the man holding a gun.

Connie sighed with relief as the last vestiges of doubt about her father fell away.

Crow: Crowther, not Crowley.

For a moment, Connie stood rooted to the spot. Then Cassie spoke.

"I knew you would come," she said.

And despite everything, Connie smiled at the sound of the beloved voice. For a single instant, she was taken back to the classroom, to happier and more innocent days. To the vanished days. And even though she knew what Cassie had done, how reliving what she'd suffered had led her to take such a revenge, Connie was glad, so glad to see her again.

"Cassie," she said softly.

The life Cassie had been forced to live showed in the lines on her tortured face. And above the collar of her man's white shirt, Connie saw a red scar where the red ribbon had almost choked the life from her.

Connie glanced to Crowther, then to her father lying unconscious on the ground.

"He's hurt, miss," said Davey. "We need to get him to a doctor."

"You won't harm Gifford," she said to Cassie. "He cares for you."

"And I for him." Cassie glanced down at Gifford. "I didn't mean to cause him pain." Her eyes narrowed. "It wasn't his fault, but they had to pay." She looked at Crowther, over Joseph's shoulder. "So must he."

Connie moved toward her father. Crowther's harsh voice stopped her.

"I wouldn't if I were you, Miss Gifford. In any case, if your father survives this, the hangman will have him. He's a murderer. A girl ten years ago, and now again. Vera Barker."

"Liar," Davey said.

"He's been blackmailing us all for years. Bleeding us dry for a crime he committed. Trying to implicate us. Woolston, White and Brook. All with connections to Gifford, all now missing. Isn't that right, Joseph?"

Connie realized, with a mixture of disgust and disbelief, that Crowther still didn't recognize who Cassie was. The girl he thought he'd killed had made so little impression on him, he didn't even know her when she was standing a few feet away, inexplicably resurrected.

Cassie seemed to realize it too. "It took Jack a moment to recognize me," she said, staring Crowther in the eye. "White and Brook were quicker to catch on. Then again, they had more time."

Crowther frowned.

"Put down the gun, sir," Joseph said. "Nobody else has to get hurt."

Leaving Joseph to occupy Crowther for a moment, Connie blocked out everything around her. Deafened herself to the sound of the sea behind them and the relentless breaking of the sky, and focused utterly on Cassie.

There was a brief lull in the wind. Connie took a step closer.

"In the cottage," she said quietly. "I understand why you did what you did, but not . . . How could you do that?"

Try as she might, she could not keep the horror of what she'd seen from her eyes. The revulsion. For a moment, sorrow flared in Cassie's gaze as she realized that Connie had been into the room and seen the dead men. But any guilt or remorse for the murders vanished almost straightaway.

"Justice," she said, in the same matter-of-fact way, as if they were talking of everyday things. Ordinary things. With a rush of pity, then horror, Connie realized that Cassie had lived away from the world for so long, planning to take revenge on the men who had ruined her life, that what was terrible and grotesque had become justified. Normal.

"But that . . ." she whispered.

"The punishment must fit the crime. Blood will have blood. I wrote it down," Cassie said. "I imagined I was telling you a story. They spoiled the museum too, don't you see? Polluted it. I took a book to help me with what to do. It seemed only right." For a moment, her eyes misted with tears. "I wish we could have been friends again. Like the old days, but it is too late. All much too late."

"We can be friends," Connie said desperately.

Cassie gave a light laugh. "I think you know that's quite impossible." She sighed. "Gifford was so proud of you. He wrote every month. He never signed the letters, we had to keep it secret, but he always let me know how you were progressing."

Connie glanced at Gifford, terrified to see how pale he now was. Davey had pressed his thin fingers against the wound in her father's side, but blood was still seeping through.

"Why didn't you tell me? Either of you? I could have helped."

Cassie didn't answer. "Gifford didn't know what I intended to do," she said calmly. "You shouldn't think he did."

Connie nodded. "Is that why you wrote from Graylingwell pretending you had died?

A look of happiness broke across Cassie's features. "You see," she said. "I knew you'd understand. Joseph knew nothing of it either, though he helped me."

From the look on Joseph's face, Connie could see Cassie wasn't lying. She hoped the same was true of her father, though soon enough everyone would know what Cassie had done. How could such a crime be covered up?

Crowther's expression suddenly changed. Finally he had realized who Cassie was.

"You died," he said. "I saw you dead."

"Put down the gun, Crowther," Joseph said again, taking another step toward him.

Connie saw how, even now, Crowther was deciding what to do. It would be easy enough for him to throw suspicion on Gifford. Then she saw his eyes harden. Joseph suddenly sprang toward him as Cassie, too, ran for him with a knife in her hand.

"Cassie!" Connie screamed.

Crowther fired. Joseph threw himself sideways, putting himself between Cassie and the gun. The blade went into the side of Crowther's neck. He fired again.

"No!" Connie screamed again.

Joseph stood motionless for a moment, as the starburst of blood spread across his chest. Then he lurched forward and threw his arms around Crowther.

Cassie tried to pull him back, but Joseph used the force of his body to drive Crowther toward the edge of the seawall. For a moment, the three of them were held there, in a violent and bloody embrace.

Then they fell.

"Cassie!" Connie shouted, rushing to the edge. Davey leaped up and grabbed hold of her to stop her being swept over.

Cassie, Joseph and Crowther sank down into the swirling black waters of the estuary. For a moment, Connie saw each of the figures, held up by the waves, tossed and hurled forward. Then they were torn apart and broken on the back of the torrent.

Cassie was the last to go under. A twist of chestnut hair, spread out on the surface of the water, then she, too, was gone.

Connie sank to her knees. She had lost her again.

EPILOGUE

One Year Later
April 1913

The Church of St. Peter & St. Mary
Fishbourne Marshes
Thursday, April 24th, 1913

Three o'clock.

In the graveyard of the Church of St. Peter & St. Mary, women and men have gathered in the gentle sunshine. Watching, waiting.

Today, the sea is as still as the surface of the mill pond and the marshes are alive with spring flowers. Blue-green water, tipped white by a gentle breeze, glinting in the sunshine. The oaten cattails like the underside of velvet ribbons. The blackthorn and the hawthorn shimmer with early white blossom. Red goosefoot and wild samphire and golden early celandine in the hedgerows.

It is a perfect spring afternoon.

*

Inside the church, soft green moss decorates every window, with bunches of wild primroses and bluebells, and purple southern marsh orchids. The wooden pews are newly polished. A smell of beeswax in the air. The tiles are washed. There is no evidence of the devastation left by last year's storms, or of the violence and death that came to this peaceful, beautiful village.

Connie's hand drifts from her side and touches Harry's fingers. He turns and smiles, then faces front again.

The two little bridesmaids fidget and hop from foot to foot, holding their posies in front of them. White ribbons, pretty skirts of tulle and lace, their hair set in curls. Awake too early and allowed to get overexcited, now that their big moment has arrived, they are too tired to enjoy it.

"Stand still, Maisie," Mary hisses.

The rector smiles at the woman and the man standing before him. The groom's face bears the scars of a life bowed down by grief, but his expression is composed and his eyes are clear. The bride, serene in her veil and lace, is radiant. This is not the first wedding the rector has conducted in this charming village church, but it is the one that gives him the most pleasure so far.

He begins the service.

"Beloved in the Lord, we are assembled here in the presence of God for the purpose of joining in marriage . . ."

There is no one in Fishbourne who does not know that several people died in the worst flood to hit the village in hundreds of years. Few were left unaffected. They are aware that something happened out on the sea wall close to Apuldram Woods.

But after a year, it is time to bring that story to a close.

Connie looks around the church and sees the smiling faces of those people she loves, and who love her. Davey, a good three inches taller now, uncomfortable in his jacket and starched collar, is standing with Sergeant Pennicott ready to make the guard of honor as they leave.

The wedding reception will be held at Blackthorn House, repaired and painted ready for its new life as a family home.

She glances, again, at Harry, knowing that he is thinking of his father and wishing he was here. He clearly feels her gaze on him, because he turns and smiles at her. Connie sighs.

She knows he understands that she is thinking about poor, wronged Cassie. Wishing she could have been present too.

Of course, it is better they are not. What they did, their different crimes, speaks too loudly. Even now, Connie cannot reconcile what she witnessed in Themis Cottage with the bright, vivid girl she remembers laughing and singing and dancing in the classroom. Only she and Harry know the true extent of what Cassie did. The cottage, so vulnerable at the water's edge, was stripped to a shell by the flood. So although three bodies were found there, the feathers and the masks had been torn away and the bodies were so battered by the surge of the torrent that destroyed the downstairs of the house, it was hard to even identify them, let alone distinguish one injury from another.

Many people died that day—in Selsey, Pagham and Bosham, as well as in Fishbourne. The most well known of them was Charles Crowther, owner of a large estate in Surrey and a weekend cottage in Fishbourne. His body was washed up at Dell Quay, but not found for days. By then, the crows—or so it was rumored—had stripped the flesh from his bones and pecked at his eyes. A huge gathering of birds, so it was said, a black cloud over the water.

A murder of crows.

Connie read Cassie's additions to her journal, and as she had promised, the explanation was there. A story of justice, not revenge. Connie still cannot accept how Cassie chose to seek retribution, but she understands why.

Blood will have blood.

Cassie's death left Gifford devastated, but Connie destroyed the pages in her journal and spared him from knowing the worst. All through the summer and autumn, they talked late into the night. Sometimes with Harry too. Until finally, as another new year dawned, they had reconciled their memories.

At last, Cassie could rest in peace.

*

"According to the laws of the state and the ordinances of the church of Christ . . ."

The rector's voice brings Connie back. She sighs. This is a day for happiness and new beginnings, not remembering the darkness.

"I now pronounce you, Crowley and Jennifer, husband and wife, in the name of the Father and of the Son and of the Holy Spirit. What therefore God has joined together let not anyone put asunder. Henceforth you go down life's pathway together, and may the Father of all mercies, who of his grace has called you to this holy state of marriage, bind you together in true love and faithfulness and grant you his blessing."

As Connie looks at her father's shining face, his pride in his new bride on his arm, she feels tears come to her eyes.

"May they live together many years, and in the hour of death may they part in the blessed hope of celebrating forever with all the saints of God the marriage of Christ and the church he loved."

The congregation stands as the new Mr. and Mrs. Gifford walk down the aisle and out into the afternoon sunshine. The choir begins to sing, their enthusiasm making up for their lack of practice.

Connie turns around and sees, framed in the doorway of the church, a shower of white rice and pink confetti as the bells begin to ring.

Finally, the congregation is outside, the churchyard filled with well-wishers.

Connie looks to her father. There is one last surprise he has arranged for his new bride. She glances toward Davey, and gives him a sign. The boy disappears around the corner of the church, then comes sauntering back and puts his thumb up.

Two white birds are set free from the porch. Everyone claps and cheers, and Mrs. Christie—Jennie, as Connie must try to call her—blushes with pleasure. Maisie and Polly shriek and let their flower baskets fall. This time, even Mary laughs.

Connie watches as the doves soar above the poplar trees, then higher into the air until they are out of sight. She feels Harry lift her hand to his lips and kiss it.

"Shall we go home?" he says.

She looks across the marshes. The spiked star-of-Bethlehem is flowering early in the meadows this year. The hedgerows are filled with purple-eyed speedwell and bluebells. On the far side of Fishbourne Creek, Blackthorn House is magnificent in the sunshine.

Connie can think of no place in the world she would rather be.

Acknowledgments

This is a work of fiction. There was no sequence of grisly murders in 1912; Fishbourne has never flooded; and the sea wall (built later) never gave way. Blackthorn House, Slay Lodge, Themis Cottage and Apuldram Woods are all imaginary. Residents past and present will, I hope, forgive me for taking liberties with geography, topography and occasionally wildlife!

All errors and mistakes are mine.

There are, however, very many people who have given support and encouragement, and have helped in making this novel what it is.

At LAW, agents Araminta Whitley, Alice Saunders and agent-editor supremo Mark Lucas. Tireless and enthusiastic, you give tip-top and immediate support, and I appreciate everything you do for me (and all your other authors too).

At Orion, Susan Lamb (and in memory of those Tappit Hen days), Mark Rusher, Gaby Young, Sophie Painter; my publisher Jon Wood and editor Genevieve Pegg, for their superb, clever editing; Laura Gerrard; my copy editor Jane Selley; Lucie Stericker, Sinem Erkas, Marissa Hussey (for transforming my digital world), Hannah Atkinson, Malcolm Edwards, David Young, Dallas Manderson and Jo Carpenter; and Preena Gadher, Anwen Hoosen, Lauren Ace and the fab Riot Team.

The novel was inspired by my long-term fascination with

taxidermy, which started when I fell in love with Walter Potter's Museum of Curiosities in Arundel in the 1970s. I am very grateful to taxidermist Jazmine Miles-Long and artist in taxidermy Rose Robson, both of whom let me pick their brains and answered my questions patiently—and Rose taught me how to skin a crow (and took over when I made a mess of things); the Guild of Taxidermists, who were kind in answering my rookie questions; John Cooper and the staff at the wonderful Booth Museum in Brighton, where we filmed, as well as the Horniman Museum in London.

I'd like to thank everyone at the West Sussex Record Office, not least of all Amanda Dalus and Corinne Burnand, but especially Katherine Slay, an invaluable—and always cheerful—guide to the archives, who found anything at a second's notice and was extremely generous with her time. Several books were invaluable, most particularly Pat Morris's *A History of Taxidermy: Art, Science and Bad Taste,* and *Walter Potter and His Museum of Curiosities*; also, local reference books including *The Fishbourne Book*, edited by Mary Hand, *Chichester Harbour* by Liz Sagues, *Fishbourne: A Village History* by Rita Blakeney, and Phil Hewitt's *Chichester Miscellany*.

Novelists are terrible friends (either too much there or vanishing toward the end of a book), and I am grateful to have such supportive friends and neighbors: in particular Jon Evans, Rachel Holmes, Peter Clayton, Tessa Ross, Clare Parsons, Tony Langham, Lucinda Montefiore, Robert Dye, Bob Pulley, Maria Pulley, Anthony Horowitz, Jill Green, Sandi Toksvig, Debbie Toksvig, Shami Chakrabati, Julie Pembery, Cath O'Hanlon, Patrick O'Hanlon, Lydia Conway, Paul Arnott, Alan Finch, Alison Finch, Dale Rooks, Jenny Ramsay, Janet Sandys-Renton, Mike Harrington, Harriet Hastings,

Marzena Baran, Phil Hewitt, Amanda Ross. Thanks, too, to my parents' old Fishbourne gang from the 1960s and 1970s, especially Jean and Ian Graham-Jones, Kate and Barry Goodchild, Helen and William Knott, Derek and Ann Annals.

For *The Taxidermist's Daughter*, we auctioned a "goodie" and a "baddie" name in aid of the St. Peter Project, to contribute toward the building of a new church hall in Fishbourne. A huge thank-you to Jennie Christie and Greg Slay for their generosity, and to everyone who came to the charity event; especially Helen Frost, Alan Frost and Nik Westacott. Thanks, also, to the Reverend Moira Wickens, rector of St. Peter & St. Mary, Fishbourne, for allowing me to play fast and loose with her graveyard.

Finally, my love and thanks to my family: my wonderful mother, Barbara Mosse—and my much-missed father, Richard Mosse—for creating such a wonderful home and always being so proud of us all; my sisters Beth Huxley and Caroline Grainge, who share the memories that inspired the novel—and also, Carrie, for the brilliant book with press-button bird song (invaluable) and advice on birdseed; my brothers and sisters-in-law, including Benjamin Graham, Mish Graham, Rachie Dunk, Mark Huxley and Chris Grainge. To my fabulous mother-in-law, Rosie, for the knitted crows and five o'clock restoratives; and massive thanks to artist Jack Penny, not only for his beautiful illustration, but also for the bird table that made the jackdaws, magpies, rooks and crows flock to our garden (sorry about that, Ma!).

In the end, though, I could do none of this without my beloved husband Greg—my first reader, my first editor, my first (and last) love—and our amazing grown-up children Martha and Felix: your enthusiasm, your help, your cooking, your support and tolerance of all the bird talk for months on end (not to mention help with #taxidermyselfies) make me the proudest—and luckiest—mother in the world.

Without you three, there'd be no point to any of it.

Kate Mosse
Chichester
May 2014

About the Author

Kate Mosse is an international bestselling author with sales of more than five million copies in forty-two languages. Her fiction includes the novels *Labyrinth*, *Sepulchre*, *The Winter Ghosts*, and *Citadel*, as well as an acclaimed collection of short stories, *The Mistletoe Bride & Other Haunting Tales*, three works of nonfiction and three plays.

Kate is the cofounder and chair of the board of the Baileys Women's Prize for Fiction (previously the Orange Prize) and in June 2013, was awarded an OBE in the Queen's Birthday Honours List for services to literature. She lives in Sussex.

www.katemosse.co.uk

 KateMosseAuthor

🐦 @katemosse